RUMORS OF HIS DEATH
MAY HAVE BEEN EXAGGERATED

In the distance, the clouds broke around the dark shape, revealing the prow of a spaceship. The clouds cleared and Jayce made out weapon emplacements—this was a warship, one larger than the flotilla it hung over. The hull was a dirty egg-shell color, marred by battle damage and scars of rough slipspace exits. Turrets along the ventral hull slewed to aim turbo laser batteries at the ships lashed together.

Giant blast doors opened slowly. Dark shapes of fighters swooped out and flew through the sky.

The last of the clouds blew past the ship, revealing a symbol on the hull made from shattered fragments of defeated ships.

Ice ran through Jayce's chest.

"The Tyrant is here!" Kay shouted, hopping up and down. "They're going to kill us all and turn us into—"

A bullet snapped over Jayce's head. He ducked down level with Kay, who'd suddenly lost interest in hopping.

A shadow roared overhead. The wake slammed the clipper a heartbeat later, sweeping water and spray into Jayce.

The ship turned away from the flotilla toward an escape. A pair of bright yellow plasma bolts slammed into the water ahead of them. Geysers shot up and rained down on Jayce and the conn.

A Tyrant fighter, the wings fashioned to resemble stretched flesh, hovered over the ship, the prows aligned. The fighter swung toward the flotilla, pointing the way for the clipper.

"How *is* the Ty   ee. "I thought he was ki

"You can tell th

T0190786

BAEN BOOKS by RICHARD FOX

THE SHATTERED STAR LEGACY
Light of the Veil

ASCENT TO EMPIRE (WITH DAVID WEBER)
Governor
Rebel

A DREAM OF HOME
Men of Bretton, forthcoming

LIGHT OF THE VEIL

THE SHATTERED STAR LEGACY
BOOK 1

RICHARD FOX

LIGHT OF THE VEIL

This is a work of fiction. All the characters and events portrayed in this book are fictional, and any resemblance to real people or incidents is purely coincidental.

A Baen Books Original

Baen Publishing Enterprises
P.O. Box 1403
Riverdale, NY 10471
www.baen.com

ISBN: 978-1-9821-9371-3

Cover art by Dominic Harman

First printing, December 2023
First mass market printing, October 2024

Distributed by Simon & Schuster
1230 Avenue of the Americas
New York, NY 10020

Library of Congress Control Number: 2023032975

Printed in the United States of America

10 9 8 7 6 5 4 3 2 1

For Dad

Prologue

Adept Carska sat in the lotus position before his Veil shrine. The spinning mandalas and fractal orbits wavered and gave way to static as they spun within the twin curved pillars. Every sound of gunfire and cry of pain from outside the small temple lessened Carska's hold on the shrine.

A stray plasma bolt blew out a stained glass window of the first Paragon. Carska fought back emotions as the battle grew closer. He knew his fate, but the artwork was irreplaceable after the death of the artist nearly two thousand standard years ago.

"Adept!" An acolyte in rough spun clothes and carrying a battered coil rifle burst into the temple. "We can't stop them! There's too man—"

A bestial claw with obsidian nails reached out of the darkness and wrapped long fingers around the acolyte's face. He vanished into the night where his muffled cries ended abruptly.

Carska tried to align his mind with the shrine. He

needed a few moments of peace to seal it shut until the next Breaking, but the chaos around him reverberated into the Veil and there he lacked the strength to overcome the disruptions caused by the death and violence all around him.

Cries came from outside. The assailants were taking their time with the last of the men and women who'd attended to the shrine alongside Carska these many decades of service to the Veil.

Heavy blows cracked the wooden doors. A slope-shouldered creature with a glowing, cybernetic eye ripped through the barricades . . . then slunk away.

Carska took a deep breath and reached into the Veil. He floated several inches off his bench as the sound of metal-shod footfalls closed in on him.

The flat of a blade made of solid light was set on his shoulder. Drops of blood hissed and snapped as the sword extended past his chin and pointed to the center of the moving rings within the Shrine.

"You'll get nothing from me," Carska said.

"I'll have what I need one way or another," a dark voice said. "I will give you a choice. Where is the next locus? Tell me where it is, and it'll be quick. Prolong the inevitable and I'll give you to my Draug to gnaw on."

"I will suffer anything you can imagine to protect the Veil," Carska said. "That is my vow to this Shrine."

"I've heard that from better men than you"—the blade turned to set the edge against his neck—"and you'd be surprised how many of them broke apart once their vows met the reality of pain . . . What are you trying to hide from me?"

The Shrine pulsed.

"Someone was here. Someone powerful. I can sense it in the Veil . . . Who?"

Carska put a hand perpendicular to his sternum in the ancient seal against fear and a crack broke through one of the pillars.

The sword lopped his head off with a quick swipe.

A lupine alien stomped into the Temple and kicked Carska's head to one side. The Dark figure lowered his blade and flicked blood away. The crack in the pillar healed itself as low chant sounded through the Temple.

"Do we have it?" the Draug asked.

The dark figure kicked Carska's corpse off its bier, then thrust his sword into the light swirling within the Shrine. Flecks of blood rose from the edge and melded into the swirl as ghostly figures and constellations manifested and disintegrated.

"The Breaking nears . . . just as was foretold. I have their next step."

"And then?" The Draug's lips pulled back, revealing metal-capped teeth.

"Vengeance."

Chapter 1

"Fight!"

Jayce Artan ducked as a reptilian alien swung a meaty fist at his face. The blow grazed the back of his head, and the stench of ozone stung his nose. Jayce shifted his left foot to one side and hooked a punch into the scaly abdomen of his opponent.

A metal plate across his knuckles crackled with electricity and the Scales delivered enough force that his Gorga opponent would actually feel it. The other fighter hissed in pain and dropped an elbow toward Jayce's skull.

Jayce bobbed to one side and a tiny claw on the Gorga's elbow sliced his shoulder.

The crowd surrounding the fighting pit howled—either in protest or joy at the sight of blood flowing down Jayce's arm. Jayce ducked and pounded a blow into the Gorga's knee. The Scales popped and the alien swiped a backhanded strike at Jayce. He covered up and the blow hit across both his forearms. His skin went numb as similar devices on the other fighter's hand reduced the force of the blow.

Without the Scales, the Gorga would have broken both Jayce's arms with ease. Jayce took a shot to the ribs and retreated back.

The Gorga stood head and shoulders over Jayce and had enough reach to keep Jayce well out of range to take much damage, but no one ever accused the Gorga of fighting smart. It growled at him through clenched teeth. A heavy wire was wound around its snout, as Gorgas had a tendency to bite when aggravated.

Jayce shot beneath a jab and landed tight punches against the Gorga's dark green abdomen and the wide muscles of its back. The Gorga stepped on Jayce's foot and shoved him back. Jayce grabbed a neck frill. The Gorga caught Jayce by the arm and stopped him from falling back and taking the frill off.

Ding ding ding.

The reptilian stepped off Jayce's foot and returned to his corner, where a pack of Simira went to work on their fighter. The three wore bright orange jumpsuits over black fur that stuck out from the sleeves and pant cuffs. Scrunch-faced, they warbled and squeaked at each other as they scrubbed bruised flesh with sponges.

Jayce didn't turn his back on the Gorga and went to his corner.

"You're doing great!" The wide, green head of his corner man bobbed up and down as he hopped around to examine Jayce's wounds.

"Little early in the fight for him to be this dirty, Kay," Jayce said as a cold spray was applied to the cut on his shoulder. He looked up at the crowd. Sure enough, a Syndicate boss was in the bottom row. He looked at Jayce, then handed off a small pack to a bookie making the rounds through the stands.

"Crowd loves the blood," the amphibian said. "You went for his frills. You know how important those are to their mating rituals?"

"Not particularly." Jayce opened his mouth and got a squirt of water. He swished it around and spat into a rusty bucket.

The Gorga's eyes were laser focused on Jayce. The break had gone on longer than usual, but taking bets was more important than pacing the fight.

"Very important. He's pissed, can you tell?" Kay barely stood up to Jayce's sternum. Jayce swiped a thin sheen of slime off his friend's head and rubbed it against his face and neck.

"So am I." Jayce stepped out of his corner and punched his knuckles together. The move was technically illegal as it could offset the force equalizers built into the Scales. They could be set to increase or decrease the impact of a blow, and tampering with them could have disastrous results for either fighter.

Jayce shook his hands down, indicating he wanted them weaker. The contempt of the gesture enraged the Gorga and it grabbed one of the Simira and threw him into the wall of the fighting pit.

The little alien squealed a number of anatomically impossible insults and the crowd went wild.

Ding ding ding.

The Gorga leapt forward, leading with its jaws that were still wired shut.

Jayce arced a downward blow and smashed the Gorga

in one eye. Its momentum kept it going and its shoulder slammed into Jayce. Jayce punched it in the ear hole and mashed the Scale against it. The power amplifiers went into a feedback loop, striking the Gorga several times like a drum roll.

The alien threw Jayce across the ring. Jayce landed hard on his already injured shoulder and looked up just in time to eat Scales. The taste of metal encrusted with the sweat and blood of a dozen different species was one of the worst things about these bouts.

Along with the pain of getting hit.

The Gorga slapped a palm against Jayce's upper chest and lifted him up and flung him into his corner. The reptilian launched a flurry of punches that buffeted Jayce from side to side. Jayce's knees buckled and he slid down the corner, catching one arm on the middle rope. The Gorga backed away, beating its chest in victory. The crowd was not pleased and pointed back at Jayce and tossed plastic cups and kelp-leaf wraps at him.

Jayce shook cobwebs away and got back to his feet.

He banged his knuckles together again and the crowd went wild.

The Gorga turned around and took a hook from Jayce, who had to jump into the air to land it. The other fighter tried to clench with Jayce, but he slipped back and landed a sharp punch to the elbow claw that had cut him, breaking the bone into pieces.

The Gorga raised both hands and hammered them at Jayce. Jayce jumped back and lost his balance. The alien looked at him with a predator's glee and sprang forward.

Jayce didn't see the rising punch that took him on the

cheek, but he saw the flash of light from the impact and felt his head wrench back. He had a brief sensation of falling and the world went to dusk and a dull buzz filled his ears.

There was a pinch at his neck and he sucked in air. He sat beside the ring, but he didn't remember how he got there.

Kay argued with the fight doctor, who feigned listening as he held his palm out. Kay finally slapped two coins in the man's hand and he went away.

Jayce tried to speak, but his jaw had swollen up.

"You back?" Kay put spindly arms on his hips.

"Did I beat 'im?" Jayce looked to one side, but stopped at a sharp pain in his neck.

"Your face didn't break any of the bones in his hand, if that's what you were after." Kay lifted a swollen eyebrow and clicked his tongue. "You got to stop doing these mismatched fights, Jayce. Feral Gorga *eat* humans, did you know that? They love it when the prey fights back."

"Always the main event. Pays better, don't it?" Jayce waved to the purser at the locker room entrance who was counting out stacks of coins.

"To *win*!" Kay's eyes bulged slightly in anger. "Every time I have to buy a shot of Cerebro to fix your concussions it eats into your margins. You know how much you pay me to be in your corner?"

"I'm paying you?" Jayce squinted at him.

"Exactly, you don't pay me at all. Except I keep getting hired for other work because you insist we're always a team on the waters," Kay said.

"'Cause you corner for me . . . for free." Jayce rubbed a split lip. "What're friends for?"

"Here." The purser put two rolls of coins in Jayce's hand. "Dock boss said you had a good fight. Covered your Cerebro. No vig attached."

Jayce looked up at the Syndicate capo in the front row. The underboss blew smoke from a pipe and raised a drink.

He hesitated, staring at the extra roll of coins in the purser's hand.

"No vig, just take the money," Kay hissed. "You trying to piss him off when he's tipping you?"

"No, I can't insult the Syndicate like that." Jayce took his winnings, then tapped his palm to his chest twice to signal thanks to the capo.

"Here's yours." The purser tossed a single, smaller roll at Kay.

"Wait a minute." Jayce took a sip of water. "Did you bet against me?"

"No! No . . . no. I bet you'd last at least one round." Kay slipped the coins into his clothes.

"You're . . . welcome?" Jayce stood up. Every step out of the fighting pit showed him where new pain was waiting for him.

"Would've been a lot more if you made it to three!" Kay stomped his webbed feet like a toddler. "We need to get to the docks and hire on for the eel run. This barely covers rent."

Chapter 2

Jayce listened to the choppy water of the Zilarra River. From his perch atop the metal box around his fishing boat's conn, every slap of the waves against the rusted metal hull spoke of the crew raising pods with wriggling slime eels or the myriad predators beneath the surface.

The thick fog, refracting pale yellow light from the dwarf star looming over most of the sky, sent semiopaque tendrils over the gunwales and around Jayce's ankles. Jayce looked over one shoulder and cocked an ear up. There'd been a splash in the distance to the starboard side.

"In the boat, not in the water!" The ship captain lunged out of the conn and grabbed the bars of a trap and heaved back as slime eels wriggled through the tight netting. The fish secreted more and more slime through their scales as their stress levels rose out of the water. Enough were escaping through the bars and netting and squirting through crewmen's hands and back into the river that the captain started counting off every quanta he lost with each escape.

"If the next two pods aren't topped off, this run'll be a loss." The captain stomped on a wiggling eel's head, then pinched a fin and tossed it into a holding tank in the middle of the ship.

The deck crew, two humans and a pair of insect-like Attorans, answered with a slew of profanity as a winch brought the empty cage onto a growing stack of empties that reeked of spoiled bait and dried slime.

The waters toward starboard swelled. A bit of foam spilled over the gunwale.

"Cap'n, there's a bull head on us." Jayce gripped a rope line that ran up toward the ship's antenna array.

The crew froze.

The captain, a fat man with eel-skin suspenders holding up rubber waders, put his hands on his hips.

"It's too late in the season for bull heads. They've all migrated east for the *kelpso* spawning—"

"Cap'n, it's already circled us once. You drop the scrammer charge now or it'll ram us. There!" Jayce pointed into the fog where a curve of shadow had just breached the water for a split second.

The captain dismissed the warning with a flick of his hand.

"Cap'n, if he's wrong it's just a scrammer," one of the human fisherman said and pointed to a barrel fixed to the port side. "He's right, and we best drop it right now, by Kaon!"

"I've been on these waters since I could walk. There's no way a bull head is—"

Jayce didn't wait for the captain to finish. He slipped a wrench out of his back pocket and cocked it behind his head. He focused on the latch holding the scrammer charge and hurled the tool at it. The head whacked the arming controls and the charge emitted ever quickening beeps and vibrated wildly against the metal bands holding it against the hull.

"Blast it!" The captain waddled over and released the charge into the water. "That's coming right out of your cut, you little—"

The scrammer ignited and tiny crackles of electricity erupted up and around the hull, snapped against Jayce's hands and face.

There was a fountain of bubbles a few yards from the ship and a predator the size of their vessel breached straight into the air. The thick frontal skull plate was marred by barnacles. Bent horns flashed rainbow colors as the scrammer's pulse continued to wreak havoc with the massive animal. It reared away from the fishing vessel and slammed into the river. The resulting wave almost knocked Jayce from his perch and sent water crashing over the deck.

The crew stood slack-jawed as the bull head rolled over and over, then swam away with a strong flap of its tail.

"See?" One of the crew wiped water off his face and pointed at Jayce. "Told you 'e's never wrong."

"Yeah." The captain shook slime off his boots. "Yeah, there's still three more lines to collect. You!" He pointed a thick finger at Jayce. "Who do you think you are, damaging my gear without my permission?"

"Sorry, Cap'n." Jayce gave him a quick bow. "It was that or swim home."

The captain grumbled and went back into the conn.

"Just keep doing what I pay you to do." He slammed the door behind him.

"Aye-aye." Jayce smiled as the boat rumbled forward.

Jayce carried a basket full of slithering eels down the gangplank and hefted it onto a scale. He swiped a sleeve across his forehead and turned his face up from the smell of the expiring catch. Latticeworks of old metal rose up around the dock, the upper levels lost in the fog. The lash up on this part of Hemenway was a conglomerate of ships and rafts lashed together, anchored to the bare rock of a short line of mountain peaks jutting up from the river. People hurried from one false island to another on suspension bridges; spun plastic ropes groaned and stretched as the boats drifted back and forth.

A rusty droid flashed the weight of the eels on its faceplate and the ship captain scratched a pencil to a notepad.

"Holds clear!" a fisherman shouted from the boat.

"Right, slime eels fresh as fresh can be." The captain held up his notepad and wagged it next to his face where a heavyset man in a long raincoat could see it.

"Buyer's agreement holds. Too bad you didn't deliver a few hours ago, would've got a better price." The man swiped his fingertips over the top of one ear and a pair of hulking guards armed with clubs stepped out of a cold storage boat and hopped up onto the pier.

"What's with the muscle if our buyer's agreement holds?" The captain glanced at his crew, none of whom seemed eager to get into a scrap with the bruisers. The captain pointed at an armband with a red-and-green binary star sewn into it on the buyer's arm. "Syndicate pays what's due."

"And the Syndicate gets what's our due." The buyer smiled. "Purchase agreement was for ninety-four quanta per bushel of eels when you signed your contract. But it didn't take effect until you delivered. Market conditions changed while you were out, plenty of other boats bringing in eel for the *Farnham* when she arrives. Oversupply. Price falls. That's the market. You get eighty-seven per bushel."

One of the guards slapped the head of a metal club against his palm.

"You want to take your catch elsewhere?" the buyer asked.

"There ain't no 'elsewhere.'" The captain's face went flush with anger. He put his fists on his waist, then spat into the water. "Just pay me, then."

"As you like." The Syndicate buyer counted out a stack of bills and handed it over. He snapped his fingers twice and the robot rumbled away, dragging baskets full of eels into cold storage.

Jayce waited until the others had been paid before stepping up to the captain.

"Funny how contracts always seem to go the Syndicate's way," Jayce said.

"They brag about how they don't levy taxes on us for them running the ports, but the Syndicate always gets their cut." The captain counted out bills rapidly and passed a handful to Jayce, then pocketed the rest.

"Hey, where's my spotter bonus?" Jayce riffled the bills with a flick of his finger.

"See, kid, that's how it goes. It rolls downhill. I've got my margins to protect, same as the Syndicate," the captain said.

"What? It's not like I can be short on my rent because of this. And food costs what food costs. Why do you get to—"

"Then don't fish with me next season." The captain lumbered up the gangplank back to his ship. "You're pretty lucky, kid, give the casino floats a shot."

"Just because I'm lucky doesn't mean I'm stupid!" Jayce shouted as the captain slammed the door to the conn. He did a quick count of the money in his hand, then stuffed it into a jacket pocket.

"Even with the spotter bonus, it still isn't enough..." Jayce turned away and walked up the pier.

He passed over a wide suspension bridge to a market where aliens and humans sold goods from boats lashed to the side of an enormous raft holding small shops. The smell of cooking fish and dried-out river kelp overpowered the lingering scent of eel clinging to Jayce.

"Hello, love!" An elderly woman held up a roasted rodent on a skewer. "Jayce, trapped 'em fresh this morning. You must be hungry."

Jayce stopped and sniffed at the rodent, then pointed to a bag of jelly cubes.

"Just some sustainers, please." He dropped two coins into a slot in a metal box.

"Saving money, are we?" The old lady smacked toothless gums. "What for...? Oh dear, are you leaving with the merchie? I heard passage costs so much more these days."

Jayce forced a smile.

"And miss your skewers? Never. Just not in the mood for...too much right now." Jayce took the bag of jelly cubes and tested their thickness with a quick squeeze.

"Now now, love, I'd never change my recipe." She gave his hand a quick pat. "You best go pack. Merchies don't come as often as they used to and Hemenway's no place to grow old. Trust me on that one."

"Blessings to you." Jayce pocketed his meal cubes and went deeper into the warren of stalls. The neighborhood changed from shops to hovels. Children laughed and played in the narrow streets. Jayce stopped for a race between two white spotted frogs as one child announced the race and the two owners yelled encouragement to their pets.

He came to a ladder and climbed up several levels. The widow on the third tier closed her blinds well before Jayce was high enough to see through her windows. He got to the fifth level and looked down—the fog nearly obscured the slum below, but the noises and smells still reached him.

Jayce stepped off the ladder to a shack made of old hull plating and corrugated metal. The light over the door flickered on and off.

"Ah, not again." Jayce went to the side of the shack and gripped a metal pole bolted to the floor. At the top was a hemisphere of black glass. Jayce gave the pole a shake and a shadow flickered over him. He kicked the pole at the base and the light from overhead changed from midday to a muted late evening brightness.

There was a rumble from the shack as solar power

returned to his home. The light trap was temperamental and unreliable, but it kept things going when it worked.

Jayce unlocked his door and stepped into his shack. The narrow bed was unmade and both his other sets of clothes were scattered around the floor. He kicked a shirt up with his foot and smelled it. More mold had gotten in while the power was out. He tossed it into a water-filled pot and flicked on the broiler.

"And it's laundry for dinner, again." Jayce sat heavily on his bed and looked at the nutrient cube bag in his hands. He didn't want to consider the weakly seasoned cubes a meal. That would mean admitting a degree of failure he wasn't ready for.

He leaned forward and pried up a floor slat and took out a small metal box. He flicked it open and sighed at the meager pile of currency. Beneath the money was a picture of him and his parents when he was a baby. One more photo of his father in a military uniform was on the very bottom. His pay from the eel fishing went in, and he shut the box.

He froze. He felt something, a presence overhead. Jayce slipped a hand under a plastic-wrapped mattress and drew out a knife. There was a scrape against the roof.

"That better be you, Kay!" Jayce shouted.

There was a thump outside the door followed by a coded knock. Jayce kept the knife in hand and cracked the door open slightly. A frog-like alien with a wide green face and bulbous eyes with milky red irises was there. A hand with four overly long fingers waved at Jayce.

"How do you always know it's me?" the alien asked.

"You're the only one that ever stands on my roof. Did you break my light trap again? Because somehow I know the price to fix it's gone sky high." Jayce returned to sit on his bed.

"*Farnham*'s coming in tomorrow." Kay stood stiffly in front of the door. His eyes twisted around in their sockets, taking in the whole of the small room without turning his head. "Prices are high on everything. Big buyers. Big prices. That's what the brood mothers always tell us."

"We're hardly big down here." Jayce rolled his eyes. "How'd it go fishing for *berthel* snipes? You get cheated at the docks?"

"You too, eh?" Kay croaked out a laugh. "The *Farnham*'s close enough in hyper to send off-world passage rates— you see 'em?"

"What? When?" Jayce flung open his nightstand and took out a battered data slate. He slapped it several times and the screen flickered on.

"Two thousand quanta for steerage class." Kay's wide purple tongue licked one if his own eyes. "Which is way too much if you ask me."

"Two . . . thousand?" Jayce pinched the screen, then tossed it back into the nightstand.

"You don't have that much," the alien croaked.

"I'm not telling you how much I have, Kay. You have the biggest mouth I've ever seen—figuratively and literally. You talk about my wad and then here comes some fee from the Syndicate I've never heard from that I have to pay if I like both my thumbs." Jayce rested his chin on his knuckles. "That's almost four hundred more than the last time a merchie came through the system . . ."

"I heard one of the Syndicate underbosses asking about you in the market." Kay scratched his feet against the floor. "Asking where your stack is. That sort of thing."

"Which boss?" Jayce rubbed a bruise from his last Scale fight.

"Same one that sprang for your Cerebro. Maybe it wasn't as free as he said it was." Kay's tongue snapped out and snagged a half-open tin of small fish. His fingers squeezed and popped the thin metal.

"He wants me in his stable of fighters." Jayce's shoulders fell. "Farm me out to different floats for fixed fights. I'll get a cut barely bigger than what I would've earned in a legit fight. Bookies will get wise and then that's the end of my fighting career. I'll be an associate or a prospect by then and end up as his muscle to collect on bets or protection money... Damn it."

"Syndicate runs the planet, Jayce. What's wrong with being on the bosses' side?"

"I'm not a thug, Kay! They've rigged everything to turn us into little more than slaves and you want me to be one of *them*? They're barely better than the Tyrant. My dad was taken away and now the same sort of authority's sniffing around to draft me too."

"What's the Syndicate going to do if you say no?" Kay hopped a few inches off the floor.

"What happens to anyone that puts up a fight? I'll get blacklisted from working fishing boats at least, broken bones... Then I'll be one of those wretches on the barnacle decks eating trash. That's why I've got to get out of here, Kay. Maybe I can get a loan from—"

"No one's loaning money to anyone when there's a

merchie in-system." Kay popped the thin metal on the tin again.

"Yeah, go ahead, its gone bad anyway," Jayce went to his window and looked out over the haze pervading through the floating town.

"You leave town with a pocketful of debt and it's the lender's problem. Can't collect if you're off-world and never coming back." Kay tossed a small fish into his mouth and swallowed it whole. "You don't have enough for a ticket out of here. It'll cost even more the next time. Makes you wonder what that new government in the Core is doing. Syndicate fees are tax. Government prints money to pay off its problems and that inflation's a tax. Scrubs like us need a big score to get anywhere in life . . . But I've got some good news. Might sound like bad news, but it's good for you. And me."

The alien tensed up.

Jayce gave him a sidelong glance.

"I'm listening," he said.

"It's not a *stupid* idea. It's a riskier one. Down on the dock's another Syndicate boss. New guy I've never seen before, but he's got the right colors on so the locals aren't hassling him. He's on the docks with a . . ." He glanced around the room and whispered, "A mystic."

Jayce let out a slow sigh.

"No, no! Hear me out. This boss is asking around for a river rat to guide them somewhere. Won't say where but the pay's good. Real good. You're the best river rat I know . . . and I owe you some favors," Kay said quickly. "They've got a clipper at the docks and they're hiring hands right now."

"Wait, our float boss doesn't let mystics touch his docks. He hates all that mumbo jumbo," Jayce said.

"New guy's from three rivers over. Must have some serious weight in the Syndicate if he can ignore local-boss rules. My eighth cousin's a prospect over there and he passed me this lead. Come on, Jayce, just hear the offer." Kay inhaled the rest of the fish and left the slimy tin on a small dresser. He went to the door and rattled the knob.

"Don't the Syndicate have rules about poaching in each other's territory?" Jayce frowned.

"Maybe that's why they're paying extra. Gotta be hush-hush. You want to sit in this dump forever or you want to find out what the chance is?" Kay asked. "Look, if the pay's not enough to get you a ticket on the merchie, I'll loan you the rest. How's that?"

"You just said that no one loans money when there's a merchie in-system." Jayce eyed the door, then looked over his meager living situation.

"Difference is I know you're good for it. And let's face it, Jayce: You're too good for this dump," Kay said.

"Hey. This dump is *my* dump and . . . Fine, let's go. But I'm not agreeing to anything unless I want to." Jayce lifted a rain slicker off a hook.

Chapter 3

Jayce and Kay walked along the edge of a massive barge. The vessel was three levels high. Open archways gave glimpses of bars, games of chance, and scantily clad workers on the uppermost level. Music and laughter spilled out like a siren's call to sailors with too much money and not enough restraint.

"Amazing how the pleasure boats always show up around the big paydays," Kay said. "We spend months earning on the docks and the waters and then the Syndicate shows up to claw it all back."

"Yet we never learn," Jayce said. "Where's this contact of yours? I don't want to go in there, but I'm getting hungry and I saw a curry shop."

"Down, down." Kay pointed to a ladder hanging over the edge of the walking deck. Jayce peered over the edge. Smaller tender boats were moored against the under-level of the barge. Syndicate guards with the same double-star armbands milled about.

One of the guards looked up to blow smoke from a

cigar into the air and saw Jayce. He removed the cigar from his mouth and pointed it down the row of boats and flicked ash away.

"I don't like this," Jayce said quietly.

"Like? There's no liking. There's making money or not. Which do you want to do?" Kay poked him in the back.

"This goes bad and I'm going swimming," Jayce said and swung a leg down to the ladder.

"That goes without saying," Kay said. "Steel carp aren't attracted to the noise and all the trash from a party like this. At all."

Jayce froze on the ladder for a moment, then kept descending. When he reached bottom, an alien Syndicate member with rubbery red skin and bristled orange hair patted Jayce down, then sent him on with a tilt of his head. More guards carrying slug throwers milled around beneath the upper deck. Thick metal walls separated the machinery and storage areas that made all the fun above possible.

Jayce and Kay went to a boat docked beneath the upper level where a pair of human Syndicate thugs stopped them on the pier.

"This him?" a lean woman asked, her eyes on Jayce.

"Yes, yes, best river rat on Hemenway," Kay said. "If there's nothing else, then I'll take my money and be—"

"You stay," a man called out from behind them. The speaker was well built, with dark hair slicked back behind his ears. He had a pistol slung low on one hip and the Syndicate binary-star symbol sewn into his jacket. A slight woman covered in a deep purple veil followed behind him. The gold threading around the binary marked him as an underboss, responsible for enough Syndicate business that his word was law most anywhere on the planet.

"You said there was a finder's fee." Kay hunched slightly and clutched his arms to his chest.

"What? Really?" Jayce gave his friend a dirty look.

"Of course there's a finder's fee." The underboss walked around the pair. "But what if you've brought me a dud? That's not fair to me and my interests if you hop back to your warren. Hard for me to collect on a bad debt."

"This is Boss Grellen's flotilla," Jayce said. "I'm not a prospect or even an associate to any boss. I don't want any trouble with the families."

"Smart kid." The man put a cigarette in his mouth, then lit it by scraping two fingernails together. Hidden cybernetics sparked and a tiny flame burnt the tip. "I'm Carotan. This is my barge. I paid the docking fees to Grellen and he'll get his cut of my profits. Everything's on the up and up, so I'm fine and that means you're fine. But there's something else I'm here for. Bellarra?"

The woman under the veil stepped closer to Jayce.

"You know the Ancients' Shrine up the Tangief Estuary?" Her voice was barely more than a whisper.

Jayce took a step back and bumped into a guard that grabbed him by his shoulders. His heart pumped harder and an old, almost forgotten fear, filled his chest.

"He knows," the woman said.

"It's been years," Jayce said. "The path there's almost always impassable because of—"

"The signs tell me it's open," the woman said. "We can get there, but we do not know the way."

"Doesn't matter." Jayce shrugged off the guard's touch. "I can't get there in any of these scows." He waved a hand at the docked tenders.

"How'd you get to the Shrine?" Carotan narrowed his eyes at Jayce.

"Pilgrims took my mother and me to the Shrine . . . We never made it inside, but we got to the entrance. I remember the way. What it looks like," Jayce said.

"Never should've let the Pilgrims get off-world," the Syndicate woman said from the boat behind Jayce. "Freaks are too valuable."

"You interfere with the Pilgrims and the Adherents come to balance the scales," Carotan said. "It's never worth it. The Founders know this and that's why anyone with the colors is forbidden to bother the Pilgrims. Get smarter, Norva."

Norva slapped the top of the gunwale and shook her head.

"I need a guide to the shrine," Carotan said to Jayce. "That's all. You get us there, you get us back. You don't even have to go inside. Then you never mention this to anyone ever again. Deal?"

He held a hand out to Jayce.

Jayce looked at the hand. "I don't work for free."

Carotan raised an eyebrow, then glanced up at the ceiling.

"It won't be as easy as potting up eels or 'dines. Say two thousand quanta." Carotan smiled.

Jayce's eyes went wide. The Syndicate underboss had read him like a book . . . or Kay had told him about Jayce's desire to get off-world.

"I'm feeling generous. Two thousand two hundred." Carotan turned his palms up. "Only way you'll make any more than that this fast is if you get lucky on my tables. And let me tell you a secret: no one gets that lucky on my tables."

"Drop the money in a Goodman account before we leave or no deal," Jayce said. A glimmer of hope rose in the back of his mind.

"This little shit thinks he can leverage us?" Norva hissed. "Let me give him a good kicking to remind him who he's dealing with."

"Now, now. The Founders insist that everyone that does business with the families gets paid. Bad business if creditors end up dead. Harder to get anyone to work with us, particularly in these trying times." Carotan poked a fingertip into a wristband and a holo screen appeared between them.

Jayce's eyes darted over the contract as Carotan filled in forms.

"Wait, is this an AI contract?" Jayce asked.

"They're only illegal in the Federation. I keep my AI core in an EMP shell with plenty of kill switches. Don't worry. No repeat of the Collapse on my watch . . . There. We get back and you cash out. No matter what we find." Carotan pressed a thumb to a blinking field.

Jayce's thumb hovered over the blinking field. "This contract is for 'services rendered.'"

"The numbers are what's important. I don't want my brother to have any worries about what we find in his territory. He might want a cut," Carotan said.

"Fair enough." Jayce put his thumb to the blinking field. "Boss Targ's skimmed plenty of money off of me."

"Inked and filed." Carotan flicked his hand through the holo and it vanished. "Get aboard. I'm told we can't take our time on this one."

"That scow?" Jayce looked back and forth from Carotan and the tender with Norva on it. "There's no way it has the range to get to the Shrine and back."

"Get up here, river rat." Norva stomped the deck. Jayce stepped onto the boat and followed Norva to the engine block at the stern. More Syndicate members came aboard; the alien bruiser had Kay by the scruff of the neck.

"Just give me my finder's fee and I'll go!" Kay's webbed feet kicked back and forth. "I'll—I'll hit the tables before I leave! Even the rounder game with the triple zeros. Everyone knows that's a rip-off!"

"You get paid when I know you've delivered what you promised." Carotan poked Kay in the chest. "You want to be a problem or you want a day's pay added to your fee?"

"You're getting paid to deliver me?" Jayce asked. "I'm hurt, Kay."

"I'll work! I'll work!" Kay squealed. The guard dropped him on the deck.

"Look here." Norva slapped Jayce on the arm. She glanced around, then lifted up a panel. Pale white light illuminated her face.

"It can't be ..." Jayce looked into the engine block. An ivory sliver no bigger than a fingertip glowed within a power cradle. "Where'd you get a phase crystal? Is it Attuned?"

"If it was Attuned it would be in a hyper ship, not down here." Norva slammed the panel shut. "Any worries about our range now? No? Good. Then add this to your list of things you never saw and get to the conn and tell Gorgi the course to the Shrine."

"A blessing." Carotan sent his men to the outer edge of the tender's deck with the words. "Bellarra, roll the bones."

The veiled woman touched a cloth bag tied to her belt.

"I rolled this morning, sir...we may anger their spirits," the mystic said.

"Can't leave the dock without a blessing." Gorgi, a rail-thin man with a cybernetic right arm, leaned out of the conn. The rest of the crew grumbled. Everyone on Hemenway lived and died on the seas and rivers and sailors' superstitions were ingrained.

Jayce reached up and gripped the upper edge of the conn booth. He heaved himself onto the top. He tested the grip of his shoes on the metal. The last lookout had kept the top free of mold and had scratched up the metal for better footing.

"As we wish." Bellarra pressed her palms together in front of her chest, then chanted as she raised her hands up overhead, then let them separate as she kept her gaze to the sky. She went to one knee, then drew the small bag. She held the opening to her mouth and exhaled, then overturned the bag.

Small flecks of what looked like silver and ivory spilled onto the deck. Each lacked the luster of the phase crystal powering the engine block, but kept a hint of internal light. The fragments rolled about...then oriented of their own accord, all pointing straight at Jayce.

The Syndicate crew looked over at him.

"Due east, three degrees off declination until we pass

Widower Rock." Jayce pointed the same direction as the flecks and out across the water.

"Our quest is true." Bellarra did a double take at Jayce, then she hurriedly scooped everything back into the bag.

"Unmoor, get us out of here." Carotan slapped the railings. "The sooner we get there..." He rubbed his hands together.

Jayce bent over the front of the conn booth and looked through the window at the pilot. "What're we even looking for?"

"You're getting paid to guide us. I'm paid to steer," Gorgi said. "Mind your own business then, yeah?"

"You don't know," Jayce deadpanned.

"No. But the boss wouldn't risk so much for something unless it was worth a hell of a lot," Gorgi said.

"Head-down-mouth-shut sort of thing." Jayce gave the side of the conn two slaps. "Watch for strangle kelp out past the first buoy. It's thick this season."

He hopped back on his feet and grabbed a bit of molded plastic around a guy wire. He leaned forward as the boat chugged away from the dock and out into the fog.

Chapter 4

Jayce put a hand over his eyes and looked out to the horizon. Scattered peaks of submerged mountain ranges cast shadows in the thinning fog. He relaxed and sat on the conn tower, feet dangling over the side.

"Hup-hup." Kay hopped onto the roof, earning a shout from the pilot. Kay passed a water bottle to Jayce. "What's going to eat us?"

"Crystal-tooth migrations cleared out last week," Jayce said. "We should be clear of anything until we reach the Misha's Wreck..." He went quiet and drank from bottle.

"You're mad at me, aren't you?" Kay asked.

"I've got reason, don't I? You should've said the work was for a boss—not even the boss of where we live. They get jealous, you know."

"OK, yes, but—"

"But I get this overpowered scow there and back again and I've got my ticket off this waterlogged nowhere. My other options are to indenture myself to the crew of the *Farnham* when it makes port, and spend the next many years scrubbing decks and having my debt increased every time I eat and breathe, or . . . stay here. Forever," Jayce said.

"It's not so bad here." Kay squatted next to Jayce, his knees bent next to his head. "There's so much family to live with."

"*You* have family. I don't. Humans tend to end up here, not grow up here. You ever even see a girl my age?" Jayce asked.

"I'm not so good with your ages. The"—Kay glanced over his shoulders—"bone speaker keeps looking at you. I owe you. How can I help with courtship?"

"By the Light, Kay, not the time. Don't worry about me and there's nothing to forgive. I don't die and you've done me a favor helping me get out of here." Jayce passed the water back.

"Where will you go?" Kay asked.

"To the sky and beyond. That's where my mother always said she'd take me after my father disappeared. There's a whole galaxy out there to see, Kay. The view out here . . . just never changes."

"My family is here. Family is future for Chorda," Kay said.

"That's great for—Don't move." Jayce thrust an arm across Kay's chest. He pointed to a pool of bubbles off the port side of the boat. Jayce tapped his heel against the conn wall and rapped out a code.

The engines cut out and the boat ran forward. Sailors stopped what they were doing and meandered toward the middle of the deck.

Jayce jabbed two fingers into his mouth and blew a high-pitched whistle. Kay was still as a statue.

Everything went quiet as the boat drifted on. Dead silent but for the slap of waves against the hull. A hatch slammed open and Norva stomped onto the deck, adjusting her belt.

"What?" she asked.

Tentacles burst out of the water and slammed onto the deck. Thick pads with throbbing suckers slithered back and forth, moving toward Norva. The Syndicate enforcer let out a cry and backpedaled. One heel clipped the open hatch and she fell back. The tentacles caught her before she hit the deck and dragged her into the water.

She screamed the whole way.

"Nautilus! Fire six yards to the east!" Jayce drew a knife from a scabbard on his hip and dove into the water as Norva was pulled under. His knife hit the water first, striking a wiggling tentacle. Tepid water enveloped Jayce as he worked the blade back and forth, cutting into the appendage. A cloud of dark blue blood blossomed in the water.

The nautilus's tentacles bumped into him, the flesh ice cold to the touch. Jayce ripped his knife down and through the wide pad at the end of the feeder tentacle. The water around him darkened with blood. Something horrible brushed against his feet and Jayce huffed out bubbles.

He kicked hard and followed the bubbles to the surface. His head and shoulders burst through a sheen of nautilus blood. Jayce moved his hands and feet in small circles to keep his head above water. Thin strands of blue goop ran down his face and over his lips.

Norva surfaced, arms flailing, her skin marred by sucker marks. She let out an awful cry and kept splashing.

"Don't move. Don't move or it'll—"

A patch of water roiled with bubbles between Norva and Jayce.

A *crack* broke through the air as a harpoon slammed into the disturbed water. Tentacles shot up around the pair, quivering rapidly before disappearing back into the dark. Someone grabbed Jayce by the collar and hauled him onto the deck.

Jayce stayed there on his hands and knees, panting as water and blood spattered onto the deck. Norva groaned in pain as Carotan's alien bruiser set her down, his other hand holding a harpoon launcher.

"That wasn't 'five yards east.'" Carotan stepped up to Jayce. The last of the nautilus's blood dappled on the Syndicate boss's boots.

"I-I thought I could get her . . . but she was too deep. Kay! Kay, get the blue injectors from the aid kit. Nautilus blood's poisonous and she'll seize up like a bad engine if too much gets into her cuts." Jayce rolled onto his back, his knife clutched to his chest.

"The rat's no good," one of the Syndicate said. "He should've seen that naut—"

"Any of *you* see it?" Carotan helped Jayce up. "'Every eye not on their job is on the water.' I hired you because you know how to crew a ship!"

Norva began coughing and wheezing as her airway constricted. Kay hopped over and pressed a corroded metal injector to her neck. There was a hiss of air and Norva's eyes went wide. She sat up, jaw slack, and gulped down air.

"N-n-not the whole thing. You idiot!" Jayce slapped his hands to the sides of his head.

Norva jumped up and began pacing up and down the deck.

"I panicked!" Kay waved the injector overhead. "I always panic! That's why I don't get hired for work on the water by myself!"

"She'll be OK in an hour or . . . three," Jayce said. "Blues dump antidote and enough synth adrenaline to counter even a full nautilus bite."

"Let's go!" Norva stomped her feet. "Why are we just sitting here?" Her teeth began chattering.

"She'll crash hard too . . . Bah." Carotan gave Jayce a pat on the shoulder. "Back to your perch, rat."

"Sure." Jayce smacked his lips. "Ah . . . there's that taste. Nautilus always makes my lips go numb. Got to love it."

"Punch it, Gorgi!" Carotan traced a circle overhead. "We're running out of daylight."

The boat lurched forward and Jayce had to rush to get back onto the conn tower. The wind caught his hair and the breeze was cool against his skin as the boat cut through white-capped waves.

The boat slowed and maneuvered around toothy rocks. Rusted-out steel and piles of fish bones littered the bare mountain cliffs and outcrops.

Jayce swung from one side of the top of the conn to the other, one hand tight on the handle on a guy wire securing an antenna to the conn.

"Deep. Five hands to starboard," Jayce called out. The boat turned to the right and chugged forward.

Sweat beaded Jayce's face and neck. The water levels on Hemenway rose and fell with the wild climate shifts on the poles that drew water into and out of continent-sized glaciers. Mountaintops could rise from the oceans and unpredictable deep currents with hazardous jagged peaks lay just below the surface.

Remnants of less careful—or lucky—vessels were scattered around them. Cargo was picked over by scavengers quickly enough, but whatever could rot was left behind. The Tangief Estuary was notorious for missing ships and sailors who never came home.

"You been through here, rat?" Gorgi asked from the conn. He spun the ship's wheel and there was a screech of metal and a bump that shook the ship.

"Two hands port, slow one quarter," Jayce said. He blocked the setting sunlight with one hand and peered deeper into the peaks. "Was here years ago. Water was lower then, not as dangerous as it is now."

"They say there's ghosts." Gorgi touched a medallion hanging from his neck then kissed the back of his hand.

"Always," Jayce whispered. The memory of freezing cold water and a woman's face underwater was just behind his thoughts.

"Jayce, how much farther?" Carotan asked from just outside the conn.

"Through there." Jayce pointed to a gap in the rocks that didn't appear to be wide enough for the ship at first glance.

"Ugh . . ." Gorgi thumped the roof. "Rat?"

"Slow down . . . half hand to port." Jayce raised a hand. He felt the breeze against his fingers and eyed small whirlpools and eddies in the water. The boat bobbled through the gap . . . then screeched to a halt.

"Rat!" Carotan shouted.

"Move everyone to port and gun the engine," Jayce said. "Hurry! There's a swell coming and if we—"

"Asses port!" Carotan clapped his hands and shoved one of his guards to one side of the boat.

The ship tilted to one side and moved forward with a scrape against rocks. It moved through the gap between mountain peaks. They came out into thick, freezing fog. Jayce stood up as they drifted into the deep blue haze.

"Stop!" Jayce stomped three times on the conn roof. He looked around, but couldn't see more than a few yards in any direction; even the stern of the boat was washed out in the fog.

"Bellarra . . . this is why you're here." Carotan motioned the mystic to him. She lifted her veil, revealing a wrinkled face. She nibbled on her bottom lip as her eyes darted from side to side.

"Come on, you're one of the Attuned." The boss's hand crept toward his holstered pistol. "I made the terms of your employment quite clear."

"Yes . . . it's just that I've never felt power like this," Bellarra said. "Give me a moment to scry." She went to her knees and opened the bag of slivers.

Jayce tilted one ear up. The sound of something . . . almost like a song was in the air, but so faint he wasn't sure if he was imagining it or not. Words carried on a breeze, and he thought he heard his mother's voice.

He turned around and stared into the fog. Something was there just beyond his sight, but he wasn't sure how he knew.

"There!" Bellarra looked up from the spilled scry

shards and pointed in the same direction Jayce was looking.

"Read the water." Carotan slapped his hand against the conn booth.

"No predators this shallow," Jayce said. "Keep speed low . . . maybe the Shrine's not flooded out."

"For the amount of money I paid for this lead it had better not be," Carotan said.

The clipper coasted forward into the murky fog. The sun's light diffused through the sky into a uniform swath. The skitter of rocks in the distance echoed around the boat. Crew drew pistols and cutlasses with no order or prompting from Carotan.

"I feel the energy." Bellarra raised a hand, fingers splayed apart. "We're so close."

A sensation rose behind Jayce's eyes. A slight pressure that added an electric taste to every breath he took.

"Conn." Jayce rapped knuckles against the roof. "Half hand to starboard. Cut engine."

"She-witch is pointing the other way," Gorgi grunted.

"You heard me." Jayce leaned out over the conn, one hand tight on the line behind him.

Gorgi mumbled curses and followed Jayce's directions. A shadow loomed out of the fog, and the helmsman stopped the clipper's forward momentum with a rumble of engines switching into reverse. A sheer cliff face appeared and Gorgi turned the boat hard to run parallel with it.

"There!" Norva cried out, pointing to a perfect circle cut into the rock. Glyphs and runes, weathered down to a faint echo of their original design, glittered around the circumference. The hole was wide enough for two men to walk through easily, with the bottom just barely touching the water line.

Jayce edged away from the opening. The sensation behind his eyes had fallen into his chest and turned into growing fear. A cold sweat broke out as his gaze stayed locked on the deep darkness of the shrine.

There was something in there. Something that wanted him.

"Drop rock anchor and kit up!" Carotan shouted. He drew a coil pistol and pressed a battery cube into a slot on top of the weapon. Magnetic coils hummed to life down the barrel. "Bellarra . . . how are the signs?"

The mystic dropped the scry shards to the deck. They rolled about, twisting from some unseen force and never resting.

"Bring the boy." She pointed at Jayce.

"Wait. What? Oh no." Jayce edged away from her, his toes keeping him on the conn. "That's not what you're paying me for. I don't—don't—"

"I don't care." Carotan leveled the pistol at him. "She says you go, you're going. Figure we can get ourselves back to the flotilla without you. Grab him."

A big hand grabbed Jayce by the belt and jerked him back. He landed in the alien's meaty arms. His heels hit the deck and the thug carried him off the ship by his collar.

Jayce struggled, then gave up as the burly alien didn't budge at all.

"Finally." Norva picked up a hydraulic piston connected to a thick chain bolted to the ship. She heaved back and slammed one end against the rock face and an anchor locked into the mountain. "We sailed halfway across the planet for this score."

The Shrine entrance was two feet over the gunwale as it bumped against the cliff. Old glyphs carved into the rock had eroded away. Dried strands of kelp marred the glittering stone of the Shrine's entrance.

"Gentle beings." Carotan stood before the hole. "The Ancients provide to the worthy. The Ancients provide to the faithful. Don't forget, everything we find in there belongs to me...then you get your cut."

The crew, armed with coil rifles and carrying packs of ammo and supplies, hopped off the boat.

The mystic held up a hand and approached the entrance.

"Do not upset the Shrine," Bellarra said. "It will reject us if we damage anything. I must appease the spirits in the great beyond before we go any closer."

She raised her palms to the sky and her sleeves fell to her shoulders, exposing old, blurry tattoos. She began chanting as she waved her hands over head, like she was trying to unravel a net.

Seawater dribbled out of the entrance to the Shrine. Jayce had a difficult time tearing his eyes away from the darkness within.

"How'd it even get here?" Kay asked. "This spot's almost always underwater and there's no trace of any scaffolding. The Ancients just...how?" He hopped up onto Jayce's vacated spot on the conn.

"It's always been here," Jayce said. "Before colonists ever came to the system."

"Huh? How do you even know that? You've been here before?" Kay asked.

"The ship that rescued me after my mom...she dropped anchor in the bay while they did some repairs." Jayce pressed a foot against the wet rock. "It was the first time I remember being on land."

"Bunch of nonsense." Norva plugged one nostril and snorted out something green into the water. "If she's Attuned, I'll eat a bowl of muck when we get back to your float."

"'Attuned' to what?" Kay's eyes shifted from side to side independent of each other.

"Mystic talk." Norva frowned. "Means they're connected to the big woo-woo in the sky. Not everyone's like them. Have to be tuned up to pull a stone from beyond the Veil. Us normals can't do that."

"That's what this Shrine's for?" Kay shifted from webbed foot to webbed foot. "Jayce...you knew where this place is and you didn't say anything?"

"It's dead," Jayce said. "Was dead. The water recedes every couple of years and there's always someone that comes looking for a Veil stone to find and sell. Most get eaten on the way. Something's different this time."

"But we've got a mystic with us. So we've got a higher chance, right?" Kay hopped slightly. "Just think of our cut!"

Bellarra glared at Kay over her shoulder. Norva raised her coil pistol slightly.

"Sorry!" Kay slunk lower and whispered. "So sorry."

"Boss thinks she's the real thing," Norva said. "If she ain't, we'll have a little less weight to haul home." She chuckled at her own joke.

"How does he know"—Jayce squeezed his eyes shut for a moment as a headache pinched his temples—"she's Attuned?"

"She's got some Veil flecks. Used them to read Carotan's mind and tell him some things that only he'd know. He's got her on the payroll to tell his fortune. He got wind of this place and some old Paragon text and he told her she was going to cast a spell and get a stone for him."

"A Paragon was here?" Jayce asked. "I thought they were a myth."

"Nah, one of their dusty old books. Paragons won't come to Syndicate territory if they know what's good for them. The Family put a kill-on-site order on any that trespass into our turf. They're too eager to enforce Governance laws in territory that's not theirs," Norva said.

"Didn't some Paragons bring down the Tyrant?" Kay asked. "How could a myth do that?"

"It is done." Bellarra bent forward and her arms swooped down. "The great spirit is appeased."

"Anyone disrespects anything in there and you swim home. Shore party, go." Carotan waved his men into the shrine. He jumped up into the opening and helped Bellarra off the boat. The boss took a small disc off his belt and squeezed it. He let it go and it lifted into the air and lit up the tunnel.

"In you go." Norva pushed Jayce toward the opening. Jayce felt like there was a force field over the entrance, but his hand passed through the threshold easily enough. He glanced at the worn runes. Their glittering continued, a steady static of weak light.

"Just my imagination," Jayce said to himself.

The tunnel angled upward, the walls slick with mold and slime. The only sound came from boots falling on the rocks. Water dripped onto Jayce's head and shoulders as they continued up the incline and deeper into the mountain.

Jayce cocked an ear up and stopped.

"You hear that?" He looked back to the brute behind him.

"Hear what?" the alien asked.

"The music . . . No." Jayce tapped an ear. "There's no echo."

"Keep moving." Norva fell a few steps behind him.

"Ha-ha!" came from farther ahead in the tunnel. Jayce tensed up and reached for his knife. "I found it!" Carotan's words reverberated down the walls.

Dread rose in Jayce's heart as he stepped out of the tunnel and into a cavern. The floor and walls were perfectly smooth, the ceiling and distant walls lost to darkness. The lights carried by the Syndicate members weakened within feet of the party.

A pair of curved crystalline posts jutted out of a slightly raised platform in the middle of the room. Jayce followed the curve of the posts and noted the arcs would join between the two, forming a circle the same width and height of the tunnel they came through.

Carotan walked around the platform, shining his light up and down the posts. The light sent cascades of sparks and tiny motes skittering through the crystal. Jayce felt an itch up and down his legs in tune with Carotan's light touching the posts.

"It's active," Carotan said. "By the will of the Tyrant, it's happening."

Several of the guards grumbled at the boss.

"Sorry, force of habit. Witch . . . summon a stone for me," he said.

"We should pray," Bellarra said. "Make an offering to the Ancients that left this bounty for us." The mystic held her hands close to her chest, pawing at her robes.

"That's not the plan." Carotan stopped his prowling. "That was never the plan. We don't have time for anything but the ritual. Get to work and do what I pay you for."

Bellarra took small steps toward the platform, flanked by two guards.

"What is this? What are you doing?" Jayce asked.

Norva edged close to him and poked him in the ribs with the barrel of a coil pistol.

"Hush, kid . . . witch says this sort of thing only happens once a generation," she said. "The Ancients built their Shrines through the galaxy. Every system they touched, they left these portals to their realm behind. These things are the only way to get new stones . . . well, the only way for us normal people to get one. Only the Attuned can touch the Ancients' realm. Which is why we need the witch."

Bellarra lifted her veil and tossed it back. Her eyes were wide, her lips so dry they were cracked. She raised her arms to her side and began chanting.

Jayce took an involuntary step forward as a pale blue light rose from the posts. Motes of light streaked toward a central point in the portal framed by the posts.

Norva grabbed him by the elbow and pulled him back.

"You screw this up and Carotan will take his time killing you," she hissed.

"Something's wrong, I can feel it." Jayce tried to swallow, but his throat had gone bone dry.

Bellarra began shaking as more motes coalesced into a glowing point. An ivory-colored stone, rent through with golden lines that pulsed in time with an unheard heartbeat, emerged in the portal. Light grew around the stone forming a flimsy plane.

Through the plane was another world. Broken mountains and a shattered sky faded in and out of reality. Grasslands and meandering streams where tall limbed creatures wandered in the distance.

Jayce reached forward. Something there felt deeply familiar.

Around the image, blazing points of light formed into constellations. The site burned into Jayce's vision, was still there even when he mashed his eyes shut and turned his gaze away.

"I have it. I have it!" Bellarra struggled to her feet and stepped onto the platform. The lights jolted with bloodred colors, washing out the glimpse of the world beyond.

"No . . . no, don't!" Jayce lunged forward.

Norva whacked the butt of her pistol against the back of his head and sent Jayce sprawling.

Bellarra snatched the stone with one hand. She tugged at the stone, but it held fast against absolutely nothing. She pulled again, then fear spread over her face.

"It won't let me go . . . it won't let me go!" she screamed and tried to yank her hand back. She gripped her wrist and kept trying.

"Don't touch her!" Carotan stepped closer to her, waving his pistol from side to side. "No one even move!"

Bellarra thrashed her bound arm, then fell to her knees, her hand still stuck to the stone. The color leached out of her fingers and she let out a wail. The gray spread up her arm, changing the purple of her robes to the same dead color. She strained her neck away from the encroachment and let out a gasp as it reached the base of her skull.

Her arm solidified and began crumbling. The mystic's face froze in terror as cracks ran through her body. Bellarra fractured and fell apart. Steam rose from her remains as every lump crumbled into loose sand.

Dust evaporated away, exposing the ivory-and-gold stone that she'd held.

The posts went dormant and cold.

"No . . . no, this is mine." Carotan drew a pair of tongs from his belt and tapped the edge against the stone. He gripped it for a split second and let it fall back into the vanishing remains of the mystic. The boss set a metal box on the floor and flipped it open. He used the tongs to set the stone into the box like he was touching a hot coal with his bare hand.

Carotan slapped the box closed and slipped it into his jacket.

Jayce drew in a ragged breath. He hadn't been breathing and air suddenly felt like a luxury he couldn't pay for.

"All right . . . all right, we've got what we came for," Carotan said. He held his coil pistol close to his face. "I'm the only one that knows the buyer. You'll all get your cut. Don't worry."

"Boss, you never said we'd get a full Veil stone!" Norva shouted. Her words did not echo off the walls. "That's worth . . . a hell of a lot more than the pot we signed up for!"

"It's not from the deep Veil. It'll never be starship grade. But it's enough to power a space station or a whole flotilla for the next standard century," Carotan said.

Some of the bruisers cracked their knuckles and swept the sides of their coats behind their holstered pistols.

"If our shares were fair . . . we'd be a lot happier," Norva said. "You think we can't find another buyer? We wear the Syndicate's colors. We've earned our cut."

"Of course. Of course!" Carotan holstered his pistol and held his hands out to his sides. "I had to keep things quiet or the other families would start sniffing around. Boss Pollara gets word and it's his right to broker the deal. You want to factor in *his* cut? Full payout for everyone. My buyer's discreet. Any of you have a contact that'll put quanta in your palm without Pollara's tax?"

Norva smiled.

"There you go, boss. We knew you were true to the colors." She aimed her pistol at Jayce's temple. "Loose end?"

"No. No, kid's solid. Besides, we need him to get us back. Then he's gonna skip the whole sector and never speak of this to anyone again. Ain't that right, kid?" Carotan put a heavy hand on Jayce's shoulder.

"Never speak about *what* again, sir?" Jayce stared at Carotan's chest. He felt a pull toward the stone, but kept his hands to his sides.

"Smart kid." Carotan gave him a pat. "Back to the clipper."

Jayce followed Norva back into the tunnel. Every time he blinked, the constellations were there, hanging in his perception. He mentally traced lines as the stars appeared in sequence. He didn't know what it was supposed to be, but he couldn't get the confusing image out of his mind.

Chapter 5

✦

Kay squatted at the front edge of the conn tower. Jayce stood behind him; his hold on the plastic grip creaked as he rolled his hand backward and forward. High thunderclouds filled the horizon, the tops stretched into anvils by high-altitude winds.

"You good, Jayce?" Kay licked an eye.

"Huh, what?" Jayce shook his head like he'd just woken up.

"You're mad at me, yeah?" The amphibian alien lifted his feet off the conn tower and flexed his toes. "I didn't know it would be so . . . weird."

"Thanks, Kay, really appreciate that," Jayce said with little sincerity. "Let's see if we actually get paid or if we get fed to the neko-fish at the bottom of the flotilla." He looked back to the engines where Carotan was alone. The Syndicate boss kept touching his jacket where he kept the Veil stone.

"See, this is when it's good to be friends with me. You? You're going off-world. No one's going to look for you. Too easy to drop you for neko food. Me? I go missing and my clan comes looking for me. Problems for the Syndicate. Questions asked. Questions that need to be answered. A cut to the big boss that wasn't paid. Cheaper to let me live. And you. You too."

"At least I've got that going for me," Jayce said. He stood up on his toes. "Flotilla, ho!"

The tops of distant stacks and lights from the vice barges appeared in the distance.

Syndicate members came onto the deck and began readying ropes and preparing to dock.

"Strange clouds," Kay said. "Too dark for the weather."

"Odd." Jayce peered at a dark mass in the storm clouds over his home flotilla. "Something's casting a shadow in the storm."

"Port authority's not coming up." Gorgi leaned out of the conn and tapped a headphone over one ear. "Your float not know how to do their job?"

"My clan works the comms. We take pride in our work," Kay said.

In the distance, the clouds broke around the shape, revealing the prow of a ship.

"Is that the *Farnham*? Is that your ride out of here?" Kay asked.

The clouds cleared and Jayce made out weapon emplacements that a merchant ship like the *Farnham* would never have carried. This was a warship, one larger than the flotilla it hung over. The hull was a dirty egg-shell color, marred by battle damage and scars of rough slipspace exits. Turrets along the ventral hull slewed to aim turbo laser batteries at the ships lashed together.

Giant blast doors opened slowly. Dark shapes of fighters swooped out and flew through the sky.

The last of the clouds blew past the ship, revealing a symbol on the hull made from shattered fragments of defeated ships.

Ice ran through Jayce's chest.

"The Tyrant is here!" Kay shouted, hopping up and down. "They're going to kill us all and turn us into—"

A bullet snapped over Jayce's head. He ducked down level with Kay, who'd lost interest in hopping. Carotan ran up to the conn, pistol barrel smoking.

"Gorgi! Turn us about and make for the Mackanara flotilla. We've got plenty of charge in the engines—"

A shadow roared overhead. The wake slammed the clipper a heartbeat later, sweeping water and spray into Jayce.

The ship turned away from the flotilla toward an escape. A pair of bright yellow plasma bolts slammed into the water ahead of them. Geysers shot up and rained down on Jayce and the conn.

A Tyrant fighter, the wings fashioned to resemble stretched flesh, hovered over the ship, the prows aligned. The fighter swung toward the flotilla, pointing the way for the clipper.

"Gorgi . . . take us in," Carotan said. "They're not here for the Veil stone. They spent more than that to get here from their territory."

"How is the Tyrant here?" Kay hugged Jayce's knee. "I thought he was killed years ago."

"You can tell them that when we dock," Jayce said. "They're not supposed to be here . . ." Jayce thought to the photo of his father in the Tyrant's uniform back in his hovel. It had come through the Net the last time he and his mother ever heard from him.

The clipper rumbled forward through choppy water.

"All of you listen up," Carotan addressed the crew. "Let me do the talking. The Tyrant's survivors aren't idiots. They know better than to mess with a Syndicate world. Our two stars have them by the throat." He touched the patch sewn into his sleeve at the shoulder. "We keep the Governance from moving on the sectors they still control, they abide by our rules in our space. Same as everyone else. They pay the vig or we take it from them."

"The Tyrant kidnaps the living and turns them into no-mind cyborgs." Kay clutched Jay harder. "I'm too young to be forced into the army!"

"Shh!" Jayce put a hand on Kay's head. "That's just a rumor. Let's just stay calm. Isn't this why the bosses always tell us they get a cut? Because they run interference for us and keep raiders away."

"There's nothing but slime eels in the tanks. What does the Tyrant want with that?" Kay asked.

"Tyrant's dead. Everyone knows that . . . so what are they even doing this far from the Core?" Jayce said. "How do they even have a battleship?"

"Do you want to ask them?" Kay slunk behind Jayce's legs.

"No . . . but I've got a bad feeling we're going to find out." Jayce spotted a navigation buoy and made a long, multi-pitched whistle. Crew went to work prepping their arrival.

"What's the boss man going to tell the Tyrant's men? That we were out fishing?" Kay asked.

"Hold's empty." Jayce shrugged.

"Maybe we're bad fisherman. We'll tell them the big one got away, yeah?" Kay mumbled as the clipper motored into the piers beneath Carotan's barge. Tall soldiers in black-and-white armor and long battle rifles waited for them at the docks.

The uniforms echoed the simple high-collared tunic his father wore in the last photo he ever sent home. The soldiers' armor was dented and scratched; the mail bodysuits under the plates had different styles, like they'd cobbled together a full set from different manufactures. The black-and-white bands of armor were woven together to give them the appearance of skeletons from a distance.

The soldiers' silhouettes looked human, except for the one crouched on the edge of the pier, clawed feet gripping the rusted wharf. Long arms that ended in skin the color of an old bruise and glittering nails that scraped against metal. The lurker's helm had an elongated snout and bared teeth worked into the faceplate.

The soldier's eye slits glowed red.

"Oh boy." Jayce swallowed hard.

"Hello!" Carotan put one foot up on the gangplank. "How can the Syndicate assist yo—ah!"

The feral-looking soldier grabbed him by the front jacket and threw him to the pier.

Coil rifles whined and targeting dots appeared on the crew's chests as the soldiers edged toward Carotan, who had his hands up.

A waft of cold air hit the back of Jayce's head. He felt something touch the side of his neck. He glanced down and saw a long blade coated in frost perilously close to his exposed skin.

"Be a dear and step off," a voice whispered in his ear. It was heavily modulated and soft. "No heroes. No trouble."

Jayce turned to look at who was behind him on the conn tower but the cold of the knife stung him without drawing blood.

The voice tsk-tsk-tsk'd at him.

"Moving," Jayce said quietly. He hopped off the conn tower and landed on the pier. He joined a line of the rest of the crew. The soldiers formed a loose perimeter around them. The wolfen soldier kept one clawed hand on Carotan's chest, drumming nail tips against his jacket.

A blur moved off the conn tower and hit the pier without a sound. The smear of light collapsed into an ivory-and-gold stone nearly identical to the one they'd recovered from the Shrine.

A lithe figure materialized behind the stone. His armor was matte black, with small horns on a skull-fronted helmet. The Veil stone glimmered until the soldier pressed a palm to it. He raised his other hand and leveled the frosted short sword at the crew.

"Which one is it, Reman?" he asked, his voice skewed by his full-faced helmet.

"They all reek of the Veil, Master." The Draug soldier removed his mask, revealing a lupine face. One cybernetic eye glowed from a dull metal plate over one side of his face that stretched partway down his snout. Cybernetic muscles flexed on one shoulder. Reman sniffed the air.

"I am Lahash, sworn officer in the Tyrant's service."

The skull-faced soldier walked slowly around the crew. His sword grew longer; the tip scratched out a line on the dock. "All artifacts of the Realm Beyond belong to him by right. All those touched by the Realm Beyond will serve the Tyrant by right."

Kay, next to Jayce, began sweating, leaving an oily sheen on his skin.

Jayce frowned at his friend, who shouldn't have anything to worry about.

"I feel it," Lahash said. "Something fresh from beyond the Veil. It's delicate . . . in need of curing to be put to proper use for the Tyrant's glory. I do not wish to damage it. I want the stone and I want the one . . . who called it forth."

"This world is under the Syndicate's protection," Carotan snarled. "There's a deal between the Tyrant and the Family. You can't just—urk!"

Reman squeezed Carotan's throat.

Lahash took his time as he walked over to Carotan as the man went blue without oxygen. He raised his hand and shuffled two fingers against each other. Reman loosened his grip.

"Does this situation"—Lahash glanced up at the edge of the warship's hull visible over the pier—"feel equal to you? The Tyrant takes what is ours. The pair of freaks running your little operation agreed to that. Now . . . give me the stone and give me the Attuned that called the stone into our realm."

"Sh-she lied to me!" Carotan laughed nervously. "The witch was never Attuned. That's why the Weeping Saint punished her. She's nothing but dust."

"Liar," Reman snorted. "The Attuned is here. One of them has the power or has the stone. You feel it?"

"I do." Lahash raised a hand and Reman hauled Carotan to his feet. "Where did you hide the stone?"

"It's mine!" Carotan canted his head to one side to glare at Norva, then one hand brushed against his jacket.

Lahash flicked his sword and the blade slashed across Carotan's chest. He cried out in surprise as he fell back onto the dock. His sliced jacket flew open and the box holding the stone taken from the Shrine flipped open. There was a glint in the air and a stone landed in Lahash's palm. The Syndicate boss pawed at his torso, but there was no injury to him.

"Now that wasn't so . . ." The skull-faced enforcer held up the stone. Its luster faded in and out. He squeezed it between his fingers, and it shattered into chalky bits and a tiny battery. "It's a fake . . . disappointing."

"What?" Carotan slapped at his jacket pockets. "No! I saw it come straight out of the Veil. Which one of you bottom-feeding trash—" He tried to sit up but Lahash stepped on his chest and pinned him to the deck.

"The stone isn't worth your life . . ." Lahash raised his sword and the blade grew longer, hissing as the metal edge seemed to build itself. "Who called it forth?"

He ground his heel against Carotan's chest.

"Sh-she's dead!" Kay stammered. "The spirits on the other side cursed her and—"

"Another liar." Reman snatched the Chorda by the collar and hoisted him up. Kay croaked and kicked at the air like he was trying to swim away. "There's an Attuned among you and they'd better . . ."

The wolfen sniffed hard, then swiped metal edged claws through Kay's flank. He kept his hold as the alien cried out; blood spurted from the gouge as Reman snatched something out of Kay's body. He tossed Kay aside like he was nothing more than garbage.

Kay rolled across the dock, leaving splotches of violet blood like footprints, and bumped into Jayce's shins. His old friend looked up at him, Kay's bulbous eyes wide with shock and disbelief.

Jayce knelt next to him and pressed his hand into the wound. Blood flowed over his fingers with each beat of Kay's weakening heart.

Reman shook one hand and Kay's torn clothes fell to the deck with a wet plop. He pinched the true Veil stone he'd ripped out of Kay between two claw tips and held it high.

"Kay? Stay with me, buddy," Jayce put a hand atop Kay's as the light went out of his eyes. Jayce lunged toward Reman but a kick to his back sent him flat against the deck. A boot against the back of his upper back pinned him down. He felt the cold muzzle of a coil rifle against his skull and he stopped struggling.

"It wasn't that one." Reman snorted at Kay's body on the ground and moved toward Lahash.

"That cheating bastard," Carotan snarled. "Wolf boy did me a favor! The Syndicate stands for honor. Brotherhood! If I was the float boss on this rust bucket I'd..." He gave Norva a quick glance. "Why, I'd want...blackjack!"

The rest of the Syndicate crew burst into action at the code word. They tackled the Tyrant soldiers and drew hidden coil guns.

Carotan thrust one hand up at Lahash and three of his fingers locked out straight.

Lahash tightened his grip on his hilt and the blade stretched out into thin vanes that whipped around him.

Hidden coil launchers snapped a trio of bullets at Lahash. Each flashed against the spinning strands and joined the moving shield as red-hot ingots. Coil-gun bullets from the rest of the fighters didn't pierce the defenses either.

"Alive!" Lahash shouted.

Jayce hugged the deck as Reman leapt over him in a blur and swiped claws through Norva's wrist. Her severed hand arced into the air before she even knew she was under attack. Reman loped forward and punched another Syndicate member in the lower back so hard Jayce heard the spine snap.

The fighting died out almost as fast as it started. The crew lay groaning across the deck, their arms and hands broken or severed. The Tyrant's soldiers kept them subdued with boot heels.

"You've made this far too difficult," Lahash said to Carotan. He flicked the hilt and one of the captured bullets shot straight through the boss's forehead. The sword returned to its normal shape. Four bullets hovered over his knuckles, spinning rapidly.

"I want the Attuned." He gave Kay's lifeless body a quick kick. "I want the location of the Shrine where you found the stone. The Tyrant is merciful to those who join his great plan. Those who act against him are his enemies. You can give me what I want or I can find it for myself. Bring one."

The soldiers grabbed the spine-broken Syndicate sailor and dragged him over to Lahash. The injured man was panting, his eyes full of faux defiance. Reman tossed the true stone at Lahash. It froze in midair and began a slow orbit around his helmet.

"Where did you find it?" he asked and reversed the grip on his sword to place the flat of the blade against his forearm and pointed the pommel at him. The captured bullets aligned toward the man's face.

"Screw you," the man snarled.

A bullet snapped through his skull and sparked off the deck. The guards dropped the twitching body. Jayce felt the vibration of footfalls as Lahash approached him. The foot on his back lifted and a kick to his shoulder rolled him onto his back. Lahash aimed his pommel at Jayce's face.

"That one doesn't even have their colors," Reman growled. "Local trash. Don't bother."

"You're close, Reman, but you missed something. Watch." Lahash tightened his grip on the hilt and one of the orbiting bullets flashed at him.

Jayce flinched back . . . and didn't feel a final jolt of pain. The bullet bounced off his nose and bounced across the deck.

Reman's ears perked up.

"This one has the touch. Here's the Attuned," Lahash said, "but he doesn't know. Do you feel his potential?"

"I'm not like you. Not yet." Reman bared his teeth and sniffed Jayce. "His scent's different than yours."

"Well, no one's like me." Lahash touched the bottom of Jayce's chin with his sword tip and lifted his gaze up.

Memories of the cave came to Jayce; the star chart

flashed across his vision several times. He imagined the stars in the wrong spot and clenched his jaw.

"He's seen it . . . this one has potential," Lahash said. "All will serve the Tyrant."

"The Tyrant's dead!" Jayce snapped.

"We are loyal to him beyond death." Lahash brought his sword to his chest, point down, in salute. "Just as he is loyal to us. Don't worry, you'll learn what it is to serve his glory . . . alive or as something greater."

Reman raised his snout and sniffed hard.

"Something's off. Something's coming." The wolfen drew a coil carbine from off the mag-locks on one leg and extended the claws farther on his other paw.

"Shunt!" Lahash flipped his sword around and put one hand to the side of his head. The stone fell to the deck and rolled away from him. "I can't stop—"

A sheet of white light opened like a window overhead. A figure in dark blue armor fell through and landed a few yards from Jayce and Lahash. The new arrival snapped up; an ornate blade glowed with pale white light in one hand. His armor was contoured to his body. The body glove beneath the plates was made of a stretched light fabric that crackled as he pointed his sword at the Tyrant leader. The vision slits on his full-faced helm were dark orbs. Lines of light ran down the sockets to the jaw line. A crest of neon blue bristles shimmered with light from the dimensional opening overhead.

A stone similar to the one on the deck glistened from a socket on his upper chest.

"Again?" The new arrival twisted his sword at Lahash. "How many times do I have to kill you?"

"Maru . . . Traitor!" Lahash launched at the other warrior and slashed at his neck. Their blades met with a flash of sparks and an electric squeal.

Jayce spotted the stone and crawled toward it as the duel continued; the blades glowed with so much power that the afterimage stung his eyes. He reached for the stone . . . only to see it skitter away from him.

The stone bounced off a boot toe and then up and into the hand of a young woman. She wore similar stretched light-and-plate armor, but her face was exposed and her blond hair was bound tightly behind her head.

Amidst the chaos, Jayce was dumbstruck by the sight of her for a heartbeat.

"Sarai! Get us out of here. Shunt by three!" The other warrior ducked a leaping strike from Reman's claws and poked his blade into the air where his head had been. The tip struck the Draug's forearm and cut down to the elbow.

Reman let out a bark of pain and shoulder-rolled to a stop, one limb clutched to his body.

Lahash slashed at the warrior, landing a glancing blow against his pauldron that let off a flash of blue light.

"What? That'll kill him!" The woman gripped the stone tightly in one hand, then thrust her palm toward the rest of the Tyrant's soldiers. Coil shots sparked off a force field that retreated toward Jayce and her with each strike.

The energy wall set Jayce's teeth on edge and sent tiny shocks through his scalp and face as it neared him. He rolled toward her and bumped against her shins.

"Do it!" The warrior punched Lahash in the face and sent him stumbling back, his mask twisted part way around.

"If you die, it wasn't intentional." Sarai pressed the stone hard against Jayce's chest. He sucked in a breath as a deep cold stabbed through his lungs. "Uusanar! Shunt by three . . . yes, three!"

Hemenway vanished around Jayce, replaced by a white abyss that flowed into the sky. Jayce felt his body unravel into the light. He couldn't scream. He couldn't fight. Everything he was had become something entirely different from what he could fathom.

The afterimage of dueling figures stayed with him, but they were different—as tall as the sky, and every clash of weapons between warriors of light and dark sent stars flowing into the endless void.

Lahash ripped his damaged faceplate away and swung blindly behind him. The warrior was gone. Along with the boy, the stone, and the girl.

"How bad is it?" he asked Reman. Lahash's voice was deep and sonorous without the mask.

"It is only pain and blood." The Draug licked the long gash down his arm. "I wouldn't let that bastard send me to the Grip. I have more to give."

"He's not one to—Stop him!" Lahash shouted as Gorgi slunk toward the end of the pier. The clipper pilot leaned over the edge to fall into the waters, but Lahash's sword flew through the air and impaled him through the calf, pinning him to the dock.

Gorgi cried out in pain.

Lahash yanked his sword out and flipped Gorgi over. Gorgi recoiled from the horror of Lahash's face and stammered out prayers to several different gods. The

Tyrant's champion grabbed the sailor by the front of his dirty tunic and jerked him up.

"You were with them. You know where they found it?" Lahash asked.

Gorgi nodded rapidly, then squeezed his eyes shut and turned his head away.

"You will take me there, won't you?" Lahash moved the flat of his blade between their faces. Its glow darkened, then the edge glowed white hot.

"Yes! Yes! Please, I'll do anything! Just don't steal my soul!" Gorgi pleaded.

"Not quite how it works. But, can't have you bleed to death, now can we?" Lahash raised his sword, which danced with flame, and hacked Gorgi's bleeding leg off at the knee, cauterizing the stump instantly.

The man stared at the stump and his dismembered foot twitching on the deck. A tiny needle-tipped strand snapped out of Lahash's wrist armor and jabbed Gorgi in the neck. Shock stopped overtaking his body but all the pain remained.

"What about the traitors?" Reman asked. "We can never let a Paragon survive."

"We're not here for them." Lahash looked at the battleship hovering over the flotilla and touched a communication panel built into the back of one glove. "But they won't get far."

More hangar bays opened and fighters swarmed into the sky.

Chapter 6

Jayce was certain he wasn't dead. There shouldn't have been that much pain in the afterlife. His whole body ached like he'd been working the haul nets for two days straight. The light shining through his eyelids was entirely too strong.

Something pawed at his face. His cheek and eye twitched from tiny pricks of pain.

Jayce groaned and opened one eye. A small, furry face looked at him. Bands of black, white, and brown fur radiated away from the cat's nose.

It meowed at him.

Jayce groaned and tried to shoo the cat away but his shoulder and elbow felt like there was broken glass in his joints. Short legs patted at his face again.

"Hurghlebablaa . . ." Jayce shook his head, trying to dissuade the cat.

"Clubby, scram before he tries to eat you," a gruff voice said. The cat scampered away on too short legs and into a duct covered by a plastic flap. "Where'd you find this one? He smells like fish."

"Maru wasn't going to leave an Attuned behind for the Tyrant," Jayce heard the young woman say from somewhere behind him. Her voice hit his ears with the thump of drums. He wanted to curl into a ball and cover his eyes and ears, but not moving or talking was the only way he knew to stem the tide of pain. "Even one this . . . pathetic."

"Well . . . if he wasn't one of you he would've been splattered through the chamber. Glad I don't have to clean it up," the other voice said.

A klaxon sounded and all lights took on a red hue.

"Attention!" a high, reedy voice said. *"It seems the Tyrant's ship isn't content to let us exit the system of our own devices. Battle stations! Should we need to repel boarders, judicious aim is appreciated. Happy ship, happy voyage."*

Jayce moved an arm and regretted it. He flopped onto his back and saw the young woman speaking to a man with his back to him. He was in thicker battle armor than hers; servos and actuators made up the helmet he could see. A compact coil blaster was held muzzle up in one hand.

"Of all the stupid—Did you tell them which ship we were in?" the gruff voice asked.

"They had their own Attuned down there. Maru wants me to do something useful with this one. Here." The woman tossed the stone at him.

The other man swatted it aside. The stone bounced off a wall and spun on a glowing panel a few inches in front of Jayce's face.

"Superstitious nonsense." The young woman rolled her eyes and ran toward a wall. A door slid open to let her pass.

The man turned to Jayce. He wasn't wearing a helmet; he was heavily augmented. Three-fourths of his face were dusky skin and one deep purple cyborg eye glowed from the metal. There was a *click* as different optic lenses cycled through the cybernetic eye socket. He bore a small badge on his Governance armor with several small stars in a single orbit around a pulsar; small text read GOVERNANCE PROTECTIVE DETAIL in a scroll at the bottom.

"Well, you're not actually *hurt* hurt." He went to one knee and held a metal hand over Jayce's face. A finger bent the wrong way and a filament snaked out of the open joint and stung Jayce in the side of the neck. "When you're shopping for replacement organs and limbs, then you'll get some sympathy from me."

The pain faded away with each heartbeat.

"*Herbablurb.*" Jayce's tongue drooped out of his mouth and touched the deck. An electric pinch snapped him out of his funk and he sat up with sudden wheeze.

"Yeah, it kicks at the end." The soldier snapped the filament back into his finger. "I'm Gunnery Sergeant Dastin, Governance Armed Forces. Adept Maru wasn't dirtside for more than a few minutes...you joined up with him that quick?"

"My name's Jayce Artan and I have ... I am so lost right now. Where am I? How did I even ...."

"You're aboard the *Iron Soul*, Governance navy special operations corvette—I shouldn't have told you that." Dastin rubbed knuckles against his chin. "You know how to use that thing?" He pointed to the stone in Jayce's hand.

It was warm to his skin, the surface smooth to the touch, with cooler threads where the golden strands moved.

"Huh? When did I—"

The ship jostled.

"That didn't take long. Come on!" Dastin grabbed Jayce by the arm and helped him to the door. Jayce stumbled and bounced off the doorframe and into the hallway. The ceiling had what Jayce thought were sea-kelp strands running down it. The bulkheads weren't uniform, but organic and shaped into giant scales.

A pair of armored Governance soldiers hustled past them.

"You should've been at your station three minutes ago!" Dastin yelled over his shoulder.

Jayce glanced out a porthole. He broke free of Dastin's hold and pressed his face to the glass. Outside the *Iron Soul*, Hemenway hung in the void. Pearl-colored clouds flowed over the glistening blue waters. He looked for the small island chains between the massive polar ice caps. Blinking lights of orbiting starships brought back memories of him and his mother watching the kindle-bug migration when he was a child.

"I'm in space. I'm actually in—Hey!"

Dastin grabbed him by the scruff of his neck with his cyborg hand and pushed him back down the passageway.

"Look, kid, I don't know what your deal is, but Adept Maru said keep you alive, and as much as I respect—"

The ship lurched suddenly as blasts stitched against the hull. Short tears scarred the passageway, giving Jayce another glimpse of his home world. A milky film of shields partially obscured his view of the void as the hull resealed itself.

"Plasma impacts are painful. Who is responding?" chimed from speakers in the ceiling.

"You keep dragging your feet, kid, and you'll get all the hard vacuum you want before you're dead." Dastin broke into a run, catching Jayce flat-footed. The soldier slid to a stop and slapped a palm to the control panel on a doorframe. The door slid open and Dastin shoved Jayce into the room.

The ship keeled to one side, throwing Jayce into a counter. His stomach hit the edge and he sprawled across the top, knocking coil weapons and ammo magazines all over the place. A scaly hand with auburn hair sticking out around the wrist slammed onto the counter in front of Jayce's face.

He looked up at a reptilian with a blunted muzzle and a long beard. A crest perked up on its head. It spoke, but it was nothing but hisses and snaps to Jayce's ear.

"Give him the old harness and get it quick," Dastin said. "This is Eabani and our resident Lirsu armorer. Eabani, new kid. Jayce or something."

Eabani hissed like a cat and bent behind the counter. Racks of coil rifles and battery packs filled the wall behind the reptilian. He slammed a coil pistol that had been knocked to the deck onto the counter with a snarl.

"Harness! No, he doesn't want to holster a weapon *there*," Dastin said as the ship bucked again.

Eabani snorted and banged around behind the counter. He tossed a dusty leather pauldron with a brass ring worked into the center at Jayce. It felt stiff with age and the Veil stone still in his hand hummed with power.

"What do I—"

Eabani slammed a palm against the counter and howled at him.

"Obviously not." Dastin slipped a loop from the harness over Jayce's neck, then fastened a line under his arm and over his shoulder. "Put your Veil stone in the emitter ring. It'll probably stop energy blasts and high-velocity slug rounds. Your shield will fail if you take too many hits too quickly—then you're easy pickin's."

"Like this?" Jayce pressed the stone to the ring and a puff of pale blue light glowed from the edge. The stone snapped into place without Jayce doing anything else. Slight pressure enveloped his body and there was a hint of ozone with every breath he took.

Eabani aimed a coil pistol at Jayce's face.

"No! Not in here!" Dastin slapped the reptilian's gun hand up. The alien replied with a dry laugh and more grumbling. "Doesn't matter if I'm not any fun. Give him a weapon."

Dastin went to a weapons rack and slapped a wire-frame gauntlet onto one forearm.

Eabani cocked his head slightly at Jayce, then tossed the coil pistol at his chest. Jayce caught it and stared at the weapon, taking in its chrome plating and smooth lines. There was a tug on the back of his harness.

"Got you tanked. Wait, you know how to use that?" Dastin asked.

"Point the part with the hole at the bad guys and pull the curvy part. Right?" Jayce held the pistol by the grip and put his finger on the trigger.

Eabani snatched the weapon out of his hand.

"You're right, he can be a meat shield and that's about it. C'mon, kid!" Dastin snapped his knuckles against Jayce's chest. There was a pulse of light from the point of impact.

"Wait, I don't even get a gun?" Jayce followed Dastin into the passageway and had to run to keep up.

"You'd be more danger to me and this ship if I gave you a weapon you don't know how to use. So you're going to do *exactly* what I tell you until we get away from the deads." Dastin racked the slide on his carbine. "We're going to secure the dorsal-point defense battery before the enemy can—"

The lights cut out and Jayce floated off the deck. Red emergency lights snapped on along the upper and lower edges of the bulkheads.

"Ah! Help! Help!" Jayce flailed his arms wildly as he went head over heels.

Dastin grabbed him by the collar and held him in the air.

"—before they can cut the power. They're more efficient than I remember." Dastin slid his feet against the deck; magnetic locks in the bottom of his boots kept him from floating around like Jayce. Jayce held onto a carry handle on the soldier's upper back. He bobbed closer and farther from Dastin and he realized how all the fish he'd caught on a line must have felt.

They dashed around a corner and Jayce's heels bounced off the bulkhead. Ahead, a pair of Governance Marines were stationed at a set of double doors.

"Gunny! Adept Maru reports a clamp assault inbound!" one shouted.

"They'll attack here first." Dastin slowed down.

Gravity suddenly returned and Jayce's stomach lurched. His discomfort got worse as he fell flat against the deck. The shield pauldron softened the impact but the landing still hurt. A muffled blast from the point defense cannons on the other side of the door boomed over and over again.

"Who the hell's that?" one of the Marines asked, indicating Jayce with a nod of his head.

"Maru picked up a stray," Dastin said as Jayce got back to his feet carefully. The gravity field must not have been functioning properly as his feet felt heavier than the rest of his body and he was lightheaded.

A heavy *bang* stung Jayce's ears. The three Marines raised their weapons toward the noise.

"Remember when you two were pissed we lost shore leave to overhaul the emitters?" Dastin flicked a switch on his coil carbine. Sparks spewed from the bulkhead farther away and began outlining a large oval.

"What—what do I do?" Jayce looked around for anything to help him.

"Stay behind us. I'll dump you in the core with Uusanar soon as we deal with this problem," Dastin said.

"Red sparks, light 'em!" one of the Marines shouted. An energy shield wavered in and out of view in front of them.

The breach point exploded into a flood of flame and shrapnel. Jayce covered his head with his arms as tendrils of fire snatched at him from beneath the shield. A wave of heat stung his arms, but the Veil shield held.

Coil guns from the Marines snapped in short bursts.

Jayce looked up at the breach. Bullets sprang off an energy shield carried by a stocky creature with a flat triangular helmet. Its head was hunched level with its shoulders, onyx-and-bone-colored armor partially visible behind the shield as bullets struck it. The breacher moved slowly—every shot from the Marines punched it back—but the advance was steady.

More boarders were just behind the shield carrier.

"Spiker!" Dastin shouted.

"Spiker, aye!" the two Marines called back.

Dastin smacked a fist against his chest and a metal launcher popped out of his back and bent over one shoulder. A Marine gripped one hand to his forearm and the shield faded out. Dastin braced himself as a pointed metal rod fired from the launcher.

The projectile struck the boarder's shield and stopped instantly. The spoke hung there, tip embedded in the face as the shaft began to turn. The Tyrant soldier grunted out a warning as a ripple spread through the shield.

The spiker pierced through and thumped into the boarder's chest. He tipped forward, revealing a half dozen more boarders who had been just behind him.

Not all of them wore the skull masks. One's face was exposed—nothing but decaying meat and glowing optics beat into the eye sockets.

"Frag ou—"

The Marine couldn't finish his warning as a hail of fire broke through his shield and punched him off his feet. The grenade in his hand fell to the deck and rolled in front of Jayce. The grenade was a small sphere, just big enough for him to grip well with three fingers.

Jayce tossed it at the boarders. The explosive sailed over their heads and rattled around the inside of their moray assault pod. One in the back of the assault stack flinched away from the opening . . . but nothing happened.

"Keep firing!" Dastin shouted.

The maskless soldier dropped to all fours and raced across the deck, bouncing off the bulkheads and gripping them with clawed fingers. Coil fire struck him in the back and legs, but the impacts failed to register with the nightmare.

The abomination leapt at Jayce, and it snatched him off the deck and rolled them both into the bulkhead. Jayce took the brunt of the impact and found himself face-to-face with the boarder. Its skin was dead and gray; decaying flecks of skin hung like ghostly sails from the crude implants.

"New meat," it hissed.

Jayce rolled an arm across his body and broke the hold on his chest. He struck the palm of his hand against the boarder's jaw. Flesh smeared against his palm, leaving part of the boarder's teeth and the bare bone of its skull exposed.

Its mouth hinged open and it mocked Jayce with a mechanical laugh.

"Hey!"

The nightmare's head snapped to one side just in time to see Dastin's boot heel kick it square in the rotting nose. Dastin pinned it against the bulkhead as it clawed at his leg.

Grenades were on the boarder's chest harness. These all had faded red buttons on top. Jayce snatched one off, clicked the button hard, and felt it buzz twice hard in his hand. He threw it into the breach point.

"Wait. No!" Dastin shouted.

"No?" Jayce looked at the Marine, a look somewhere between confusion and fear on his face.

This grenade functioned as expected. The blast cracked the seal over the breach point and the assault craft wagged like a stiff flag.

There was a sudden breeze against Jayce's body. The assault ship broke away and a hurricane of venting atmosphere carried Jayce out into the void. The body of one of the boarders bumped into him as he tumbled head over heels through space. He caught quick glimpses of the *Iron Soul* as water vapor in the ship's air froze in the cold of space, sending ice flurries all around him.

Jayce managed a shout that echoed around him . . . which struck the last calm part of his mind as impossible as he was in the void. His tumbling slowed and he saw the Tyrant battleship in stark contrast against the north polar ice cap of Hemenway. It shrank ever so slowly along with his home world.

"What is this?" He looked down at his Veil-stone harness and saw it glowed brightly. There was a tug on his ankle and he looked "down" at the *Iron Soul*.

Maru was on the hull, one hand held out to him. Rich blue light roiled across his fingers and up his arm. Jayce remembered the Elman Fire he'd seen on the masts of fishing ships, a warning that a bad electrical storm was coming. The Adept was in his battle armor; the solid light under the plates crackled with brief static.

Maru reached his glowing hand back like he was

drawing an arrow and Jayce hurtled toward him. The Adept pointed at the breach in the hull and Jayce flew through a weak shield membrane over the gap. He bounced off a bulkhead and skidded across the deck.

Dastin lifted a foot and stopped him.

"Were you trying to kill us all?" the Marine asked.

Jayce exhaled, his breath fogging in a cold he didn't understand.

"I was . . . I was trying to help." He waved behind him. "They're all gone? Right?" He got to his hands and knees and felt something. He looked over at the rotting boarder, who was pinned to the bulkhead with another spiker. Its jaw clicked as it tried to speak.

"By the Depths!" Jayce scrambled to the other side of the passageway.

Maru landed in the passageway and put one hand to the side of his helm.

"Uusanar. Hull is clear. Get us out of here," he said.

"It will sting to leave this close to the gravity well, but I'll take that over a Tyrant battleship on our tail," came Uusanar's voice over the ship's loudspeakers.

The prow of the ship reared up like a speedboat suddenly gunning its engines, and the view of the void through the breach changed to a kaleidoscope of smeared colors.

Maru marched over to Jayce, Dastin, and the incapacitated boarder.

"Nemal's down," Dastin said. "Ickena's taking him to stores." He aimed his coil gun at the boarder's forehead. "I don't like giving them mercy, but this is your ship, your mission, sir."

"This one..." Maru squatted in front of the boarder. "There's not much left of him, but I still feel a spark of consciousness in there. With enough time I could glean something of how a Tyrant capital ship made it this far from their home stars."

"The blasted Syndicate gave them passage," Dastin said. "They always do."

"Not this far." Maru shook his head. "Not with something so...obvious. I need answers. Can you secure it safely?"

"Yes, if you basket-case him for me." Dastin scooted away.

Maru looked over the boarder. "They're prosthetics, no pain receptors installed."

He snapped his hilt off his leg and a short energy blade materialized from the hilt. Two swift cuts and the boarder's mechanical arms and legs fell to the deck.

"Loyal beyond," the cyborg rasped from a speaker embedded at the base of his neck. "Loyal beyond the Veil. For the truly faithful will never know death."

"I will give you true peace as soon as I can," Maru said to it. "Forgive me."

Dastin grabbed the limbless cyborg by the back of the neck and pulled him off the spike and carried him away.

"Are you hurt?" Maru asked as he helped Jayce up.

"I don't know why I'm alive." Jayce touched the stone on his harness.

"Come on, let's get you to Uusanar before anything else unexpected happens." Maru put a hand on Jayce's shoulder. A hand with only four fingers. "I will explain everything I can as soon as there's time."

"Is there time for me to"—Jayce shook goo off his fingers—"wash my hands? Please."

"Mmm...indeed. You'll need to know where the facilities are eventually. Follow me," Maru said.

Chapter 7

Jayce followed Maru deeper into the ship. He glanced at the taller alien every few steps, his eyes lingering on the pair of weapon hilts attached to Maru's belt and the harness incorporated into his body armor.

"You need not be so silent," Maru said. "I'm happy to answer your questions."

"'Bout that... why didn't I die when I was sucked out of the ship? I've never left my planet before, but I've seen enough vids to know—"

"Your Veil harness enveloped you in a force field strong enough to keep you from depressurizing and causing a lung embolism. The air tank Dastin had the foresight to install fed you oxygen, and the field prevented most high-energy particles from damaging you. You would have survived for maybe half an hour if you remained calm."

"Calm? Oh, totally." Maru looked at him. "Not at all, actually. Thanks for using... pulling... what did you do to me?"

"I am a Paragon of the Sodality." Maru tapped the

79

stone on his harness. "I wield the Light of the Veil for the benefit of all. Have you heard of us?"

"That's real?" Jayce frowned at him. "You're real? I thought it was a bunch of rumors cooked up by Governance rebels before the Tyrant was killed."

Maru stopped and held up a hand. He pinched three fingers together, then flicked Jayce's earlobe.

"What? Ow!" Jayce rubbed his ear.

"If I'm not real, then where did that come from?" Maru asked. "And I apologize for inflicting pain. Sometimes it can convey a message far better than words."

"I didn't doubt that *you* were real. I meant the whole Paragon part." Jayce was caught flat-footed as Maru began walking again.

"I fell from the sky in a dimensional slide, fought off one of the Tyrant's Blades, and pulled you back from the void using a graviton well I projected from my hand. Would you like to play with my Prestor Hilts to satisfy your curiosity?" Maru asked.

"Can I?" Jayce reached for one of the hilts on Maru's belt and got his hand slapped.

"No. I was attempting human sarcasm. Sarai is rather fond of it. As you've never been in a ship's soul before, let me give you some critical instructions: Do not touch the stone." Maru stopped at a vault door and brandished a finger at Jayce.

"You understand?" the alien asked.

"Don't touch the stone. I just saw someone get turned into dust from one of these things. If this one hadn't saved my life, I wouldn't want it at all," Jayce said.

"Then you're aware of the risk." Maru raised a hand

and pale blue flames danced through his fingers. The vault door slid open.

Inside, a Veil stone the size of Jayce's head hung at the center of an hourglass-shaped force field. Energy flowed out of the stone in motes of light like sand in an hourglass, but it originated at the stone and flowed up and down. The chamber was brightly lit, but Jayce couldn't pinpoint the light source.

Sarai sat on a small bench, the cat that woke him after his shunt aboard the *Iron Soul* on her lap.

"Ah-ha! He is here at last," a reedy voice said from the other side of the stone. "Come . . . let me learn of him."

"No touching," Maru said to Jayce.

"No touching." Jayce put his hands into his pockets and realized his pants had a long gash down one leg that hadn't been there before all the excitement.

"Nemal didn't make it," Sarai said. She scratched the cat's ear. "Dastin requests you perform the rites."

"I shall. We are less without him." Maru brought the back of his knuckles to the chin of his helmet, then placed his palm over his harness stone. Sarai did the same.

Jayce copied them both and got a mean look from Sarai.

"Come, come . . . a soul leaves us. A new soul arrives. Such is the cycle," the reedy voice said. Jayce kept his distance from the large stone and followed Maru around it.

A being with spindly limbs and a long neck sat in a crystalline throne built into the vault wall. A tunic of silver thread covered most of its body; its gray skin looked dry. Large, all-black eyes fixed on Jayce. It raised a hand to

Jayce and the digits twisted in ways Jayce's human joints never could.

"This is Uusanar," Maru said by way of introduction.

"Ah . . . he's new," Uusanar said.

"I did . . . just get here." Jayce looked down at his feet.

"No, no, fresh soul, you are new to the Veil. I see it clinging to your aura, probing for the right fit to merge with you. But are you young enough to be of greater service to the Sodality? Sarai? How far beyond his first maturity is he? You two seem matched." Uusanar leaned forward slightly. Wires attached to the back of his skull stretched from the throne.

"That's not how it works for humans." Sarai rolled her eyes. "How many years standard are you, new guy?" she asked.

"Standard? Almost . . . twenty-two, I think. My mother came from a Core world where that was used. Age wasn't that important on Hemenway. All that matters is if you can work or not."

"Then he's able." Uusanar flicked his fingernails against his thumb. "What a boon for the Governance. What a find for the Cycle."

"What are we talking about, exactly?" Jayce inched away from the crystal throne.

"He's lived under a rock his whole life." Sarai shook her head.

"No one lives on land back home. It's boats. All boats," Jayce said.

Sarai put a hand to her face.

Jayce rubbed an itch away from his nose.

"Jayce," Maru said. "You were exposed to a Shrine.

That's where your stone came through from the Veil itself. Such exposure leaves an imprint on your aura and Shrines—at this time in the Cycle—direct the penitent to a greater, more stable rift into the Veil. Uusanar needs to see the map you found. It's of vital importance to the Governance and to the war against the Tyrant. Would you let him read you? It won't hurt."

"About that . . ." Jayce looked over his shoulder to the exit. "I saw a woman get turned into dust when she used one of those Shrines. So this stuff definitely hurt her."

"A charlatan," Sarai said. "Let me guess? She had some Veil stone flecks and used them to scry? Read the future? They're always on fringe worlds. Some may be Attuned, but they're untrained. Or they follow the Path that's been passed down through generations and the proper rituals have been corrupted through time. Was she old? Likely midtwenties standard or older?"

Jayce thought for a moment.

"OK, everything you said described her," he said.

"The powers of the Veil are not to be trifled with," Maru said. "Attuned require many years of training before they can wield it properly and become a Paragon. Less time for Shrine tenders. Uusanar is well versed in aura reading. There is no danger to you. You have my word."

"We don't *need* his permission, Master." Sarai tried to push the cat off her lap, but it dug claws into her pants. "If the nexus is on Illara, then we don't have time to waste. There's too much at stake."

"If you make your path with pain and deception, you will carry that through the Veil," Maru said. "Besides, the signs point to Besh VIII."

"I'm close to the junction." Uusanar raised a hand and a star chart projected from the stone floating in the center of the vault. "If I have to make a radical course change ... there's risk to me. To the ship."

"What are you looking for? Is there time to tell me?" Jayce asked.

"Let me show you," Uusanar said. "Behold ..."

The holo changed to a map of the entire galaxy. Beacons lit up within each spiral arm, fewer on the fringe and none in the center. Ley lines spread from the beacons and extended from star to star.

"Before recorded history, there was a galactic civilization that included most of the races we know now," Maru said. "Travel between the stars was nearly instantaneous and it is believed that every world that could support intelligent life as we know it ... did. The Ancients had peace and prosperity for uncounted years until ..."

The beacons failed and the links between the stars vanished.

"We don't know how the collapse happened, but from what fragmented stories remain it seems that artificial intelligences were to blame," Maru said. "AI were destroyed or dismantled across the galaxy at the same time as the collapse. We're not sure if that happened before or just after all faster-than-light travel ended. For over six thousand years, star systems were largely cut off from each other. Civilization at the galactic level collapsed and populated systems survived on their own. We still find dead worlds in the Deep."

"The Deep?" Jayce asked.

Maru held up a hand.

"Not long after the Collapse," Maru said, "the first Attuned were found. Sentients connected to the Light beyond the Veil. They called the first Veil stones to them from the Shrines that appeared at the same time the Attuned were born. These smaller stones could power a ship into the brane between our reality and the Veil where faster-than-light travel is possible, and the Governance began."

"That's what I am?" Jayce said. "What all of us in this room are? 'Attuned' to this Light?"

"Correct," Maru nodded. "It is not a biological mutation, rather it is something innate to the Attuned when they're born. Most Attuned never know what they are, but they're known to be particularly lucky and are more spiritually inclined. It is not an inherited trait, but the children of the Attuned have a statistically higher chance of being born with the gift." He glanced at Sarai, who looked away.

"You no doubt had quite the experience when you went to the Shrine," Maru said.

"But I'd been there before. No crazy visions or anything that time," Jayce said.

"Your earlier visit must have been while it was dormant. The Veil thins when a Breaking nears," Uusanar said.

"It is not a Breaking," Maru shook his head. "The Veil wanes and ebbs on a cycle. Do not use that word lightly."

"My apologies, Paragon," Uusanar said.

"Paragons and other trained Adepts can sense the Attuned," Maru continued quickly. "We do our best to give them the opportunity to serve the Governance as best they can. Some choose to tend Shrines and call forth stones, which is the only option for those we find too far into adulthood. Some choose to become Paragons or shipmasters, but that is a difficult path for anyone to take."

"What is it Paragons like you do?" Jayce asked him.

Sarai cleared her throat loudly.

"Paragons serve the Cycle and maintain the balance between our reality and the Veil," Maru said. "For millennia we were scholars and explorers. In recent decades we've adopted the warrior's role to—"

"To fight the Tyrant, right? Didn't you Paragons kill him and bring back the Governance?" Jayce asked.

"He's never heard of you." Sarai raised an eyebrow. "This is new."

"What does she mean?" Jayce looked from Maru to Sarai and back to Maru.

"Quite refreshing that I am not living up to someone's expectations or hearsay. Jayce has the opportunity to know me as me, and not from any media nonsense," the Paragon said. "You are correct, young man, the Paragons did defeat the Tyrant. At great cost."

"And you're still fighting the remnants? Why did I ask? I just saw you do it back home. Let me join you. I hate the Tyrant and—"

Maru held up a hand. "You do not know what you're asking."

"I've been training since before I could even walk," Sarai said. "You think you can just waltz in here and expect Maru and the rest of us to take you beyond the Veil?"

"I'm Attuned and I'm young enough, aren't I? The Tyrant took my father from me. Those bastards back on the dock killed my friend. Let me fight back!"

The light in the vault went crimson. Uusanar pressed his palms together and lowered his head.

"Aggression has consequences," Maru said. "Please, do not let your emotions flare."

"I'm not sorry. I'm sick of being under any tyrant's boot—Syndicate or otherwise," Jayce said. "I've worked deep-water boats for years and fought in the pits. What's out there to be scared of?"

"He has no idea." Sarai shook her head. "Can we stop wasting our time? Just get the path from him and we'll dump him on a Governance world with enough quanta in his pocket to get him to a military recruiter station. The Marines always need cannon fodder."

"Is that what Gunney Dastin is to you?" Maru asked her. "An expendable hero?"

"Well . . . no," she demurred.

"Jayce, most Paragons go through years of training in the academy on Primus," Maru said to him. "Most. If I enrolled you there, you would be too old to claim a stone beyond the Veil by the time you're trained well enough to plausibly survive the journey. If I do take you with Sarai and the rest of the team . . . you will likely perish."

"I've been dodging death from predators, the Syndicate, and now the Tyrant. How bad can this Veil place be? Take me with you . . . please," Jayce said.

"You *really* don't know what you're asking," Sarai said.

"If I regret it, then that's my responsibility. My problem," Jayce said.

"Very well, I will take you through the Veil to claim a suitable stone, and train you to become a Paragon," Maru said.

"*What?* No!" Sarai's fists shook at her side. "He *just* got here!"

"Our options are limited. If the Tyrant's loyalists are bold enough to venture this far from their sanctuary, then the Governance will need all the Paragons it can find to finish the war," Maru said. "Now, Jayce, in order for you and Sarai to become actual Paragons, we need to know where we can enter the Veil. You have that knowledge."

"I . . . do?" Jayce pursed his lips.

"You saw the path at the Shrine. Active Shrines point to where we can cross into the Veil. Every decade or so, the Veil thins in certain places and we can travel to the Veil itself." He noted Jayce's blank expression. "Some call it the Foundation. The reality connected to our own. That's where we get the finest Veil stones from."

"I see." Jayce put his hands on his hips and nodded slowly. "I mean, I don't see. Why go there when you can just call them out from a Shrine?"

"Flawed. Imperfect," Uusanar said, pointing to the one in Jayce's harness. "Useful for personal shields, perhaps as an energy source, but to ply the star ways you must travel to the Veil and bring forth more perfect samples. Whoever attunes to a stone like mine can grow it like a seed into something wonderful."

The lanky alien clicked his tongue and opened a small tin holding morsels of food. Clubby leapt off Sarai's lap and snuggled up to Uusanar.

"Little mercenary." Sarai brushed loose hair from her clothes.

"We are close to losing our chance," Maru said. "Word

reached the Governance of a possible access point in this sector, and I brought Sarai with me to investigate. Shrines point the way, but we didn't get the last part of the map from your world. There are several possible gate worlds in the Deep, but we have only have enough time left to go to one of them. We can take a chance . . . or we can read your aura and know for sure."

"Governance can pay you," Sarai said, "if that's what you're holding out for. The navy needs Veil stones like Uusanar has for larger ships."

"Additionally"—Maru put a hand on Jayce's shoulder—"Attuned can only claim an empowered stone beyond the Veil within a single cellular regeneration cycle after puberty. Perhaps ten years for most humans. The stones reject any who are too old."

"What? That seems weird." Jayce's brow furrowed.

"Despite nearly nine thousand years of regular journeys through the Veil, we don't have all the answers." Maru took his hand back. "But this is Sarai's only opportunity to claim a stone . . . yours as well."

"Master, you can't be serious!" Sarai stood up. "He has no training. He barely knows what planet he's from and you think he can survive beyond the Veil?"

"And how many expeditions have you led, young one?" Maru asked her. "How many times have you crossed the Veil?"

"Well . . . none." She crossed her arms.

"I took your father and half a dozen other Attuned through the Veil and all lived to tell the tale. Jayce—as he's chosen to join us—will be fine," Maru said. "Probably. If he listens to me."

"Wait, so I go with you and get one of those?" Jayce pointed to the Veil stone. "But then I don't—"

"Once you claim a stone from beyond the Veil, you can use it to create a hilt." Maru detached his from his belt. "It is only by creating your own link to the Veil that a Paragon can achieve his full potential. Using another's stone hobbles your abilities. If you can use it at all," Maru said.

"You're not trying to convince him to become a shipmaster? It may look boring"—Uusanar leaned back in his throne—"but I love my job."

Maru bowed slightly and lowered his helmet's eye slit to be even with Jayce's face.

"If you change your mind," he said, "I will not abandon you. Help us find the next step on the path and I will help you make *your* next steps. No matter where you choose to tread."

"Then . . . let's do this. What do I need to do? Meditate in front of that stone or—"

Maru slapped his hand onto Jayce's forehead and squeezed his temples. Jayce gasped as his vision went white. He felt like he was floating as memories from his childhood rose and fell like bits of a broken ship surfacing during a storm. There was a glimpse of his father in the Tyrant's colors, his mother playing with him in their hovel when he was a child. Moments with Kay that brought a fresh ache to his heart. Then his mother's hand as she slipped into the dark waters all those years ago.

The vault returned and Jayce stumbled into Sarai. She gave him a not-so-gentle push to the bench as his vision swam. He grabbed the bottom of the seat, then slapped a hand over his mouth.

"Do not vomit in my sanctum!" Uusanar hissed as his head undulated from side to side. "I don't even let Clubby have his litter box in here."

"I have it." Maru held his palm up to the Veil stone and constellations appeared against the energy field, then swirled around it as the coordinates melded into the stone.

"The Gate is on . . . Illara," Uusanar said. "I'll redirect at the next lay junction."

"I knew it!" Sarai shook her fists next to her face.

"Mmm . . . I may be losing my touch," Maru said.

"Peanut gloves sad barnacles." Jayce tried to wipe drool from his mouth and bonked his nose.

"An aura reading can be a bit dissociative." Maru waggled his fingertips in front of one of Jayce's eyes, then the other. He snapped his fingers and Jayce reared back like he'd been shoved. "Better?"

"Can I have some water, please?" Jayce asked.

"He can share a berth with Sarai," Uusanar said.

"Oh no, he cannot," Sarai snapped.

"That's not appropriate. Sarai, take him to Holden's quarters and see that he's comfortable." Maru went to the vault door. "I must attend to Nemal's service."

"But I want to be there. He was my friend too." Sarai looked away.

"I will wait for you. Now go." Maru tapped a control and left the vault.

"When do I start my training? Can I have a gun now?" Jayce asked Sarai.

"By the Path of Light." Sarai motioned for him to stand. "You're still pissing planet water and you think you're going to be Paragon Mathas the Great. Let's see if you can get to your bunk without throwing up everywhere first, yeah?"

"I . . ." Jayce swallowed hard and made a face. "I promise nothing."

Chapter 8

✳

A door slid open and lights flickered on inside a small berthing. Inside was a well-made bunk, closet, single chair at a desk, and a sink.

Jayce put a hand on the doorframe and ran his touch down the strange polymer.

"Wow, this is really nice. What's the hot water ration?" he asked Sarai, who was two steps behind him.

"Water ration? The *Iron Soul* can carry an entire Intervention platoon and still have room for support staff. There's no rationing on anything," she said. "You've really never left your home world, have you?"

"Nope." Jayce went inside and ran his touch over the blanket. "This is all for me? Really?"

"Listen to me, bumpkin, you need to get over this starry-eyed wonder thing real quick. When we land on Illara, we're not going there with the rank and authority of the Governance. This is a wild world in the Deep. Less law and order than your wet bucket of a planet. You better obey everything Master and Dastin tell you, because we're not going down there for a picnic."

"I thought the Syndicate was in control of every world the Governance had abandoned after the revolt." Jayce sat on the bed and pushed on the mattress. "This is so soft."

"And who told you that about the Syndicate?" Sarai leaned one shoulder against the doorframe.

"The . . . Syndicate," Jayce said.

"Let me tell you something true about the Syndicate: they're thugs. Criminals. They gave the enemy that survived the Battle of Tyrant's Bane an escape from the Governance fleet. The Tyrant's lieutenants would be done and dusted if it wasn't for the Syndicate. The same Syndicate who've kept trade routes open to every last fringe kingdom, barony, and pirate band that sprang up after the Tyrant was killed. Governance would have brought peace to every star of the old order by now if it wasn't for the Syndicate."

"I don't doubt you, but on Hemenway the Syndicate kept the peace. Mostly treated everyone fairly except . . . that slime eel. What's this worth on the open market?" Jayce touched his harness.

"Couple hundred thousand quanta," she said. "That's got a Governance serial number in it. You try and sell it outside the Adept network and it's an automatic prison sentence. You really think you could just cash out that easily?"

"No. I was going to get paid two thousand and a little more for navigating the Syndicate boss to and from the Shrine. He could've paid more. Lot more." Jayce fumed for a moment. "And Kay got killed because he was greedy. The Syndicate got killed because the boss was greedy. All I wanted was a ticket off-world. Least I got that . . . sort of.

These stones seem like a lot of trouble. What did you say about a network?"

"The galaxy is full of Shrines. Some more active than others. Ones in the Deep can pull several stones a year, almost all graded for harnesses or power plants." Sarai tapped a fingertip against her harness stone. "More perfect stones for slip drives, planetary shields, and hilts only come from beyond the Veil. Attuned with the right training can crew a Shrine and deliver stones to the Governance, which has right of first refusal on any Veil stone. We pay excellent rates for them. Better for that power to be used for good than in the wrong hands."

"People trade the Veil stones for Governance quanta?" Jayce scrunched his nose. "Something of actual value for what the government creates out of thin air and has an endless supply of?"

"You sound like the Syndicate. There's quite the black market for them." Sarai shrugged. "The Shrine Adepts live quite comfortably, and rampant materialism tends to affect how well they can call a stone through the Veil. The greedier they are, the poorer they become."

"Huh, just like what happened on the docks." Jayce smiled slightly. His mind drifted to Kay and his final moments. Would he still be alive if he hadn't swapped Carotan's stone and swallowed it? Probably. Kay wasn't one for brawling.

"Oh no, bunch of Syndicate got killed. Anyway..." Sarai leaned back and glanced down the passageway. "What do you know about crossing the Veil? About the Foundation?"

"Growing up, it was a lot of superstitious nonsense. I didn't think the Paragons were real until ... very recently.

We were worried about floods, changing supercurrents that could tear a flotilla apart or send us to the poles to die in the ice. No one had time for the old legends."

"I've been preparing for this moment since before I could walk. Master Maru's made the pilgrimage more times than anyone else alive. You are one giant liability. So, you just keep your head down, mouth shut, and don't ruin this for anyone, you understand me?" She stared at him.

A whistle sounded through the ship.

"That's the call to mourning. Just stay here until someone comes and gets you." She turned away and the door slid shut behind her.

"See you." Jayce kicked a boot off and rubbed sore, waterlogged feet. He slapped the pillow twice, noting that the foam melded around each hit. His other boot came off and he flexed his feet against the deck.

"What am I doing here?" He opened the closet and touched the Governance shipboard uniforms hanging inside. He pulled one out and read the name stitched over a breast pocket.

HOLDEN BIN WOLECH.

He put it back, then felt around on a high shelf. He pushed boots aside and removed a data slate.

"Wow . . . it's so new." He tapped a corner and Standard text fields appeared. When his thumbprint didn't unlock the screen, he tossed it back.

"Kay could've hacked it." He sat on his bunk. He wiped his face and caught a glimpse of all the grime and filth marring his skin and hair. "What am I *doing* here?"

He set his elbows on his knees and buried his face in his hands.

Jayce sat in silence until he ran his hand over the shoulder harness. He slipped his arm out of it and examined the stone embedded in the ring. It had shrunk slightly, and he could jiggle it from side to side in the mount by tilting the harness.

"What am I even *doing* here?" He looked up, then tossed the harness onto the bed.

Lahash set hands before bent knees and pressed his forehead to the triangle shape made by his thumb and fingers.

The ship stone at the heart of his battleship pulsed and sparked. The stone master was bound into the bulkheads. Cybernetics and lobotomy implants strained as the slave moaned from pain.

A shadow formed around the stone and frost grew from the deck.

"My lord." Lahash leaned back and rested his palms on bent knees. "We've found the Aperture world. We will be through the Veil soon."

Lahash tensed as a hand made of smoke passed over his face. Memories of the duel against Maru and glimpses of Sarai passed through his mind. A deep hatred rose in his chest as his spirit resonated with the one that manifested from the stone.

"Of course I will kill him." Lahash's jaw clenched. "But the signs . . . the signs point to something monumental. Something I hadn't anticipated."

"Bring me the child." The apparition touched Lahash's face then melded back into the stone.

Lahash sucked in air and fell over, his body shivering.

He coughed as warmth came back to his chest. He slapped a comms button on a forearm panel.

"Bridge! Set course for Illara. Now. Run this ship as hard as you can." He clicked the button again and went to the doors. He gave the slave synched to the stone a playful pat on his way out.

Chapter 9

Jayce ran through a passageway to a lift where Maru and Sarai waited. He skidded into the lift and bumped Sarai with his shoulder.

"Sorry," he said. "Got my hilt. Wearing good boots just like you said. Where we going?"

"Not someplace you're going to like," Sarai said. The lift doors closed and it rose slowly.

"You will be in no danger," Maru said. "The FTL bubble is absolute and Uusanar has pressurized it from the ship's emergency atmosphere tanks."

"Wait." Jayce frowned. "Where are we going? Exactly?"

The lift doors opened to the outer hull. A gust of cool air washed over them as the stretched light of the FTL passage danced in a kaleidoscope of colors and patterns.

Jayce choked down a mouthful of something that came up from his stomach.

"It takes a little getting used to," Maru said, "but being this close to the Veil can be rather soothing to those of us Attuned to its energies. Sarai, would you be so kind as to begin the kata?"

Sarai stepped out onto a wide, flat space on the *Iron Soul*'s hull and ignited her hilt. The blade was translucent, but the shape was stronger than Jayce had seen before. She bowed toward the prow and the onrushing Veil.

She stepped back into a fighting stance and raised the flat of her blade parallel to her forehead, then hopped forward and cut across her body in a fluid motion. The sword dance continued, her blade catching light from the Veil and flashing as she struck and flowed from one move to another.

"I glimpsed memories of you fighting in some sort of sanctioned fight," Maru said. "How much combatives training have you had?"

"Scale bouts are more about hurting the other guy faster than he can hurt you," Jayce said. "There wasn't anything elegant about getting punched in the face. But I learned rhythms. How to read a defense and how to duck and weave. Punches that miss don't hurt."

"Interesting," Maru said. "We call this kata the Flow. It is not meant to teach you how to defend yourself or others with your Fulcrum blade. Rather, it is meant to train you to release your mind and act with the Veil."

"She started over," Jayce said. "Same moves again from the same starting spot."

"Very good," Maru nodded. "Perceptive."

"How does doing the same dance over and over again help in a fight? The Veil wants us to run around in circles?" Jayce asked.

"In order to manifest the Veil's influence on our dimension, one must 'attune' at a higher level. Manipulating causality is no simple feat. But after training generations of

Paragons, I've learned that the Veil must be felt. Words are inadequate. Would you like to begin?" Maru stepped out of the lift.

"How do I do it? I don't even have one of those swords," Jayce said.

"Here." Maru handed him a wooden handle with a brass cross guard. "This is a training device. Veil-stone dust is embued through it, but it is useless anywhere but the hull during FTL. It will suffice until I can help find a hilt suitable for you."

Jayce squeezed the training hilt and a ghostly long sword appeared. He touched the flat of the blade near the tip and his touch passed through it slowly. He winced as a slight cut drew blood from the side of a finger.

"Always treat your weapon as if it were real." Maru took a single part of his glaive hilt off his belt and a wavy short-sword blade manifested.

"But you fight with the whole hilt," Jayce said. "Why only use part?"

"Flow is not about fighting, it is about acting without acting. No mind but the will of the Veil," Maru said. "It is only performed with blades at this length and style."

"Why?" Jayce tested the heft of his weapon.

"Questions are not helping you. Now, let us begin the ninety-seven steps. Right foot back, blade at ready. Good. Now watch me."

Jayce went through the moves step by step. He stumbled through the first few moves and was told to start again by Maru after every mistake. Much to his surprise, he retained the movements and was able to complete the entire kata after an hour of constant practice.

He thrust his sword forward for the final move, then swept back to the starting position.

Maru clapped politely.

"How?" Jayce asked. "I'm kind of a dummy. Why does it feel . . . feel like I've always known how to do it? Like I still can swim even after months stuck on the decks from an injury."

"The Attuned are of the Veil and the Veil is of us," Maru said. "The first members of the Sodality thought they came up with the Flow—though they were separated by hundreds of light-years and had no FTL communications— at the same time. When they gathered at the first Shrine world many thousands of years ago, they realized that they all knew the Flow. The identical kata to what you've performed."

"Huh . . . weird," Jayce said.

"Their summation was a bit more verbose but the gist was the same," Maru said. "You do not need to be on the hull of a ship to enter the Flow. Frequent practice is encouraged. The challenge is to perform it perfectly without conscious thought."

"Have you been able to do that?" Jayce asked.

"No. Perfection is unattainable, but through trying to reach it we can discover mysteries we never knew existed. I may reach that point eventually, but listening to the Veil as I perform is the true purpose. You need to increase the range of motion in your shoulders for the thirty-seventh step, your riposte is too slow."

"Right, I'll work on that." Jayce watched as Sarai began the kata again. "Hold on, the Veil somehow taught the first Adepts this dance before they'd ever met each other?"

"Kata. It is an active meditation."

"But . . . why?"

"You will never find the answer if you ask the question," Maru said.

"That doesn't make sense. How am I supposed to learn if I don't ask?"

Maru flicked Jayce's ear lobe.

"Ow!" Jayce rubbed his ear furiously. "Stop doing that."

"I had to snap you from a harmful thought spiral. Do not seek reasons while you perform the Flow. Your mind will keep you from hearing."

"What do you learn when *you* listen?" Jayce asked Maru.

Maru raised a hand to the practice area. Jayce shrugged and began the kata. Halfway through, he braced his hand against the lower third of his blade and forced it downward, then stabbed the tip forward and ducked an imaginary blow. He stopped . . . then looked at Maru.

"Finish," the Paragon said. "You must always finish."

Jayce did as instructed, but his footing was off and he nearly slipped several times. He returned to the starting position, breathing hard.

"Maru, is there another kata after this one?" Jayce asked.

Sarai flowed to the end of her practice and stopped.

"Why do you ask?" Maru clasped his hands behind his back and paced back and forth in front of his students.

"Because we're not shadowboxing." Jayce made a face. "I don't know a right way to say this. When I prepped for bouts, I'd warm up with a lot of punches, but it wasn't like sparring. This kata, this Flow . . . we're fighting someone else the whole time. I feel the momentum shifting. I can almost feel the other blade against mine. And there's only one other fighter."

"Pssh." Sarai became annoyed. "Who told you that? Was it Eabani?"

"No one told me. It's just there," Jayce said.

"Very good." Maru gave Jayce a pat on his shoulder. "You're learning."

"So, do we learn the other side of the kata?" Jayce asked.

Maru looked him in the eye, then motioned toward the training area.

"Keep practicing. You'll know when you're ready. Let us Flow together as one, yes? You've both made so much progress." Maru ignited his sword.

Chapter 10

A knock on the door woke Jayce up from the small desk. He blinked hard and glanced around, reorienting to his new surroundings. He knocked over his chair and lunged for the door as a louder knock came. Jayce poked at the door controls and a bolt slammed shut.

"Press and hold the green button!" Dastin shouted through the door.

The door slid open. Dastin wasn't in his Marine battle armor, but a padded bodysuit under a dusty leather trench coat.

Jayce looked down at his torn and burnt civilian clothes.

Dastin glanced into the closet.

"Why didn't you change?" the Marine asked.

"I didn't want to wear Holden's stuff. Doubt he'd appreciate it," Jayce said.

"Holden died two months ago on Fesh. Paragon Maru was hunting down one of the Tyrant's agents near a Shrine and we got ambushed. I collected his personal stuff and got it boxed . . . forgot to go through his shipboard utilities."

He sniffed the air.

"Ugh. You smell like Maru's quarters. Fish. So, you're going through the Veil with us?"

"With . . . you? I thought it was for Attuned only," Jayce said.

"Ha! I wish. No, you glitter guys and gals can bring us knobs with you. We keep you safe and carry gear while you're doing all your hoodoo . . . stuff," Dastin said. "C'mon. Can't send you down to Illara dressed like you fell off a shrimp boat."

"Do I get a gun?" Jayce hopped over the threshold and rubbed his hands together as he followed Dastin.

"No! You can carry food and water so someone who does know how to shoot and fight can concentrate on shooting and fighting without the burden of carrying food and water."

"That . . . makes a lot of sense."

"I'm not an officer. I don't make things needlessly complicated," Dastin said. "You know how to handle yourself at all?"

"I'm a docker. Ratted for crews that went out to the dark currents and made it back. So if we'll be doing anything on a ship—wet ship—I'm set."

"You ever been in a fight?" Dastin gave him a sidelong look.

"Couple. I knocked a Bril out in a sanctioned fight once." Jayce rubbed a phantom bruise on his jaw.

"Oh? And how'd you manage to do that with their keratin plating?"

"They have nerve clusters in the armpits. Sharp poke and they lock up. Lot like us humans getting punted in our . . . favorite nerve cluster."

"How'd you get away with a dirty shot like that?" the Marine asked.

"It was a sanctioned bout. Only rule is no killing. Break bones or eyes and winner forfeits the pot to pay the apothecaries." Jayce shrugged.

"We get in a scuffle and you better be ready for killing, because the only way to win the fights we get into is to survive. Best way to do that is to kill the other guy before he kills you." Dastin whacked knuckles to a door panel and a reinforced door slid open.

Battle armor stood in recesses through the room. Eabani grunted at them from an open locker as the shaggy lizard alien fiddled with a breast plate. He hissed and snapped, then slapped a small box onto the workbench.

"No, he would've said something if he could understand you," Dastin said. "Any implants, kid? Anything that'll fritz your nervous system if you get anything conflicting?"

"All meat and bone," Jayce said. "Why?"

"You need a Babel Dot." Dastin picked up the box. "It'll translate most anything you hear and can link to the Dot of any language it doesn't know and train itself. Hack-proof tech. Cheap. Biologically based so it'll work in the Veil. It's standard for any spacer and if you don't have one down on Illara it'll beg questions we don't want to answer. No one just washes up on a planet that far in in the Deep."

"Will it hurt?" Jayce asked.

"Nope." Dastin grabbed the side of Jayce's head with his cyborg hand and held him firmly as he moved the small box toward Jayce's ear. There was a snap and Jayce cried out in pain.

"Ow!" He pulled back, rubbing a growing welt where his ear met his jaw. "What the hell?"

"*Ralllghshtar* dropped last fortnight," a low voice growled.

Jayce twisted around to look at Eabani, who was tapping a screen with a short talon.

"Hey, I understood him!" Jayce pointed at the Lirsu.

"Congrats, squeak, you want to sniff my scent glands and be my friend?" A forked tongue wagged briefly from his jaws.

"Do I?" Jayce asked Dastin.

"No! Quit wasting time and hop on up." Dastin pointed to three stairs leading to a glowing ring in the middle of the armory. Jayce skipped the stairs and jumped into the circle. Small cube-shaped drones floated up from the platform and spun around Jayce slowly. Laser arcs swept over him.

"Suppose I should've asked if this was going to hurt, but I wouldn't trust the answer," Jayce said.

"Hurts less if it's a surprise. You're welcome." Dastin went to the workstation and spoke with Eabani as the drones kept moving around Jayce.

"I'm getting Governance Marine armor?" Jayce asked.

"No," Dastin said. "It would be a waste if you become a baby Paragon. Maru wants a Light Armor suit for you. Takes days for a fully fitted set to come out of the printers we have aboard. You'll get a suit eventually. Mostly so we don't accidently shoot you during a fight because you're not dressed like the rest of us."

The lights on the drones pulsed and sank back into their recesses.

"His dirtside gear won't take too long," Eabani said. "He's mostly skin and bones. My clan wouldn't even have him for a feast." The alien turned to a cabinet, which thrummed and bumped as it worked. "You should show him. Bet he doesn't know his ass from a hole in the ground."

"Show me what?" Jayce hopped down from the scanner.

"Nothing good. Come here." Dastin went to a larger locker and pressed his bare palm to a reader. He drew a pistol and stepped back. The locker swung open, and Jayce cried out in shock.

The Tyrant's soldier he had fought face-to-face was inside a cage, its torso strapped to the back of the locker. The head was held back with a dark band across the forehead. Broken cyborg joints at the shoulders and hips squeaked as actuators kept functioning. The bare-boned jaw opened and closed slowly. Milky white eyes stared at nothing.

"Why is that thing here?" Jayce edged toward Dastin, thinking to put the Marine between him and the nightmare, but forced himself to stay still and exposed to the limbless soldier. "I thought it was . . . dead."

"He is. He's not. The Grip has him." Dastin stepped closer. "Come closer. He bites but he can't get out of his crib. You see the metal in his flesh? Starts at the back of his neck and base of the skull, extends over the forehead and around the neck." The Marine tapped the muzzle of his pistol against the cage in front of the prisoner's face.

"I see it." Jayce took hesitant steps closer. "What do they mean?"

"They mean he should've died a long time ago," Dastin said. "The Tyrant's Grip. It's pre-Collapse technology. Ancients used it as last-ditch life preservation technology. It was meant to shut down and keep the nervous system alive if the rest of the body failed. Too much blood loss? Fatal trauma? The Grip activates and keeps the brain alive long enough to stabilize the user until a clone's ready or the survivor gets dumped into a cyborg rig. Call it stasis. Hibernation. Not optimal but it's better than dying—at least that's my guess on what the Ancients were thinking."

"So, he's not . . . dead?" Jayce sniffed the air and caught a whiff of formaldehyde.

"Not completely." Dastin rapped his muzzle against the cage and the prisoner grunted. His head lolled from side to side. "His brain is still functional and it never ceased functioning. He's not much more than a vegetable now. The ones with all the augmentation can get their synapses burnt out if they take too much damage. I don't know how much of the original person's still in there. Likely doesn't matter, the Grip . . . it changes you."

"The Ancients did this to themselves?"

"It wasn't the same back then. The Tyrant rediscovered the technology during the Black Chanid Invasion. Back when he was still a hero of the Governance . . . he twisted the Grip. A device about the size of a small-caliber bullet gets surgically implanted into the nervous system"—he tapped the base of his skull—"and then nano-filaments start growing through the brain and spine. Can't feel it at all. And when a soldier falls in battle, it doesn't just keep their mind alive, it twists who they were into someone utterly loyal to the Tyrant."

"And the old Council just let that happen?" Jayce touched the back of his own head, then looked to one side, his mind piecing things together.

"The Chanid Invasion was before my time, but the Governance was losing that war until the Tyrant managed to turn the tide. When you're facing annihilation, it's amazing what the brass will let slip by. Legend is the Tyrant was the first to take the Grip; most of his soldiers followed. But instead of a long sleep after getting hit in battle, the Grip brought them back. Got them into the fight within minutes of being mortally wounded so long as they still had enough of a body left over to keep moving."

Dastin holstered his pistol and his voice spoke softly to someone far away.

"You ever see the dead come back? A whole field of corpses rising up, praising the Tyrant. All of them even deadlier than they were before they were knocked down . . ."

"Can't say I have," Jayce said.

Dastin shook his head quickly.

"Tyrant was smart." He rubbed his chin. "He didn't want revenants as simple terror troops, he wanted to keep skills and experiences. Turns out, the longer you've got the Grip on you before it activates, the more of your mind you keep. Manage to survive for years and you're not all that different. Thing is, the Grip works to keep the nervous system functional. The rest of the body will rot away. Some of the Gripped went pretty far to keep their bodies functional—artificial hearts and blood replaced with hyper-oxygenated fluid that kept the rot away. Those the Tyrant used to favor were almost perfect. They just never aged again. The cannon fodder, like this basket case, went full cyborg as the meat failed."

"This is how he overthrew the Council?" Jayce asked. "By the time he defeated the Chanid he had an army loyal only to him?"

"There were plenty of powerful people that didn't care for the Council and how they were running things. The Tyrant's coup was a pretty bloodless affair. The purges came later and that sparked the revolt."

"Did . . . did *every* soldier that fought for the Tyrant have the Grip?"

"No. It was voluntary. The Tyrant swore to be loyal to his soldiers beyond death. He was persuasive and charismatic when he needed to be, and most of his soldiers took the Grip. It seemed better than dying. Is my guess, anyway."

"My father—" Jayce swallowed hard. "At the beginning of the Revolt, the Tyrant sent a ship to my home world. They ordered a tithe, one out of five fighting-age adults. Volunteers got a signing bonus, but the flotillas weren't exactly eager to send their workers off to a war that hadn't touched us out so close to the Deep. So, then there was a mobilization and my mother's number came up. I was just a baby . . ."

"Your father took your mother's place?" Dastin said.

Jayce nodded.

"Mom got a little money, and the Tyrant sent her his paycheck every month. Wasn't a lot, but it kept us from starving while she raised me. My dad didn't know his letters, but we got a message from him and a picture after he finished training. He never said where he was being sent, only that he loved us and he'd come back soon as the fighting ended. That was the last we heard from him. Then the Tyrant was killed, and the new Governance took over and his pay stopped coming. Mom and I figured he was dead. Probably not long after he was taken away . . . the Tyrant was known to keep paying families of the fallen."

"Your planet wasn't the only place the Tyrant mobilized," Dastin said. "I've heard your story before. Shame it had to happen."

"Yeah, well, the new Governance wasn't too eager to keep paying the families of the Tyrant's soldiers, and with all the trade routes failing things on Hemenway got worse. Mom took me to another flotilla to find work and our ship sank during a bad storm. She had to fight for a life vest for me . . . then she drowned. Survivors got picked up a day later and I was all alone at nine years standard."

"Sorry, kid. Sounds like both your parents loved you more than life itself. Doesn't bring them back, but you're still alive. Speaking of alive, you need to know how to kill these meat sacks." The Marine pointed at the soldier in the cage. "We train to aim center mass on targets. Less chance you'll miss. With the Tyrant's soldiers you have to destroy the nervous system. Two rounds in the pink meat." Dastin tapped the side of his head. "If they're already Gripped, hitting them in the chest might disable them if you sever the spine. Take off a limb? That'll just piss 'em off. Decapitation works most of the time. Most."

"Why is this one still here? All alive . . . alive-ish?" Jayce asked.

"We try and free them from the Grip," Dastin said. "They're not of their own free will anymore. If we can right some of the Tyrant's wrongs, then we should do it. And there are some who were Gripped unwillingly. They deserve to die clean, not in the service of a monster that wanted everyone to be 'loyal beyond death.'"

"We'll take this one back to Governance space." Eabani thumped a plastic-wrapped package into Jayce's chest. "They'll transfer him to a lab to be worked on. Right now, we've got him on a numbing drip. He's not lucid at all and probably having a great time in there."

"Is this my glowy armor?" Jayce tested the heft on the thick package.

"No, that's your outfit for when we hit Illara." Eabani handed him a pair of boots. "It's not a Governance world. Not even a Syndicate outpost. We have to blend in while we're down there. Plan on self-rescue."

"Your shinies will be done in a couple of days," Dastin said. "Now get changed and dump your fish-bait-smelling rags in the trash. Then come back here for another assignment. You're a part of this crew, you're a part of the work schedule."

"I don't know how to do anything on a starship." Jayce shouldered a large jacket from Eabani.

"Do you know how to clean? You think you can do what I tell you to do without me having to kick your ass until you do it?" Dastin asked.

"Yeah . . ."

Dastin gave him a quasi-gentle kick to the rear end.

"Then why are you standing there looking at me like an idiot? Go get changed like I told you to and come back here!" Dastin kicked at Jayce again, but the younger man hopped out of the way.

"Moving!" Jayce hurried out of the armory.

"Maru's going to get him killed," Eabani said after the door shut behind Jayce. "He recruited us all for missions through the Veil. Trained us. Now he's going to throw that fish"—he sniffed twice—"into the fire? Kinder to shoot him in the leg now."

"For as long as I've served with Maru, I've never fully understood him. This is some Paragon thing we don't get, and we're not going to get it. So we do our job and do our best to keep everyone alive. Same as it ever was." Dastin gave the limbless prisoner one last look and closed the locker.

"You remember your promise to me, Eabani," he said.

"Always." The alien raised an arm and gave the shorter Marine a paternal pat on the head.

Chapter 11

✳

Jayce jogged down a passageway in the lower decks of the *Iron Soul*. He carried a sheet of polymer paper and an electro-pen in one hand; the other pointed at numbers on doorways until he skidded to a halt.

"Squiggly mark . . . little house . . . eel-looking thing. Is this it?" Jayce held his paper up to the door panel, then knocked several times. The door slid open and a wall of very hot and humid air hit him. An earthy smell of vegetation with a hint of decay stung his nose. Ferns and neon-green plants swayed in a heavy breeze from vents in the ceiling.

"What the hell?" He looked at the paper.

"Come in, Jayce." Maru's voice carried through the foliage. "Hurry, I don't want my frogs to get out."

Jayce ducked into the room. He began sweating immediately in the heat and moisture. A brightly colored animal the size of a fingernail leapt from a leaf and landed on the back of his hand. Its coloring changed to match his skin and where it sat began to itch.

"No. No, you shoo!" He shook his hand gently but it didn't budge.

"Don't." A webbed, scaly hand passed over Jayce's. An alien with neck gills, forward-facing eyes, no nose, and azure colorings brought the same hand up to his face, then flicked the frog into his mouth.

Jayce let out series of vowels and backed into a fern. Water shook off like he was in a brief shower. More of the little frogs jumped onto him.

"My, they like your new clothes," the alien—Maru—said. He gave a low croak and the frogs hopped away.

"What is happening?" Jayce said, afraid to move.

"Didn't Sarai send you over? I asked her to fetch you for me." Maru's gills flexed and spat out a spray of water.

"I'm looking for"—he glanced at his paper—"ten units of gig line and a left-handed void hammer. Eabani says we need it before we leave FTL or the ship will invert its gravity axis and—"

"There are no such things," Maru said. "You've been sent on a fool's errand. Several all at once, interestingly enough."

"But—but I ran into Sarai and she said this bay would have all—"

"She sent you here as I wished to speak to you, and it seems she took part in the joke as well. No surprise, she was on the hunt for a mail buoy hook for several days when she first came aboard."

"Mail buoy?" Jayce held his list up to his face. "That's the next thing I'm supposed to get. So, she knows where that is?"

"No, young one, there is no such thing as a mail buoy. You're going through a bit of harmless hazing."

"She did roll her eyes when I asked questions about the buoy. That should've been a hint," Jayce said.

"Indeed. I was informed by her mother that human females rolling their eyes is a predominate trait in their late standard teen years. She assured me that Sarai will grow out of it, but Dastin tells me human females reacquire the habit once they marry."

"This is like that time I had to bite the head off the first slime eel on my greenhorn trip." Jayce crushed the paper in his hand. "Rest of the crew said it was good luck if I did that. We didn't catch a damn thing that trip. Funny how I still got blamed."

"Traditions. They matter." Maru motioned toward a bulkhead and vines stretched to one side, revealing several small hatches. "You aren't as bothered by the humidity or even my exposed face. Most of the humans aboard find either to be rather off-putting."

"Is that why you wear the helmet?" Jayce pointed to a shelf with the same helm he'd seen Maru wear, along with several others in different styles.

"My Veil-powered armor has a number of environmental systems that keep me comfortable. Species that only breathe air prefer things far too dry for my species."

"You're . . . Wottan? I saw some of you back home. They did underwater repairs."

"Wottan. Correct. Oh, and don't eat my *chickle* frogs. They're rather difficult to raise and they are rather poisonous to humans if ingested." Maru caught one of the tiny frogs as it jumped from one vine to another and swallowed it whole.

"Or . . . they're not poisonous at all and you just don't want anyone else after them." Jayce smiled.

"Would you like to test your theory?" One of Maru's large fish eyes twitched.

"No. My apologies. I'm not used to people being honest with me. The Syndicate preferred to keep things under control through violence and corruption. Crews could trust each other as we were all in the same boat. Trust on the docks was harder to find."

"I understand. Good that you are here as I wish for you to understand something before we land on Illara. How much do you know of the Veil and its effects on us?"

"Other than what I've learned since I've been aboard? I heard about Veil flecks being used to power some ships. Rumor was the boss for all of Hemenway had flecks for his antigrav yacht. That tech's way too expensive for fishing. My mother said the Tyrant used the Veil somehow in his coup. I remember she paid for an amulet to ward off the Veil's influence a few months before she died."

"Mmm . . . observe." Maru held out a hand toward Jayce's chest and the Veil stone in the alien's harness glowed softly. Strands of light flowed from the stone and wrapped around his arm and coalesced at his fingertips.

"Our reality, our dimension, is built atop another. Our laws of physics and everything we can perceive flow from the conditions in the Veil. The Veil itself is not the base upon which we derive, but where the two dimensions meld with each other. It is like the brane between air and water." Maru's fingers twitched, and a coin appeared floating over his palm.

"That's an impressive holo," Jayce said as he stared at the coin.

"Take it. It's yours."

Jayce shook his head in disbelief and swiped his hand over Maru's. He tensed up, feeling the coin in his grasp. He rubbed the coin between his thumb and forefinger.

"Where'd this even come—"

Maru huffed air at the coin and it vanished.

Jayce shook his hand like he'd touched something slimy at the bottom of a fish bucket.

"With a stone of sufficient power, our reality can be manipulated," Maru said. "It dips into the brane between the Veil and our reality. That is how this ship breaks the laws of physics to travel faster than light. That is how Veil flecks and shards can provide power without changing the state of matter as fuel."

"Can I learn how to do that?" Jayce touched the stone in his harness.

"Not with that bauble, no. The deeper one travels into the Veil, the more powerful and influential stones can be found. But it is unwise to travel too far through it if you are unprepared. There are intelligences within the Veil we do not fully understand—reflections of creatures here twisted into monstrosities that are hostile to anything not of the Veil. And we will not be the only ones searching for things of value."

"What happens if we come across these . . . intelligences?" Jayce asked.

"I don't want to frighten you, and we won't be going

anywhere that far into the Veil. You and Sarai should be able to find a sufficient stone not far from the entrance. But there is a choice for you to make, Jayce, one that's better to be made before the journey." Maru unhooked a pair of hilts from his belt and pressed the ends together. He twisted them against each other, and the combined hilts snapped out to form a shaft. A glowing glaive blade materialized at one end, strands of light flowing up and down the weapon. He set the metal end cap of the glaive against the deck.

"There are stones that can be cultivated into a ship drive like Uusanar controls, or there are stones that can be wielded for a different purpose. They can be used for great good, or evil. I chose to become a Paragon and my master guided me to the right stone when I crossed the Veil. This manifestation, this weapon, is a small part of what I can accomplish." Maru unfastened a tie on his shoulder and exposed the stone in his harness to Jayce.

Maru's stone was a spinning star, its orientation changing rapidly. Jayce had to look away.

"It's . . . There's something wrong with it," he said.

"It is not of this reality, but of the Veil. The more powerful it is, the more disconcerting most find it." Maru covered up his harness. "When we cross the Veil, you will have a choice to make."

"Why do I get the feeling the ship stones are easier to find while yours is a lot harder?" Jayce asked.

"It's not that the ship stones are difficult, it's that we are not the only ones who'll be looking for them. Possession of a ship stone makes the bearer a quantity that's very much in demand. Claiming a Paragon stone does not come with the same material benefits," Maru said.

"If I want to be a Paragon, then I'm not going to be rich, that's what you're saying." Jayce tapped the stone in his harness.

"Correct." Maru shrugged. "I won't give you any kind of antimaterialism diatribe. Both Paragons and shipmasters are necessary. The Governance will be strengthened, no matter which you choose."

"Why would anyone choose to be a Paragon when they could be rich?" Jayce asked.

Maru went to the wall of small cabinets and touched one.

"If you understand our true mission, then it becomes easier to understand why we take up the mantle. Do you know how the Tyrant fell?"

"It wasn't the decade-long rebellion?" Jayce frowned. "News from the Tyrant's government didn't say the rebellion was much more than a nuisance. Then the Tyrant was gone overnight, and the Syndicate took over my home. There were rumors of a new Governance, but we never saw it."

"The rebellion was a factor, certainly. But his true death came at the hands of the Paragons . . . I was there when it happened," Maru said. "We lost many good men and women that day, but we saved all we know from the final darkness."

"*You* killed the Tyrant?" Jayce asked.

"It was the work of many. I did my part. The Paragon Sodality fought the Tyrant from the beginning of his reign. So many of us fell during the rebellion . . . but the price we paid was worthy of the cost. Rebuilding has been a challenge as some in the Governance don't trust us, not fully. But all that has no bearing on you and the journey before you. It is dangerous in the Veil, and it is best to enter well armed and well prepared. Or at least . . . better armed and prepared than you are now. Here. Hold this."

Maru proffered the long-handled glaive to Jayce.

Jayce tapped the shaft, then gripped it. The wide blade flickered on and off, then vanished with a pop. Maru took it back and the blade returned. He twisted a grip on the glaive and it collapsed back into a pair of hilts.

"They're called Fulcrum blades and a Paragon's first weapon is always inherited—in a way—from one generation to the next. They can't be wielded by another unless they pass through the Veil to unbind them. But every blade carries an echo of former wielders. To reach the rank of Exemplar, one must forge their own Fulcrum after many journeys into the Veil."

"Fulcrum?" Jayce asked.

"It is by the power of the Veil that our Sodality acts, and these weapons are the will of the Veil. The Balance is everything."

"I don't really understand what you just said, but do I need one of these Fulcrums if I'm going to become a Paragon?" Jayce asked.

"You will need one—for protection. Things work differently beyond the Veil. Coil weapons won't function. It's rather analog in there. Having a Fulcrum weapon can be the difference between success and . . . less success," Maru said.

"You'll teach me how to use it?" Jayce asked.

"First things first. Let's see if any I have with me are right for you. Sometimes the wielder chooses, other times it is the blade. Choose." Maru gestured to the cabinets.

Jayce frowned. He raised a finger and waved it back and forth before seemingly stabbing at random at a box on the upper row.

"Hmm." Maru tapped the latch and it popped open with a hiss. He removed a felt-lined box and angled it toward Jayce. The hilt within was lined with glittering strands and a crest that looked like it was solidified wax.

"Nice!" Jayce snatched it up and yelped as a jolt of electricity ran down his arm. The hilt landed back into the box and Maru returned it to the vault.

"Ow! What the hell?" Jayce shook his hand. "I'm all . . . tingly."

"Paragon Yun'tar Nafftesh did not care for humans. While we are carriers of ancient truths and act for the good of everyone within the Governance, some of us still fall short of expectations. Another?" Maru asked.

"Is there some sort of a trick or do I stick my hand in another box and find more pain?" Jayce asked. "Maybe you can do that thumb-to-my-head trick and help me sort out—"

"You forced the choice. That is the mistake. Clear your mind and simply let the choice come to you. And we do not force our will onto the Fulcrum blades. That way lies darkness. Breathe and decide. That's all."

"Fine fine . . . just drift away and . . ." Jayce closed his eyes and raised his hands slightly.

There was a bump behind him. Jayce opened one eye

and glanced at Maru. He closed the eye and the bump happened again from the same place.

"No . . . no it can't be that one." Maru stroked his chin and turned toward the noise. A rattling began behind a painting of Maru and several humans in Governance military uniforms. All sat around a holo table, their attention on a wire diagram of a pyramidal structure floating before them. A man and woman sitting opposite of Maru held hands.

"I know I'm new here, but is that painting a Fulcrum?" Jayce asked.

"*The Final Oath.* It captures the moment that the Tyrant's fate was decided. But no, it's not the blade." Maru went to the painting and ran his hand across the top of the frame. The painting vanished, revealing a safe. Maru cupped his webbed fingers over a dial and light glowed from his palm. There was a heavy snap of metal and the safe opened. Maru repositioned himself so Jayce couldn't see what was in there, then shut the safe and turned with a wooden case in his hand.

Jayce felt drawn to the box, like he was starving and a long-desired meal was inside.

"What's in that one?" Jayce asked.

Maru rubbed a thumb against the top and half turned back to the hidden safe.

"This belonged to a friend," Maru said. "I thought it would go to another, but sometimes the Veil does what the Veil chooses to do, and it is not my place to second-guess that decision."

He flicked a latch and opened the box.

The hilt inside was made of a silver metal inlaid with

glittering strands. The cross guard was circular, made of what looked like glass full of a golden filigree that moved of its own accord. The strands ended in a carved jade pommel.

"Wow..." Jayce's jaw went slack.

Maru sighed.

"Take it." The alien held the box to him. "I haven't felt his spirit so strongly in a long time."

Jayce gripped the hilt and held it up. It felt right, like it had belonged to him for years and he'd just found it again. His fingers squeezed in sequence and a column of diffuse light shot out almost a yard long. Motes swarmed around the long axis and lit up his face.

"How did you know the activation sequence?" Maru asked.

"I just...did," Jayce said as the mental picture of a slightly curved blade came to him. The motes coalesced to match his vision and a sudden weight came to the weapon. Jayce fumbled with the hilt and dragged the edge across the deck, slicing through roots and plating.

"Oops!" Jayce fought to keep his hold on the hilt, and it nearly pulled away from himself. He settled into a fighting stance, the weapon held at middle guard.

"Your stance is correct." Maru stood to one side of Jayce. "You even hold it like him."

"Wait, am I possessed?" Jayce looked at the hilt in horror.

"No, but the spirit of passed wielders persists in the weapon. The motes that make up the blade are from stones found deep in the Veil. By tradition, a mentor will claim a stone when they lead an aspirant into the other realm. The stone is broken within the Veil and returned to our realm to be forged into a Fulcrum. This creates a chain-of-duty obligation that's stretched back to the very beginning of the Sodality." Maru stared at the blade for a moment. "Why would he choose you and not her?"

"Who?" Jayce brought the cross guard close to his face. "When can I practice? Can I change the way the blade is shaped like you can?"

"You can manifest it while we're under Slip Drive. The inherent closeness to the Veil amplifies your resonance. Once you claim a stone within the Veil, you'll be able to better meld with the weapon and the spirit of those within will help guide you."

"So, it's haunted?" Jayce moved the blade a few inches away from his face.

"It retains the spirit of those who've wielded it before. It is not connected to souls that have . . . moved on," Maru said. "The most important thing for you to understand right now is that it is a weapon and not—"

"It feels like I have so much power!" Jayce thrust the blade up and the blade extended. The tip pierced the ceiling. There was a wet hiss.

"Uh-oh." Jayce jerked the weapon down. Water sprayed out of the cut and soaked Jayce's hair and jacket.

A double chime sounded from a speaker near the door.

"Maru, what in the name of the Eternal Egg Sack are you doing to my ship?" Uusanar asked.

Jayce looked from the Fulcrum blade to Maru, his panic rising.

"It is through failure that we learn the fastest." Maru swiped his hand at Jayce's hilt and the blade disintegrated into motes and the specks of light flowed into the cross guard. The weight suddenly lightened in Jayce's hand and he scrunched his face at it, testing the heft.

The water spray stopped.

Maru cocked an earhole up and looked at the door to his quarters, which was open. Sarai was there, her arms crossed and her face fuming.

"Do not activate it again until we have more time for lessons." Maru touched Jayce's arm. "Now report to the bridge and tell them the emergency glow sticks need new batteries. Take them to Dastin as soon as you have them."

"Yes, sir." Jayce hooked his new weapon to his belt and avoided Sarai's gaze as he left.

"Come in." Maru sighed and went to the holo painting. He clasped his hands behind his back and refused to look at Sarai.

"How dare you," she said after the door shut.

"Don't start, Sarai. We've been over this," Maru said. "The blade chooses. Not me."

"He doesn't deserve that hilt. It should be mine!" Sarai shouted.

"And if the Tyrant's agents weren't on our heels the situation might be different. The Sodality needs every Paragon it can find and—"

"He is fringe trash!" Sarai pointed at the door. "He's no one. He just had his first touch of the Veil and you think he's ready for the journey? You think he'll even survive? I've trained for this since before I could walk, Maru, and you just go and give away my legacy to him?"

"If we impose our will and desires on the Veil, we are

not Paragons," Maru said evenly. "The blade chooses. How many times did you try and bond with that Fulcrum and how many times did it reject you?"

"Every time, but you told me that the closer we get to the Veil the likelier it would be that he would change his mind," Sarai said.

"We stand on the cusp of the final path and the Fulcrum made its choice, Sarai. The more I ponder this . . . issue, the more I realize that this may be my fault. I never told you this, but your father didn't want this life for you."

Sarai took an involuntary step back.

"No. No, if I wasn't meant for this, then I would never have felt the touch. I never would have been Attuned," she said. "He would never have . . . he . . ."

"I knew him, Sarai. I guided him through the Veil and we fought side by side every step of the way until the Tyrant was destroyed. Before that last fight"—Maru bent his head slightly to the painting—"he told me that he didn't want you join the Sodality."

"I don't believe that. Mom said she didn't tell him she was pregnant with me."

"It is true that your mother kept that from him. From everyone. Else we would never have let her join the mission. But your father knew her quirks from when she carried your brother and it didn't take the power of the Veil for him to know she was pregnant again," Maru said. "It was still wrong to bring your mother. No one should ever see their loved ones die. But if we didn't win that day, everything would have been lost."

"Maru, you've . . . you've been there for me ever since I was a little girl. You're not the type to lie. Why wouldn't my father want me to be part of the Sodality? There's no way he could have known I'd be Attuned."

"Your family line has a number of statistical anomalies when it comes to being Attuned. He knew the chances were higher for you after your brother didn't develop the touch. Right after we made the decision to assassinate the Tyrant, he pulled me aside and begged me to keep you from joining the Sodality in case he fell in battle."

"You're not the type to lie," Sarai said.

"I did not. When I asked why he would forbid a path to his child that he himself walked . . . he told me he had a premonition. He saw that the Veil would be your undoing. Something worse than the premature death he faced."

Sarai was quiet for a moment.

"And what did he see, exactly?"

"He wouldn't tell me. But I told him that it was not up to me what path you would choose, Attuned or not. I am a Paragon—it is my duty to listen to that still, quiet voice that whispers through the Veil and carry out that will. I have sat in meditation many times since taking you under my wing and I have never felt the same dread that your father felt. Though, he was the best of us."

"So, you didn't believe him?" she asked.

"You are not a parent. I am. While I am not human like your father, the worries we have for our children are universal. I *wanted* to believe him, understood his fears and his love for you, but refusing to train you always felt contrary to the will of the Veil. He died with his hilt in hand, Sarai. His final thoughts were of you, your mother, and Kaisen. Such emotions imprint on the Fulcrum blade—that is why it always rejected you. The blade chooses, Sarai."

"Why would it choose that scum?" Sarai glared at the door.

"He has a good heart. There is potential there." Maru shrugged.

"He's an idiot!"

"He is inexperienced."

"He's an inexperienced idiot!"

Maru glanced up at the gash in the ceiling.

"You have your own Fulcrum, one with a legacy thousands of years old. Why do *you* think that blade chose Jayce?" Maru asked.

"What? Why would it . . ." She frowned. "Why *would* it pick him? Do you know?"

"Mmm. I will let you consider the answer for yourself. When you know, you'll learn a greater truth." Maru touched her shoulder. "Now, go find Jayce before Eabani tells him to go test out the emergency overrides in the airlock."

Sarai nodded. "That is exactly what Eabani would do."

"Then you'd better hurry."

Maru stared at the holo painting for a long time after she left.

Chapter 12

✳

The night sky was full of stars, but the ground around Jayce was as bright as if it were daytime. Salt flats stretched to the horizon, ivory planes shimmered under the phantom light. A dark peak loomed ahead of him.

Jayce spun around, the scrape of his boots against the grit the only sound. The Fulcrum hilt in his hand refused to ignite.

He called out a name, but there was no sound.

A low rumble shook the ground. A salt haze rose up to his knees. He wiped his other hand against his thigh and looked at the residue. It glinted from an internal source, and he realized it wasn't salt.

It was Veil stone.

The giant shadow shifted, and Jayce froze. The mountain shifted and an enormous man's face turned up. One side was skeletal, the other decaying flesh. Empty eye sockets lit up with a baleful green light.

Jayce felt ice in his chest as the gaze focused on him.

"You will die . . ." rolled across the plain.

* * *

Jayce sat bolt upright. He swiped a hand across his chest in the darkness and whacked fingers against the bulkhead. He yelped in pain and swung his legs over the side of his cot and stuffed his feet into his boots.

The door slid open, and Gunny Dastin burst inside with a large metal can and a rod. He banged the rod against the inside of the can as Eabani reached in behind him and slapped the lights on.

"On your feet, maggot! You think just because you're— Oh, you're already up." Dastin rattled the rod one last time.

Jayce stood up quickly and stumbled in his half-on/half-off boots and fell against his wall locker.

"Do we really have to take him?" Eabani growled. "He can barely wear boots."

"No, no, I'm good." Jayce got to his feet. "Where are we? Where are we going?"

"We just came out of FTL. Should be in Illara orbit in the next few hours but this far into the Deep we're at higher risk of corsair attack and all sorts of otherwise awful encounters." Dastin grabbed the small backpack hanging from a hook on the wall. "This feels light. Did you follow the packing list?"

"It was too heavy." Jayce pushed a foot into a boot. "So, I—oof!"

The thrown bag careened off his shoulder.

"How many trips into the Veil have you made?" Dastin's one flesh eye widened, and a vein pulsed on his forehead.

"None . . ." Jayce picked up his Fulcrum hilt from the sink countertop. "But look what I got!" He squeezed the activation code into the hilt and there was a sputtering sound. He shook the hilt and tried the code again.

"We're out of Veil space." Dastin shook his head.

"Won't work until you take it through and do all the Paragon mumbo jumbo Maru knows all about."

"Oh. Does this mean I get a gun?" Jayce's face lit up.

"No!" Dastin and Eabani replied as one.

"I have to drop some crap off at the armory. Eabani, instruct him how to pack correctly and find out how much more this cherry knows about Veil expeditions than I do." Dastin flung the garbage can against the wall and stormed off.

"You have the packing list." Eabani kicked a plastic bag full of gear Jayce had received earlier at him. "You didn't even pack your hydralizer?"

The reptilian's goatee swung as he shook his head.

"You mean this thing?" Jayce picked up a plastic tube. "What does it do?"

"It converts your urine into drinkable water. The Veil's not the most hospitable place, kid," Eabani said.

"I have to drink my own pee?" Jayce dropped the hydralizer like it was hot.

"I'm not going to let you drink mine."

"No, I mean—"

"I doubt anyone will let you drink theirs either."

"I don't want to drink anyone else's pee!"

"Then you'd better pack your hydralizer." Eabani tapped his foot. "We'll die for each other in there, but we still have limits."

"Fine!" Jayce shoved the device into his bag.

"Better put it in the outer pocket. They tend to leak," Eabani said.

"Thank you, Mr. Lizard Soldier." Jayce moved the hydralizer. "I'm pretty new at all this and—"

"I'm a Lirsu, not a 'Mr. Lizard Soldier.' You're not a Governance Marine, or Dastin and I would have turned you into paste by now for a long list of failures. But your cluelessness helps our image and our backstop when we hit dirtside. We'll start fixing you soon as we get back."

"And what does 'fixing me' mean?" Jayce glanced at a printout on his desk, then shoved three pairs of socks into the rucksack.

Eabani cracked his knuckles.

"Governance Marines and the Paragons have fought together since the earliest days of the Restoration. We know your ways and capabilities. You must know ours. This is how we fight, win, and survive." Eabani said.

"So, once I'm 'fixed' I can have a gun?" Jayce shoved a polymer blanket into the sack.

"Don't get ahead of yourself. But let me tell you something: when we get down there, you keep your head down and your mouth shut, you understand? Plenty of Deep crooks and criminals would love to get their hands on an unbound Attuned like you."

"And do what?" Jayce asked.

"Head down! Mouth shut! Complete your task!" Eabani snapped. "You're already not listening."

Jayce opened his mouth to respond, but Eabani pointed a knife hand at his sternum. Jayce drew air in and Eabani raised the knife hand to Jayce's chest. Jayce exhaled and met the reptilian's gaze for a moment, then went back to packing.

"There may be hope for you yet."

Chapter 13

✳

Jayce's knees ached with every step as he ran down a passageway, heavy pack on his back. Eabani kept an easy pace behind him.

"Why—why do I have to carry *everything*?" Jayce asked between pants.

"No quartermaster beyond the Veil, squeaky. You need it, you better have it," Eabani said.

Jayce focused on the end of the passageway and ran past tall double doors.

"Ack!" Jayce's feet flew out in front of him when Eabani grabbed him by the pack and jerked him back. The alien held Jayce a few inches over the deck with one hand as the other punched in a code to the door controls.

"Why aren't you the one carrying all this?" Jayce wiggled amidst the pack straps holding him aloft.

Eabani dropped him and the doors slid open, revealing a hangar. Inside was a small ship slightly bigger than the fishing cutters he crewed back home. The hull was blocky with sharp angles and obvious point-defense turrets and missile ports. A ramp from the dorsal side was down. Maru and Sarai chatted at the base of the ramp. The Paragon turned his helmet to the door, then back to Sarai.

Dastin came clomping down the ramp. His one cyborg hand had been replaced with a crude claw. His bale eye was gone, a dark patch over the socket. A crossbow was slung over his back.

None wore their Governance uniforms and instead wore rougher climate gear like Jayce.

"Preflight checks are done." Dastin hooked a thumb over his shoulder up the ramp. "Daylight's burning. Let's get dirtside before we see anyone in orbit that's got it out for us."

"What is this?" Jayce asked as he waddled forward under his heavy pack. He ran a hand down the reentry-scorched hull.

"You like? Inner Core smuggler didn't pay her license and registration fees for this cutter and she decided to surrender it before she had to pay even more fines." Dastin winked at Jayce, then went back up the ramp.

"I seized this ship several years ago as part of an operation against smugglers," Maru said. "The integrated stealth systems are rather useful when we need to hide the Governance's hand during an operation."

"We're not going to do that shunting thing up and down?" Jayce asked.

"Only works on latents and Attuned," Sarai said. "If the *Iron Soul* shunts anyone else..."

"Can barely lock onto us." Eabani nudged Jayce aside with his shoulder as he ascended the ramp. "I saw the aftermath of a shunting from some fraud that had a

Fulcrum on him and claimed to be some long-lost Attuned. It was messy." Eabani's frills shivered.

"Damn fools should know when they're in over their heads." Sarai gave Jayce a look and followed Eabani up the ramp.

Jayce bowed slightly and hefted his pack higher onto his shoulders with a quick thrust from his hips.

"Why do I feel like she wasn't talking about some generic fraud just then?" he asked Maru.

"Every journey into the Veil has its dangers," Maru said. "But you are in good company, Jayce. I have yet to die during any of my pilgrimages. Only had to break my anchor twice." He started up the ramp.

"That 'yet' word bothers me." Jayce raised a foot to step onto the ramp. "Where are my manners? Permission to come aboard, sir."

Maru canted his head slightly at him.

"Permission granted. Welcome aboard the *Thorn*."

Jayce took small steps up the ramp. The incline and the weight on him kept his pace slow. Inside the cargo bay of the ship were smaller recesses for containers, all blocked off with thick webbing. The place smelled of old oil and ozone. Dark starbursts on the hull framing and a few too-clean patches on the deck gave Jayce pause.

"I thought you said this ship was seized for taxes or something. Looks like there was a fight," he said to Sarai.

"There was. Previous owner had some disagreements with her suppliers before we caught up to her. The aggrieved party's probably the one that tipped us off that this ship was running under a false transponder." Sarai shrugged. "Criminals. Never trust them."

A sailor in mufti took Jayce's pack from him and tossed it into a recess along with four other packs. Another sailor climbed into the upper turret and was sealed inside.

"They're not coming with us?" Jayce rolled sore shoulders and pointed at the four other sailors moving around the cutter.

"Why do you think that?" Maru asked.

"They're not carrying all the heavy shit we are," Jayce said.

"They are not." Maru sat in a crash seat and buckled himself in. Jayce and Sarai sat on either side of him. "The larger our party, the more attention we'll garner. With the Tyrant's agents involved, it's best to avoid them until we have the strength to deal with a battleship once and for all."

"Are they going to be down there?" Jayce asked. His heart beat faster as the memory of his dream came back.

"Possibly." Maru signaled to a crewman and the ramp rose with a hydraulic hiss. "Uusanar didn't detect them when we came out of FTL. But that doesn't mean they didn't beat us here and are elsewhere in-system keeping a low profile."

"How could something that big beat the *Iron Soul*?" Jayce asked as he buckled himself in.

"Mass does not matter in FTL space," Maru said. "If the stone master has the skill to guide his ship through the fasted paths, he can take them—though there is much more risk maneuvering a ship like that. I don't suggest you ask Uusanar about it, he will not shut up about the topic."

"Unless you want to be a stone master." Sarai leaned forward to look at Jayce. "But you probably should've done that before you got aboard, hmm?" She leaned back.

"And what if we see the Tyrant's own again?" Jayce asked. "What's Dastin going to do to them with a crossbow?"

"No projectile weapons allowed in a Belmont town," Maru said. "No open violence either. We come across the Tyrant's own and the smart thing to do is keep your distance from them. Outside the town is a different matter."

"Why would they do 'the smart thing'?" Sarai asked.

"I have dealt with the Tyrant's agents and soldiers for many years, Sarai. They're not stupid. We're far from the few systems they control on the edge of the Deep, just as we are far from Governance space. Belmont towns earned their reputations for neutrality and swift justice. Let's not be the stupid ones down there, agreed?"

"Yes, Adept." Sarai glared at Jayce.

"What? I haven't done anything down there yet!" Jayce tossed his hands up.

"Don't worry. There's a big difference between ignorance and stupidity. I'm sure if you make any mistakes, it'll be from one and not the other," Maru said.

"Thank you, Adept . . . Wait a minute. Which one do you think I'll do?" Jayce furrowed his brow.

"Thorn *ready to depart*," Uusanar's voice boomed through the ship. "*I want all of you to come back whole. We would be less without you.* Iron Soul, *out.*"

"Hold on." Maru nestled back into his seat.

There was a *clank* and the cutter fell out of the larger ship and nosedived toward a brown, cloudy planet. The *Thorn* rattled as turbulence shook the small vessel. Licks of flame cast red light through the portholes and into the cargo bay.

Jayce held onto his shoulder straps and squeezed his eyes shut as his last meal threatened to jump out of his mouth with each jolt to the ship.

Dastin let out a long hoot.

"Ha-ha! Who doesn't love a good old-fashioned death drop?" the gunnery sergeant shouted from his crash seat on the other side of the cargo bay. Eabani thumped a fist into Dastin's chest to quell his enthusiasm, but the Marine only laughed harder.

Jayce looked to Maru for any kind of reassurance, but the Adept's helm hid his emotions. The *Thorn* leveled out and blood rushed out of his head. He fought to breathe and his face suddenly went cold.

"Tighten your thigh and stomach muscles," Maru said. "It will help."

Jayce grunted and squirmed in his seat.

A few moments later, the awful sensation of too much gravity pulling in strange directions faded away.

"Contact with port authority established. You're not going to like the parking fees, Adept," came from the ceiling.

"This is good news." Maru unbuckled his harness and went to the cockpit.

"How are high mooring fees 'good news'?" Jayce wondered out loud.

"It means there are a lot of . . . pilgrims here." Sarai touched her buckle, but a sudden bout of turbulence sent her hand to grip a strap. "If there's that many, then we didn't miss the Aperture and our only chance to become Adepts and claim a stone. If we were too late, they'd all be gone and parking would be cheap. This isn't hard to figure out."

"He's not going to spew." Eabani held a palm out to Dastin. "Pay up."

"Kid keeps letting me down." Dastin slapped a pair of coins in the alien's hand.

"We shouldn't have to pay anything." Sarai unlocked her hilt and twisted it in her hand. "The Governance—or even the Sodality—needs to control these Aperture worlds. We just leave it to the Syndicate and the freaks."

"Governance doesn't have the manpower to put outposts on the tens of thousands of potential Aperture systems," Dastin said. "Then there's the logistics chain to hard-bore worlds. Something comes out of the Deep for the outpost and there's no way we could get to them in time, ma'am."

"We had the strength before the Tyrant's coup," she muttered.

"What kind of coin do they use down there?" Jayce rubbed his thighs. "This place a trade lash-up or a service flotilla?"

"Your feet ever touch grass before?" Dastin narrowed his eyes at him.

"I walked around the Dry Caldera a couple of times. It's the top of a dead volcano," Jayce said.

Eabani laughed, short *keek-keek-keek* hisses at Jayce. "Best stay close to us, kid. Young Miss is about to graduate from ever needing us again, but that doesn't mean our priorities will get confused if you get into trouble."

"I do *not* need you two." Sarai rolled her eyes. "When am I ever out of Adept Maru's gaze?"

"That time on Borshalt Station. That dock arm was obviously damaged, but you went in there anyway. Or the tectonic resonance facility on that dead Aperture world."

"How many times do I have to tell you that wasn't my fault?"

"The safety overrides said, 'Don't Touch,' in thirty-seven different human and alien languages." Eabani worked his lower jaw from side to side. "We saw what you did."

"I didn't—"

"Got the video right here." Dastin unsnapped a ruggedized data slate off his thigh armor.

"You said you deleted that! Don't make me—don't make me tell my mom you lied to me," she said.

"But then she'd see this." Dastin waggled his one eyebrow at her.

"Ugh! You two can go be 'real Marines' again after this," she said. "I won't need you at all."

"My people demand a hatchling draw blood from their brood tenders in ritual combat to prove they can survive beyond the nest," Eabani said. "What is the human equivalent?"

"Defiance of authority followed by minimal communication and a whole bunch of avoidable mistakes. You're seeing it happen right in front of you," Dastin said. "Honestly, your way sounds a bit cleaner for all involved."

The shuttle rolled slightly from side to side.

"Landing zone ID'd." Dastin pointed at Sarai and Jayce. "Keep your hilts hidden. Don't need to flag what you are. Assume everyone we see's smart enough to figure out what you are if you act stupid, so act as knob as possible. Get me?"

Jayce unbuckled and moved his hilt to a back pocket on his belt that must have been purpose built to conceal the weapon.

"Here." Dastin tossed Sarai and Jayce small sacks of coins.

Jayce felt a tiny shock when he squeezed the bag. He opened the purse and shook up a bunch of glittering coins. They were all the same size, but each was designed differently: simple stamps of runes on one, an intricate depiction of an ancient battle on another, reliefs of humans and aliens. He plucked one up and held it to the light.

"Is that Adept Maru?" he asked.

"Yes, from when he returned from his Adept pilgrimage," Sarai said. "That was over a century ago. You feel that twinge? Means there's Veil-stone fragments imbued in the coins. It's the only currency accepted on Aperture worlds. Each are worth a couple hundred quanta, so don't waste them."

"Wow." Jayce tested the weight again. "I've never had this much money in my hand before. How can things be so expensive down there?"

"Boomtown, kid," Dastin said. "The guys selling shovels and wheelbarrows are going to make plenty of money while the ones who take all the risk in the Veil may or may not come out with enough stones and flecks to cover their expenses. Couple will end up wealthy. If they're lucky."

"Another reason for the Governance to take over Aperture worlds," Sarai said. "Too much opportunity for abuse."

"Governance tries to muscle out the players out in the Deep and all of a sudden the prices for Veil stones are going to get really high, really quick . . . assuming we could even find another seller," Dastin said. "The Tyrant never even tried to do that."

"The Tyrant took three fleets into the Deep two seasons into his reign," Sarai said. "No one knows what he found, and the crooks running Aperture worlds never tried to squeeze him on prices."

"He must have gone to an Aperture world they didn't control," Jayce said. "No harm, no foul. How far into the Deep are there gates into the Veil?"

"The farthest one goes from the center of the galaxy." Maru came down the ladder leading to the cockpit and jumped off halfway. "The farther into the Veil you can enter, the deeper into the Veil you travel, the more pure and larger stones can be found. It is a curious relationship."

"The Tyrant came back from that expedition with only one ship," Sarai said. "He never went into the Deep again."

"Mysteries persist but we're not here for that." Maru adjusted lines that ran from the underside of his helmet and underneath his tunic. Mist sprayed out as he snapped one into place. "Remember, discretion is paramount in the camp. We have no friends here."

The *Thorn* set down with a rumble.

Chapter 14

✳

Maru led Sarai and Jayce down the ramp, the pair of Marines on their flanks. None carried weapons openly. Dastin's crossbow was secured against the side of his pack. Eabani carried the heaviest load, though he didn't seem to be bothered by the weight. The landing pad was poorly leveled quick-crete marred by scorch marks and gouges. The shadow of other ships loomed in thick fog.

Jayce fought to keep the heavy pack on his back from fouling his steps down the ramp. It seemed lighter than when aboard the *Iron Soul* and he considered asking if the gravity on this planet was different from what he was used to.

Lights and signs flickered in the distance.

The clink of bells and chains sounded in the fog, growing closer.

Maru stopped at the edge of the ramp and held up a hand to the rest of the party. A squat figure came out of the fog, an alien with mud-colored skin and a cone-shaped head. It wore little more than a sack and its feet were caked in dirt. Chains imbued with Veil stone hung from its chest and arms, glittering with internal lights.

Jayce couldn't tell if it was male or female and didn't know if that species even had such distinctions.

"Welcome, pilgrims," the alien said. "I am Charok, herald of the Faithful. Welcome to Illara, blessed by the Veil and the Great Ones beyond."

"We are humble travelers come to accept whatever bounty the Great Ones give to us." Maru bowed deeply. "May we tread on this place so blessed?"

"Ah . . . you're no stranger to our customs." Charok's nostrils flared. The alien snorted out of ducts on its temples. An earpiece buzzed on one side of its head. "Respect the peace we provide. Donations are accepted."

Maru reached into a pocket and handed over a golden rod, segmented with platinum bands. He put his thumbs on a crevice then said, "We prefer our arrival remain off record."

Charok raised a finger and waggled it to the left. Maru moved his thumbs one segment over. Charok waggled his finger again.

"We're being robbed," Sarai protested.

Maru looked over his shoulder at her, then back to Charok. He moved his fingers two segments and broke the rod and handed over the longer piece. Charok sniffed it, then squeezed its lips onto one end and tilted its head back and swallowed the rod.

"Respect the peace." Charok turned to one side, which didn't accomplish much as the alien was uniformly round at the waist, and raised a hand.

"We shall," Maru said. "Any bounty we receive shall be

taken from this world and used to spread the good word of the Great Ones."

"Yes, yes, your business is your own. We only provide peace to those who respect it," Charok said. The earpiece buzzed again, and the sound of engines carried through the fog.

Charok waddled away.

"That wasn't so bad," Maru said. "Come."

Jayce stayed a step behind the Adept as the party walked toward the lights. He stepped off the quick-crete and into a puddle. His heel sank into mud and Jayce stopped, confused at the suction on his boot.

Maru pulled him forward with a quick tug to his arm.

"What is the ancient human curse for one who spends too much time not at sea? A dirt lubber?" Maru asked.

"Landlubber," Jayce said. "Weird, I don't feel the deck moving at all."

"It's not a deck. It's ground," Sarai said. "What're you going to do when you see your first *trika* bull or a pterra-squirel? They're like fish, but on land. And they breathe air. And walk. OK, they're not like fish at all."

"Stop giving squeaky such a hard time, little miss," Dastin said. "He's finally getting his land legs. Where to, boss?" he asked Maru.

"I don't know how long we have until the Aperture opens," Maru said. "We'll need a Docent."

"Master, why do *you* need a Docent? You could be—" Sarai glanced around. "You could be the most experienced pilgrim on the entire planet. The galaxy, even."

"Something is . . . off. I can feel the bright points of Aperture gates most of the time. Here it's all diffuse.

Nebulous. I don't like it. If I had a few days to meditate I could sort out the signal from the noise, but we may not have that much time," Maru said. "Perhaps he is here."

"Oh no, not that asshole," Dastin said. "Sir, the chance that scumbag is here has to be a million to one."

"He may be a rectal sphincter but I'd rather have him be *our* rectal sphincter than anyone else's," Maru said. "We need to find the Ahura lodge. There's always at least one this close to a Pilgrimage."

"Should I ask my dumb question or will someone tell me what an Ahura is?" Jayce asked.

"Head down. Mouth shut." Dastin poked him in the shoulder. "Eyes open and mind alert. There's a peace so you'll get your scales balanced if you're killed, but you'll still be dead."

The sound of voices and laughter carried through the fog as they stepped out of the muddy field and onto a raised sidewalk. Buildings made of repurposed cargo containers lined an equally muddy street. Sprinkles of rain tickled Jayce's face and kept up an unceasing drizzle off eaves and awnings.

Storefronts carried packs of food and tools. Rows of pickaxes and shovels were set out close to the sidewalks. More than one store had bows and arrows for sale.

"Perfect stasis locks!" a woman called out from atop a box. She had small, lacquered cases in each hand. "Don't risk imperfections. Secure your claims!"

"Make way!" came from behind Jayce.

He turned and saw torches lighting up the fog. A procession of humans and aliens, their skin daubed in gray mud and their clothes little more than rags, marched down the street. Some had fake Veil stones around their necks or carried crude approximations over their heads.

"Fanatics." Sarai shook her head. "How much did they pay to be brought here?"

"None of our business, little miss," Dastin said.

"Latents!" An alien similar to Eabani—yet somehow uglier—banged two bells together on one side of the procession. "Latents come forth and the Church of the Divine Light will take you to the Promised Land! Latents, join us and return paradise to this existence!"

Eabani barred needly teeth at the other Lirsa, who returned the greeting.

"Sarai"—Jayce leaned toward her—"what in the Cold Depths is going on?"

"Your planet had Veil mystics, didn't it? Your backwater wasn't unique in that regard. Too many cultures and fools worship the Veil and those who can use its power. Every season draws in the gullible and the desperate to try and claim a stone, or even a few flakes, with the hope of becoming more than they believe they are. The Sodality works against . . . veneration like this, but it doesn't work. It's never worked. And some Adepts end up believing the same pack of lies we're supposed to fight."

Maru slipped a coin into the palm of a clerk selling dried rodents and stomped twice on the sidewalk.

"Follow the boss," Dastin said. Jayce was flat-footed until Eabani stiff-armed him toward the Adept.

"Anchors!" A man held up an arm to them as they passed. Leather straps with a flat ivory-colored disc in the center swayed from rings attached to his sleeve. "Exit locations guaranteed. You, young man, don't risk your life on a fake. I'll give you and your girlfriend a bargain, seven coins each!" He waved at Jayce.

Jayce ignored him.

"Hey! You're going to need one of these." The vendor reached for Jayce.

Eabani put a hand on the man's chest and shoved him off the sidewalk. He landed flat in a wide puddle and mud sprayed over him.

A drone descended from the fog and spun around. Camera lenses clicked and changed focus, then the drone rose again.

"That was too close," Dastin said.

"Drone saw him go for the squeaker. Defense against unwelcome contact's not against the peace. And if he got hurt the fine'd be a coin." Eabani shrugged. "I've got plenty of coins."

"Why didn't we buy an anchor if we need one?" Jayce asked.

"One can guarantee a product if the buyer will never return to collect," Maru said. "We're not risking anchors from someone off the street. I've never been that stupid, and I've never known anyone that bought one and survived."

They continued deeper into the camp, which was street after street of prefabricated buildings and a never-ending stream of aliens Jayce had never seen before. He wanted to gawk at an avian with legs as tall as him and rainbow plumage marching down the street, but he kept his head forward.

A hooked beak snapped at the edge of the sidewalk and plucked up a squealing rodent. The animal was swallowed a moment later.

Maru stopped at a ramshackle structure made of planks of rotting wood. The upper floors were lost in the fog. He tapped a pair of coins against a locked door. A panel opened at thigh level and a thin, hairy arm thrust out a chipped cup. Maru dropped the coins in and waited.

The hand holding the cup swirled the coins around, then jiggled it.

Maru plunked in another coin with a decent amount of force.

"Is it me, or is everyone greedy down here?" Jayce asked.

"Shh!" Dastin snapped. "You want to pay extra for pissing them off?"

"Back home we could haggle the price on anything. You take the first offer and it was seen as an insult to—"

"Shh!"

"Back to 'head down and mouth shut,'" Jayce muttered.

The cup withdrew into the building and there were rapid-fire whispers and squeaks. A peephole opened in the wall and a jaundiced yellow eye looked at Jayce for a split second. The hole snapped shut and a door creaked open after several locks unbolted.

"I'm the only one going in," Maru said. "Dastin, go to the bazaar and procure a pond skipper. Most range you can find."

"Aye, sir . . . you know where we're going?" Dastin asked.

"No . . . not yet." Maru nodded at the Marine, then opened the door slowly with his shoulder. It shut behind him with the rapid clicks and clacks of locks.

"Let's go." Dastin knocked a heel against the sidewalk twice. "Bazaar's always in the center of the camp."

Maru stood in darkness. Rays of feeble light shone through gaps in the boards. Shadows darted in the corners. He looked up at dozens of shining sets of eyes in the gloom.

"Not really him. Can't be," a reedy voice whispered. A chorus of hisses and clicks rustled around him.

"Den Mother Charro . . . I know you're here," Maru said.

"We have rules in my house, fish man. Many, many rules," a resonating voice said.

Maru gripped both sides of his helmet and environmental lines unplugged from the feeds. He removed his helm and tucked it under one arm. He heard claws scramble up and down wood, accompanied by panicked squeaks.

"The prophecy! The prophecy!" was repeated over and over.

"Silence! Or I'll put you back in your eggs." A figure barely three feet tall shuffled out of the darkness. A canid snout with blue fur going white from age stuck out from beneath a hood. "Every time he comes to us you all go so silly about the prophecy. All existence is still here. Foolish hatchlings." The alien spoke with an odd tempo, speaking some words almost too quickly to be understood and drawing out others.

"Charro, you're looking well," Maru said.

"How do you know what I'm supposed to look like? I'm old! Everything hurts. Nothing works right." Charro shuffled closer to him.

"You said that when we first met. Almost—"

"I know how long ago that was! I feel it in my hips every day. Where is your crutch? Do things get all soft and droopy on you fish men?" Charro looked up at him. Her eyes glowed softly within the hood. "But you do look good. I envy you. And hate you too."

"That you've made it here for this Pilgrimage is both a good sign and a bad sign," Maru said.

"Symbols! Portents!" rattled from above. Long, bluish-green tails dangled from the rafters.

"You are disturbing my children," Charro said. "I felt the two latents with you." She sniffed hard. "One is familiar . . . connected to a soul you've brought to me before. The other is . . . off. You brought the daughter—didn't you?"

Charro kicked Maru in the shin.

"Yes, one is his daughter. There was no stopping her. She is determined to cross the Veil and if I'm not with her it could be a disaster. We can guide children as best we can, but they won't always listen. No matter how wise we are."

"Ha. Ha-ha." Charro turned around and Maru saw her tail had lost some of its fur. She rapped a small hand on a long box. "They never learn, do they? But you're not here to trade stories. Show me pictures of follow-on-follow generation and brag of their intelligence, Maru. Ask so I refuse and send you away. That is polite."

"This may be the Breaking, Charro. If it is, then we must be the ones to claim the prize, not him. Not the darkness," he said.

"Can't be!" Charro waved a fist at the ceiling. "I don't want it to be. No. Go away."

"What we want is irrelevant. What is happening will

happen no matter our feelings on the matter. Ignoring it changes nothing. It will only put us all in peril. You've felt it, haven't you? The Veil's changing. It's never been this way before." Maru sat on the long box.

"They are so close to each other now. The clash . . . no one is ready for it. It destroyed the Ancients and they were far beyond us. Fear! Uncertainty! Doubt! Too much for me to worry about. Why not retire to a beach and eat candied roaches and have my feet rubbed by well-fed males until the end comes, eh?"

The voices above quaked in fear.

"Ah! Now you all pay attention to me." She scratched toe claws against the floor. "Doom and gloom gets their attention when patience and wisdom won't. Did you try that on the daughter? Of course you didn't, too pure and noble, Maru. Learn to lie—exaggerate! Makes everything easier."

"In the short run. Every lie has its price to pay and the longer it takes for that to come due . . . the worse it is," Maru said.

"And how long have you lied to the daughter?" Charro clicked her teeth together. "You tried to keep her away from the Veil, she persists. She has the whole of the Governance to choose from for her future and she wants her father's path. How many times did the Veil lay the stones for your journey to me? To this time and place?"

"I do not believe in fate. Though the number of helpful coincidences were hard to ignore," Maru said.

"Then break the cycle! Refuse her. Why take the chance?"

"The final part of the prophecy was lost, Charro. We

don't know if it means to tell us how to break the cycle or continue it. Without certainty I cannot know what to do. I must travel into the Veil with them—her—and see it for myself. Then I can make the hard decision."

"Why 'them'? Why the more than one of your silly tongue? Why risk bringing two if it is what you fear?"

"Better the Sodality have both parts than only one. The other . . . I intended to bring to the summit died during our journey here."

"Sodality! Amateurs! Look what they did to the galaxy!"

"We are not perfect. We set the scales right in the end and paid for our mistake in blood. You're going to help, Charro. I can feel it in your aura. You can feel the determination in mine. I need him."

"So much trouble this one! Debts debts debts. He is a shame to the Docents. If we did not have the protection of the peace, I would have auctioned him off to the one that promised him the swiftest balancing." Charro knocked on the box.

"No, you wouldn't have. He's your favorite," Maru said.

"Bah! But I could have scared him into better behavior. Fine fine fine. Standard contract." Charro clapped her hands twice and a pressboard with a metal clasp at the top was handed to her. "Food. Equipment. All your expense. Absolutely no eating of limbs."

"Never my intent." Maru took the clipboard from her and glanced at the bottom of a yellowed and curled page. "This fee is a bit more than 'standard.'"

"Inflation! Inflation and taxes, same thing. More mouths to feed. Since when do Sodality care about money?" Her snout pulled into a snarl.

"Since no one else in the galaxy accepts good intentions as payment." Maru reached into his jacket and removed a brace of glittering coins.

Oohs and aahs came from above. Charro sniffed them, then scratched her palm.

Maru handed over the rest of the golden rod he used to pay the dockmaster.

"Ha! You got ripped off again at the gate. When will you learn?" Charro snatched the payment away and hid it inside her rags.

"A little overpayment fosters good will. Keeps the greedy attentive to another bloated payment. Makes things easier for me. I'll take good care of him, Charro. Now, I need Neff . . . and six anchors."

Groans of disappointment echoed up and down the layers of rafters.

"You hush hush! If you knew, you wouldn't want to go with him." Charro shook her head. She clicked her tongue several times and a Docent scrambled across a rafter and dropped a small sack into Maru's hand. Then she shooed the Adept off the box and pointed to the latch. There was a rasp of moving gears and the top popped open.

Maru slipped the bag into his jacket.

"Not even going to inspect them?" Charro asked.

"Never has a Docent ever sold a bad anchor. Which is why you can command such a high price for them."

"Never has anyone with a false anchor ever returned. The real reason you trust is because I would not doom any of my children to the Void. Polite polite, yes . . . Neff! Neff, get your lazy bones up and up!" Charro reached into the box and shook something.

A Docent with short green fur and floppy outer ears looked over the edge and sniffed the air. The canid alien bent his tail up and scratched under its snout.

"What?" Neff rubbed his eyes. "I didn't do it. I was asleep," he slurred.

"Job job chop chop." Charro snapped her fingers next to Neff's ear and both went flat against his head.

Neff's eyes lit up with an inner light as he focused on Maru.

"Oh no!" Neff ducked back into the box. "Don't sell me off! I'll earn the money back, I swear!"

"You're under contract, Neff. You work for me now. That incident on Golda is forgiven," Maru said. "By me. We shouldn't run into any Nalaaks."

"You have a gambling problem!" Charro grabbed him by the ear and pulled him up and out of the box. Neff wore a long, coarse tunic cut at the thighs and at the back to accommodate bent knees and his tail.

"No dice! No cards! No spinny-wheel machines that rob you," she chided.

"I don't have a gambling problem. I have a *losing* at gambling problem," Neff said. "Where's he need me to take him this time? The poison marshes? The Infinite Cliffs?"

"We'll find out once we're through the Veil. The geography is never the same." Maru turned to Charro. "I will take care of him like he is one of my own."

"I wish you a dull crossing and may you find nothing but flecks!" Charro shook a fist at him. "Prophecy! Pah!" She spat on the ground.

Neff gave his rear end a vigorous scratching. He raised his snout and sniffed hard.

"Two? Just two this time? You must have lots of confidence in them or you lost your mojo, walking fish." Neff hopped onto Maru's shoulder and wrapped his tail around his neck. His hands and feet bent at unnatural angles and gripped each other to anchor him to the Adept's body.

"Food, yes yes? Flecks always appreciated," Neff said.

Maru flicked an imbued coin into the air and the Docent caught it with his teeth and swallowed the money whole.

Plaintive wails came from the rafters.

"Now look what you've done." Charro put her hands on her hips.

"Apologies." Maru passed off his sack of coins to her, then put his helmet back on.

"Wasn't talking to you! Greedy greedy. Come home with a decent story, Neff, and no new debts! Now out out before next customer comes knocking." She prodded Maru toward the door.

Neff let out a slow howl that made the walls vibrate.

Maru shut the door behind him and a low-frequency echo from the rest of the Docents set his teeth on edge.

"Where we going this time, bossy boss fish man?" Neff asked. "Grand adventure or just a trip to the Lake of Sorrows to pick at the shore?"

"I don't know yet . . . but we'll need your talents for sure. How far to an over-the-horizon Aperture?" Maru asked.

Neff began pulling away from Maru's shoulder. The Adept put a gentle hand on the back of the Docent's neck.

"I don't want the horrors." Neff began shivering.

"We're not going for that, we just need a head start,"

Maru said. "You know an Aperture that won't attract attention?"

"'Course I do, boss boss. Just need fast transpo. You have?" Neff nestled back onto Maru's shoulder.

"We should have it by the time we reach the rest of the party," Maru said.

"Good. Don't go past the Xert Quarter. They have no sense of humor," Neff said.

"You have quite the price on your head with them." Maru gave the Docent a quick scratch behind an ear.

"Because they want to eat me! They believe all those lies about Docents—at least you know the truth! Besides, Xert have no use for money, they're so boring."

Jayce sat on a pile of rucksacks against a long chain-link fence. On the other side was a parking lot partially full of air skiffs, all bobbing a few feet off the ground. All were open topped with a standing control rig at the front. Jayce scratched his chin as he looked them over.

Sarai sat on the other side of the pile. Eabani was a step away. The alien looked out over the muddy road running parallel to the park, glowering at anyone who got too close. The Lirsu's aura of menace kept a bubble a few feet wide clear of pedestrians from their packs.

Dastin stood atop one of the wooden staircases up against the fence, its twin on the other side directly across from him. The Marine had been in animated, profanity-laced negotiations with another human from the skiff park, who was just as willing to use colorful metaphors about Dastin.

The pairs of stairs on either side of the fence ran down

its entire length, where similar negotiations took place, albeit with less invective than Dastin's discussion.

"You want me to sign over my mother's eyes too? No percentage!" Dastin pointed a knife hand at the other man's chest.

"You want a rental with *that* range and carrying capacity? Then you pay!" The merchant stabbed a finger into his palm.

Jayce leaned over to one side to speak with Sarai. "Should we be worried?"

"It's fine." Sarai glanced over her shoulder. "He's not pointing at the guy's chin yet. That's when he's really angry."

"Oh . . . I couldn't tell," Jayce said. He sniffed the air, then looked down a side street to a long line of street vendors. "Anyone else hungry?"

"Bit peckish." Sarai pressed her lips to a thin line. "We *should* get something to eat here. Doesn't make sense to eat the supplies we're going to need through the Veil before we cross it. And Gunny's already talked the price for the skiff down to less than he's got on him . . ."

"Not the worst idea." Eabani sniffed several times. "Most of the vendors over there sell human-edible food. Squeaker. Go to the sixth stall on the left and get enough *chorzo* sausage and cheese *tapals* for all of us. Don't spend more than two coins. Stay where I can see you."

"Ooo and get extra of the purple onion slices," Sarai said. "Loved those when I was a kid."

"Move it." Eabani raised his chin toward the vendors.

"No problem . . . What the heck is *chorzo*?" he muttered to himself and crossed the road. Rickshaws pulled by thick-legged aliens with tentacles for arms snorted at him as he maneuvered through traffic.

The first vendor was an elderly human woman with pots of steaming broth around her. She ladled out cooked noodles and soup into plastic bowls and slid the soup onto a shelf where a coin went into a wooden box and the bowl was carried over to the side of a building and consumed without any utensils by a dirty-looking teenager.

An alien that looked like puffs of dark brown fur stacked atop each other slurped wiggling worms the size of Jayce's fingers, straight off a stick hanging over burning coals at the next vendor.

A large humanoid shape stepped out of a building and directly in front of Jayce. Jayce bumped into the figure and stepped back as it turned around. It was in an environmental suit, solid armor with flexible joints made from chain mail. The head was a blunt cone full of lime-green fluid.

It turned to Jayce and a human skull with augmented optics in the eye sockets leered at him.

"There a problem, meat?" The bone jaw moved but the words came from a speaker at the base of the dome. Jayce took another step back and saw the double-star Syndicate insignia on the dead thing's shoulder.

"I am no one's prospect," Jayce snapped out of reflex. "No affiliation."

"This isn't Syndicate territory," the skull said. "You lost, meat? Need a crew to get you through the Veil? Attuned command a high price right now."

"I-I-I'm just here to buy sausage." Jayce felt like the skull could see straight into his soul.

"Food...what a crutch." The Syndicate member shouldered passed him, almost knocking Jayce off his feet. Jayce hurried over to the vendor that had happy holographic meat links in buns dancing up and down the side of his stall.

"I don't like them either," an obese man in a tight white undershirt and apron said from the other side of the grill. Jayce wasn't sure if his skin glistened from sweat or the incessant humidity. "Can never trust the Gripped. Even if they look like they're fresh out of the grave like the Tyrant's ministers. Dead should be dead, I say."

"I've never seen one"—Jayce held up a hand to block view of his other that pointed at the Syndicate—"like a skeleton that *talked,* and can I get four *chorzos*? Oh, and cheese...tarps?"

"Four *chorzos*. You want *tripasas* or *tapals*?" The vendor flipped a hatch over and used tongs to pull out sausage links.

"Yes." Jayce began to panic internally.

"*Tripasas*." The vendor used a ladle and scooped up a gray soup of what looked like fish maws that Jayce only ate when he was on the verge of being flat broke.

"*Tapals*." The vendor flicked a fingernail at a glass case with breaded wedges that leaked off-white goo from the corners.

"Those." Jayce tapped on the glass too.

The man chuckled.

"Sure hope you're the real thing, son. Hate to see another bright-eyed kid with his whole life ahead of him get conned through the Veil only to figure out he ain't one of the Attuned." The man pulled down the collar of his shirt and revealed a slave brand. "You always have to pay. Least I can eat well."

"Uh ..." Jayce looked at the menu, which was written in a script he couldn't read.

"Yeah, best to keep things quiet." The man dropped Jayce's order into a paper bag. "Two." He whacked the side of his hand against a metal box on the cart.

Jayce dug into a jacket pocket and rubbed the two coins together so the merchant could see them and dropped them one at a time through a slot on the box and they landed with a clink.

"Good journey." The sack of food was handed over.

Jayce muttered thanks and started back toward Sarai and Eabani. The Lirsu snarled at a beggar shaking a tin cup at him. Sarai had both hands on the pile of backpacks and seemed tense.

Jayce started walking faster.

The beggar flicked the cup toward Eabani, and a cloud of white powder burst out and hit him in the face. The Marine reared back, slapping at his mouth and eyes.

A large skiff bike, atop which sat two riders in full leather gear, veered sharply around a corner. The rider on the back snatched Sarai off the packs. Sarai cried out as electric shocks from the kidnapper's hands jolted her entire body. She was tossed over the bike between the riders like a bedroll.

The crowds froze as the bike turned down the street and raced toward Jayce.

Jayce flung the sack of food into the driver's face. The impact sent his control off, and the skiff careened from side to side until it passed Jayce and the rear antigrav engine clipped a food stall and blasted the stall like it had been struck by a sudden gale.

The bike rolled over, sending all three aboard tumbling into the mud.

"Sarai!" Jayce ran toward her. She lay on her side in a mud puddle, her face turned away from him.

The rider on the back got to his feet first and knocked his knuckles together. Sparks and thin lightning bolts burst from the impacts. Scale fighting gloves, but with significant after-market modifications.

Jayce brought his guard up in a boxer's stance and bobbed from side to side slightly. His first instinct that the kidnapper was a prizefighter proved correct when the other man mimicked his stance and laughed at him.

Jayce ducked a crackling punch, but static leapt off the gloves, jumped out at his face and stung his cheek. Jayce didn't close the distance and threw an uppercut too short to strike the kidnapper's jaw.

Instead, the punch landed right where the outstretched arm met the shoulder. There was a wet snap as the shoulder dislocated from the socket. The kidnapper yelped and the arm fell dead against his side.

Jayce swung an arm out and clotheslined the other man across the upper chest and wrapped an arm around his neck. The assailant struck with his other hand at Jayce, but the safety settings still on the Scale gloves wouldn't activate the power field so close to the user. Jayce got behind the kidnapper with one arm around the man's neck, then raised a foot and stomped on the back of the kidnapper's knee, breaking it with a wet pop.

Jayce shoved the crippled man away and turned back to Sarai.

The driver stood over her. He held a crude knife made from a sharpened hunk of metal with cord wrapped around the base for a handle.

"Don't you come any closer!" The driver tore off her helmet and blond hair spilled out. Her skin was sallow and she had the wide, uneven, dilated eyes of a crash addict. "We're not staying here any longer!"

She pulled Sarai up and set her knife against her neck.

Jayce reached behind his back and drew his Veil-stone hilt and thumbed the activation switch.

"Ha!" he shouted.

The hilt sputtered and gave a dying buzz.

"Huh?" Jayce gave it a quick shake.

"I'll split—I'll split the price for her!" the driver shouted.

A lit Fulcrum blade touched the driver's shoulder from behind. Maru lengthened the blade so the driver could see it. A creature with big eyes glanced over Maru's shoulder, then ducked back behind him.

"It is time to stop," Maru said. "Drop the knife. No one else needs to get hurt."

The driver's breathing got faster and faster, then she looked up.

Several drones descended from the overhead gloom.

"No sudden movements!" came from the drones. The command was repeated in several languages.

"No. No no no`... please." The driver tossed her knife into the mud and raised her hands. "We didn't hurt—we didn't hurt anyone!"

Maru bent his arm and raised the blade from her shoulder.

"Violation." The pronouncement was followed a moment later by a solid green bolt that struck the driver in the chest. She disintegrated from the inside out, leaving only a dark cloud that drifted over Maru.

The drone swung its weapon toward Jayce. He froze. He dared a glance at Maru, who shook his head ever so slightly.

A flash of green light stung Jayce's eyes as the bolt snapped over his shoulder and erased the other kidnapper where he cowered in the mud.

"Respect the peace." The drones lifted back into the fog. Activity returned to normal on the street within a few seconds. The owner of the wrecked stall jumped into the middle of the street and waved his fists at the sky, shouting at the drones.

Eabani stumbled over to Sarai. His face and neck were badly swollen and his eyes could barely see through fat lids. He shook her shoulder and growled nothing but vowels. Sarai pushed him away and put a muddy hand to her temple.

Maru retracted his blade to the hilt and touched her cheek. There was a dull glow from his fingers and Sarai straightened up with a gasp.

"Jayce. Our equipment," Maru said as he and Eabani helped Sarai to her feet.

"It's back there." Jayce pointed behind him.

"I know that. Put your currently useless weapon away and get back to our gear," the Adept said.

"Yes. Right." It took him two tries to put the hilt back into the sheath on the back of his belt. He spotted the meat and cheese he'd bought strewn across the road, covered in mud. A few rats had already come out from beneath the sidewalks to carry away the food.

Dastin was at the packs, his face set like stone but red with fury.

"Uh...I went to get food." Jayce slowed as he approached the Marine. "And then—"

"Shut. Up," Dastin snapped. "I can't believe how I screwed this up."

"You...did?" Jayce frowned.

"Do we have transportation?" Maru slid an arm through the strap of Sarai's pack and shouldered it. The creature peeked over the other shoulder at Jayce and its eyes lit up. Sarai was woozy on her feet but had a hand on Eabani to keep her balance.

"Oh, Maru has so much potential with him. Shame shame to lose either," it said.

"What is—Never mind." Jayce shook his head.

"Yes, sir. Pick up at lot thirty-seven," Dastin said.

"Then we best be on our way. Seems we've been noticed by the wrong sorts around here," Maru said.

The party picked up their gear and followed Dastin into the skiff lot. Jayce felt a bit safer once the fence closed behind them. They walked past skiffs floating in their parking spaces. The quality and upkeep on the skiffs improved as they went.

"Jayce, did you forget that a Fulcrum will not fully manifest in this realm until you've bonded with a stone beyond the Veil?" Maru asked.

"A little. I was trying to do something constructive," Jayce said.

"The drones look for restraint during altercations. If you'd ignited your weapon, they may have viewed you as an aggressor. Remember this," the Adept said.

"But when I threw our lunch in the driver's face that was OK?" Jayce asked.

Eabani growled and coughed. Jayce poked a finger against the sore lump behind his ear and waggled the translation bead.

"Yes, his quick thinking was a useful, albeit crude, solution, but I am more curious how Sarai was snatched away from you," Maru said.

"A beggar hit him with…shells? From some crustacean, is my guess." Sarai brushed white powder from her jacket. Eabani sneezed again. "They must have known Lirsu are allergic to that."

Eabani put one thumb to a nostril and exhaled sharply. Something green plopped into a puddle.

"A beggar distracted us, then hit him with the powder," she continued. "He was working with the kidnappers."

"Kidnappings aren't uncommon in boomtowns like this," Maru said. "An Attuned is worth the risk if they can bring back a ship stone to sell on the open market. The peace isn't concerned with crime, but it is concerned with violence."

"Here." Dastin banged a fist against a skiff and a ladder unwound from the prow down to the walkway. The vehicle was matte black and a good seven paces long and four wide. It had rails around the deck that concerned Jayce. No sailor on Hemenway would have risked choppy seas in that thing.

Dastin tossed his bag onto the deck and climbed up the ladder.

"Get up here, you puffy bastard," the gunnery sergeant said to Eabani, who wheezed through swollen nasal passages as he climbed the ladder. "Check the power supply and get ready to cut the grav anchor."

Sarai touched her forehead and wobbled on her feet. Jayce gripped her arm, but she dismissed it with a shrug.

"There was this dead guy," Jayce said. "Had Syndicate colors on him. He talked to me, but I didn't tell him anything."

"Not dead dead," Maru's passenger said. "Dead have died. Brain still talk talk."

"Ah!" Jayce composed himself. He had been startled for a moment.

"Sarai, Jayce, meet our Docent. He is called Neff and he's going to lead us to an Aperture," Maru said.

Eabani growled and beat a fist against the skiff's railing. Jayce hefted up his and Sarai's bags.

"It would be the Syndicate that tries and ruin everything." Sarai opened and closed her hands several times, but they kept shaking. "What did they hit me with?"

"Hacked Scales," Jayce said. "You foul the capacitors with a spike made from a gold-and-copper alloy and it'll futz with the power levels. Do that in a sanctioned match and you'll end up scav fish food. Thing is, the safety sensors stay on." He extended one arm. "Strike and you'll hit with all the power you want from the hack." He pulled it back into a guard. "But you pull in too close and it goes neutral. Stops you from frying yourself."

"I never thought getting punched in the face for money would ever be useful," Sarai said.

"Jitters go away in about an hour," Jayce said. "My

friend Kay once hit me with a hack 'just to see what would happen.'"

"Some friend." Sarai started up the ladder.

"It was OK. I hit him back with the other one and he hit the ceiling. For real. Dent's still there," Jayce said. He put a foot on the ladder, but Maru stopped him from climbing.

"Jayce . . . you need to know that the danger we've faced thus far is nothing compared to what's beyond the Veil," the Adept said. "You don't have to go with us. I can place you in a school or find you work on a variety of vessels."

"What? I've come this far and you want me to turn back now? Did I . . . did I do something wrong? Did I pick the wrong hilt?" Jayce reached behind him and lifted the scabbard. Sarai leaned over the railing to watch them.

"The path of the Adept is difficult. Shipmasters can be even more difficult to learn and many don't even leave their stones after they're interred in a vessel," Maru said. "There is no happiness on the other side of the Veil. Not when you go through. Not when you come back."

"Then why did *you* go?" Jayce asked him.

Maru's head tilted back slightly, as if stung by the question.

"Purpose," the Adept answered.

"Aren't you Adepts out there killing tyrants and winning wars for the Governance?" Jayce asked.

"Some of us are."

"This one so young . . . so stupid stupid. But he shines bright." Neff crawled up on Maru's shoulder and sniffed the air. "Don't like. Won't make it. Send him home."

"I don't remember anyone asking you. Neff. Docent.

Thing. Sir, what is he . . . exactly?" Jayce put his hands on his hips.

Dastin stomped on the deck and the skiff wobbled ever so slightly.

"Don't decide now," Maru said. "I wouldn't leave you here, not when we're so close to the Apertures opening. Too dangerous. Let's go."

"Hungry," Eabani grumbled as Jayce climbed aboard.

"You shut up!" Dastin kicked at the Lirsu. "Your damn stomach's already caused enough trouble. Raise the grav anchor. Neff! Where we going?"

"East to fifth road marker, then turn south." Neff glanced around. "Tell you more later later."

The skiff rose several yards and Jayce felt the familiar unease of a deck beneath his feet. Dastin turned it around and the skiff jolted forward.

Chapter 15

Jayce held onto the prow railing as the skiff flew over treetops. He laughed as flocks of colorful birds were spooked from branches and scattered through the sky. Maru was at the controls, speaking with Neff quietly as he drove them all toward a distant mountain peak.

"Nothing, sir." Dastin, standing watch on the port side, lowered a pair of binoculars from his eyes.

"No one knows my entrance, no one one!" Neff stretched his limbs across Maru's back. The Docent's skin stretched like a bat's and caught some of the breeze. The skiff nosed down slightly and skirted over a deep ravine.

"I love all those standing kelp beds," Jayce said. "What do you call them again?"

"Trees. They're all trees," Maru said. "Go take Sarai's post. I wish to speak to her."

"Aye, sir." Jayce pushed off the rail and ran to the back of the deck where Sarai clutched the railing for dear life with one hand; the other clutched an optic to her chest. She'd gone pale and her knees wobbled.

"You OK?" he asked.

"By the Light of the Veil, this is miserable," she said. "How are you so damned cheerful?"

"What's wrong? There aren't even sea swells to deal with. No spray either. This is the best ship I've ever been on," Jayce said. "Aren't you having a good—"

Sarai leaned over the railing and vomited.

"Guess not." Jayce plucked her water bottle from the side of her pack and handed it to her.

"I hate you so much." She spat out the last of her breakfast. "And thanks."

"Maru wants to talk to you." He took the binoculars from her.

"I don't want to walk right now. Did it seem urgent?" she asked.

Jayce looked over his shoulder. Maru's attention was on piloting and whatever Neff was jabbering into his ear.

"Not particularly." Jayce looked around with the binoculars. "This is easier than watching out for snatch squids or crimson sharks . . . Can I ask you a question?"

"You just did." Sarai set her forearms on the railing and lowered her head between them. "This is miserable. I want to be back in the void."

"Adept Maru asked me why I want to go through the Veil with him. Why are you going?" he asked.

Sarai turned her head to look at him, then walked toward the prow. Jayce stayed at his post until the sun began to fall and Maru tapped him on the shoulder. Jayce didn't look away from the back of the ship.

"Neff needs to get to know you," Maru said. "It's necessary, but a bit uncomfortable."

"Uncomfortable ho-ow!" Jayce shouted as Neff stuck his snout into Jayce's ear and sniffed quickly.

"Just stand still." Maru took the binoculars from him. Neff jumped from Maru's shoulder to Jayce's and continued nosing around Jayce's head and shoulders.

"Why why so much fish smell?" Neff scratched Jayce's hair, then shook dandruff from his claws. "Human male child. Bad breath breath. Otherwise viable."

"What are you doing?" Jayce asked.

"I am Docent. I find you right Veil stone. Bad stone won't let you take through. Waste waste of time and chance. You're a year or so away from being too old . . . last chance. Only chance!" Neff held Jayce's left eye open for a second, then huffed.

"The Docents are something of a mystery," Maru said. "There's no record of them from before the Collapse, and they were encountered by the first Adepts when they crossed into the Veil."

"Lucky those ones were. We have anchors for them. Never any Adepts without Docents. Hands. Hands!" Neff scratched at Jayce's arm. Jayce brought a hand up to Neff and the Docent meticulously inspected his fingers.

"This is an anchor." Maru pulled out a small disc from his jacket and let Jayce see it. He put it back before Jayce could reach for it. "It will be tethered to our Aperture gate. When you are ready to leave the Veil, you must break the anchor. It's the only way out if you can't return to the gate."

"Time-lost treasures from beyond the Veil. Don't forget the price!" Neff set Jayce's hand on his head like a hat and peered through his fingers.

"I never do," Maru said. "There will be temptations on

the other side, Jayce. Not every stone you'll come across is a prize. Some are false. Others are traps."

"How do I know the difference?" Jayce asked.

"That's what I'm for." Neff turned upside down and wrapped his tail around Jayce's forehead. "Ha! Have cut cut stone already. Familiar it . . ."

Neff jumped onto Maru and bared his tiny teeth at Jayce.

"Where you get get that? How dare you steal!" Neff swiped at the air between them.

"It chose him, Neff. Adept Holden has gone beyond the Veil," Maru said. "Jayce is a good man. Holden's spirit would not choose anyone else."

"Did I do something wrong?" Jayce asked.

"Owe that one! Saved me from Docent eaters at great risk to himself. Never met him before but still saved me," Neff snarled. Maru scratched the Docent behind the ear and that seemed to calm the small alien down.

"A lot has happened since we last met, Neff," Maru said. "The galaxy is a different place now. Your aura is too much right now. There's something else, isn't there?"

"The Below clings to the stone. Old blood that never washes out," Neff said. "Bad omen for the crossing. Don't like . . . no."

The Docent sniffed Maru's neck, then snorted.

"Yours too. No good! No good, I say!" Neff jumped off and ran on all fours to Dastin. He climbed up the Marine and perched on his shoulder, tail swinging back and forth angrily.

"Is he always like that?" Jayce asked.

"He has a flair for the dramatic. Don't worry about

what he said, he'll lead you and Sarai to excellent Veil stones. He always does."

"That dead man I spoke to—"

"Not dead dead!" Neff shouted.

"I talked to a skull! He's dead enough!" Jayce shouted back. He cleared his voice and continued speaking with Maru. "Aren't all the Gripped like we saw on the *Iron Soul* loyal to the Tyrant?"

"Technology is an incredible thing. Once word gets out of a new use for something, everyone knows that it is possible. The Tyrant's nobles were a significant part of his rule. Some with the money and expertise found a way to use the Grip to prolong their lives without having their wills bent to the Tyrant."

"Why doesn't everyone want to get one? Not dying seems desirable."

Maru removed his helmet and tucked it under his arm. The strong breeze wicked moisture away from his face.

"There is a cycle, Jayce. What lives must die. What endures from our lives after our passing is the greatest gift we can give to those we leave behind. Those who take the Grip do not live as you know it. Sensation is greatly muted. The vessel of life rots away without intervention. It is an abomination in every way. The Tyrant used the Grip to enslave his soldiers and his court; there was no life for them to live. Most of those that take on the Grip voluntarily succumb to madness and despair within a few years. The mind is alive, but it is trapped in a rotting cage. Those that trade the cycle of life and death for a pale reflection of how they lived almost always regret it."

"Then why did that Syndicate shot-caller do it?"

"Some enjoy the power. Others fear death so much they will do anything to stave it off, no matter the cost," Maru said. "Can you feel them? The gates."

Jayce leaned against the railing.

"I don't know why... but maybe there's something really interesting over there." He pointed west, toward a small hill.

"Bad bad spot," Neff said. "Takers know it, have it monitored. Gate goes to island with bad flecks and nothing more. Young one has the touch."

"Not bad," Maru said.

"What are these gates?" Jayce asked.

"This was once a Shrine world of the Ancients. Perhaps they were beings from beyond the Veil who came to our dimension, maybe they were an advanced race native to our galaxy that found a way into the Veil and went on to exploit it, but this is one of the systems where the gap between becomes very thin. From time to time."

"We couldn't go through at the Shrine back home?"

"Too far. Too much needed." Neff shifted between Dastin's shoulders. "Apertures only a few tens of systems at a time. Good nose, good instincts needed to know which ones to go to. No pattern."

"We must beware our return," Maru said. "The entrance and exit points are the same for all who travel beyond the Veil. It's easier and more cost efficient to take from those who make the journey instead of making it oneself."

"How is that an advantage? Say someone comes back with an FTL stone, they can't just take it. Doesn't it have to stay with the Attuned who found it?" Jayce asked.

"Correct. But most who return do so with power flecks

and stones rated for harness, if they're lucky. Neither of those need Attuned for them to function. No one who makes a Pilgrimage for those is safe until they return to Illara and auction off what they found . . . or they get off-world with their bounty. There's less risk of being ambushed for those that go deeper into the Veil to bond with a more powerful artifact."

"Soon soon, be there soon." Neff stood on his hind legs and wafted air toward his snout with his fleshy wings.

"The Docents can sense where the gates are," Maru said. "But they're more valuable within the Veil."

"How do they—"

"Mind your business!" Neff barred teeth at Jayce. "Don't believe lie that eating us can give you our gifts. It is lie! Also don't believe eating Docents gives long life. More lies! We taste terrible terrible. Very poisonous to all."

"You don't even have any meat on you," Jayce said.

"Adept! Protect me!" Neff clung to Maru and inched his body around to put the Adept between him and Jayce.

"He's not serious." Maru gave Neff a pat on the head, then narrowed his eyes at Jayce.

"No one's going to eat you while I'm around, Neff," Jayce said. "You have my word."

"Watching you!" Neff swiped at the air and gave him a double take, then pointed at his eyes and swung the same fingers at Jayce. "Tell unfunny man to turn forty degrees east and stop ten klick klicks at the clearing surrounded by red blossoms."

"Will do." Jayce handed over the binoculars to Maru and jogged to the conn at the prow.

* * *

Dastin set the skiff down in a clearing as the sun set. He and Eabani leapt off the deck and raced to opposite sides of the wood line. Maru ignited his glaive and walked off the skiff. He stood in the middle of the clearing and looked around.

"Finally." Sarai shut down the skiff. Her eyes lingered on Maru.

"Feels like . . . feels like my teeth are humming," Jayce said.

"Squeaker! Open the big pocket on the left side of my pack!" Dastin called out from the woods.

Jayce pulled his pack off the pile and unsnapped the pocket. Crabs crawled out and skittered over his hand. Jayce snapped back as the crabs sprouted wings and flew away. They spiraled overhead, then spread out into the woods.

Jayce hopped off the skiff and tested his footing. He went to one knee and touched a thick weave of vegetation. He snapped a blade off and held it up to the waning sky. He rubbed it between his fingers and sniffed it.

"What are you doing?" Sarai asked.

"Is this that 'grass' you've mentioned?" He pressed his palm against the ground. "It's . . . neat."

"Don't go hugging any trees just yet," Sarai said. "Unless you want to figure out if you're allergic to the bark."

"Come here." Maru tossed his helmet toward the skiff. He pointed to an armband with an anchor stone fastened to it. He snapped similar devices onto both their arms. "These anchor stones will bind to this Aperture as we pass through. If there's an emergency or you're injured, break the stone with one solid blow. Cracking it can offset the recall and you could end up inside one of those trees or half-in, half-out of the gate."

"I can't believe this is finally happening," Sarai said. "Now I can finally know which stories are true and which were lies Dastin would tell to scare me when I was little."

Jayce looked at the Anchor stone, then glanced around. Dastin and Eabani emerged from the woods and brought over the packs.

"Listen to me." Maru locked eyes with Jayce. "When the Aperture opens, you must keep moving. Do not stop for anyone or anything. You linger too long in the Between and you'll end up like them."

"There's a 'them'?" Jayce asked.

"There is only one direction. Keep moving until you find us on the other side. Everyone goes through alone. Such is the way of things." Maru helped Sarai shoulder her pack, then spoke to Jayce. "Know this: any water you drink from the Veil will not quench your thirst. Any food you did not bring with you will not stop your hunger. The Veil underpins our reality, but it is not of us and we are not of it. Do you understand?"

"Only eat and drink what I've packed. Got it." Jayce snapped his waist strap together.

"Sarai, tell him about the dilation. I must prepare." Maru went to the center of the clearing and spun his glaive around and stabbed the blade into the grass.

"Time isn't the same in there," she said. "We will feel time passing. We'll get hungry and thirsty and need to sleep, but when we leave . . . everyone comes out at the exact same time. All across the Aperture world. The gates will open for about an hour or so, but when everyone comes out can be a bit funny. Longest is six standard days. Usually only a few minutes pass out here."

"Then why are we carrying all this crap if we're only going to be gone for—"

"Say an hour passes out here before the Return. You can stay in the Veil indefinitely if you have enough food and water and don't get killed by anything. Or anyone. Some aliens don't have the same bio needs we do and they've stayed there for years."

"Ugh . . ."

"We get through the Between and I decide I'm not going to put up with your crap and snap your anchor. Poof! You're gone from the Veil and you'll be right back here. Maybe a couple of minutes have passed. I go on and it takes me days to find the right Veil stone to synch with. I crack my anchor and poof! Right back here at the exact same time you arrive. But I've lived all that extra time and you haven't. I can't make it any simpler without drawing stick figures."

"I get it now. Weird."

"Also: don't die in the Veil," she said.

"I wasn't planning on it."

"You die there and you won't come back. You'll . . . you'll see." She drew her hilt and spun it in her hand. "I'm going to become an Adept. Finally."

"Good luck." Jayce tried to reach for his hilt, but his pack was in the way.

She grabbed him by the front of his jacket.

"Do not get in my way. The Docent finds a stone worthy of me, you keep your thieving mitts to yourself. Understand?"

"I haven't stolen anything," Jayce raised his hands to the side.

Sarai's face contorted with anger, but she didn't elaborate. She pushed him away.

"Adept, perimeter defenses are in place," Dastin said. He and Eabani pulled out their crossbows and checked the strings.

"Soon! Soon so very soon!" Neff jumped into the air and flapped his wings, slowing his fall slightly.

Maru began chanting. The words were low and indistinguishable. A vibration in tune with the invocation resonated through Jayce's feet and he lifted one foot up and hopped to the other in panic.

Dastin grabbed him by the arm.

"It's OK, kid. This is how it goes," the gunnery sergeant said.

Jayce tried to pull away, but the older man's grip was iron.

A dull glow appeared beneath the grass and grew more intense with every passing moment.

"Maybe . . . maybe this was a bad idea!" Jayce shouted as a rush of wind came from the ground and blew grass and dirt around him.

"Keep moving!" Dastin shook Jayce. "One foot in front of the oth—"

Jayce fell into white light.

Chapter 16

Jayce screamed, but there was no sound. Rays of white and ivory light broke around him. He spun around, but no matter where he looked, he saw the same long fractals.

His feet touched down with no impact. He stood in a white abyss; the fractal rays dissipated overhead.

"Hello?" His word was muted with nothing to echo off of. There was a tug against him. He turned around, but the tug was always to his back.

"Maru! Anybody!"

His heels sank into the ground, and he took a step back to balance himself. His rear foot sank halfway up to the ankle in broken shards of white glass. He fell forward and pulled his foot out. Both hands hit the ground and the surface broke into tiny pellets that rolled behind him.

Jayce pushed himself up, struggling against the weight of his pack and the growing pull behind him. He took a step forward and the ground held. He kept moving through the blank canvas of the reality all around him.

"What if I break it now?" He touched the anchor band

around his upper arm. "No. No, I didn't come all this way to quit now." He kept moving, the drag behind him constant no matter how fast he went.

He didn't know how long the march lasted, but after counting enough steps he realized that he'd walked the distance of the largest flotilla he'd ever visited back on Hemenway. His legs began to ache, and his shoulders burned from the straps and heavy pack.

He bent forward and thrust his legs up to kick the pack higher and reduce some of the strain. When he raised his head, there was something in the distance.

"Hey!" Jayce waved a hand overhead. "Hey, Dastin, is that you?" He broke into a jog. The figure ahead of him was moving toward the direction of the pull, which broke what little Jayce knew of this Between place.

No matter how fast he moved, the figure approached at the same rate.

"Ah, this is eel slime!" He stopped for a second and his feet began sinking again. "Crap. Crap!" He started forward again.

The figure was on a path parallel to him. Jayce made out the same sort of Veil energy armor that Maru wore, but the helmet was different. The other man was about the same size as Jayce but wasn't carrying anything with him.

"Hello?" Jayce tried to move at an angle toward the other, but the ground began to give way and the pull suddenly got stronger. It felt like he was walking through a headwind as the new Adept came within a few steps of him.

"How can you go that way? What's behind you?" Jayce asked.

The Adept covered his Veil hilt with one hand and patted his chest twice. They passed each other without another word.

"Why didn't Maru tell me there'd be others in here? What's that?" Light blue stumps appeared ahead of him. A path just wide enough for his pack cut through the sudden obstacle. The stumps became posts of varying height as he got closer.

More details on the objects didn't become clearer until he neared, like ancient ice melting off some long-lost object buried in a glacier.

The first one he could make out clearly was of a man with one hand to his chest, his arm reaching up to the sky. His face was contorted in pain. Jayce kept walking, afraid to touch the statue.

The next was of a woman in fatigues. She was on her knees, a cracked anchor in her hands. Her face was perfect, but her look of pure shock and horror was frozen in time. A cut appeared on one side of her neck, then her entire head fell forward like an axe had severed it.

Jayce cried out and broke into a run through the forest of statues. All were of people in their final moment before death. Emaciated, starving men. Sunken-eyed adventurers with distended bellies and their hands cupped with water at their mouths. Too many had signs of violence on their bodies.

"Maru! Maru, where are you?" Jayce ran down the open path past all the horrors.

Reality blinked several times, like when he'd take a hard blow to the head during Scale bouts, and Jayce fell forward. He landed in blue-green gravel and the pack knocked most of the air from his lungs when it landed on him.

"There he is!" he heard Eabani shout.

Rough hands rolled him onto his side. Dastin and Eabani stood over him, their crossbows in hand.

"Well, did you die?" Dastin asked.

"What in the hell was all that?" Jayce touched the gravel and when his hand didn't sink into any arcane strangeness, he opted to just lay there and catch his breath.

"The Between. Weird, ain't it?" Dastin chuckled.

"The statues! The other guy! What was that?" Jayce sucked in cold, moist air.

"Let me see him." Maru knelt next to him and lifted his chin. "What did you see?"

Jayce gave him the barest of details while he checked his hands and clothes for any glass dust from the Between. Maru listened carefully and nodded.

"Attuned experience things differently when they cross over," Maru said. "Dastin and Eabani saw nothingness until the Between released them. I saw the dead, same as you. Same as Sarai."

"Dead? What all those statues were . . ."

"It's best not to die here," Maru said. "There is much debate as to what happens to a soul when the vessel ends beyond the Veil, but no certainty."

"A little more warning would've been nice," Jayce said.

"The more one knows about the Between, the more the Between can latch onto thoughts. Some have reported seeing dead loved ones, their very heart's desires. All meant to slow Pilgrims down as they cross. Hesitation is death in the Between," Maru said. "If I warned you of any sort of high strangeness that you might encounter, it could have been the end of you. So, I asked Gunny Dastin to give you clear and simple instructions that only a combat-tested Marine can give."

"I didn't even have to cuss or bring out the big guns." Dastin raised a knife hand.

"Where's Sarai?" Jayce asked.

"Still not through." Maru looked up.

The sky was an infinite sheet of cracked ice. Light shined through shifting cracks of the frozen river and cast long rays toward the ground in many different spots and at different angles. Tufts of clouds meandered below the high ceiling of the world.

"Whoa. That . . . that doesn't seem right," Jayce said.

"Welcome to the Veil, kid. It's only gonna get weirder from here." Dastin pulled Jayce to his feet. Behind him was a spinning loop of glistening wire large enough for two people to step through easily. Veil stones were wrapped in the gate like lost gems enveloped by tree roots.

"This is our gate," Eabani grunted. "Go through and you'll be dropped back at the Aperture. Return trip's a lot faster."

Neff pawed the ground, then sniffed at something. He followed his nose to a sapling and began digging. He came up a moment later, Veil flecks glowing between his small fingers.

"Aren't those worth a lot of money?" Jayce asked Dastin.

"He's contracted to lead us to stones. Any flecks or flawed stones we don't want are his," Dastin said. "He brings them back to his nest and they feed the next generation."

"Ah-ha! Good good omens." Neff swallowed the flecks. "Very valuable." Neff tapped his stomach.

They were atop a gently sloped hill. The aquamarine pebble field spread across rolling hills. Two more gates spun in the distance.

"What if we go through one of those?" Jayce asked.

"Don't." Maru held a palm out to the gate and thin filaments of light appeared connecting his fingertips to the stones. "She's close. Still moving... Every Aperture gate in the galaxy is open right now. Very few of them will lead back to Illara. You step through another gate and you could be ejected to an uncharted planet or a world with no atmosphere."

"Even if you do end up on Illara, we wouldn't know where it would be. Most of the gates are camped by Syndicate who'd rob you blind and then kill you," Dastin said.

"Or eat you. The order they do all that's up to them." Eabani hefted his crossbow and looked through optics. "Little early for Sniffers."

"Don't antagonize it," Maru said softly. "We can't take trophies back. You know that."

"Probably best." He lowered the weapon. "Imagine if the Drakes could pass through."

"Let's not." Dastin tapped the stock of his crossbow. "Adept? I'm getting worried about her."

"Shh..." Maru's eyes closed. "She's close..."

Jayce looked out to the horizon, which was lost to a distant haze all around them. Snow-covered mountains were behind the gate, a turquoise sea to the left and right, but it was far more distant than felt right. He was used to the horizons on Hemenway, but there didn't seem to be any sort of curve to this planet.

If it even was a planet.

He turned around right as Sarai snapped into existence and fell against him.

She screamed and beat at his chest and pushed him away. Her face was wet with tears and dreadfully pale.

"Whoa! Whoa! We're all friends here." Jayce backed away.

"Maru?" She swiped a sleeve across her eyes and dropped her pack. "Maru, where are you?"

"Here." The Adept grabbed her by the shoulders and held her firmly. She slipped forward and hugged him. "I saw you. I saw you in the graveyard."

"I haven't died, little one." He stroked the back of her head. "I'm just fine. See?"

"Then who . . . ?" She pulled back to look at him again.

"It could have been any Wottan that's died here. I'm told we look alike," Maru said.

"You could have warned me better." She wiped her face and composed herself.

"You got warned?" Jayce flopped his arms against his sides.

"I've been preparing for this since I was a child," she snapped at him. "Have you read the epics of Veddan the Pure? Seen the art hanging in the grand walkway of the Sodality's Grand Temple?"

"No. But maybe I was better off when I was in the Between knowing next to nothing." Jayce shrugged.

"Told you." Dastin handed a small box to Sarai. "Not every secret makes you happy."

"I'll take dangerous knowledge over blissful ignorance." She gave Jayce a dirty look, then flipped open the box.

"Kid." Eabani held up a similar box and gave it a shake. "This is your other insurance policy. It points back to this gate, but it's offset for a bit more security."

"Like a compass?" He flipped the box open, and a needle spun several tens of degrees away from the gate.

"Sorta. It'll point back here in case you lose your anchor. But the needle is offset by nineteen degrees. That means—"

"So, it's like a declination off magnetic north from true north." He held the compass in front of him and turned toward the gate.

"You know the offset. Don't tell anyone. Keeps anyone who might get it from following it back to our gate," Eabani said.

"Are you going to tell me how it works?" Jayce asked.

"No. Governance military secret. Which means we spent entirely too much money for the tech, and we don't want looters across the galaxy having an easier way out. Keeps competition down."

"Won't that mean more people will die in here?" Jayce asked.

"Someone chooses to come through, it's on them. Governance can't save everyone all the time," Eabani said. "No one in here but us is your friend, you get me? We're not here to save anyone. We get you two the shinies you need, then we bounce out. Understand?"

"Yeah, I got it," Jayce said.

"Neff, are you ready to scry?" Maru asked.

The Docent paced around the party on all fours, pausing to shake pebbles from his paws. He sniffed at the air, then sneezed.

"Bad bad air here. We need to go move. Something is different this time. Something is wrong," Neff said.

"Let me scry for a moment." Maru clapped his hands together. He kept his pointer fingers together and threaded the rest of his digits together. Tiny motes appeared and spun around his fingertips. The spinning grew faster and faster as Maru murmured.

A song rose in the distance. Jayce cocked an ear up and leaned toward the sound. The words were strange but felt familiar and were sung along with long notes of bells and chimes.

"Ahs sodame ko dahl . . . tad arima na egur methar . . ."

"Stop!" Maru's command jolted Jayce out of his reverie. The Adept drew his hilt and ignited the blade with a quick motion. "How do you know the words?"

"What? I don't—I was just listening and—"

"You were singing." Dastin lowered his crossbow. "So was Sarai."

"I was?" She looked as confused as Jayce.

"Oh no . . . no no no!" Neff ran for the portal. He leapt toward the opening but Maru caught him by the tail and threw him back. Neff tumbled through the pebbles, then curled into a ball with only his snout and eyes sticking out.

"Omens! I must tell the clan." The Docent snuggled into the rocks.

"If it's true, then we must remain here," Maru said. "Your mother was right . . . I should never have doubted her." The Adept retracted his blade with a snap and returned the hilt to his belt.

"What is that?" Sarai pointed to a distant plain of ice-white reeds.

Jayce peered at the horizon. A solitary mountain peak formed just above the far horizon. The cliffs looked like stretched glass, glowing with silver and gold from within. The peak was shorn off and perfectly flat. Starlight pulsed irregularly from the top.

"Why why do they have to see it? Send me back, full refund!" Neff began shivering.

"If they can see it, so can everyone else," Maru said. "Which way?"

Sarai and Jayce pointed to the peak as it faded away.

"Sir?" Dastin stepped between the two Attuned. "Sir, this isn't like our last trip."

"There may be...a complication." Maru's face scrunched for a moment. "The Pinnacle is never in the same place. It's been seen before, but that doesn't mean we can reach it. It may just be an afterimage."

"Go back now?" Neff perked his ears up.

"No!" Maru snapped. "My apologies. It may mean nothing."

"Or...?" Jayce raised a hand.

"Or we dare not leave. Not when the Pinnacle has manifested," Maru said. "We need to move deeper into the Veil...then we'll know more."

Maru started down the hill.

Jayce looked at Sarai. They both shrugged and followed the Paragon.

"What's the 'Pinnacle'?" he whispered to her.

"A myth from the first Adepts," she said. "It's supposed to be the very edge of the Veil where an object of great power is located. Something that can destroy the balance between our reality and the Veil."

"How many Adepts have been there?" Jayce asked.

"None. But enough have felt its presence. Maru never gave me a straight answer when I've asked about it. Neither did any of the other Paragons on Primus. They told me, 'You'll understand when you're older,' or words to that effect," she said. "They don't tell baby Paragons everything, Jayce."

"Why don't we ask him now?" Jayce lengthened his stride to catch up with Maru.

The Wottan flicked a hand up and a root sprang from the ground and nearly tripped Jayce. He fell back and matched pace with Sarai.

"Maybe later."

Chapter 17

The party walked through a field of knee-high grass, the tops bent with heavy nodules. Eabani and Dastin were on the flanks, Maru and Neff were a few steps ahead of Sarai and Jayce. Jayce plucked up a stalk and bent the silver-blue length in two spots. It bruised black and little seeds fell off.

"Do you know what that is?" Sarai asked.

"No idea, but it does seem kinda neat," he said.

"So, you don't know if it's poisonous or toxic," she said flatly.

"I figured it wouldn't be. Water won't stop thirst. Food won't feed us. Why would there be anything that'll give us allergies or be poisonous?" Jayce asked.

"Thank the Great Egg." Eabani rubbed his still slightly swollen nose.

"The Veil—here, things will become different as we travel farther—is close to the reality we know," Maru said. "Flora and fauna from the other side of the gate are reflected on this side of the Aperture, but with elements of the deep Veil."

"If it's a reflection, what if this plant thing and the eggs on the top—"

"You're holding *bragga* wheat, it's a staple across the galaxy," Sarai said.

"—are the original and the wheat stuff she's talking about is changed by our side? Our reality. How do you know which is the real one?" Jayce asked.

Maru looked over his shoulder at him.

"Go on . . ." the Adept said.

"If this place gets weirder with every step we take . . . but it doesn't when we're back home . . . then . . ." Jayce turned the stalk around in front of him, then tossed it aside.

"Philosophies across centuries and empires have pondered these questions," Maru said. "No one has a definitive answer. The best stance I've learned is to accept the reality you're in, and not layer on reasoning that does not apply to where you are."

"We're here for your Veil stones," Dastin said. "Not big thinking problems."

"There's still value in asking the questions." Maru raised a finger. "Even if we do not learn the complete solution to the Veil and its relationship to our reality, searching for the solution led to knowledge of how to survive here. How to harvest Veil stones."

"Is there an end to it?" Jayce asked. "The horizon here is . . . not right."

"There's a theory," Maru said. "But it is neither here nor there while we—"

Eabani raised a fist.

"Contact left." He swung his pack into the field and went prone behind it.

"I don't see—Ah!" Dastin pulled Jayce to the ground. His pack rose up his back and smushed his face into the ground. The dirt smelled like citrus and dust stung his eyes.

"Take cover behind your gear." Dastin put the buttstock of his crossbow to one shoulder and kept the weapon amongst the wheat stalks.

"I see them." Maru had a monocle to one eye. "Half dozen Vishar. They're armed."

The monocle landed next to Jayce, and he looked through it. In the distance were a group of tripedal aliens. Their insectoid exoskeletons were covered in a thin brown skin, their bulbous heads had several antennae that bent and twitched toward the party.

"I've never seen those before," Jayce said. One of the Vishar held a longbow made of chitin.

"Vishar have an enclave in the galactic southeast," Sarai said. "They hate humans for reasons no one knows but them. No trade with the Governance. Not even with the Syndicate."

"I've encountered them a few times," Maru said. "Best to keep your distance from them. They will fight for Veil stones."

"And they will eat us," Neff said. "Bug bug men have big appetites, weak backs. Don't carry much on them."

"They have a weapon like you, Dastin," Jayce said. "Bigger arrows, though."

"What's it doing with it?" the Marine asked.

"Holding it up in the air toward us," Jayce said. "Pulling an arm back and—"

"Down, you idiot!" Dastin reached out and shoved

Jayce's face into the dirt. A second later an arrow as long as Jayce's arm thumped into Eabani's pack.

"Message for us, sir," Dastin said.

"They want us to keep our distance," Maru said. "Which we shall do."

Clouds rolled across the field and fog enveloped the distant Vishar.

"Forest there there." Neff pointed ahead and to the right. "Better protection."

"Is there a mirror storm coming?" Maru asked.

Neff took a deep sniff of the air.

"One's out there, but it hasn't decided to come for us yet," the Docent said.

"Up. Follow me," Maru said.

Jayce grumbled and cussed as he got up and brushed seeds and dust off him. He swung the pack on and nearly lost his balance. He stumbled toward the Vishar arrow and reached for it. A flash of blue light redirected his hand, knocking it high.

One foot stepped on the arrow shaft and flattened it to the ground. There was a hiss and pop as some caustic substance leaked out of the arrow.

"Nothing poisonous on this side of the Veil." Blue light faded from Maru's hand as he pulled Jayce away from the weapon. "But the Vishar are rather fond of it and coated their arrows in something we don't have an antidote for."

"Not real friendly, are they?" Jayce asked. His ears perked up on their own, listening for the sound of another arrow incoming.

"Assholes, the whole lot of them," Eabani said. "Good

thing you stomped it down. Give those bugs a harder time finding it."

"Yeah, that's what I meant to do." Jayce nodded quickly. "Swear."

"Storm closing fast fast." Neff slapped Maru on the back of the head, then slunk back against his shoulder. "Faster. Faster!"

"Step it out." Dastin jogged ahead, his pack seeming like another part of his body as he sped up. Jayce broke into a run and his pack jumped against his shoulders and lower back. His knees ached by the time the party reached the edge of the forest.

Only Sarai was more out of breath than him when they stopped just beyond the wood line. Wind howled through the upper branches and the sky darkened with thick clouds.

"So much . . ." Jayce tried to swallow down his dry throat. "So much walking."

"Throw up shelter, sir?" Dastin asked.

"Not so close to the edge. We need some breathing space if another group comes in here for refuge." Maru drew his hilt and stalked into the woods. Jayce marveled at the trees; some were as tall as the biggest barges back home. Spear-tip-shaped leaves and branches brushed against Jayce's shoulder. Clusters of nuts surrounded by jackets of short spikes and white flowers hung from high branches.

Jayce kicked a pile of brown, oblong seeds, by accident.

"Ah . . . now this is a treat." Maru knelt behind a tree and signaled the others to take cover.

Jayce felt sweat up and down his back. Leaning against

the rough, brown-and-silver bark of a tree trunk didn't do much to reduce the load on his back.

"Ooo, is that a barnacled tower turtle?" Sarai drew a small notepad and pencil from a shoulder pocket.

Jayce calmed his breathing and heard something big moving through the woods. There was the burble of running water and the occasional snap of tree branches.

He inched around the trunk and saw what Sarai was so enamored with.

The turtle had a circular shell with a diameter as wide as Jayce was tall. The flesh of its legs was sky blue and each was thick as a skiff mast. Its back was flat, with slithering appendages that reached up and stripped seeds off the branches. The seeds were strewn ahead of the turtle's face, where it cracked the food in thick jaws. Bits of shell fell from its mouth as it ground the inner nut to paste.

"Where's that alien from?" Jayce asked.

"It's native to the Veil," Maru said. "Docile, unless provoked or bothered while feeding. The barnacles are a different creature from the turtle. Seems they've developed a symbiotic relationship with each other."

A pile of steaming waste fell from the back of the turtle. A stalk reached over the tail and ejected what looked like pollen onto the droppings.

"Yum," Jayce said. "Does this mean there are intelligent species native to the Veil?"

"Yes, but no. Mostly no," Maru said as the wind picked up. Freezing cold rain spattered against the trees and dropped onto the party.

"Worse worse coming," Neff said. His tail shot out and quivered like a plucked string.

"Set up the shelter," Maru said.

"Aye, sir." Dastin dropped his pack and pulled out a plank from between his pack and the frame and shook it out into a semirigid tarp. He and Eabani gathered up more sections and joined them together to form a low tent frame. The party moved their gear underneath and the Marines unrolled flaps down the sides and tied them to plastic legs. The flaps went clear, but they still blocked the gusts of wind abusing the forest.

"Hydrate. Eat," Dastin said to the pair of Attuned. "Sleep cycle, sir?"

Rain thumped against the tent roof.

"Not too long." Neff opened Sarai's pack and rummaged inside. "Tuna and noodles where where? Always yum."

"Adept Maru?" Jayce kicked his legs out in front of him and dug his heels into the dirt as he leaned against his pack. "What would have happened if I'd touched that arrow?"

"Nothing good, which is why I risked using my Veil stone to save you." Maru moved between Jayce and Sarai and squatted between them. He opened his harness with a tug on the leather cover and plucked his stone out. It glowed more sharply than the last time Jayce saw it on the other side of the Aperture gates.

"Look at yours," Maru said.

Jayce's harness stone was dull and cool to the touch.

"I used mine and now it's a beacon to every creature behind the Veil. Attuned can sense it, but it should work to keep others away more than inviting trouble," Maru said. "My hilt carries less of an aura to it right now. When you two claim a proper stone, it will shine. We will be in even greater danger as neither of you have the training to mute the power. I've found it best to break anchor once you have a stone."

"Wait, are our hilts working now?" Jayce fumbled with his belt.

"They are." Maru touched his arm. "But it will attract attention if you use it."

"What will come for us?" Jayce asked.

"Other Pilgrims, possibly. Veil predators, more likely. The Veil tries to defend itself when stones are disturbed," Maru said. "Now . . . there's more we need to discuss. Something is different this time. Something potentially dangerous."

Neff sat on top of Sarai's pack. The Docent had an open pouch of food in hand. His tongue darted into the pouch and snapped tan glops into his mouth.

"Tell truth whole truth," Neff said. "You knew. You brought them."

"I suspected." One of Maru's fish eyes turned to Neff, the other stayed on Sarai. "Now I'm surer."

"Sure of what?" Sarai asked.

"I want you both to clear your minds and listen to me." Maru pressed his palms and fingers together. "What do you feel above us?"

"The tent."

"Jayce . . ." Maru tapped his fingertips together. "Above the false sky."

Jayce looked up, then to Sarai. She sat in the lotus position and had her hands on her knees, eyes closed. Jayce mimicked her and tried to calm his thoughts. He felt a pull against him, and his eyes popped open.

"It's OK, you can see it without worry," Maru said.

Sarai was breathing deeply, though her chest moved in starts and fits.

Jayce closed his eyes and relaxed again. He felt a pull up and the sensation of the ground against his body lessened but didn't leave completely. His mind floated up through the forest and to the sky. White birds flapped in the upper clouds, unperturbed by the buffeting winds and rain. He came to the great barrier of ivory glass and blue ice . . . then drifted through.

The sky plate was so thin Jayce barely had time to register that he'd passed through when he found himself standing on top of the icy sheet. Darkness was all above him, but the sky plate lit up below him. Sarai was nowhere to be found.

There were no stars in the sky, not at first. Pinpricks of light appeared slowly, then flooded into shoals of swirling galactic arms that twisted around each other and coalesced into a figure: a man made of stars.

The celestial being wore plate armor, his face hidden by a helm. His arm drew back and a spear materialized in his hand. The star man flung the spear away and it speared across the sky, a contrail of nebulae and burning stars left in its wake.

It struck something and a blinding flash of a supernova spread. A wall of unimaginable force struck the false sky, shattering it. Jayce was too terrified to run as the wave of destruction swept over him.

There was no pain. He regained his bearings and saw the galaxy, the home galaxy he recognized from star maps, drop away from him, like he was hundreds of thousands of light-years above the galactic plain.

Fragments of the broken sky collided with the galaxy. Stars were snuffed out by the millions, then a pinprick of darkness at the center grew . . . and grew. A singularity devoured the galaxy, sucking in stars and releasing only fatal radiation.

Everything collapsed onto the black hole . . . then there was nothing left.

Snap.

Jayce sucked in air and opened his eyes. Maru had his fingertips together to snap again at his ear, but Jayce was wholly returned to the shelter.

Sarai was there, her eyes wide and her knuckles pressed to her mouth.

"What did I just see?" Jayce asked.

"Some call him Michael the Sainted. Or Georgias the Sainted. Or Tulkaran. My people call him *Ghur'kulk*, the Final Champion. He is the guardian of the Celestial Cycle. The distance between our reality and the Veil is variable. The closer the two, the stronger the Veil's influence. Ships can travel faster. Manipulating stone energy is easier. Other times we are farther apart and things become more difficult. There was a century-long period where off-ley-line travel was extremely difficult. It gave rise to several of the Deep kingdoms and nations that are still not part of the Governance. After thousands of years of gathering data, we of the Sodality detected the Cycle."

Maru opened his hands and a light grid appeared between the three. A horizontal dark red line and a blue line moved closer and farther from each other as a bright dot moved from one side of the graph to the other. Every time the two lines came perilously close, they would separate widely.

"Our reality and the Veil come perilously close to a Breaking every thousand standard years or so," Maru said and his demeanor hardened. "The Sodality believes that the Cataclysm that destroyed the Ancients' civilization came about after a Breaking was manipulated to merge the dimensions."

"How is that possible?" Sarai asked.

"You don't know?" Jayce gave her a quizzical glance.

"Only senior members of the Sodality know this. We only share it with other Adepts once they've proven themselves after many years of service . . . and only if they need to know," Maru said.

"Did my father know this?" Sarai asked.

"He did indeed. He was one of the first voices to rise against the Tyrant after the Sodality helped him take power."

"Wait . . . 'helped'?" Sarai leaned forward slightly.

"The Tyrant began as a particularly talented and charismatic military commander during the Black Chanid Invasion. The Governance at the time of that crisis was particularly corrupt and inefficient. We were losing that war on all fronts and the Governance was making things worse. A decision was made by the Sodality and others to install General Mutarin as Tyrant until the Chanid were defeated. We believed the Tyrant's promise to relinquish power."

"Which he didn't," Jayce said.

"We had the choice between hundreds of billions consumed by the Chanid or trusting the Tyrant. In hindsight, we should have taken our chances to defeat the Chanid. The Tyrant was more than we thought he was—he was well aware of the Cycle, and once he had the Governance under his control, he began work to disrupt the Cycle and bring about another Collapse. Once the Sodality learned of this, the rebellion began. We were fooled and betrayed, and the Sodality paid the price."

"Why are you telling us this now?" Sarai asked.

"Because we are perilously close to a Breaking. The Pinnacle appears only when such an event is nigh. It is from the Pinnacle that a Veil stone powerful enough to prevent another Cataclysm can be claimed. Some of us within the Sodality believe that there is a higher intelligence within the Veil that works to prevent such disasters, as the Veil is as affected as our own reality."

"The god here is the Sainted guy?" Jayce asked. "That's who I saw fighting above the sky?"

"That is the strongest theory," Maru said. "The intelligence is too divergent from us to communicate directly. How would you teach a fish to avoid an ecological disaster on your home world?"

"I . . . have no idea," Jayce said.

"What does this have to do with me?" Sarai asked.

"There is a Veil stone atop the Pinnacle. I need one of you to claim it before the Tyrant's agents. While the Tyrant is dead, his lieutenants likely still believe in his quest to end the Cycle. The consequences could be cataclysmic."

"Wait, why is there even a stone like that?" Jayce asked.

"It is a gift from the Sainted One," Maru said. "The *Iron Soul* did not bring us here by happenstance—too many coincidences happened along the way. Neff should've been sold off to repay his debts, but the creditor that was coming to collect had her ship knocked off course before it could reach Illara."

"Wait wait . . . Ollian knew where I was?" Neff's ears perked up.

"Yes, she mentioned she was coming for you and asked for passage when I encountered her on Nivan Station. I didn't respond to her request, but I appreciate that she pointed the way to you. The Shrine on Hemenway confirmed Illara was the place for us to cross into the Veil."

"Thank you," Neff said. "Ollian has no patience. No options for more credit and would eat eat me given the chance. I am poisonous!"

"She's eaten at least three Docents and is still alive," Maru deadpanned.

"New one!" Neff jumped onto Jayce's shoulder and snuggled against him like a living shawl. "Protect protect, yes? Like you promised."

"This Ollian lady's not here, is she?" Jayce asked as Neff's claws tested for solid footing against his clothes.

"Highly unlikely," Maru said. "The most important thing we must do is to reach the Pinnacle. Claim the stones before the Tyrant's agents can—or anyone else— and bring this news back to the Sodality. Other Adepts are likely here, but none will have entered so deeply into the Veil as we have."

"Den mother Charro would have come with you had she known." Neff hopped back onto Maru's shoulder.

"She suspected, but she feared to trust her instincts," Maru said.

"Who else knows?" Jayce asked. "Wouldn't other Attuned have seen the Pinnacle?"

"Indeed," Maru sat back. "Indeed. The Tyrant's agent we encountered is likely here . . . but did she have an Attuned with her? It was too chaotic on the dock for me to have sensed any with her."

"You can crack your anchor now if you're scared," Sarai said.

"I'm not scared," Jayce snapped back. "Just in over my head. A bit."

"We will continue to the Pinnacle," Maru said. "Perhaps it is unreachable like almost every time we cross over. It is possible I am wrong. I often am."

"Storms getting worse, sir," Dastin said.

Through the semiopaque tent sides, leaf-shaped hail cut through the trees and shattered against the ground and tree trunks. The crack of glass sounded through the forest over and over again. Tiny indentations appeared and disappeared against the tent roof.

"Doesn't look too bad," Eabani grumbled. "But the mirror flecks will slice you up in minutes without shielding."

"Why doesn't it tear up all the trees?" Jayce asked.

"We're not of the Veil," Maru said. "The mirror flecks are imbued with Veil energy, just as everything else here. There is a planet close to the galactic core where hydrofluoric-acid rains from the sky. The Crathul native to the planet can stroll through the acid storms without issue. The rest of us? Not advised."

"Chow." Dastin tossed a tube at Jayce's chest. He caught it and turned it over in his hands and squinted at the writing.

"What is 'potato'?" Jayce asked.

"Ground tuber, human favorite." Maru peeled the top off a tin. "They don't sit well with my species."

"Ugh, do you have to eat that in here?" Sarai scrunched her nose at Maru. "Not everyone likes the smell of—"

"Canned ass." Dastin put the back of his hand over his nose.

"It is fermented shrimp in a *falhtun* brine." Maru stuck a pinky into the can and plucked out something still wriggling. "A delicacy." He crunched the shrimp between his jaws and there was a brief squeal.

"Trade you for beetle casserole." Eabani shook a box.

"I hope 'potato' is better." Jayce squeezed some of the paste into his mouth. His jaw worked from side to side. "It's . . . good."

"What'd you grow up on, kid?" Dastin asked.

"Fish, crab, kelps. So many kinds of kelps." Jayce looked in the same pocket on his pack that Dastin pulled food from and looked through more tubes. "Pound cake with popping seeds? Chilly macs and . . . cheese?"

"You don't want those," Dastin shook his head. "No good for your stomach if you've never had that before. Here, I'll trade you for the vegetable omelet and chicken fit for a king."

"Sweet, thank you." Jayce handed over the tubes and stuffed them all into his pack.

Sarai shook her head.

"Maru, what if we get to this Pinnacle place and find these super stones you're talking about?" Jayce asked. "What then?"

Maru closed his tin.

"We will deal with that when we need to," Maru said. "Hopefully anyone else heading there will be slowed by this weather. If the wrong people get there first . . . things become more difficult."

Outside the tent, the storm raged on.

Chapter 18

✳

"No, that's not where that goes." Dastin shook his head at Jayce. The gunnery sergeant reached into Jayce's pack and pulled out a small cylinder. He stretched it open, then snapped it shut and screwed it into a ring on Jayce's belt.

"What happens if you have to drop your pack and run for your life?" Dastin slapped his palm on Jayce's waist. "And if you can't get your pack again? Then what?"

"I won't have to carry this damn thing anymore?" Jayce asked.

Eabani's raspy laugh came from the half-dissembled tent.

"If you're going to lose gear, squeaker, lose what'll keep you alive *last*," Dastin said. "Lack of water will take you down in three days. Food?" He flapped his hand against Jayce's stomach. "You can go maybe two weeks without a calorie before your body starts eating your organs. Veil will take you down long before it comes to that."

"So, I've got that going for me." Jayce thought back to the statues of emaciated Pilgrims during his talk through the Between and realized that starving to death was entirely possible.

"Come." Maru waved to the party from atop a boulder. "I've found something for us."

Jayce started toward him. Eabani stopped him and slid a part of the tent's shield roof into the back of his carry rig.

"Haul your own gear," the Lirsu grunted at him.

"Of course." Jayce jogged to Maru, and joined him and Sarai as the Adept led them deeper into the forest. "I can tell why the Sodality never let word about all this walking and carrying heavy crap come out. Wouldn't have nearly as many recruits if this was on the posters."

"What did you learn of the Sodality before you met us?" Maru asked.

The trees grew taller as they continued through the forest. The sky was lost to double layers of canopy, but glowing grasses cast an eerie light around them.

"Stories of Alcaeus the Savior since I was a kid," Jayce said. "How he helped start the Governance and discovered the first FTL stones. Defeated the star beast of Neman. Drove off the giant aliens from Scinar."

"Interesting," Maru said.

"Why's that? Are you going to tell me he wasn't real?" Jayce asked.

"Alcaeus was indeed real, but his contribution to the galaxy lies more in establishing the Sodality and learning how to access the Veil soon after the Cataclysm. This we know for sure; I've been to his tomb and read his writings. But over the millennia he's been credited with feats that were done by others."

"When planets and races began to reconnect with each other, Alcaeus became the default hero," Sarai said. "Some great deeds happened and the name was similar to Alcaeus or was done by an Adept? Must have been done by Alcaeus. Not an unusual thing to happen after a long enough time span."

"Why not tell everyone that?" Jayce frowned. "Why let people believe in something that's untrue?"

"Changing people's beliefs is a fool's errand," Maru said. "Most sentients will decide on the truth and cling to it; to change means that all beliefs are suspect. People would rather willfully believe a lie than admit their core tenets are incorrect. The Sodality doesn't seek to influence beliefs, we exist to maintain a balance."

"News to me." Jayce hiked his pack higher onto his back. "I never heard much about you all during the revolt. The Tyrant's governor back home assured us everything was normal. Keep working. Keep paying your tithes. Keep sending people to the military to never return."

"You never wondered if there was more to the story?" Sarai asked.

"I had to work. I was saving money to get off-world, then y'all took me away for free. Sort of . . . I wonder who's going to clear out my room. Bet it'll be old man Franks. He was always trying to sell me stuff so he could pay for *tvass*—alcohol made from fermented kelp and fish mash."

"He doesn't know anything." Sarai shook her head.

"Sorry, we didn't have a Ley Link on the planet to keep up with the latest fashions and holo dramas," Jayce said. "What have I missed?"

"If it's relevant, we'll share it," Maru said. "For now . . . we should practice Flow." The Adept dropped his pack at the edge of a clearing with a brook running through it.

"Flow? Now?" Sarai dumped her gear. "Don't we have to reach the Pinnacle before anyone else?"

"Good, keep that in the front of your mind." Maru clicked his hilts together and twisted them. They linked and popped out into a glaive handle. "Can you feel where the Pinnacle is now?"

Sarai closed her eyes for a moment, then shook her head.

"Neither can I." Maru looked at Jayce, who shrugged.

Jayce dumped his gear. The Marines took cover nearby.

"This time will be different," Maru said. "Ignite your blades."

"Won't that attract . . . bad stuff?" Jayce looked to the tall trees. A flock of birds with glowing wings flew from a deep knot of branches and glided across the clearing.

"The Veil energy from the hilts will resonate as stone concentrations." Maru fired up his glaive. Pale blue light broke against his face. The short grass of the clearing reflected a rainbow of colors where the glaive shined upon it.

Jayce felt a tingling off to one side and from Maru's weapon. He pointed toward the distant sensation.

"What's over there?" Jayce asked.

"Later. Ready your weapon. Ready yourself," Maru said.

Jayce unsnapped his hilt and keyed in the activation sequence. A straight solid blade materialized from the hilt and almost cut his other hand. The balance point remained in the cross guard, no different from the practice session aboard the *Iron Soul*.

But this blade was real, no ersatz holo. He looked down the length of the weapon and made out runes in the fuller, a faint groove running down the center of the blade. Jayce moved to the kata starting position, the blade held flat and parallel to his forehead, off hand out and forming a ninety-degree line from the tip.

Sarai looked at Jayce's lit blade and a tear rolled down her face. She wiped it away and ignited her hilt with a snap of her hand. Her weapon was a saber with a slight curve to the blade.

Maru stared at Jayce's blade.

"What?" Jayce swiped his weapon down and cut through blades of grass.

"It has been a long time since I've seen that weapon activated," Maru said. "Emotions . . . emotions I thought I was ready for, but I was wrong. No more time to waste. Ready your weapon. Ready yourself."

The three went through the first ten moves of Flow when a shock went through Jayce's body. He froze up and fell out of synch with the others. He jabbed the sword into the ground and fell to his side, his lungs refusing to breathe. One hand clung to the hilt.

Lightning cracked beneath the solid sky and a shadow fell across the shattered ice.

An ice-deep cold spread through his hand. Jayce's breath fogged with each exhalation. He tried to pull his hand away, but it was caught firm.

"Maru . . . help!" he called out.

Maru deactivated his glaive and holstered the two halves

of the hilt in one smooth motion. He held a straight-fingered hand over the hilt, then ran it down Jayce's arm.

Jayce's fingers began to crystalize.

Maru chanted and traced runes in the air close to the hilt; his fingertips left bright lines in the air, like the afterimage of a red-hot poker, then slapped his palm against the pommel. An inky shadow leapt from the blade and rolled across the clearing. The amorphous blob spat away grass until it flopped into the brook with a splash of icy white water.

Jayce pulled his hand away from the hilt and the blade dissolved into bright motes that were sucked into the stone set in the cross guard.

"Stay back." Maru reassembled his glaive and ignited the blade. The edge burned with white fire that clung to the back of the energy projection like Elman Fire against a mast. Jayce had inquired among his other sailors back home why the phenomena was named that, but no one had an explanation.

An inky darkness arose from the stream. A constellation of eyes lit up on a mass hanging between slumped shoulders. Forelimbs as thick as tree trunks dragged the rest of its bulk from the stream. The eyes narrowed at Maru and a deep rumble emanated from the creature. It raised an arm and struck toward the Paragon.

Maru sprinted toward the monster. He swiped his glaive up and across his body, striking the monster's amorphous limb and impaling it on the blade. Maru used the impalement to twist over the arm as he leapt up and landed on the outside of the attack. He snapped the glaive down and severed the arm.

The limb hit the ground and burnt away to nothing.

Maru rolled under a swipe and thrust his glaive at the beast's face. It vanished before the blade could hit home, leaving a dissolving shadow where it had been.

The beast reappeared behind Maru and lunged at him, dark tentacles writhing out of its mouth. Maru spun and swept his blade across his body. He nicked several of the tentacles, but the beast's head punched into his chest and sent him flying backward.

"Maru!" Sarai raised her Veil saber and started toward him.

"Oh no, you don't!" Dastin grabbed her by the collar and yanked her back. "He knows what he's doing."

Maru slid across the grass and planted his glaive hilt behind his head and kicked his feet up, then pushed off the ground and flipped toward a sturdy-looking tree on the wood line. He squatted against the tree and jumped toward the beast, who was charging right after him.

Jayce's eyes went wide with shock as the beast roared and smashed into the tree, knocking needles loose from the branches.

Maru was gone.

There was a sudden rustle from the tree and Maru dove down, spearing the beast between the shoulders and pinning it to the ground. Maru twisted his weapon and a bolt of silver light shot down the length and blew the shadow creature apart.

Maru was still for a moment, then spun his glaive behind his back with a flourish. The Wottan went to one knee, breathing heavily.

Jayce and Sarai ran to him. Purple blood dribbled from gashes down his chin and chest.

"Are you all right?" Sarai asked.

"I dislike displacement maneuvers." Maru looked up at the tree. "But needs must. At times."

"What was that thing?" Jayce asked.

"You! It came from you!" Sarai swung her saber at Jayce's anchor band. Maru's hand snapped out and caught her by the wrist, stopping the attack inches from Jayce's arm.

"It did not," Maru said. "Compose yourself, Sarai, this is not how Adepts behave."

She looked at him like he'd just betrayed her, and pulled at his grip, which didn't waver in the slightest.

"I saw it," she said.

"Ferr tok!" Maru tapped the side of his hand against her fingers and the hilt deactivated. "It did not. The specter I destroyed was a corrupt remnant imbued into the weapon. May I?" He held a hand to Jayce, who gave him his hilt.

Maru held it high and turned it around.

"I felt an echo from the corruption. A memory of the Tyrant's soul that clung to the Veil stone in the hilt." He lowered it to chin level. "It must have been dormant until Jayce synched with it and the disparity between him and the last wielder must have awoken it. Curious . . ."

"Some warning would have been appreciated." Jayce hesitantly took the hilt back from Maru. "Is there any more?"

"The Tyrant had knowledge and powers that the Sodality still does not understand," Maru said. "That his essence remained on the weapon that slayed him . . . I should have anticipated it. We all should have. Sloppy. My apologies to you all."

"Told told you!" Neff hopped onto Maru's shoulder and sniffed at the air. "Told you there was a darkness to squeaking male child."

"Is it still there?" Maru asked.

"Is over there." Neff pointed to the ground. "There. There . . . not on boy. Is going away. Not on any of us anymore."

"Then this is a valuable lesson we must pass on to the Sodality." Maru touched his bleeding chin. "The price was minimal."

"Here." Dastin shook a small bottle, then sprayed bubbling foam against Maru's lacerations. "How bad is it?"

"Flesh wounds." Maru squinted one eye closed and the cuts healed rapidly. "Food? Who has food?" He turned off his glaive blade and set the handle onto a brace across his back. Eabani tossed him a tin and Maru devoured wriggling shrimp.

"How'd you do that?" Jayce asked.

"The displacement or the healing?" Maru turned around and Jayce saw several tree branches embedded in the back of Maru's clothes. "Walk and talk. No doubt we've attracted some attention."

"The—Oof!" Jayce caught his pack and swung the straps onto his shoulders as he followed Maru. "The displacement. That demon thing did it and then—"

"Just as we can shunt from the *Iron Soul* to planetside, one with the right training, attunement"—he tapped the glowing stone in his harness—"and concentration can do the same. It is inherently dangerous. The slightest error can result in catastrophe."

"Every Attuned has to walk past the skeleton of

Paragon Bulsarra on the way to the training halls," Sarai said. "He almost shunted through the doors. Almost."

"That sounds terrifying." Jayce glanced at his Veil hilt. "Hold on, did you say this is the thing that killed the Tyrant?"

"As I told you before, it was a group effort," Maru said, "but it struck the final blow."

"That would've been something cool to tell me when I got it." Jayce smiled.

Maru stopped and put a hand to Jayce's chest.

"Weapons are nothing, young one. There are no dangerous weapons. Only dangerous people. The last man to carry that blade into battle was far braver and determined than anyone I have ever met. He would have torn the life from the Tyrant with his bare hands if he had to. That hilt has no legacy." He looked at Sarai, then back at Jayce. "Only history."

"But it had an . . . ink monster," Jayce said.

Maru snorted and continued walking.

"The Veil's mysteries shall endure for all time," the Paragon said. "Once we assume to know too much, the Veil will humble us with our ignorance. Now, return to proper march order and let us cease our prattle before Gunny Dastin has an aneurysm."

"My eye wasn't twitching that badly," Dastin said.

Jayce kept the hilt in his hand as they continued through the forest. The stone in the hilt glowed softly and he felt like something inside was watching him.

Chapter 19

Dead undergrowth snapped beneath Jayce's boots as they continued through the forest. Needles fell from the branches and a chill nipped at his ears and nose.

"It me, or is it getting cold out here?" Jayce asked.

"Does feel like winter." Sarai shivered and zipped up the front of her jacket.

"The song, can you both still hear it?" Maru asked.

Jayce turned away from the group and cocked an ear up. He hummed the first few stanzas, then pointed at an angle to the left of the way they'd been walking. He turned around and found Sarai pointing the same way.

"It isn't any weaker or stronger," she said. "What does that mean?"

"I'm not sure." Maru stroked his chin. "Sodality records of this particular apparition are contradictory."

"We spread them out and basic land-navigation techniques can tell us how far the tower is," Dastin said. "We only have a direction now. Two different vectors to the same point and some trigonometry will—"

"If we were anywhere but the Veil that would be an

excellent idea," Maru said. "But the Veil has a way of changing the rules. Look."

He pointed his glaive staff toward the direction Sarai and Dastin had given. Ruins made of white, chalky bricks were just visible through the fog.

Eabani growled and readied his crossbow. His goatee flapped from side to side, and he spit toward the buildings.

"Where'd those come from?" he asked. "Wasn't there a second ago."

"Doesn't matter," Maru said. "That is the way we need to go."

"Principals fall back to center, close on them." Dastin and Maru led the Attuned pair into the ruins. Eabani kept watch behind them.

Jayce fiddled with his hilt as they crossed the threshold between the ruins and the forest. The buildings were mostly single storied with no roofs. The brickwork changed from building to building, the orientation and size of the bricks different, as well as the height of the doorways.

"Who built all this?" Jayce whispered.

"We did." Maru did a combat peek around a corner, then waved the rest of them across a street with deep ruts from countless carts that had rolled down the street. He bounded across the street and took his place in the lead. "At least, these are buildings from our home reality that have been imbued with Veil flecks. Shrines. Houses of healing. These structures are a reflection of what is there . . . and are also here."

"But why are they all *here*?" Jayce rubbed knuckles on one wall and it flaked off into clumps of chalky dust.

"Because the Veil wants them here," Maru said.

Dastin held up a fist and the party froze. He made quick hand gestures and ducked as he went to a low wall. Eabani clicked the safety switch off his crossbow. Sarai tapped Jayce on the shoulder twice, then pointed one finger up and then at a mound of rubble behind them.

Jayce raised his hands in confusion.

Sarai rolled her eyes and then leaned closer to his ear.

"Dastin saw hostiles. Take cover while Maru scouts a way around. We get separated, that pile of crap back there is our rally point." She pushed him toward a half-crumbled wall. Jayce dropped his pack as quietly as he could against the wall.

Jayce took a sip from a hose connected to a water bladder on his back. Dastin took a crossbow bolt from the bandolier across his chest and tapped the arrowhead against the wall, then pointed at Jayce, then to a hole in the wall.

Jayce got the hint and crawled to the hole and looked through.

They were on a steep hillside. Below was a dead city with a hodgepodge of quarters, none with the same architectural style. A crumbling dome rose over the distant fog, an enormous crack riven through the top. Roads connected through each quarter but didn't run from one to the other.

A river ran through the city; bridges made of crude wood and rope connected to suspended segments. Other bridges were floating slabs of masonry that led halfway across and became elegant arches to the other bank.

"It's a bloody labyrinth down there," he whispered.

"Shh!" Dastin snapped. He tapped the arrowhead again and then angled it down. Jayce looked down the slope and his breath caught in his throat. There was a temple of sorts at the lower level. The roof was gone, but an altar with ivory statues around it was visible. In the center of the altar was a Veil stone.

It glowed with a magnificence that was still there when he closed his eyes and turned his face away. He touched the stone in his harness and felt that it was a pale reflection of the power and potential of what was on the altar.

"I think that's a ship stone." Sarai peeked over his shoulder. "Oh, it's beautiful, isn't it?"

"Sure is." Jayce licked his lips, suddenly thirsty. "How would . . . how does someone claim it? Synch with it?"

Sarai mimed reaching out and grabbing it, then pressed her hand to her chest.

"That's all," she said. "You should go get it. Then break your anchor and go go go back to the Aperture. We'll meet you there in no time flat."

"Maru needs us to synch with the stones at the Pinnacle," Jayce said. "We can only do it once, right?"

"Right," Neff whispered in Jayce's ear. Jayce seized up out of shock and the Docent slapped a furry paw over Jayce's mouth. "I see the stone fever fever in your eyes. Always like this, so close to the prize you've wanted for so long and you want to take the first one you can get your dirty hands on. Can't you tell?"

"Tell what?" Sarai asked.

Jayce tried to talk, but his words died against Neff's paw.

"Someone's already watching it," Neff said. "Someone has designs for it. I feel the greed. Long snout. Claws. Predator intelligence."

"It's a trap," Maru said. Jayce did a double take at the Paragon, who appeared seemingly out of nowhere. "Powerful stones must be found, they don't give themselves away."

"Then what's that one doing there?" Jayce asked.

"You've been to a Shrine, what did you see around the altar?" Maru asked.

"Symbols without any repetition. The—Look!" Jayce pressed his face against the hole in the wall. Below, at the altar, ghostly figures appeared. All bowed and prayed toward the altar.

"They're summoning a stone from our reality," Maru said. "Interesting. They appear to be from the Star Cult from the Occarian sector, by their robes at least. I've found a way down. Leave them to their business and follow me."

"Wrong souls. There's others down there." Neff hopped to Maru's shoulder.

"Then we best avoid them," Maru said. The party came to a spiral staircase that ran perpendicular to a sheer cliff. The staircase ended in broken blocks a few feet over the top of the cliff, but there was no connection to the hilltop or even handrails.

"Nope." Eabani tried to back away. Dastin grabbed him by the collar and kept him from moving farther. "No no no, I don't do heights."

"You're gonna have to." Dastin shook Eabani. "There's a faster way down, but you're not going to like the sudden stop at the bottom."

"Just knock me out." Eabani nodded quickly. "Toss me across the gap and carry me down. Much better way."

"Wouldn't we all just love to be carried everywhere and

wake up after a good nap to a nice stretch and tea?" Dastin's voice grew slightly louder. "Are you going to leave our little miss behind because you're a chicken shit?"

"I am not a prey avian!" Eabani shouted, then hunched his shoulders as he heard his words echo off the forest.

"Help? Help!" came from the fog.

Dastin let Eabani go, then held up a knife hand cocked next to his face.

"Toss me the gear." Eabani dropped his pack, then got a running start and jumped across the gap. He hit the central pillar and fell back. His claws scratched long gouges against the flaky bricks and stopped himself before he could fall.

A sharp whistle went over Jayce's head. At the edge of the fog, dark figures emerged, all with bows in hand. One took aim at the party and let loose. Maru knocked the arrow away with his glaive.

"I don't think they want help," Jayce said.

"You're figuring this out real quick, aren't you?" Dastin smacked him on the shoulder. "Toss your gear to 'Bani—hurry!"

Jayce heard the crack of more arrows against Maru's blade and chucked his pack to Eabani. It almost fell short and Eabani caught it with his arms extended. The counterbalance almost tipped him over the edge of the stairs.

Eabani let out a roar that sent more fear through Jayce than the raiders firing arrows.

"Here goes!" Sarai jumped off the cliff and into Eabani's arms.

"Your turn." Dastin prodded Jayce on his back.

"I don't think he'll catch me," Jayce said to him.

"You either jump in the next two seconds or we'll see if I can kick your ass across the gap!" Dastin shouldered his crossbow and fired at the bowmen. One went down with a cry, grasping his thigh.

"Sure wish I could do that shunt thing." Jayce ran toward the stairwell. He planted his last step to propel himself forward...and lost his footing to a loose pebble. Jayce got some momentum to clear the gap, but not enough.

His heels went over his head, and he spun his arms as he got a very clear look at the chasm leading all the way down to a river white with rapids.

Eabani caught him by the ankle and swung him to the level below him on the circular stairway. Jayce thumped against the central pillar and fell against the stairs.

"Move it!" Dastin yelled down at him. The gunnery sergeant hesitated for a heartbeat when he looked all the way down, then jumped the gap. Maru landed next to Jayce and helped him up.

"I miss my boats and all the water monsters," Jayce said as Sarai came around the stairs and motioned at him to get moving. Eabani had all the packs either on his back or had their straps in hand.

"It spirals down, keep going," Maru said to him.

Jayce concentrated on the steps and put one foot in front of the other as fast as he could. He didn't know what the species that made the staircase had against handrails, but he hoped he never had to visit their planet.

There was a hoot from the cliff side and a sharp pain against his shin. An arrow sprang off the steps and went tumbling through the air. A bloody gash flapped from his pants a few inches over his ankle.

"Ah, damn it!" Jayce leaned against the central pillar.

"He's got a hilt! I claim it!" came from the cliff.

Jayce looked up as a wild-eyed young man with dark skin hopped off the hill and locked a metal brace on his arm against the rock to slow his fall. The bandit braced both feet against the cliff and leapt at Jayce, one hand reaching for the hilt on Jayce's belt.

Jayce turned aside and the bandit got one foot on the staircase, then went flailing over the edge. His screams trailed off to nothing quickly.

"I'll handle this." Eabani raced up the stairs three at a time and came around the bend and bumped into a rather surprised marauder. Eabani gave him a quick shove and launched the man into the air. He caught the bow before it could fall and swung the bent end around the center column. The point struck the next marauder in the sternum with a crack of bone.

Eabani grabbed the stunned man by the shoulder and bashed him against the column and let him stumble into gravity's embrace. He seized the final marauder under the arms and snarled in the man's face, then lifted him up and crushed his head against the stairway. He flung the body off the stairs and went down the stairs.

Jayce and Sarai clutched their packs as Eabani shouldered his load. Both stared at him in shock.

"What?" Eabani asked.

"It was raining people." Jayce pointed toward the city.

"Better them than us," Eabani said. "Get moving, I'm not carrying your crap if I don't have to."

Chapter 20

Jayce stumbled off the bottom stair and leaned a shoulder against a building with a slanted wall.

"Knees . . . hurt so much," he panted.

"You aren't even in your thirties," Dastin said to him. "You have no idea how all this rucking and hiking will catch up to your knees. And back. Neck. Ankles."

"Where are they?" Sarai drew her hilt. "Where are the bandits?"

Maru held his glaive staff to one side and looked around slowly.

"Those that die in the Veil discorporate," Maru said. He swept a foot through a smattering of marble dust on the solid concrete ground. "I didn't see wings on any of them. Did you?"

"Was that a joke?" Jayce asked. "Did he just crack a joke?" He put a hand against the wall and ran his touch down the seams of the stones. He stepped back and looked over the construction. None of the bricks were uniform, all were shaped differently and fit together like a massive jigsaw puzzle.

"Ah, polygonal masonry." Maru held the cross guard of his bladeless glaive up to the wall. "We've seen this on some Ancient worlds. This construction proved resilient to natural disasters and earthquakes. Built to last, not to impress."

"We can spelunk archaeological sites later, sir," Dastin said. "How do we get through this city? Looked like a labyrinth from up there."

"Got a feeling there's going to be lots of walking." Jayce sat against the slanted wall and slid down. He rolled up a pant leg and winced at a cut down his shin.

"Bah, rub some dirt on it," Dastin grumbled and pulled out a first aid kit.

"We can't afford a limp." Maru lifted Jayce's injured leg and set it across his knee.

"Ooh, are we going to eat his limb?" Neff sniffed at the wound.

"Wait. What's happening?" Jayce's eyes lingered on a combat knife attached to Dastin's gear.

"Just relax." Maru slapped his hands together and a glow grew between his palms. He spread his hands apart as thin plasma streams jumped between his digits. He clamped onto Jayce's injury and a shock ran up Jayce's leg.

Pain seared from the injury and burned like Maru was somehow cauterizing the wound. Maru pulled his hands away and he collapsed to his side.

Jayce cried out and squeezed his shin. Dried blood sloughed off, but the cut was gone. He scratched at the wound, and it felt normal. Not even a scar.

Maru gasped and sat up. He covered his mouth and

coughed. Water sprayed out of his gills and splashed against Jayce and Dastin.

"How'd you do that?" Jayce asked.

"It's very . . ." Maru coughed and bent forward to rest his forehead against the ground. ". . . It takes a great deal out of me. Please . . . no one else get injured."

Sarai rubbed Maru's back as she helped him up.

"You can't strain yourself like this, Master. You're not as young as you used to be," she said.

"None of us are." Maru leaned heavily on his glaive staff. "We need a way through the city. Suggestions?"

"Haven't you been through here before?" Jayce asked. "Or someone from the Sodality?"

Maru touched his forehead, then raised an empty hand to the sky.

"The labyrinth is . . . difficult. The layout changes as the distance between the Veil and our reality shifts. Most who enter lose their way and break anchor to return home."

"And the rest?" Jayce asked.

"They never return." Maru lowered his hand.

"I should've figured." Jayce laced his fingers behind his head and leaned back against the wall. He stared at the sky and worked his jaw from side to side.

"We have a bearing toward the Pinnacle," Sarai said. "So long as we can sense where it is, we know which way to go . . . but we need to be in Flow state and there may not be room to do the kata properly."

"Maru?" Jayce asked. "Does the sky ever change?"

"How do you mean?" the Wottan asked.

"The cracks in the ice—or whatever it is—I haven't noticed a difference. We'd use the stars to navigate the seas back home when the geo-positioning satellites would fritz out . . . and we all saw that river, right?" He stood up and quickly tested putting weight on his newly healed leg. "We just get to the river and follow the current and it'll dump us out on the other side of the city. Not too far off if we walked a straight line through the labyrinth—which we can't."

"Every time we jump a wall we skyline ourselves to anyone else nearby," Dastin said. "Squeaker may be on to something."

"The sky wall is consistent," Maru said. "But the river . . . there are risks."

"It's my first time here, but what's the least risky option?" Jayce asked.

"Orient to the features in the sky wall and head toward the Pinnacle." Maru pointed a weak hand into the polygonal masonry quarter. "Then we follow the river. If a better opportunity presents itself, we'll seize it."

"I smell the water." Eabani pointed the same direction. "Cold . . . sterile."

"Same march order," Dastin said. When they were moving again, he got closer to Maru. "We may need to stop for a few hours to sleep, sir."

"Not here." Maru shook his head. "There's a presence around us, a darkness like we faced in the clearing."

"Where?" Dastin scanned the walls.

"I . . . I can't tell. Most distressing," Maru said. "I've never felt anything quite like it within the Veil."

"What about outside the Veil?" Dastin asked. Neff curled tighter against the Paragon's shoulder.

Maru didn't answer. He stopped relying on his staff and walked faster.

Jayce felt blisters rising on his feet as they continued through the silent city. They doubled backed more than once when their route led to a dead end. Eabani drew a knife and pressed the tip against a wall they'd just turned around.

"No, others can follow any mark you leave," Maru said.

"I'll carve arrows pointing the wrong way." Eabani plucked the knife tip a few inches off the wall. "We just have to remember to go the opposite direction."

"When is it ever wise to assume your foe is a fool?" Maru asked.

Eabani considered the question for a moment, then sheathed his knife.

"Water's this way. You blunt noses should at least *hear* it by now," Eabani said. "No? Then follow me."

The party went through a zigzagging passageway. Jayce saw the river between Maru's and Dastin's shoulders. He looked behind them, then turned back.

Jayce smacked into a wall. He was in a dead end and there was no one around.

"Maru? Dastin?" Jayce spun around. "What is wrong with this—sky wall?" He looked straight up and pointed at the cracks in the faux-ice. "Eel switchback next to the trident break in the hull. OK, using the sky as an atlas still works."

He jogged back the way he came, then turned around to see if the new wall had vanished. Still there. He returned to a courtyard with a sunken path through the center and went toward an exit that he prayed would still get him to the river.

"Maru must've had an excellent reason not to tell me

the labyrinth could *move*," he muttered. "Unless he didn't know. How could he not know? He's super old and knows everything. Why am I talking to myself?"

A chill rose as he moved deeper down the narrow corridor. The polygonal masonry blocks became larger the farther he went. Then the rocks began to show signs of wear—cracks from damage and stress split through many and pebbles rolled down the slanted walls. He came to a T-intersection and turned to the right.

The quarter had collapsed into a cave entrance. Blue and white bones littered the outside.

"That's . . . don't think so." He backed away. A glowing yellow eye lit up from the abyss. Jayce dropped his pack and ignited his hilt. He thrust the blade in front of him, hoping the light would scare off whatever predator was inside.

"I'll always find you," came from the cave. Reman stepped partway out of the cave, his head visible. The Draug's cyborg eye had been replaced with a dark orb. One arm was stiff against his body, and the augmented muscles were missing, giving him a weakened, lopsided appearance. Reman spat a bone to the ground.

"Back! I know how to use this," Jayce said, the sword shaking in his hand.

"I doubt that . . . I doubt that very much," Reman said. "The meat here has no taste. It is like eating air, but one doesn't learn unless one tries. We are of the same plain . . . could I feast on you before the Veil takes your soul? Human meat has a particular flavor if it's seasoned with fear."

"Come closer, you'll see how well I can use this. Lot of talk from some space dog with one good—"

Reman flicked out his good arm and long Fulcrum

blades appeared from a converted hilt on his wrist. Wisps of plasma danced between the blades.

"OK, OK you've got one too. Good for you." Jayce looked around for an exit, but the only escape route was behind him, and turning his back on Reman did not strike him as a good idea.

"They've initiated you into the cult," Reman growled. "Lies atop lies to bring you here—for what? What did they promise you? Coin? Mates? None of it will matter soon."

"You killed my friend. I owe you for Kay," Jayce said.

"Death is a concern for lesser beings. The Tyrant's path can save everyone from it . . . You haven't claimed a stone yet." Reman took a step closer, and Jayce scrambled back. "But you must have seen the prize in the old cathedral from the forest. Why risk this place when you could have that kind of power in your grasp?"

"Kay had . . . a lot of cousins, brothers, and sisters. The number changed based on how desperate he was for money. He used to catch star perch for me when I couldn't buy food. Why'd you have to kill him? He was never any threat to you." Jayce took a step forward.

"Because I knew I would enjoy it."

Reman sprang forward, lightning claw driving straight at Jayce's face. Jayce swiped a parry across his body and deflected the strike into the wall. The blade sank easily up to the hilt rig over the alien's knuckles.

Jayce raised his blade to strike, and put too much strength into the attack. He lost his footing as the blade sailed over the wolfen alien's head. Reman kicked Jayce in the chest and sent him tumbling backward. The hilt skittered across the solid stone walkway.

Reman howled as he fought to extricate his weapon from the wall. The rig ran up to his elbow and wouldn't give. His other arm was too crippled to undo the straps.

Jayce rolled over and scooped up his hilt and ran. His chest ached from the blow and he careened from one wall to another. He lost track of where he was or where he was going, all he needed to do was get away from the terror behind him.

Reman's howl cut him to his core, and Jayce ran faster, an atavistic fear driving him into a panic. He swore he could smell Reman's breath on the back of his neck. He turned a corner and saw the river through a tight gap in the walls.

Jayce called out for help. Reman swiped at him; the claws knocked off a hunk of rock and sent a cloud of dust into Jayce's eyes. He ran blind and wiped his face just in time to see the gap was only a few steps ahead.

Jayce dove through the gap, but his foot caught on the edge. He rolled to his back and swiped his weapon in a wild cut across his body. His hand hit the ground and the hilt bounced out of the grip.

Jayce raised his arms to cover his face . . . and only heard the burble of running water.

"Jayce . . . what the hell are you doing?" Dastin asked. The gunnery sergeant stood next to him, his hands on his hips.

"Huh? I found you? Tyrant soldier!" He pointed at the gap . . . which was now a solid wall.

"How'd you get over here?" Dastin turned to an exit several yards away. "You were behind me."

"Wall! Wall there." Jayce clutched the hilt to his chest

as he fought to breathe. "Wall then maze and wolf—wolf thing! Chased me. Big claws. Teeth. Going to eat me!"

"Not funny funny is it?" Neff called out from atop Maru's shoulder.

"Where's your gear?" Dastin crossed his arms over his chest. Jayce pointed at the wall.

"Give him a minute." Maru hurried over. "How long were you separated from us?"

"Couple of minutes at least." Jayce rinsed his mouth out with water from the tube connected to his harness. "Why weren't any of you looking for me? There was a wolf thing!"

"Calm down." Maru patted his shoulder. "You haven't been gone that long. We just crossed the threshold to the river moments ago."

Jayce thrust his finger at the wall several times. The terror in his chest was subsiding, and he felt like he was about to cry.

"I believe you." Maru touched Jayce's hand. The Wottan's skin was clammy, but the contact helped calm him down. "Perhaps this is why so few can get through the labyrinth . . . it may have a mind of its own."

"It was—it was the one from the docks. The cyborg wolf, but his machine parts were missing. Like Dastin," Jayce said.

"Likely not an apparition, then. Those are details your mind wouldn't have created. We best not tarry here," Maru said.

"He has Draug scent to him." Neff slunk behind Maru's back. "They eat Docents. They eat everything. Bad bad clients."

"You lost your gear." Dastin's good eye began to twitch.

"Wolf alien was chasing me." Jayce stood up and brushed himself off. "I regret nothing."

"Not yet you don't," Dastin said.

"The bridge is stable!" Sarai shouted from a series of floating steps that crossed halfway over the river. The water was fast and turbulent, nothing Jayce wanted to wade into. Sarai put her hands on a floating block and pressed hard. It didn't budge.

"Both banks lead to the same place," Jayce said. "No reason to be up there."

"There's more room on the other side." Sarai shook her head and went up a step. Even with the extra weight of her pack, the floating step was perfectly still.

"Antigrav like that's expensive," Dastin said. "Only see it in research labs or the megacorporation headquarters back on Cadorra."

Jayce scratched the back of his shoulder and felt a claw mark through the fabric. He stopped a few steps shy of the riverbank and paused. He looked over the water, his attention lingering on a still patch on the other side. A shadow shifted beneath the water.

"Sarai . . . stop. Don't move!" Jayce yelled.

"Why?" She put her hands on a floating platform and tested if it would move or not. She scraped her boots across the stone she was on and raised a knee onto the next step.

Bubbles broke against the surface of the still section of the river.

"Moving moving," Neff pointed to the river.

Sarai stood up on the next stone.

"Whoever built this side must've been larger than most sentients," she said. "The height of these stairs—"

A dark green hydra burst from the river. Its three heads had no eyes but the wide mouth of needle teeth snapping all around would eventually chomp onto something. A pair of heads latched onto a floating stone and tore it to pieces. Another head knocked against the step holding Sarai and flipped her backward.

Her head banged against another stone and Jayce watched her fall limp and unconscious into the raging water.

"Sarai!" Jayce ran to the river, ignoring whatever commands or warnings Maru and the Marines shouted after him. He locked his hilt to his belt and dived headfirst into the river. He dove deep and saw Sarai rolling just beneath the rapids. Her pack dragged her deeper and deeper.

He kicked his legs and stroked hard to reach her. His first grab at her missed her ankles. He swam harder, feeling a slow burn rising in his lungs the longer he was underwater.

Jayce ripped one strap off her shoulder, and was dragged deeper with her. They hit the bottom and the current pushed him down the river. He kept hold of her wrist and the force of the rushing water rolled her out from the other strap and she bumped into his chest.

A hydra head struck the pack and shook it apart.

He got an arm around her waist and kicked up to the surface.

Jayce sucked in a deep breath and rolled Sarai's head over the water. The rapids buffeted them back and forth but didn't move them any closer to either bank.

An ululating roar carried over the sound of the rapids. Jayce spun around and saw the hydra diving up and down through the water toward them. A head rose on a tall neck, the skin had scales and old scars running up and down it. Nostrils flared and the head snapped toward Jayce and Sarai.

Flesh rolled back from rotting teeth and the ancient hydra head reared back to strike.

A crossbow bolt struck the head from behind and pierced through the eye. Jayce kicked hard, trying to get them both away from the wounded beast. The hydra thrashed from one side of the river to the other as the lesser heads went berserk. The beast stopped chasing them but wasn't going to give the rest of the party an easy time getting passed it.

Jayce checked that Sarai was still breathing, then tried to prop her body horizontal to the surface to help their buoyancy. His boots had filled with water and Sarai was growing heavier as her clothes soaked through.

The river banked suddenly and Jayce looked over his shoulder. The ruins of a collapsed building had spilled over the banks. The current carried him straight toward a dragon's teeth of blocks jutting out of the river. He tried to grab one but bounced hard off it instead.

Jayce cried out in pain but kept himself between Sarai and more of the broken walls. He careened off another, scraping one side of his face against rough masonry. His leg struck something hard and unforgiving beneath the surface, but he kept his hold on Sarai.

Blood stung one eye and Jayce kicked to move them closer to the center of the river as the current sped up.

"Ah . . . ah, Sarai, you want to wake up?" he panted. "Could use some . . . participation here."

The cityscape changed to smaller buildings and degraded to wide fields of grain after several minutes. Jayce kept kicking to keep them afloat, but his muscles burned and his head began to dip below the surface between every pulse.

The current slowed and Jayce spied a sandy bend in the river. He used his last bit of strength to get them to the bank and one foot touched mud. He dragged Sarai off the bank and laid her next to a massive, dead tree.

Jayce rolled her to her side and she coughed several times. He fell face-first into the sand, exhausted. Blood from the cut on one side of his head seeped into grains of sand the size of ball bearings and got snorted into his nose during massive heaves of his chest.

He rolled to his back and touched his belt. The hilt was still there, as were the hydrator and a small emergency pack on his hip. He raised a waterlogged boot and let it fall back to the bank with a wet squish.

"I should've . . . I should've stayed home." He put a hand over the cut and winced at how much blood came away from the touch.

"Ow," Sarai stirred. "Ow, what . . . what?"

"Everything sucks," Jayce groaned. "But there's some good news. We don't have to carry that shit anymore."

"There was . . . What was that thing?" Sarai put a hand to her head. She tried to get up but lost her balance and crashed onto Jayce.

"You are not OK." Jayce steadied her. "Stay still, wait for your—wait." He opened the emergency case on his belt and fiddled with an injector and tiny pellets in color-coded boxes on the case. He snapped a yellow one into the base and jabbed the other end into Sarai's neck.

"Ow!" She slapped his hand away. "What did you just give to me—ugh!" She retched water and the remnants of her last nutrient-paste meal into the sand.

"Cerebro injection." Jayce scooted his leg away from the vomit. "Treats the concussion and wards off any permanent injury. It'll make you woozy for a bit."

Sarai went to the river and splashed water in her mouth and spat it out.

"Mouth's still dry, but at least I got the taste out," she said. Her hands trembled and she clutched them against her chest.

"Tremors are normal too. Means the medicine's working. But if there's any facial paralysis and everything turns yellow, then you got a bad batch," Jayce said. "Cerebro's great for prizefighters, extends our careers and keeps most of us from becoming punch-drunk dock trash before our time. Good promoters would give us a dose after a fight if the crowd was happy with the show."

"Getting punched in the head so much . . . did it mean you were good or bad at fighting?" Sarai asked.

"I had to eat, and glove leather has a crap taste to it." Jayce sat up.

Another large tree was in the middle of the field. The horizon was dark with the promise of another rainstorm.

"We're going to need cover," Jayce said. He looked over the tree near the bank and kicked at the roots. "I'd rather not be too close to the water. That hydra might still be alive and it was *pissed*."

"Help me." She held up a hand. He lifted her up and held her steady as they slowly made their way to the other tree. She glanced at him every few steps.

"Why'd you save me? I am . . . awful to you," she said.

"I'm a river rat. Ratter's job is to watch out for shipmates and keep predators away. That thing back there? Way worse than anything on Hemenway," he said.

They reached the tree, which was several stories high. The root swells were almost as tall as Jayce in some spots. Sarai found a depression under one of the roots just large enough for the both of them as the crystal rain began to fall.

"Here." Sarai gave him a shiny folded square, which blossomed into a rigid board. He set the board over the gap beneath the root as the rain picked up.

"Ow!" Jayce pulled back his hand from the outside. A flake of crystal was embedded between two knuckles.

"Let me get it." Sarai took a plastic tube from her emergency pack and cracked it. It lit up with a pale green light, and she tucked it into a fold of the roots to illuminate the shelter. She plucked the crystal out of his skin, and it disintegrated into steam while she held it.

Rain broke against the cover with cracks of collapsing ice and dropped mirrors.

"Thanks," Jayce said.

"Let me get that cut." She turned his head and dabbed at the laceration with a buzzing applicator from his kit. The smell of burning hair and singed flesh filled the small space. She sat back against the dirt wall, her shoulder against his in the tight space.

She sighed. "It wasn't supposed to be like this."

"You don't say?" Jayce smiled, and that hurt too.

"We had one of the best Docents in the business. Should've just been an easy get in—get stone—get out. Instead, Maru's trying to get us to the Pinnacle, which I thought was either a myth or a tall tale they tell baby Attuned to keep their eyes wide and tails bushy for this."

"And now there's one of the Tyrant's killers after us. At least one," Jayce said. "Are there high casualty rates for Pilgrims and Attuned that come here? Because this is a garbage tourist destination."

"Most Pilgrims stay in the shallow part of the Veil. They commune with whatever deities they think are here and they hop right back through the gate they entered. No need for anchors. The more adventurous—or greedy— enter deeper and try to bring back every last fleck and stone they can get their hands on. Most of them get hurt or killed *after* they come back, as fewer survivors mean bigger cuts for anyone that's left. Those that go after ship-class stones or need to synch with a Veil stone like we do to be full Adepts . . . it's harder."

"You don't say." Jayce sighed. "How many Attuned from your Sodality academies drop anchor before they can get a stone?"

"We say 'crack anchor,' and it's around half. They get here and realize it's not as easy and magical as the holos made it out to be, or they figure out that if they claim a stone, then their life as Paragon in service to the Sodality and the Governance will be nothing but pain and sacrifice. Which is why the Sodality and Marines work so closely. Most Attuned go through their training to weed out the weak ones."

"Did you do that?" Jayce asked.

"No . . . no, I had Dastin and Eabani with me since I was a little girl. Two full-time tutors was better than going through boot camp with the commoners—at least that's how my mother rationalized it."

Jayce patted at the cut.

"You'd make a good corner. Your mom hold the keys to a planet or territory or something?" Jayce asked.

She gave him a dirty look. "Why do you think she's some sort of Syndicate criminal?"

"Sorry, Syndicate are the only power structure I'm familiar with."

"She's important enough. How connected are you to the Syndicate?"

"I wasn't even a hanger-on. Never a prospect. Good thing I was a prizefighter, 'cause if you were affiliated no one would bet on you. Everyone'd assume the fight was fixed. Syndicate got their cut on all the books and the purses. They made more money off me *not* being affiliated than if I did work for them."

"That sounds like the Syndicate. Bunch of greedy criminals." Sarai crossed her arms and began shivering. "Can't drink the water here, but it'll sure make you wet and cold."

Jayce took his jacket off and squeezed water out. He put it to one side and rubbed his arms.

"Get the wet fabric away from your skin. You'll be warmer than with it on," he said.

"This how you get the girls back home?" She snorted and shivered harder. The cold made her breath fog.

"Be cold. Or don't. It's up to you, but hypothermia's no

fun. I almost died on a fishing run to the southern pole two seasons ago. Weather didn't cooperate but the captain had to pull all his crab pots or he'd lose his boat. So what if some crew don't make it home?"

"Of all the laws of physics to stay the same, why does thermodynamics have to be so consistent?" She stripped off her wet jacket and threw it at her feet. She plucked at her undershirt as her lips went blue.

"You're warm?" she asked.

"I'm OK."

"Can you put your arm over my shoulders—in the most platonic way possible—please?"

"I don't know what plate tonics are, but sure." He raised an arm and she snuggled up to him. Her shivering subsided after a few minutes.

"It means don't try anything. I bite," she said. "Thank you for not losing your hilt . . . Can I see it?"

Jayce unsnapped it and handed it to her. She held it like it was delicate and ran her fingertips across the stone in the cross guard.

"Why don't you want me?" she asked, staring at the hilt. "Can you hear me this deep in the Veil?" She held her arm out and squeezed, trying to activate it, but it didn't respond.

"What's so special about it?" Jayce asked. "Why'd Maru keep it away from the other hilts he had?"

"Out of respect for me . . . and my father." She held the hilt up to the light. "This was his Fulcrum. It even manifests the same way for you as it did for him."

"Wait . . . wait, hold on." Jayce's eyes darted from side to side.

"Paragon Taras is my father. He died before I was born. He died before my mother told him she was pregnant. She thinks he didn't know, but Paragons can feel auras. Maru's let slip enough times that he can tell when women are with child. He knew my mother was carrying me. My father was just as strong as Maru."

"Why keep that secret?" Jayce asked.

"You don't know anything about the final days of the revolt? Nothing about the Battle of Tyrant's Bane?"

"I was a toddler. My mother told me the only difference the Tyrant's death made for us was that we paid taxes to different assholes," he said. "She hated taxes."

"The Sodality lured the Tyrant to a star system far in the Deep. The rebels didn't have the ships or the firepower to destroy his war barque, the *Purgation*. But something about the star system disrupted large-scale Veil systems. A skilled enough pilot could slip through the shields and deliver a kill team onto the *Purgation*. The pilot Maru and my father wanted for the mission got herself killed days before the mission, and my mother was the only other option."

"Brave of them," Jayce said.

"She got the kill team through the shields just like she needed to, then my father sent her away before the Tyrant knew he was under attack. It was a suicide mission for him, he knew that. They all did. But the Tyrant had to be thrown down or his plan . . . there was too much at stake. Either he and the others killed the Tyrant or we'd all be doomed. My father loved me enough that he was willing to die so I could have a future."

"Good man," Jayce said.

"He struck the killing blow and died aboard the *Purgation*. Maru and Marshall Tulkan got the survivors off the ship before the rest of the sabotage bombs went off. Dastin was there too." She snuggled closer to Jayce.

"Why assassinate the Tyrant if they were going to blow his ship up?" Jayce asked.

"The bombs were the distraction to pull the Tyrant's bodyguards away from him." She smirked. "The ship ended up being disabled and not destroyed. Most of the Tyrant's court survived and escaped to the Deep.

"I was born nine standard months later in the middle of all the chaos before the new Governance was established . . . Few years later and Maru realized I was Attuned. My mother didn't take it well. Since my brother's a knob, and she's a knob, she assumed I would be too." She held up her hilt and motes swirled around the cross guard. "Sorry, Mom, someone had to follow in Father's footsteps."

"But my hilt—I mean your father's—"

"Rejects me. Every single time I tried, it rejected me. I carried it with me for over a year, hoping that whatever part of my father's still in there would recognize me. See me . . . accept me, but . . . never. I gave up and the blade of Xerrval the XIV practically leapt into my hand." She looked at the pommel.

"Who's that?" Jayce asked.

"No one's sure. That's the name inscribed on the bottom." She laughed and handed the hilt back to Jayce. "I thought I'd carry my father's weapon, the one that destroyed the Tyrant . . . but no. That wasn't to be."

"I'm still pretty new to all this," Jayce said. "Are hilts usually inherited?"

"Maru always said 'it depends,' which is his way of politely telling me that I won't like the answer and I should stop inquiring. Wottan aren't known for their tact, but he's old and has figured out how to deal with humans."

"You know, what you have with your father's still pretty good," Jayce said. "My father was drafted by the Tyrant when I was a baby and my mother and I only ever heard from him one time after he was gone. He was a nobody. Just a dock rat like me."

"Do you have a brother that's a golden child? One that's done everything perfectly his entire life?"

"No. Been just me for a long time. So how do we find the others?"

"Maru can scry and find us that way. Neff can sniff us out, but we were in the water and there'll be a gap in our scent trail." She pursed her lips. "But should we stay in one place until they find us or keep going toward the Pinnacle?"

"Dastin gave us a rally point. But that was back up the stairwell and there's that hydra between us and that spot. Doubling back doesn't feel like the right thing to do. But we're not lost children, are we?"

"We're hiding under a tree during a storm and we don't know where the 'adults' are. All our water is on our backs or in our bladders. Food?" She dug a nutrient tube from her pocket. Little bits of brown goop dripped out of a large tear in the bottom.

"I don't have anything, sorry," Jayce said.

The storm continued; more razor flecks scratched at the shield.

"Why are you even here, Jayce? You barely knew what

the Sodality was until we found you. I thought you just wanted a way off the Syndicate world. We gave that to you—the *Iron Soul* will take you anywhere and drop you with enough quanta to keep you in room and board until you get your feet under you."

"Huh." Jayce scratched the cut on the side of his head. "You ever grow up small? The only value I had was what others could squeeze out of me. Fight until your face is mush. Get up there, rat. Be thankful we pay you at all. The Syndicate would've paid me a fraction of what that stone was worth. There are posted rates for work that the Syndicate set, in case you didn't know. Then the Tyrant's people show up and kill Kay and who knows what they were going to do with me."

"You're Attuned. They would've kept you alive and forced you into here until you found a ship stone. If it makes you feel any better, the Tyrant and his lieutenants were known for taking good care of their shipmasters. All the girls and pharmaceuticals you'd care for. A well-compensated slave."

"Keeps their shipmasters from drifting off course at critical moments," Jayce said. "How are the Tyrant's forces still around? Who's even in charge?"

"That . . . is a tough question. There was anarchy for years after the Tyrant was killed. The Sodality's forces weren't exactly numerous. They had just enough to occupy Primus. While they were trying to convince everyone to return to the Governance we had before the Tyrant, a full-bore civil war broke out between the Tyrant's marshals. Which ended up saving the Governance, as their infighting kept them busy. Sectors under control of the Tyrant's lieutenants eroded until they held two-star clusters out on the edge of the Deep; they don't even control a Ley Junction. The Governance has let them fester out on the fringe for too long. That battleship we saw over your planet's dingy collection? First capital ship sighting from the Tyrant's forces in years. Which is concerning."

"How many people died after the Tyrant was killed?" Jayce asked.

"We're still counting. The bloodshed was a catalyst to reform the Governance, at least. But during the years where there was no central government, star systems had to fend for themselves. Some turned to piracy. Some decided that was the time to settle scores against their neighbors. Enough of the Tyrant's officers who weren't Gripped opted for piracy or becoming warlords over their sectors. I was a child through most of the bad years. But once the Governance and the Sodality were organized enough to strong-arm rogue systems and leaders . . . most fell back in line. Peace and prosperity are better than anarchy and terror, as they figured out.

"The Governance didn't have the economy or manpower to restore itself to her former glory everywhere. Systems in the Deep were too far and too difficult to reach. The Tyrant's loyalists fled to the rim and the Syndicate formed between the Governance and the loyalists. Now the Syndicate has metastasized into a shadow economy and they've corrupted enough systems away from the Core that it's near impossible to root them out. But the Syndicate's not interested in being the new Governance. They're content to control the bottom-tier systems," Sarai said.

"The Syndicate had pretty strict rules about who controlled territory and who owed tribute to who. Most of the gangs they absorbed needed protection just like those governors you were talking about. No one gets all the money and power, but the guys that bent the knee to the Syndicate still ended up with more money and power than they knew what to do with," he said.

"Don't compare the Governance with those criminals. The Syndicate exists only to exploit people." She stiffened beneath his arm.

"Yeah, I lived that for years. So, nobody gets exploited in Governance systems? Aren't there taxes and military drafts and corruption?"

"No system is perfect, but the Governance is always trying to become more perfect."

"How's that working out?"

"It's better than civil war and mass death across countless star systems."

"That does sound better. But who's in charge of the Tyrant's forces? Who does that wolf alien answer to?"

"Latest intelligence we have is that a Count Nabren calls the shots. We found documents with his name on them recalling all loyal to the Tyrant's dream to their stronghold in the Ogdru sector." She pondered something for a moment. "When I take the stone from the Pinnacle, then I can lead a crusade to finally erase the Tyrant's memory from the galaxy. I'll finish what my father started."

Jayce felt an awareness from the hilt on his hip, like something had awoken for a moment then fallen back to sleep.

"You think that's what your father would want you to do?" he asked.

"What about *your* father? Think he'd be happy you're with the Sodality when he went off to fight for the Tyrant?" she snapped.

"He was drafted. It's not like he had the choice of being a slave soldier or not. And his salary kept my mother and me from starving for years. I think he'd be happy I'm doing this instead of working the docks until rot lung or a maw beast takes me out."

"Do you think he's alive?" she asked.

"No . . . I mean, Mom said he didn't know how to read or write. But he could've sent word back if he was alive out there somewhere. If he is, and he's gone this long without even trying to come home or something . . . Nah, he's dead. Dead as he can be," Jayce said. "I don't spend a lot of time thinking about him. Wouldn't make much difference."

"Then you're lucky. My father was the martyr that ended the Tyrant. His sacrifice was the rallying call to rebuild the Governance. When a hero dies, and anyone less than that hero fights against the cause?" She shook her head. "It puts people on one side of the moral authority line pretty easily. I see his statues everywhere. You should see the recruitment posters with him and my brother on them. It's brilliant. My mother is a master propagandist."

"Well, I hope you get a stone from the Pinnacle," Jayce said. "My mom wanted my life to be better than hers. Pretty sure every parent wants that."

"Again, you haven't met my mother," she said.

Jayce opened his mouth to speak but opted to stay silent.

"Say it," she said. "I know what you're thinking. There's a giant hole in my story that you want to point out, but you're just too polite to say it. Go on."

"I don't"—he shifted uncomfortably—"don't know what you're going on about."

"If my father wanted me to become a Paragon of the Sodality and hoped I'd carry on his legacy . . . why has his Fulcrum rejected me? And it why did it choose you, of all people?"

"I was thinking that, a little bit, but I don't have an answer. I'm guessing you don't either."

"At least you're honest. And no . . . I don't have the answer either. I thought I'd find it in the Veil, but no such luck yet. Maybe at the Pinnacle." She snuggled against him and closed her eyes.

"What does the Sodality say is up there?" he asked.

"A test . . . and the key to the salvation or ruin of our reality and this place," she said. "You mind keeping watch? I'm so tired . . ."

"No problem." Jayce unlocked his hilt and kept it in hand as Sarai dozed off.

He listened to the rain fall and the steady cadence of her breathing for hours.

Reman marched into the crumbling temple. Lahash knelt before the Veil stone floating in the shrine.

"The targets are separated from the Paragon." Reman knelt beside Lahash. "Though I lost their scent."

"You rely upon your strength from our home realm,"

Lahash said. "The Veil is a different place. We must adapt to where we are."

"I do not have a Veil stone yet," Reman snarled. "I am not as synched as you are."

"This stone is worthy of you," he said. "Take it."

"I'll have to leave to complete the resonance. You'll be without me. There is a greater prize, isn't there? Why settle for something lesser?"

"Because it serves our Lord's purpose. Are you here for yourself?" Lahash asked.

"I am here for the paradise to come." Reman snorted and approached the stone.

Chapter 21

Jayce jolted awake. Sarai wasn't in the shelter, but the cover was still in place.

"Sarai?" Jayce cracked the cover open and made sure razors weren't still falling, then charged out of the nook, his hilt in hand. The only sound was the rustle of the tall grasses all around the tree. The same haze obscured the horizon.

The sky wall hadn't changed, and he quickly found the direction toward the Pinnacle. He put a hand on the tree and looked around the other side in case Sarai was hiding there.

Nothing.

"Sarai!"

Jayce's flapped his arms against his side in frustration. She'd taken over the watch after a few hours of sleep. He'd fully expected her to be there when he woke up, or at least she'd give him a kick if there was a threat or if she wanted to get moving sooner.

He looked at the soil around the tree and there were only two sets of footprints.

"Sarai!" He went around the tree looking for more clues. He did a double take at two words carved into the bark.

GO HOME.

Jayce yelled at the sky and kicked a rock into the grass.

"Maybe I will! Maybe I'll drop my anchor and meet you all at the gate. You think I need this?" Jayce sat on a root arch for a moment, then stood back up. "Spoiled brat doesn't have all the attention in the galaxy put on her and she goes and leaves a shipmate behind. You'd get black-marked on my docks for that!"

He shook a fist at nothing.

Jayce put his hands on his hips for a moment, then looked around.

"Well . . . shit. Do I stay here and wait for Maru to find me? Who am I kidding, he'll go find little miss princess first. Then she'll pout and whine until she gets her way, and they'll keep going to the Pinnacle while I sit here with an un-baited line in my hand like some kind of an idiot. An idiot that's talking to himself in the middle of no-gods-damn-where. I'll catch up to them. Decent idea. Maybe I won't get killed before I find them. I love this place so much." Jayce felt the hilt buzz in his hand.

"Oh, you've got an opinion all of a sudden?"

His hilt hand raised of its own volition to the start position for the Flow kata.

"That? Now? You know you could've given her even a little bit of acknowledgment or encouragement. She might be a nicer person," Jayce said as the hilt pointed toward the direction of the Pinnacle and then twisted back to the Flow stance. The blade materialized without Jayce's action.

In the distance, a song began.

All of Jayce's frustrations faded away as he moved through the kata. Each strike and block flowed from one to the next and he made every jump and thrust with ease. His mind went still as he flowed to the end and to the final salute of the weapon's cross guard against his brows, the stone over the center of his forehead.

The hilt jumped out of his hand and landed with one side of the cross guard plugged into the ground, the blade vertical to the ground. It pointed two hands off from the direction he felt toward the Pinnacle.

"OK, I'm not going to pretend that's an accident. Is she that way?" Jayce picked the sword up. The blade disintegrated and the motes flowed back into the hilt. "Maybe if you'd done something sooner, she wouldn't have left."

The hilt didn't react.

"Now you're quiet. Fine! Let's go get her." Jayce took off at a jog.

He doubled back at a run and picked up the shield over the shelter and struggled to fold it back up as he ran after Sarai.

Jayce pushed a cobalt frond out of his way. The endless fields of grain had ended abruptly almost half an hour ago and transitioned to a jungle biome full of plants with the same ivory trunks he'd seen before, but the leaves were a spectrum of blues.

Birds the size of his thumb flitted from branch to branch. None made so much as a chirp at him or each other.

He'd reoriented himself every time he could see

through the upper canopy. Following the direction he'd received from the hilt hadn't been too difficult, so long as he could see the cracks and features in the sky wall.

"Am I lost?" He stopped and took a sip from the water bladder on his back. "Would I even know? Being lost implies having a correct place to be, or the right way to go. I'm running on faith here."

He pushed through the brush and came to a steep ravine. A stream ran through the bottom.

"More water, lovely," he said. Something drew his attention to the right, like there was a live wire buzzing on a ship that needed to be grounded or shut off before it could hurt someone. He drew his hilt and slid down the embankment. His boots splashed in the water, and he hopped out before they could soak through.

He crept around a bend in the stream and kicked a broken brick. An overgrown Shrine was the source of the stream, water flowing from the bottom of an altar. Floating a few inches over the altar was a Void stone.

The stone was almost the size of his palm and pulsed in tune with the thunder of Jayce's heart.

"Whoa." Jayce reached for it . . . then paused. He could almost taste the power of the stone. A vision of him aboard a trade galley with a loyal crew looking to him for command as he plied the star routes trading and adventuring his way to fame and fortune came to him.

All he had to do was take it.

He reached again, then pulled his hand back.

"You too?" he asked the hilt. "You want me to get what's good enough and go home, eh? And here I thought you cared about—"

A twig snapped in the jungle. Jayce ducked and moved into the undergrowth and tried to breathe as quietly as possible as more rustling approached.

"You're not going to find it, you git," a reedy voice said. "You think walking another circle's going to get us there? Give me the diviner and I'll find the bloody thing."

"You had it for two hours and where'd you take us, eh? Right back where we fargging started with the wench," another voice said.

"Neither you lot know where we is, so how'd you know if we's in a circle or not?" a deeper voice asked.

"Shut up, Mort, or I'll crack your tether and then there's no bonus for ya," the first voice said.

Jayce spied a pair of men in dark clothes and hoods several yards away. One had a pair of leg bones lashed together at the joints with a Veil-fleck talisman hanging from the front. A larger figure followed behind them.

"I knew that fortune-teller back at the Pilgrim rendezvous was selling us a bill o' goods," the one without the bones said. "Spent all that coin on a trinket, we did."

One turned his head toward Jayce, and he realized it wasn't a man, but an alien with one eye over a bulbous nose and lime-green skin.

"They're legitimate Docent bones, they are!" The one with the divining sticks slapped the other on the shoulder. "Docents find stones. Is what they do."

"Oh yeah?" The second kicked the other in the rear end. "Which way's it telling us to go find our fortunes now?"

"That way!" The alien pointed straight to the Shrine hidden behind bushes.

"I's hungry." A hulking mass of alien pushed a branch

down and snapped it from the tree. Jayce recognized an Ogroid when he saw one. They were cheap muscle, known for violence and the inability to count their pay correctly. "Can we eat her?"

The Ogroid pulled on a chain and another figure behind him fell to the ground.

"No, we can't eat her, Grug!" The one with the divining rod shook the talisman at him. "How we supposed to sell off a stone-bounded Attuned if she's in your stomach?"

"She won't be in there forever," the other alien giggled. He had the same single eye, but it was milky on one side from an old scar. All of them had Syndicate colors on their chests and armbands.

"Don't even let him think it's a good idea," the one with the divining rod said. "Why don't you let him snack on you? I'll buy you a new arm when we get out."

"Blet won't taste good," Grug rubbed a thick hand against a wary nose. "He don't smell good. What don't smell good don't taste good."

"The hungrier he gets the better I'll smell." Blet cowered behind the leader. "Let's get our little prize to a stone and be done, yeah? Doesn't have to be that shiny, grab some flecks from that stream bed and that'll cover our costs, won't it?"

"Boss Zallak didn't fund us to break even." The leader shook the divining rod again and pointed toward the Shrine. "We's been blessed by capturing this little prize. We best come back with more than just flecks and we'll be able to buy our own territory with our cut. Now quiet down, we're close. I can feel it in the bones."

Jayce waited for them to break through the underbrush

and used the noise to cover his movement behind them. He couldn't get a perfect look at the one in chains behind Grug the Ogroid, but the figure looked female enough.

"Blight my eye!" The leader stopped at the edge of the stream. "Would you look at the size of that one?"

"Whazzat? I've still got me trousers on," Blet chuckled.

"No, you git!" The leader grabbed Blet and pointed him toward the altar. "That one good enough?"

"We'll need Grug to carry all the coin we'll get when we sell 'er off," Blet said. "Grug, bring her up! Keep her leash tight, don't want any funny business this close to payday."

Jayce waited for the lumbering Ogroid to pass him. The figure behind him tripped and sprawled out.

Grug turned back as he tugged the chain . . . and stared right at Jayce with his single porcine eye.

"Boss!"

Jayce burst out of the brush and ignited his Fulcrum. Grug snapped a punch at him with the arm holding the chain, and had the blow slowed by the weight of the woman on the other end.

Jayce stabbed Grug in the chest. The blade flashed and sent a bolt of energy down the length that knocked the Ogroid off his feet and into a tree trunk.

"Kill 'im! Kill 'im!" The leader chucked the divining bones at Jayce. He raised his blade and swatted the bones away. His vision was blocked for a split second, which was just enough for the leader to pull out a small hand crossbow from off his belt.

Time slowed as the Syndicate member unsnapped a bolt from the top of the crossbow.

Jayce gave a war cry and charged. The leader shrieked

and set the bolt, then pulled it back with the string, but fumbled the weapon and sent the bolt spinning into the air. Jayce struck and cut the one-eyed alien from shoulder to hip. The leader spun around and transformed into icy chalk before he could hit the ground.

The statue of the dead alien landed in the stream and crumbled into dust. All that was left of him was washed away.

Blet jumped onto Jayce's back and beat Jayce's head and face with his fists. Jayce reached up and seized the Syndicate thug's hood and flipped him off. The alien dug long, jaundiced fingernails into Jayce's sleeve with one hand.

Jayce raised his trapped arm and swiped his blade at Blet's grip. His sword chopped through the alien's arm, straight through the anchor band. There was a flash of light and Blet vanished.

Most of him vanished. The severed arm still clung to Jayce's sleeve, the fingers twitching as the color drained from the cut and swept up the limb until it crumbled.

"Wait . . ." Jayce kicked at the debris left by the alien, then to the stream, then at the felled tree where Grug's foot was propped over the broken stump. "Wait. Why didn't . . ."

Grug sat up suddenly. The Ogroid bayed like a pack animal and picked up the fallen tree. Jayce's eyes went from his Veil sword to the much larger tree.

"Crush your bones!" Grug stomped toward him, the bleeding and burnt gash on his chest not slowing him down. Grug swung the tree with a long windup. Jayce noticed something the Ogroid hadn't and charged him.

Grug's tree smashed into another, startling a flock of bats with glowing wings from their roosts. The improvised club bounced out of Grug's hands and landed on his foot.

"Ow!" The Ogroid bent down to toss the tree aside and Jayce used his lowered height to decapitate him with a single stroke.

Grug crumbled into sand and grit, his head disintegrated before it even hit the ground.

"There, that did . . . Ow!" Jayce shook the arm that Blet had latched onto as blood ran down his fingers. "Sarai? Sarai!"

Jayce splashed through the stream and found the chains leading around a large tree. A hooded woman cowered against a fern.

"Don't worry, it's me." Jayce pulled the hood off.

A pair of blue eyes stared up at him under loose dark hair. The young woman gave him a nervous smile, which was something Sarai would never have done.

"Wait a minute." Jayce looked at the Veil stone in his cross guard, then deactivated the weapon.

"Standard, *yej*? Friend. No hurt." She held her cuffed hands up to her chin. Her accent wasn't like anything he'd ever heard before. Something about her face made Jayce's heart skip a beat.

"I thought you were—yes, Standard. Are you hurt?" he asked. "Name. Name? You have a name?"

"Leeta, Eshanti tribe of the Minari clan." She wiggled her hands back and forth. "Don't suppose you got the keys for these? They were on the dowsing bones the ugliest one carried."

"He threw them at me, hold on—" Jayce turned away, then back to her. "Don't go anywhere. I'm Jayce."

Leeta raised and lowered the heavy chains, making them clink together. The entire length was too long and too massive for any human to move around easily with.

Jayce brought the broken bones over. The charm on one end had a key and several coins and carved amulets. He pulled the key off and tossed the rest to the side. Their hands brushed together as he unlocked the cuffs.

They fell to the ground and Leeta shoved Jayce back. He hit the ground with an "*Oof!*" She scooped up the pile of charms and gripped an anchor stone between her fingers.

"No! Stay back or I'll do it!" she cried.

Jayce sat up.

"Do what? Send yourself back to your Aperture gate?" Jayce asked. "I'm not going to hurt you, Leeta. I meant to . . . to help someone else, but I'm not regretting anything. Let me guess . . . you're Attuned just like me, but no stone yet."

Leeta brushed hair from her face and Jayce's heart did that thing again.

"Are you a Paragon? You have that special sword they use," she said.

"Yes. Well, no. Not yet. That's . . . why I'm here," he said. "I need to find the people I came in here with. We're on a mission. That is secret. Forget I said that."

Leeta gave him a smile. She rubbed the anchor stone between her fingers.

"Don't suppose you've got someone with you that might be able to help with a little problem? See, I crack this now and it'll send me back to my gate on Succarran III where a gang of Syndicate is just waiting to auction me—a me with a Veil stone—off to the highest bidder."

"I doubt ... I doubt you'll be any better off if you go back without a stone." Jayce got to his feet. "I don't have one yet either."

"There's one right over there." She rubbed her wrists, then pointed to the shrine. "Be my guest."

"Wait, you don't want one?"

"You think I'd be here in chains and carted around by three scum grunts if I wanted a stone, you silly? I get a stone and I'll always be someone's property or running from people that want me to be their property. No thank you." She looked around and sniffed the air. "This whole place is just ... wrong."

"That's ... a way to look at it. You leave now and the Syndicate is waiting for you. Well, you can come with me. Hopefully my master can help you. When we find him."

"Did you really kill all three of them?" She pulled off her tattered cloak. She wore a loose blouse and shorts underneath along with a tight bodysuit.

"Pretty sure." He rubbed the scratches on his one arm.

"Oh, thank you!" She hugged him and kissed him on both cheeks. She wiggled the tip of her nose against his and skipped away.

Jayce was flat-footed for a second, then went after her. Leeta leaned against a tree and stretched from side to side.

"You're awfully happy about that," Jayce said.

"They kidnapped me from my clan holdings and were going to sell me into slavery. You want me to boo-hoo-hoo for them? No...anyway. How're you going to find the super Paragon that'll help me?"

"I know where he's heading. Which is where I'm heading. So, we'll meet there," Jayce said. "Which is this way. Follow me."

"Did you have to get here through the swamp with all the fire plumes? There were more than three of them when we first came through."

"No, the labyrinth with the hydra monster in the river. Doesn't everyone have to go over the hydra river?"

"This place isn't right." Leeta shook her head. "Which is weird because it feels...Does it feel like home to you?"

Jayce thought for a moment.

"It does, come to think of it," he said. "If anyone explained it before I came through, I don't think I would've come. Ice skies? Water that isn't water? Maybe that's why I didn't get all the details. Funny how that works."

"And yet we're both oddly comfortable with how we are here. I assume you are." She unzipped the front of her body suit to reveal just a bit of cleavage.

"Dry ground is starting to appeal to me. I'm from a— Hold on. What if my...master can't help you? I don't even know if he can."

"Legend in my clan is that Paragons can do anything their heart desires in the Veil. Healing. Magic. Moving my anchor point doesn't seem impossible. And if he can't... I'll find a gate. Any gate but the one I came through."

"Without knowing what's on the other side?"

"A chance at living is better than certainly dying," she said. "And let me guess what you were about to say, you grew up on a water world?"

"How'd you know?"

"Months at sea with my clan. You're still walking like there's a swell to the deck," she said.

"You got me." Jayce raised his hands.

Leeta lifted a tube from the open collar of her body suit and took a sip. She frowned at him with the tube still in her mouth.

"You don't want any of this," she said.

"I've got my own . . . and likewise." He took a drink from his water pack.

Chapter 22

The storm had congealed beneath the sky wall and descended on Sarai within minutes. Gales buffeted her from several directions, as if ghostly hands from the Veil were trying to disorient her.

Sarai pulled a flimsy hood closer to her face as snow and ice stung her exposed skin. Fractal flakes the size of her palm were accumulating on the ground, snapping with every step she took.

"Don't judge me. He doesn't deserve to be here. He didn't earn this. He didn't earn any of this!" The cold leached feeling from her arms and face. "I'm going to reach the Pinnacle on my own if I have to. I don't need him. I don't need anyone!"

The storm washed out the horizon. Sarai couldn't see the sky wall either. She stopped and tried to calm her mind to sense the Pinnacle, but her thoughts were as scattered as the sudden gusts of winds.

"Damn it!" She kept walking. "This isn't going to stop me!"

Cold bit her ears and lips. Every breath stung her nose and throat as the temperature dropped. She kept moving as the snowdrifts grew deeper, almost to her knees. A gust pushed her from behind and she stumbled forward. The oversized flakes crumbled beneath her hands and knees. Her bones ached from the cold, and she trudged forward, unsure if she was even going the right direction.

"You can't stop me!" she yelled at the storm.

She dragged a foot through the growing snowdrifts when the movement suddenly became unhindered. She lost her balance and rolled into a field with boulders strewn all about. The crystalline rocks ranged in size from cargo trunks to small homes. The sky wall was clear overhead.

She looked behind her at a wall of snow and ice sweeping across an invisible barrier. Sarai brushed icy crystals off her clothes.

"Well . . . how about that?" She scrunched her face as feeling returned to her skin.

Pebbles clattered down a nearby boulder. Sarai drew her hilt and ignited the saber. The blade pulsed in time with beats of faint light from the rocks.

A pair of wide eyes peeked over the top of the boulder, then ducked down again.

"You leave me alone, I'll leave you alone, fair?" Sarai carried her weapon at high guard and kept her distance from the creature as she walked around.

"Friends friends we are," came from behind her.

Sarai spun around and cut across her body, leaving the blade pointed down and behind her.

A Docent—what looked like a Docent—crept over a

boulder. Its skin was mottled white, with yellow-ringed splotches of black. Its face looked diseased, with lips curled hard over pointy teeth and a rotted-out eye in one socket.

"Such a strong one yes yes." The Docent crawled closer; its wing flaps were torn and decayed in several places. "This one will surely make it to the Pinnacle."

"That where you're heading?" she asked.

The scratch of claws against rock sounded from several more boulders and more eyes peeked out at her.

"If it's a way way out," the Docent said. "You have one? Yes, smell your anchor stone." The alien sniffed at the air. "You got it from one of us. Very kind. Too kind."

"Why waste so much food?" A Docent leaned over a boulder and spoke down at her.

Sarai raised her saber.

"I don't have anything for you," she said. "I'll be on my way. You go about yours."

"How long has this human skin skin been here, clan?" the dead-eyed one asked. "Felt the tears from the lower world we just did. Not greedy this one . . . has one morsel on her she does. Tastes old. So old."

Sarai brushed her finger against the edge of the Veil stone set into the cross guard of her hilt.

"We're so hungry." A sickly Docent tugged at her sleeve from the side of a boulder. She slapped the hand away and hurried on.

The dead-eyed alien leapt from boulder to boulder, then got ahead of Sarai. Dozens of the small creatures showed themselves. Diseased and rotting Docents surrounded her, all clinging to rocks.

"We are in need. So so much need," the dead-eyed one said. "Haven't had a stone in year years. Look what's happened to us. All of us."

"Abandoned by the matriarch! Cheated by creditors! Food stolen back by the Veil!"

New excuses and pleas came from the pack of Docents. Their needly teeth chattered and snapped, all eyes on the stone in her hilt.

"As you can see," Sarai raised the blade to high guard, "I have a need for this."

"What 'need'?" Dead Eye snarled. "Your flesh glows with health. You don't need the stone. We we do or the hunger will eat us!"

"Pain! Pain!" came from the pack.

"Just a taste." Dead Eye put a paw onto the grass and crept toward her. "Just give us your food. One of us gave you an anchor, yes yes? Only fair!"

"Fair is fair!" hissed the Docents as they closed in on her.

"Stop!" she swept her blade across her body, but the Docents didn't flinch back. "Stop! I—I can lead you to other stones. I'm Attuned and can sense them."

Dead Eye's face twitched.

"Only two left this far from the gates, you think we haven't tried to reach them? We are hungry hungry *now*!" Dead Eye scratched out a quick signal on a rock and the Docents attacked.

One landed on her shoulder and bit into her harness. Sarai cried out and grabbed it by the neck. She threw the weak creature to the ground and kicked it away. More jumped on her, their claws scratching and ripping at her.

Sarai cut one in half with a quick swipe, then slapped the flat of the blade against one on her hip. A pulse of thought sent a searing light down the saber and the Docent cried out as it ignited. The alien ran off, yipping as it sprang from stone to stone, trying to outrun the fire on its back.

Dead Eye clutched Sarai's sword arm and dragged it down. More and more Docents piled onto her, but she kept her grip on the hilt. Dead Eye swiped his foot at her, and claws raked across her face.

Sarai cried out and let go of the weapon. Some of the Docents jumped off to mob Dead Eye and the hilt. They formed a swirling mass of wings and claws all fighting for the saber. The ones still clinging to her began biting and chewing her clothes.

Sarai couldn't throw any off and she fell to the ground.

A flash of light sent a wave of heat and pain across her arms. The Docents panicked into squawking. Meaty thumps sounded around her, and Sarai grabbed a Docent on her chest by the neck and slammed its face into a nearby boulder.

The chaos died away as the Docents fled.

Sarai put a hand to her cheek as blood seeped through her fingers. Dead and burnt Docents were everywhere; a sizzling hole through a rock over a pair of smoking feet were all that remained of Dead Eye.

"Sarai? Sarai!" Dastin came around a boulder. He froze, his face just like her mother's the time she fell down a set of stairs and broke her arm. Sarai choked back tears and held out a hand to him.

He scooped her up and hugged her, rubbing blood

across his armor. He looked her over, his eyes full of worry and fear. "How bad are you hurt? Just your face?"

"Find my hilt." She spat blood and tamped down emotions that shouldn't have troubled a Paragon like her.

"How is she?" Eabani stomped the life out of an injured Docent, his crossbow in hand. "I think the rest are gone."

"Banged up." Dastin pulled her hand from her face and winced at the damage. He took out his med pack and inserted a medicine cap into an injector. "They're from our realm. Infection is a risk." He stung her neck with the injector, then took out a pair of large tweezers with tiny inward-facing needles at the top.

"Sarai?" Maru squatted next to her, his glaive in one hand and the base planted firmly in the ground. The blade glowed from the blast he'd just channeled through it. Neff peeked over his shoulder, then slunk behind him.

"Sarai, where is Jayce?" the Paragon asked.

"We got separated." She pointed to the blizzard behind him. "Can't you scry him?"

Maru's hand twisted his glaive haft from side to side.

"I cannot," he said. "I felt you together for a time, then there was a darkness before it faded away. Now we're too close to the Pinnacle for me to reach out to him . . . too much interference in the air."

"My hilt! Someone find my hilt!" She turned away just as Dastin was about to pinch her lacerated face with the tweezers.

"Gone gone, it is," Neff said. "So sorry."

"Nope! Found it." Eabani scooped up the hilt and tossed it to Maru. Held it where Sarai could see it, then flipped it around. The stone inlay was empty. Bits of Veil fragments glittered in the recession.

"Oh no." Sarai's shoulders fell. "Oh no, what do I do now?"

"You hold still so I can stop the bleeding, little miss." Dastin snapped the tweezers together and pain pinched her cheek.

"Ow!"

"Stop squirming or you'll end up with a bad scar," he said. "Nothing that can't be fixed, but I want your mother to be able to recognize you when she sees you again."

"That doesn't matter!" She slapped Dastin's wrist away. "I came here to become a Paragon and how am I supposed to do that if I don't have a Paragon's weapon? The symbol!"

Maru put a gentle hand on her shoulder.

"Sarai, does Shipmaster Uusanar have a hilt?" he asked calmly.

"Well . . . no," she pouted.

"Yet he was able to claim a stone when I led him through the Veil. Do you think you are the first Attuned— or even the first Paragon—to lose a hilt?" he asked.

"I-I should be better than that," she said. "How can I fight without a hilt? How can I be a Paragon?"

"Another hilt will choose you," Maru said. "This is my third." He shook his glaive. "The Sodality cares so much about the hilts because they are very difficult to replace. You lost yours in the course of . . . something awful. Not negligence. Another will choose you."

"Sodality won't even make you buy it." Dastin stung her face again with the tweezers. "Big Marine Corps would take the price of Eabani or my crossbow out of our pay if we lost ours."

"That's why these ugly things could pry mine out of my cold dead claws." Eabani punted a dead Docent over a boulder.

"There . . . not quite like new." Dastin swiped blood off Sarai's cheek. "Don't scare me like that again, little miss." He gave her a long hug.

"Hasn't been intentional." She hugged him back. "Where's your packs? What happened back at the river?"

"Eabani, get the gear," Dastin said. He stood and helped her up. "Maru and me had to kill that hydra thing on our own as *someone* got a little bit scared during the fight."

"I don't like tentacles!" Eabani shouted from behind a distant boulder. "You know that!"

"He doesn't," Sarai said. "Remember that time he ran from that seafood restaurant on Cardin VII?"

"Being scared's one thing." Eabani stomped over, two packs on his back. "Doesn't mean I didn't help. Who shot the hydra in the head? Was that you or me, Gunny?"

"And then I hit it four more times while Maru finished it off," Dastin snapped. "Then I had to drag you out from under a rock. I'm still pissed about that."

"It's instinctual." Eabani lifted his snub nose and his goatee swayed from side to side. "I can't change my evolution."

"Onward." Maru disassembled his glaive with a twist of the haft and snapped the two halves to his belt. "Dastin . . . I need a moment with Sarai, if you please."

Sarai's jaw tightened and she walked faster to keep pace beside the Paragon.

"I am worried about Jayce," Maru said. "How was he when you last saw him?"

"Safe. Safe as he could be in that storm. I've never seen anything like that." She waved a hand behind her. "Will there be more?"

"Manifestations," Neff said. "This far in and home knows us better than we know ourselves. Too much emotion and that will resonate resonate through the ether. Why storms for you and the other Attuned, hmm?"

"He was scared," Sarai said. "He tried to be a big strong man around me and when I didn't need him, his ego must have—"

"Jayce dove into the river and saved you," Maru said. "You were unconscious. His split-second decision saved you and put himself in great danger at the same time. I do not believe Jayce had much to prove to you. Or anyone."

"I hope he's as smart as he is brave. Maybe he's already cracked his anchor and we'll all see each other again soon."

"Neff?" Maru scratched the Docent's ear. "Can you sense his anchor?"

The Docent worked his claws into Maru's harness and lifted his snout to sniff the air.

"I cannot not tell. There's patch of night out there . . . distant. Could be there," Neff said. "If we get closer then—"

"What were those things?" Sarai snapped. "Aren't Docents supposed to be guides? Why did an entire pack of your kind attack me?"

"Bad bad blood." Neff cowered against Maru. "Long

long time since the kin entered the Veil as a clan to feed. Eat too much. No stones for the Pilgrims. No stones for the Sodality. Too many attacks on us inside and outside the Veil. Jealousy! That kindred . . . no idea how long they've been in—Fleck!"

Neff hopped off Maru and scrambled up a boulder. He stuck a paw into a crevice and fished out a handful of glowing shards. He gobbled them down without chewing and jumped back onto Maru. The shards clinked in his stomach.

"Been in the Veil," Neff continued. "My kin are proper Docents, only send scouts scouts who return with flecks for the egg time. Earn our keep like everyone else. Keeps customers from eating us. Poison!" He pointed at his chest. "Poison!"

"You encountered the first feral population of Docents in nearly a century," Maru said. "The Sodality will be interested in your report."

"Some warning would have been nice," she said.

"Shall I tell you of every potential threat here?" Maru asked.

"I'll settle for knowing about the Pinnacle and why it's so important for us to reach it." She grabbed Maru by the arm. "We came here for Veil stones—ones strong enough for me to build my own hilt and become a full Paragon. How many stones matching that description have we passed, Neff?"

The Docent counted on his fingers, then slunk away from Maru's gaze.

"Enough, yes yes," Neff muttered.

"If we can reach the Pinnacle . . . I will tell you. If you

carry the answer in your mind, it can attract more manifestation. Please, let me concentrate on the Pinnacle so we don't walk in circles. I will tell you everything when the time is right. But the Tyrant's blades are here and . . ." He held up two fingers pressed together.

In the distance, the Pinnacle wavered in and out of existence.

"No more for now . . . please." Maru kept walking and the Pinnacle solidified.

Sarai fell back to Dastin. The Marine offered her a nutrient tube.

"White fish and noodles, your favorite," the Marine said.

"Thanks." She slipped it into a shoulder pocket. "Not a lot of appetite right now."

"Adrenaline does that. Soon as it wears off, you'll be hungry. Don't go swimming anymore, OK?"

"That worried about me?" she smirked.

"Always, little miss. When your father saved me from the Tyrant's prisoner camp, I swore I'd return the favor to him one day. I was on the team that planted the bomb aboard that monster's ship while you shiny types dealt with the Tyrant. I wasn't there when he needed me . . ."

"How much of a difference would you have made against the Tyrant?" she asked.

"Doesn't matter. I should have been there. When you were swept away, I had that same . . . there was this pit in my stomach. Felt the same way when your father, Maru, and Marshall Tulkan split off from the rest of us knobs aboard the Tyrant's barque. I'm so glad we found you."

"I'm a big girl, Dastin. I can take care of myself."

"You had everything under control back there?" He jerked a thumb over his shoulder.

"It was like being bitten by butterflies. I had it under control," she said.

Maru looked back at her for a moment.

"Eaten by Docents isn't how I want to go," Eabani said. "Too embarrassing. No one would believe it."

"But hiding under a rock because of some wacky waving arms is acceptable?" Dastin sneered.

"Everyone back home would understand." Eabani snorted.

"There's going to come a time when I don't need you, Dastin. Mom assigned you to me to keep me safe until I'm a Paragon. I'm almost there," Sarai said.

Dastin's bottom lip quivered for a heartbeat, then his face went to stone.

"I know . . . you won't always need me, little miss. Just been with you since you were five years standard. I'll just go back to the line and—"

"No." Sarai squeezed his arm with both hands. "No, don't talk like that. Just because I won't *need* you doesn't mean I don't *want* you around, Das-das." She set her head against his shoulder.

The Marine's eyes moistened, and he leaned his head over to touch hers.

"Eabani too," she said.

"Someone has to scare the boys away," the Lirsu said.

Neff sniffed Maru's ear, then snorted off to one side.

"Problem?" the Paragon asked.

"I lied because you lied lied," the Docent whispered.

"Why aren't we telling the truth?"

Maru scratched Neff under his chin.

"Because we must. There's too much at stake. Now keep your senses open for anything coming for us. We're close now." Maru pointed in the distance. A gleaming peak shined through the gloom.

Chapter 23

"And then the *farggle* birds fly into the air and drop spoors all through the boughs." Leeta spread her arms and spun around. She and Jayce made their way up a slightly inclined hill. A fog surrounded them. Small blue flowers sprouted from the grass that bloomed and died back within a few seconds.

"Sounds amazing," Jayce said. "We had *scharple* squid migrations twice a year. But there wasn't any sort of celebration. Those squid would eat anyone too close to the water."

"Your planet doesn't sound . . . the best." She scrunched her nose at him. "Are you going back?"

"Not if I can help it. The Tyrant's forces were there, and the Syndicate probably won't be too happy to see me again."

"Then where will you go?" she asked.

"Paragons go most anywhere, don't they? The whole galaxy needs them. Us."

Leeta sighed.

"I had a great-aunt that was touched. Attuned? Is that what you call us? She was eight years old when a Paragon came to our tribe lands. The Paragon was some sort of outlander with skin the color of lava and thick scabs all over." She waved at her face. "He demanded her, he demanded a little girl and promised she'd be well taken care of and put to work for 'the greater good.' My grandparents were . . . not convinced."

"Not convinced he was a Paragon?" Jayce raised his hilt. "Did he have one of these?"

"Not convinced she wouldn't just be some sort of slave. The tribes had rebelled from outlander control a generation before and they didn't want to invite new overlords. They refused the Paragon and asked him to leave. He took her anyway. Killed my grandfather to do it."

"What? That's horrible," Jayce said. "How could a Paragon do that?"

"He must have bragged to the rest of his order because every generation more and more slavers came looking for Attuned in my tribe lands. We had little in the way of weapons, so we hid our children every time the omens said the sky gates were about to open. The Syndicate were . . . were more thorough than others." Her mouth pressed into a thin line. "They had one of those vile beasts with them—the one with the magic bones— and it found me in the deep forest."

"I'm sorry, but we'll get you back home," Jayce said.

"Where is Illara? Because Kelku'i is in the Tasshal Arm, eighty-five light-years off galactic north."

"Kelku'i? I'm not exactly sure . . . three days in FTL from Hemenway where I'm from. I'm not exactly an expert on interstellar travel. Need to take a skiff from one trade lash-up to another? Easy work," he said. "But I heard Syndicate complain about coming out to the Navras Arm."

"Then your home is tens of thousands of light-years from mine . . . Illara is likely that far as well." She stopped and put her hands in her face.

"Hey, hey, no reason to cry." He rubbed her shoulder.

"How can I ever get home?" she sobbed.

"I'll help you, don't worry." Jayce smiled.

Leeta hugged him and the press of her chest against his caught most of his attention. She kissed him on his cheek, then grabbed him by the hand and led him up the hill.

"There anyone waiting for you back home? Besides family?"

"No. I'm one season away from betrothal. My father hopes he can get at least two cows for me as dowry."

"Two? Why not ten?" Jayce asked.

"No wife has ever gone for ten cows. Ever." She squeezed his hand.

"Well, you should be the first," Jayce said.

"That's sweet of you . . . Jayce, why do you want to be a Paragon?" she asked.

They continued walking toward the Pinnacle; its needle shape glistened in the distance, the base still lost to the haze.

"To matter. Be more than some dock rat. And fighting the last of the Tyrant's followers will be a bonus."

Leeta lessened her hold on his hand but didn't pull it back entirely.

"The Tyrant never came to Kelku'i, but when he was

in power, no Syndicate came to steal me away. No one from the Sodality either."

"Huh. I didn't know. The Tyrant cost me my father . . . and my mother, in a roundabout sort of way. No Tyrant, no draft. No draft, no soldier's salary to my mother. If the salary didn't stop when the Tyrant was killed, my mother wouldn't have had to go looking for work and she might not have drowned in that storm. So, no Tyrant and my father would've stayed with us."

"That's good reasoning," Leeta said. "We live in peace on my world. We're poor. Nothing worthwhile but the clans and kin. Sometimes slavers will come, but we fight. They found me, so they might think there are more Attuned for them to take the next time one of these Pilgrimages comes about. I wish there was a way to cut my planet off from all this."

"You need more protectors."

"You think the Governance will do it? The Sodality?"

"Isn't that what they're for?" he asked.

"Not in my experience. Not in my part of the galaxy. The less we're involved with all this business, the better off my clan and kin will be."

"That sounds like a good life," Jayce said as he pulled ahead of her and let her hand go. "Your clan and kin know anything about . . . here? Sometimes it seems like we're closer to the Pinnacle, other times I can barely see it."

"No. Anyone taken by the Paragons or the criminals never comes back." She squatted down and plucked the blossoming flowers and began twisting them together.

"Hours!" Jayce raised a hand to the distant Pinnacle. "Hours walking and it's still *all* the way over there."

"Shouldn't we have come across your mentor by now?"

"Uh . . . should've. I need to clear my mind and try and focus. I'm going to practice the kata and see if I can enter the Flow." Jayce drew his hilt.

Leeta clutched a pile of flowers to her chest and took a step back.

"Don't be afraid." He flicked his hand and the sword came to life. Motes sprang out and formed a lattice of the blade, then it appeared as dull, solid, light.

"Don't leave me." She buried her nose in the flowers and looked at him with wide eyes.

"I won't." Jayce sank into the starting position, then raised the first deflection and stepped into the spin-and-slash. His mind didn't focus on the kata, his thoughts were on the look Leeta had just given him.

He felt a presence behind him, and he shifted to the next deflection and a phantom blade struck toward him and was pushed away by Jayce's kata step. Jayce didn't feel the impact as he snapped a high stab, then ducked another ghostly attack. He continued through the kata and drew in a deep breath for the final strike.

He cried out and stabbed forward. The tip of his sword glanced off a polished wall and the hilt jumped from his hand. The blade collapsed back into the hilt, which clattered onto the second step of a stairway.

The Pinnacle scraped against infinity; the heavens behind the Pinnacle were not the creaking sky wall, but the dark of the space surrounding a swirling pool of stars. The apex may have pierced the fountain of light from the center point of the pool.

"Ooh . . . whoa!" He stepped back into the grass and bumped into Leeta.

"How did you do that?" She slunk behind him.

"I am not entirely sure, but we're here now. Or it came to us. I'm not entirely sure of that either." Jayce moved slowly toward the stairs leading to a flat area before the Pinnacle. The Pinnacle was a dark gray; its shape wasn't fixed, but roiled slowly with fractals and geometric shapes. The stairs were made of basalt so polished that they had a mirrorlike sheen.

His reflection was a bit rougher than he thought he looked. He felt Leeta clutch his arm. Her reflection wavered for a moment, then resolved into a fanged monster with stormy skin and red eyes.

He flinched away. The Leeta next to him was just as beautiful and human as the moment he first laid eyes on her.

"You OK?" She smiled.

"Yes, sorry, it's all . . . it's all a lot, all of a sudden," he said. "And I'm suddenly very tired. Are you?"

"I am, but I don't want to stop. What if your master's ahead of us?" She fiddled with the flowers.

"I don't think they'd wait out here in the open. The top of the stairs and that super-tall doorway that just appeared out of nowhere . . . more likely. That's where I'd find him." He glanced at her reflection on the stairs. Normal.

"Maybe not." Her front foot grazed the bottom step, and she pulled back. "We still have our anchors. We don't have to do this. Let's just break them and leave before—"

"What? You'd go straight back to being sold into slavery or killed. We can't give up now." He took her by the hand.

"What if the anchors don't even work in there? What if we can't leave?"

"You don't know that." Jayce tugged her hand.

"And you do?"

"What happened to wanting a chance at life instead of a sure death? The chance is there." He pointed up the stairs. "That's the only place where I know I can find Maru. He's an expert at all of . . . this."

Leeta frowned.

"You're lucky we're just getting to know each other and I can still say you were right about things." She moved a woven flower bracelet from her wrist to Jayce's, leaving a second one behind. "Let's go."

Chapter 24

✦

Jayce and Leeta walked off the top step and onto a plaza that stretched to the massive doors. Trash and debris littered the plaza. Against the wall of the Pinnacle were chalky, coral-like statues of dead Pilgrims who had come before.

The doors were taller than any ship he'd seen back on Hemenway. They were built for giants, not those who'd died at the threshold.

"Ah, no more steps." Leeta leaned forward and rested her hands on her knees.

"Well, there's good news and bad news. Bad news is that I don't see my group, good news is that they're not any of the dead ones either." Jayce kept his hilt in hand and walked across the line of statues.

"Now we wait?" Leeta kicked a bag away from a statue and pawed through the contents.

"Doesn't seem to have worked for any of these guys," Jayce said. "There's a way inside, I can feel it."

"Bet they could feel it too." Leeta pulled out a rotten blanket and tossed it back into the bag.

Jayce started up at eternity, then looked away.

"Stings my eyes for some reason." He put a hand against the Pinnacle to prop himself up as he yawned. "Tired. Yeah, tired right now."

"Could it have something to do with all the walking we've been doing and not eating?" Leeta fiddled with the crochet of talismans and charms from the Syndicate slaver's divining rods. "What're we missing? There's got to be some clue on how to get inside."

"Dunno." Jayce found a space between all the statues and set his back against it. "Maybe we should rest a bit."

He slid down, already feeling relief in his legs and feet. He had almost reached the floor when Leeta grabbed him by the jacket and jerked him away with a surprising amount of force. He went sprawling across the plaza.

"Hey! What was that for?" He rubbed his chin where it had struck the polished stones.

"All of them"—Leeta shuffled backward—"none of the bodies died from violence. No defensive wounds. No shock or horror on their faces. *Look.*"

She was right. All the statues looked almost comfortable in the moment they had died. Some were still wrapped in blankets or had borrowed the shoulder of the dead next to them for a pillow.

Jayce hopped to his feet.

"Thanks." He yawned hard, and Leeta followed suit.

"Stop it." She pinched the flesh of one hand between the thumb and pointer finger. "There's something in the air here . . . something making us tired."

"Then we'd better think fast or start slapping ourselves." Jayce went to the enormous door and ran his hand along the mirror-smooth surface. He felt a slight depression but couldn't see it when he took his hand away. He touched it again, then detected another one a few steps closer to the center of the door.

"What are you doing?" Leeta asked.

"Something here . . ." He ran his thumb over the stone in his hilt, then felt the edges of the invisible groove in the door. "Leeta, any of the statues have Veil weapons like I do?"

"No. Some had blades and arrows," she said.

"None are dressed like Sodality either. If the Sodality knows about this place, and what's in it, then they must have gotten inside. Paragons all have Veil stone hilts. Come here." He motioned her over.

His eyelids became heavy, and his head drooped forward.

A sharp slap to his cheek jolted him away from the cusp of sleep.

"Sorry." Leeta kissed him on the same cheek. "Do whatever it is you're going to do quick before we both get too woozy."

"Let's give this a try." He wrapped an arm around her waist and pressed the Veil stone on his hilt into one of the small indentations.

The light around them dimmed. Jayce felt his consciousness blink and he was inside a long, narrow hallway with a curved ceiling. He stepped toward the lit end of the passage and ignited his veil sword. The blade was solid and glowed white hot along the edges.

It cast ivory light against the walls. Sections of polygonal masonry blended into simple bricks, then into scales and tight grids. The tunnel looked like it had been built one small section at a time by different cultures over thousands of years, all of them a mishmash of styles and material.

He looked back for his companion, but he was alone.

"Leeta?" He turned back but all that was behind him was a solid wall, no depressions for keys or Veil stones.

"Jayce?" He heard her voice like she was just on the other side of the wall, but there was no way to get to her.

"Damn this place. Leeta! Get to the end of the tunnel and I'll meet you there!" He took off at a slow jog. The brightness at the end dimmed the closer he got to it. He exited the tunnel and skidded to a stop and nearly fell over the edge of a drop-off. He was in a circular room with several more tunnel exits. In the center was an oblong Veil stone several times his size, floating over the chasm he'd nearly fallen into.

Cold fog fell from the large stone. Beneath it, the galaxy turned ever so slowly. Stars winked and flashed as the fog drifted through it.

"This has not been my best idea," he said to himself.

"Jayce!" Leeta came out of a tunnel adjacent to his. "What happened?"

"We made it inside . . . I presume," he said. "Wow. Do you think this is the stone I'm supposed to—No, can't be."

"Jayce, I don't like this anymore. Your master's not here and we should've seen him by now, don't you think? Some sign of him." She rubbed her hands together.

"They couldn't wait at the door or the sleep would've got them. They didn't die there either, so they must've come inside." He walked around the large Veil stone. "Or we're ahead of them. That's not a good . . . Hey, look at the size of this one. It could power an entire planet, couldn't it?"

He came to the other side and found an open doorway, the arc curved to a sharp upward point. Across the threshold was a disc that bobbed up and down ever so slightly.

"Oh," Leeta said from behind him. "That seems to be our only way onward and upward. I'm helping, by the way."

"Let's get on it at the same time. It'll be tight but there's room." He took her hand and they stepped onto the disc as one. Leeta put her head against Jayce's chest.

Jayce didn't feel any acceleration. One moment they were on the disc, the next they rose through the air without any sensation at all.

"I just want to go home," Leeta said.

"We're getting there." Jayce hugged her with his non-weapon arm. "Worse comes to worst . . . you take my anchor. Drop it and you'll be with the rest of my party when they leave. I'll take yours and deal with the Syndicate waiting for you."

"You won't make it." She nuzzled against him.

"They're expecting you—all bound up and helpless—not a Paragon with a fully powered Veil hilt and harness." He looked down at the empty ring on the front of one shoulder. "I'll have all that *and* the element of surprise."

"We'll be on the wrong side of the galaxy from each other," she said.

"Have them bring you to Primus, the capital world. I'll meet you there eventually," he said.

"There's a hundred billion souls on that world," she said. "You think we'd just bump into each other?"

"But only one Citadel. That's where the Paragons are headquartered. I'll meet you there . . . or I'll find someone there that knows where you are."

"Why are you so kind to me?" She hugged him harder.

"I have a better chance at life with your anchor than you do with it, so I ca—" The tube blinked and Jayce glimpsed a throne room full of figures in dark armor. It blinked again and there was a balcony looking over an endless cityscape.

The disc stopped. It rotated slowly and stopped in front of a set of double doors that didn't so much as open as crumble down the center line, the broken bits moving perpendicular to gravity and molding back into the tube wall. Beyond was an onyx statue of a Paragon, a short sword run through his chest, Veil hilt in hand. His face was hidden by his helmet, but the figure appeared human. The statue reached to the sky; motes of light floated down the statue's arm like it was hollow inside.

"Creepy." Leeta clutched his arm.

"Let's get off at the same time and I'll check it out," he said, and they stepped off the disc. He pulled away from her and her touch ran down his hand and brushed against his fingertips. The statue changed as he walked around it, an internal light source giving him glimpses of star clusters and nebulae. The blade at the base was carved from the same material and couldn't be moved.

"I think it's OK."

Jayce turned around, but there was no one to hear him.

"Leeta? Leeta!" He ran to the lift. The disc was still there, but there was no trace of the young woman.

"Damn it!" Jayce swiped his sword across the lift entrance

and left cuts on both sides. The damage repaired itself within moments. Jayce ran a hand through his hair. He touched his anchor band and felt the talisman was still there.

Jayce raised a hand to the statue. "Who're you supposed to be? What's with the levels and the giant stones and...where did Leeta go? Where's Maru? Dastin? Anybody? I'll take Sarai at this point."

Jayce sat on the statue's pedestal.

"I saw people in that throne room...didn't look friendly. Giant city place? How did they fit that in here? You know"—he looked up at the statue of the mortally wounded Paragon—"I'm an excellent river rat. Bad ones get eaten. Maybe I should've stayed at home. Kept at the Scales until my brain went to mush and I turned to the rotgut and burnt out at forty-five. Don't knock it. Lots of fighters better than me went that way."

He frowned at the disc.

"That would be a life without meaning or purpose. I wouldn't have been living, I'd just be...being." He looked back at the statue. "Bet you went looking for something greater and look how you ended up. You saw Leeta, right? Pretty. Nice. Smells like flowers and vanilla, somehow. I turned my back on her and *poof*."

He stood up and paced around the statue.

"Now here I am talking to some kind of volcanic glass art piece that doesn't answer and I'm about to annoy myself." Jayce poked a finger at the dropped blade, which struck him as being oddly familiar. The statue's weapon nudged slightly at his touch.

"Ahh!" the statue cried out and bent forward, its dark shell cracking as the man within broke out.

Jayce backpedaled, his mind wild with fear and flailing to react to the insanity as the statue stepped off its dais and hit the floor.

Jayce wasn't in the lift station anymore; he was on a starship. A large chamber opened out to an enormous viewing window. A dusty red world turned beneath the ship; a yellow-and-orange nebula stretched across the distant void. The Paragon was no longer a towering statue, but a human-sized warrior. The Paragon thrust an arm out and stopped himself from falling against the deck. Blood dripped down the knife in his chest and spattered against the dark metal plating and his hand.

"What the—" Jayce raised his sword arm, but his hilt was gone.

It lay next to the injured Paragon.

"Why are you fighting me?" a dark voice rumbled. Jayce spun around. A tall man in onyx armor with a bloodred-light weave beneath the plates was propped against a throne. The chair was made up of the same clear stone run through with stars and galactic phenomena like so much of what he'd seen in the Veil. Long white hair dangled from the speaker's scalp, but he didn't look up at Jayce or the Paragon.

"You . . . you'll end it all," the Paragon said. He swiped at the side of his helmet, and it fell away. Blood sprang up from the inside when it bounced against the deck. He was human with blond hair and green eyes, his face in agony, blood seeping from his mouth and down his chin with every breath.

"No, I'll save everyone." The other man's voice cut through Jayce like ice. He gave off an aura that made Jayce's skin crawl. "You've seen the truth, haven't you?"

He looked up and Jayce cried out. The face of the man in the black-and-red armor was half flesh, half skull. The same visage Jayce saw when his spirit had traveled over the sky wall. Neither of the fighters reacted to Jayce's cries or even to his presence.

The Paragon pulled the knife from his chest and a glut of blood splattered against Jayce's hilt next to him on the deck. The Paragon picked it up, and his wound glowed with Veil light. He got to his feet and ignited his blade with a flick of his wrist, just like Jayce had learned to do.

"The Cycle will only destroy us." The half-skull man raised an arm and shadows emanated from him. "We break free and our destiny will be ours, Taras. Why do you want to end here? Because of some prophecy you'll die to fulfill?"

Taras. That was the name carved into the hilt. The Paragon was Sarai's father. If this was his final moment, then the other man must be the Tyrant. Jayce froze. Part of him wondered if Sarai should have been here to see this.

"There is no freedom in slavery, Mutarin," Taras said. "We must live. We must die. This is the Cycle and you can't control it."

The Tyrant laughed.

"I have already freed myself from death. You should see the glory that's waiting for us, Taras. In fact . . . let me show you." The Tyrant raised a double-handed hilt overhead and a massive broadsword sprang into being. He lunged at Taras and the Paragon deflected the strike with the first move of the Flow kata.

Jayce backed away as the two attacked each other. His

foot bumped into something, and he looked down at an alien with short brown fur over his face. One arm was missing at the elbow and a leg was lopped off above the knee. The stumps oozed blood, and Jayce was pretty sure he was already dead.

Beside the alien lay Maru. The Wottan was deathly pale, a gash across his stomach and one arm pressed against the cut to keep his intestines inside his body. His skin was tighter than Jayce remembered; then he realized he was looking at a much younger version of Maru.

"Maru!" Jayce touched the Paragon's shoulder.

A blow from out of nowhere landed against his chin and sent him reeling back. His head bounced off a wall. His hilt was back in his hand, and he waved it at whatever had just struck him.

"Jayce? My goodness, I'm so sorry." Maru put the knife edge of his hand against Jayce's wrist and kept the blade angled away from him.

Jayce's eyes went wide with surprise. Maru wasn't injured—at all—and they were back in the long hallway full of statues in their recesses.

"Why did you punch me?" Jayce felt a welt forming under his bottom lip.

"You appeared out of nowhere and my reflexes got the better of me. Are you injured? How did you get here?" Maru asked.

Jayce raised his hands in despair. He looked over the hilt, which was devoid of any of blood. He read the name engraved on the end cap, then looked back down the hallway for Taras.

"Where's . . . anyone else?" Jayce asked. "Leeta? Have

you seen her? Human. Female. Really pretty. Seems to like me. I don't find that combination that often."

Maru's brow perked up.

"Sarai and I became separated when we came through the doors," Maru said. "She wasn't in the giant stone chamber. I have been alone for several hours. Who is Leeta? She must be an Attuned like you or of a different Veil school."

"She's Attuned. Got kidnapped from her world and brought here to pull a stone out for the Syndicate," Jayce said. "Can you scry for her? She's all alone and unarmed. We need you to—"

"Only Attuned with a Veil stone can enter the Pinnacle, Jayce," Maru said. "You had to use it to get through the Gate of Eternal Slumber."

"One, you could've warned me about the sleeping trap. Two, that's not right because I got her through with just my stone. I had my arm around her when I plugged it in." Jayce mimed using his hilt as a key.

"That's not possible," Maru said, shaking his head. "That's why only Sarai and I entered the Pinnacle. Dastin, Neff, and Eabani are waiting for us at the base of the stairs. I told them to wait ten hours for us, then break their anchors if we haven't returned. I assumed we'd reach the Pinnacle before you. As for the sleeping ward . . . I didn't know about it. This other person . . . the Veil tests us. It will tempt us with our deepest desires to keep us from the Pinnacle. Are you sure she's real?"

"I'm not making Leeta up." Jayce pointed to the flower bracelet she'd given him. "You think I'd make one of these for myself for kicks and giggles?"

Maru held up a hand. "I believe you. But Sarai and I had to use our blade stones as keys individually. We came through and she was in a tunnel next to mine that led to a massive way stone."

"That's what happened to us—Wait, hold on." Jayce put his hands on his hips. "But Leeta doesn't have a blade stone."

"Knowledge learned through millennia of Sodality expeditions into the Veil and to the Pinnacle are consistent: a blade stone is needed to pass the Gate of Everlasting Dawn." Maru paused. "Hmm, High Paragon Vitrix the Seventh once wrote a rather lengthy codicil on how our translations of the first records were likely incorrect from linguistic shifts over thousands of years. He speculated that the Gate of Everlasting Dawn should be the Gate of Eternal Slumber. I will most certainly add this information to the Paragon archives once we return home. As for this Leeta, perhaps I am wrong now, I often am. But if you carried her across the threshold, then that is certainly in contravention of the sacred texts."

"Which you just realized are wrong," Jayce said.

"The name was wrong. The method to access the— Perhaps your judgment is clouded by a hormonal surge. Dastin tells me this is rather common in postadolescent humans. You and Sarai are of that age."

"No surging with Sarai. None! She left me behind after I dragged her out of the river. She mention any of that to you?"

"No, but I suspected," Maru said. "Curious that she and I were separated after entering the Pinnacle but you and this Leeta were not."

"Why do you . . . not know the reason that happened?" Jayce asked.

"I assume it is the Pinnacle continuing to test all who enter. The Sodality has speculations on this phenomenon, but no concrete theories or explanations. Paragons strive toward a more perfect understanding of all things. But some puzzles are more difficult than others. Come, let us keep moving. Tell me what's happened to you."

Jayce got Maru up to speed, giving extra details about Leeta to prove to Maru—and himself—that she was a real person.

Maru listened attentively, then stopped when they reached a statue of a four-armed warrior wielding a pole arm on either side of his body.

"Sarai said you two became separated in the river. Likely she did not want you to reach the Pinnacle and claim the stone at the top," Maru said. "She has a number of insecurities that I have been unable to train out of her."

"And when were you going to tell me that this hilt belonged to her father?" Jayce asked.

"When the time was right," Maru said. "I worried that knowing you had such an auspicious weapon would go to your head. Make you overly confident in dangerous situations."

"Maru . . . can we stop with the secrets? Because now I'm paranoid that if I blink too hard you'll disappear and then I'll be left here with absolutely no clues as to what to do next. And it's not just me, Leeta needs you. You can do something with these, right?" He pointed to his anchor.

"The anchors are locked to the gates they came from, but if they're damaged before the seal breaks, it can release the bearer in the vicinity of their home gate," Maru said. "It's not recommended. You could reincorporate inside a wall or underground or—"

"Not what I want to hear!" Jayce shouted. "I just— Damn it!"

"I understand your frustration," Maru said.

"Do you? I told someone that needed help—your help—that there was a chance she might be able to survive this nightmare." Jayce turned away and crossed his arms.

"Did you tell her I had the skills and ability you hoped I had?" Maru asked.

"No, I just said you're one of the most skilled Paragons in the entire Sodality and if anyone would be able to help her, it would be you." Jayce lowered his head.

"Then you told the truth and acted with kindness to one in need. What more could anyone ask of you?"

"I was going to swap anchors with her if you couldn't help," Jayce said.

"There's altruism, and then there's stupidity," Maru said. "Are you prepared to wield a soul stone from the Pinnacle, Jayce?"

"As I have no idea how to do that, I'll go with no."

"If you returned to her gate to fight the Syndicate, you'd likely explode trying to control powers you do not understand. We cannot save everyone, Jayce. We must save those we can when we can," Maru said. "Being a Paragon is not easy. Even we have limits."

"I couldn't help Kay," Jayce said. "I feel guilty enough for losing a friend. I'd rather not lose anyone else if I can help it."

"Sarai didn't need you when she fell into the river?" Maru asked.

"Well, that . . . that shouldn't count."

"It certainly mattered to her. And me. And countless others across the Governance," Maru said. "Many Attuned lack your essential humanity, Jayce. You will become a great Paragon one day and I will be honored to continue your training. Now, I fear for both Sarai and this Leeta person right now. We need to find them."

"And we do that by . . ."

"We continue the ascent. The Pinnacle is the domain of the Sainted One. I suspect he is the intelligence that tests everyone who enters. The soul stones he protects are of particular importance," Maru said.

"They have something to do with the Cycle?"

"That is the assumption, but no one has ever made it this far before," Maru said.

"I'm honored. Hold on, what was that vision with Taras and the Tyrant that I had?" Jayce asked. "Did that really happen?"

"It was not a vision. You stepped into the past," Maru said. "Marshall Tulkan and I were gravely injured during the initial fight with the Tyrant. Tulkan, he is a Borasti. Downy fur. Arm. Leg?" Maru touched himself where Jayce had seen the other alien injured.

"That's him," Jayce said.

"You were definitely shown the past. Sarai's father struck down the Tyrant and stopped him from reaching the . . . It isn't relevant. We need to find Sarai before she's tested beyond her abilities."

"No, no! I want to know everything, Maru. Why are

you hiding things from me? Is this a Paragon trait or a you thing?"

"Not every secret will make you happy, Jayce. You know as much as Sarai at the moment, and if we dither here, she is at risk. Do you want to have a tantrum or do you want to find her?"

"Tantrum? I wasn't—Let's keep moving, then." Jayce looked away, embarrassed.

"Then to that stairwell." Maru pointed to a corner at the end of the statuary hall and an opening to stairs leading upward.

"Where did that—You know what? I don't need to understand everything. Let's keep going. Leeta and Sarai need me. Us. Mostly you."

Chapter 25

Sarai leaned through the opening of the tube and looked around the chamber beyond. The disc had stopped on its own and her heel stomps against it had no effect. The chamber's walls across from her were lost in shadow. The only thing in the room was a tall mirror with an ornately carved wooden frame. It was angled away from her, showing only the dark reflection of the curved wall near the tube.

She stepped out and the door closed behind her; the ivory and glass of the tube grew toward a center point. The disc in the tube sank into darkness without a sound.

"Oh no no no!" She slapped a palm against the lift, then ignited her hilt and swept its projected light across the room. She'd stumbled across Maru and the rest of their party a few hours before they all reached the Pinnacle. There'd been an enormous relief when Jayce was *not* there waiting for them. Maru and Dastin accepted her explanation that he'd been washed ashore before her and she hadn't seen him since. Dastin was fine with waiting at the base of the Pinnacle to tell Jayce that he'd lost his chance to go any farther as Maru was escorting *her* inside.

Which suited her just fine. The Pinnacle was her destiny, not his. Though, leaving him behind seemed to have caught up to her now. Maru had warned of trials within the Pinnacle. Being forced to act on her own suited her just fine, as the Pinnacle would find her worthy or not. She didn't need Maru or anyone else as a crutch.

Sarai braced her saber in front of her and stepped in front of the mirror. It was wide enough to show two people standing shoulder to shoulder and several feet taller than her. But she wasn't in the mirror; rather, on the other side was an identical chamber. She gave her hilt a waggle, and the light around her and in the reflection shifted.

"What in the Veil is happening?"

The reflection shifted without the mirror moving and came to a stop. There was a man in ornate armor kneeling in prayer on the other side. A Fulcrum formed into a broadsword glowed in front of a bent knee, his head bowed. The man had short, platinum-blond hair and dusky skin. He spoke in a low tone, repeating the same few sentences over and over again. She didn't recognize his armor or the style of his weapon.

Sarai canted her blade from side to side, and its light washed over the knight. He looked up, steel blue eyes focusing on her.

"Stay back!" She raised her saber. The glow from it both reflected off the mirror and shone through the glass to light up the man's face.

The knight reached forward and flicked a finger against

the glass. It rang like a bell for several seconds. One side of his face was badly scarred. He regarded her with something between surprise and scorn.

"I am safe from you," he said, his voice raspy.

"Something tells me you can hold your own." She kept her guard up. "How long have you been in here? Do you know a way out?"

"Time is different here," he said. "The better question is, which of us is in the future and which is in the past?"

"Why? Why is it like this?" She glanced around.

"They want it this way. It's all part of their game. They need the Cycle to continue, no matter how much damage it causes," he said. "No matter how much suffering it causes. But we are stronger than them . . . little one."

"That's why you're here?" she asked. "To stop this Cycle?"

The knight exhaled slowly.

"Why are *you* here?" he asked. "All alone in this place."

"Maybe it's best we don't share with each other." Sarai lowered her blade slightly. "If the Pinnacle wants us to see each other, there must be a reason for it."

"They say if you reach the Pinnacle you can see one of them. Stare a god in the face and demand to know why they have set us into this life just to suffer. We can free ourselves from them. Do you know the myth of the crippled saint?"

"Can't say I do," she said.

"Some say she created the Cycle with an iron-hearted demon. They wanted to bring all souls to divinity, but their conflict trapped us all here. Life. Death. Pain. Suffering. Over and over again. All for nothing," he said. "I must end it. Save us all."

"Mighty noble of you," she said. "How're you going to do that stuck in here?"

"One of the gods wants the Cycle to end. He said I can find the key here . . ."

Sarai swallowed hard. An icy fear grew in her chest.

"How long have you been waiting? How will you know if you find it?"

"I will wait until the stars burn out. What is the price of time when all souls can be saved?" The knight leaned back slightly, and dust fell from his shoulders and arms. "Do you enjoy your suffering?"

"I don't know who or what you are, but this conversation is over," She touched the mirror frame and tried to lift it up, but it had solidified with age. In the mirror, light coalesced behind the knight into a humanoid figure. A spear made of light formed in its hand and it readied a strike.

"Look out!" Sarai sidestepped, avoiding the spear out of instinct.

A spear tip made from solid light thrust through the knight and burst through the faux-mirror where she'd just stood. Glass shattered and fell to the floor. The spear held in place as the glass within the mirror disintegrated into dust.

A golem of ensorcelled armor plates kicked the frame away. The armor was hollow; strands of plasma and lightning made up the inside of the armor. The helmet snapped toward her; there were no eyes within, yet Sarai felt a presence that was deeply hostile. The thing had found a way through the mirror and had come for her.

Sarai ducked and rolled under the sword as it swiped

at her. She stabbed her saber into the golem's knee and the plasma strands coalesced around the tip and slapped it away with a snap and a sudden tang of ozone in the air.

The golem raised a foot and stomped at her. Sarai braced the flat of her blade against her hand and caught the stomp. Energy flowed through her saber and the sabaton burst apart in a flash of light.

The golem reared back. It stuck its damaged leg into the floor and chopped at her. Sarai knocked the blade aside and cut through the golem's arm with a quick back slash. She thrust the saber beneath the chin of the golem's helmet and twisted hard. Its helm popped off and the plasma roiling through its form died back with snaps and pops.

"What . . . what the hell was that?" Sarai kicked one of the armor plates away. The wood of the mirror frame rotted away before her eyes, filling the chamber with the smell of a deep forest.

She lifted her face to the ceiling lost to the darkness overhead.

"This all part of the test?" she asked. "Send the rest! I'm sick of these games." Sarai lifted her arms to her side and spun around slowly.

A small point on the lift tube crumbled; the disintegration radiated outward until a portal to a waiting disc appeared.

"More? Yeah? Fine. I will make it to the top." She shook her saber slightly and deactivated it. "I will finish what my father started. That stone will be mine."

Sarai hopped onto the disc.

* * *

Jayce came out of the stairwell and leaned against the wall, his chest heaving and hands on his thighs. Maru stepped past him, his glaive ignited and ready. The chamber dissolved into darkness. A narrow walkway appeared. It glowed from within and led into the deep night. A doorway of solid light rose in the distance.

"So. Many. Steps," Jayce said between breaths.

"No excuse to lower your guard," Maru said. "We're close to the top . . . I can sense it."

"Maru . . . what is all this? I don't like it," Jayce said.

"The path forward is quite clear. Come." Maru went toward the beginning of the walkway.

"No!" Jayce straightened up. "I'm sick of being carted around like a hull full of fish. What's so damn important in here? Why aren't you telling me everything? Why haven't we found Leeta yet?"

"No concern for Sarai?" Maru lowered his glaive.

Jayce rolled his eyes. "Her too. I want some answers, Maru. Where are we going and why?"

"As you need to catch your breath after that exertion . . . and as I have not earned your complete trust, then let us discuss the end of all things." Maru fiddled with his glaive, tapping the flat of his blade against his shin. "Do you believe life is a natural occurrence in the universe?"

"Wow, starting off with the easy questions, huh? I haven't put a lot of thought into that." Jayce took a sip from the canteen on his belt.

"Even before the Collapse, records from civilizations— active and extinct—never found any trace of life anywhere in the galaxy before about six and a half million years ago. Despite worlds existing in the golden zone that would support and nurture life for billions of years before that ... nothing. Not even microbial fossils. Then, for reasons we don't have a full explanation for, life began all across the galaxy at exactly the same time."

"I know how to read water, fish, and fight in the Scale pits. I haven't been through a whole lot of fancy schoolin' like Sarai, but ... that doesn't seem natural." Jayce swished water around his mouth and swallowed. "Religion back home was all about warning off bad luck. Never got into any deep discussions about where life came from. So how does life just happen everywhere all at once?"

"The chance of that is quite improbable. Some theorize an intelligence from beyond the galaxy seeded the stars for reasons unknown to us. Others believe that the Veil was involved. One glaring problem is that if an intelligence was capable of creating life as we know it, why create so many diverse species? Why design it to end in death?"

"I don't have answers to that. Been a rough couple of days, Maru."

"You demanded answers, and I am giving them to you as best I can. The cycle of life and death has been with us for longer than we've been able to contemplate it. The Sodality believes the Collapse of the Ancients had something to do with attempts to break the Cycle."

"Not thinking machines that went rogue?"

"AIs are a particularly dangerous invention. Once given enough power and freedom, they always eclipse what their biological creators are capable of. Their rate of evolution and advancement are terrifying to behold. Species that unleash AIs quickly go extinct as their creations find them ... limiting. We've seen this happen on planets after the Collapse. The Ancients seem to have kept their AI on a short leash, never giving them full freedom. But, at some point, the Ancients attempted to use their AI to solve the final mystery: death," Maru said.

"How is a computer supposed to stop things from dying?" Jayce asked.

"The Veil is eternal and unchanging. What we see and experience here is a reflection of our dimension. The Ancients attempted to ... merge this reality with ours. Create bodies free from the decay of entropy and join their souls with these new constructs that the AI designed for them after enough study of the Veil. They were not afraid of death. Rather, they believed it was their purpose to conquer death after being placed in this universe by ... whatever created them and us."

"What? The Ancients aren't us. Us in ancient times, I mean," Jayce said.

"The Ancients were a cybernetically enhanced species from what few remains we've found. Many species we know—including humans like you—were uplifted to serve them. Whatever species they were originally was lost in the Collapse. The current hypothesis is that the Ancients feared AI, but modified themselves to compete with AIs' capability. At some point, they decided to unleash the potential of AI and when the AI proposed a way for the Ancients to transfer their souls to vessels drawn from the Veil ... something catastrophic happened. The more religiously inclined among the Paragons believed they were punished by the Veil for their hubris to escape the inevitability of death."

"And the more science minded?" Jayce touched the crystalline wall next to the stairwell.

"They postulate that the Ancients made a mistake. One they could correct with enough time and study," Maru said.

"That sounds stupid. What makes them think they can improve on what a civilization that ruled the entire— They've tried, haven't they?" Jayce put a hand to his face.

"Perceptive of you. During the Black Chanid Invasion, the man who became the Tyrant found an Ancient codex that laid out the final stages of their attempt. He needed two artifacts to recreate the ritual—or experiment. One was a spirit vessel created by the Ancients, an artificial body that would be immune to entropy once the final prize was obtained. The Sodality defeated him before he could obtain the vessel . . . we assumed."

"That's not a good word," Jayce said.

"The Tyrant seemed quite dead when we left him aboard the *Purgation* before it exploded. His forces collapsed and the Governance returned, but we still came across the Tyrant's agents from time to time. They always had a purpose. Most of the time we caught or detected them searching for some bit of esoteric knowledge regarding the Ancients. Always toward the missing piece of the Ancients' riddle."

"Which would mean that the Tyrant had the machine or body the Ancients invented," Jayce said.

Maru nodded. "You are very perceptive. Sarai's initial impression of you was highly inaccurate. It doesn't necessarily mean that the Tyrant is still alive, but at the very least, someone is continuing his work."

"Oh. Oh! Oh no." Jayce frowned. "And the second artifact they need to repeat what the Ancients tried to do is..."

"The Saint's soul stone"—Maru pointed up—"which lies, according to legend, at the top of the Pinnacle. The Saint has many forms...you've seen him? The manifestations are different."

"I believe so." Jayce looked down the hallway.

"That stone has been sighted, but never claimed since the Collapse. I believe you or Sarai could be the first to claim it, but it *needs* to be you, Jayce," Maru said.

One of Jayce's eyebrows cocked up.

"Me? Me, the Deep-world scum that's brand new to all this, and not the golden child that's been raised to do this since birth like Sarai?" Jayce asked.

"Jayce, I have been Sarai's mentor and instructor for many years. She is not the right person to wield such power. Her intentions are not altruistic. She wants revenge against the Tyrant who killed her father and the Syndicate that she believes has frustrated her mother's efforts to repair the Governance. She would be an avenger with the Saint's stone."

"I'm all for taking down the Tyrant too. Remember? I want to become a Paragon for exactly that," Jayce said. "Maybe we should just crack our anchors and not let anyone go any farther—"

"Why did you try to help this Leeta person?" Maru asked.

"Because she needed the help. She'll end up as a slave if I don't help her."

"And why did Sarai abandon you after you escaped the

hydra? I know what she did. I'm no fool, my boy," Maru said.

"You'd have to ask her." Jayce looked aside. "If you know she's the wrong person, why bring her this far?"

"It is better for her to claim it than any Tyrant's agent. She's not lost, she can still be led to the light," Maru said. "The Sodality does not demand perfection from anyone."

"Good news for me, then," Jayce said. "But what happens if the Tyrant gets the stone?"

"There may be another intervention from the Saint. The Ancients tried to break the Cycle, they wanted to end death. When they came too close to breaking the natural order, their empire was cast down. Reduced the galaxy to base survival. Another Collapse would be cataclysmic, Jayce. The Sodality exists to prevent this."

"That's why you've brought me this far? To stop this disaster that *might* happen?" Jayce looked down at himself, then at Maru.

"You've accomplished a great deal on your own, young one. Do not doubt yourself. The Veil influences our reality. I do not believe our meeting was by accident or happenstance," Maru said.

"But why?" Jayce raised his voice. "Why would some superpowerful intelligence create life and then just leave the way to wreck it all just laying around?"

"Jayce, are there no sayings about tempting fate on your world?" Maru used the rather loose joints in his hands to wrap two fingers around each other in what Jayce assumed was a gesture to ward off evil.

"It's been a long day and I'm running out of patience," Jayce said.

"What brought life to the galaxy may not have been able to do it by simple command. There is a saying that the Sodality has uncovered through our quest, in many places and in many different languages. We do not know who originated it, but it says, 'As above, so below.' There is a reciprocal relationship between our reality and the Veil. One we do not fully understand. But we know what the Ancients did before they were cast down. We know what the Tyrant attempted. And what he may still be after. As such, I suggest we tarry no longer."

"This is a lot to take in," Jayce said.

"You asked."

"Then what—what do we do? We get the Pinnacle stone and then what?"

Maru tapped a claw tip on the empty ring on Jayce's harness.

"Let us get you to the stones before others can. Then get you back to the Sodality and keep it safe from the Tyrant," Maru said.

"You can't expect *me* to do this! F-find Sarai. She's the important one, not me. I don't know how to deal with all of this." Jayce edged back toward the stairs.

Maru put a hand on his shoulder.

"Power and authority are dangerous things in the wrong hands. The Tyrant nearly destroyed the galaxy because he was entrusted with too much by the old Governance. You would not have come this far if you were the wrong person, but we need to continue on. You've been given a gift, Jayce; you can find out exactly what you're capable of in here. Not many get that chance," Maru said.

"I'm starting to realize that working a trawler and taking Scale dives for the Syndicate may not have been that bad—Wait, did you say 'stones' earlier? How many are there?"

"Did I?" Maru got a faraway look to his eyes, then focused back on Jayce. "I must have misspoken. Stay close to me on the path, Jayce. There's something in the darkness watching us."

Maru stepped onto the glowing stone. Faint musical notes sounded with each footfall. The glow intensified around the edge of his boots each time he took a step.

"Ahs sodame ko dahl ... tad arima na egur methar ..." Jayce sang softly along as they walked toward the distant door of light.

"I do not recommend looking down," Maru said.

"Why?" Jayce peeked over the side. There was nothing but pure darkness below. "Nope. Mistake." Jayce fought a moment of vertigo.

"Young humans never listen. I wonder if it is genetic." Maru readied his glaive and moved with his feet in a combat stance. They continued on until the stairwell and the starting platform were lost to darkness.

"Jayce?" a voice sounded from the darkness.

Jayce froze.

"Jayce! Help me!" The voice was closer now. A woman's voice.

"Mom?" Jayce lowered his sword. "Mom, is that you?"

"No, Jayce, no—"

Jayce ignored Maru's warning and turned around. Behind him, a woman in tattered clothes clung to the edge of the glowing pathway.

"Mom!" Jayce ran to her and slid feetfirst to stop in front of her. Her eyes were the same auburn, full of terror from the last moment he saw her years ago. She grabbed him by the wrist and her feet swayed like they were underwater. Her touch was cold and slimy, like anything dredged off the ocean floor on Hemenway.

"Don't leave me again, please!" she pleaded.

"Mom . . ." An icy mote formed in his chest; old grief spread through his spirit. "I saw you go under. How can you be here if I lost you . . . but not Dad too?"

"He's not here. You should come to the depths with me," she said. "The dark welcomes everyone. You can be with me forever," Her face changed to a waterlogged and decayed gray. One eye sank back into her skull and her hair thinned and fell out. Her hands sprouted claws, the flesh decaying swiftly to expose bones.

Seawater gurgled out of her mouth, and she reached for the back of Jayce's head.

Maru's glaive severed her forearm. His strike continued to the mother's other wrist. She fell into the abyss, her body returned to the last living moments Jayce remembered of her. Her amputated limbs dissolved into motes of light and rose into the air.

"No!" Jayce thrust an arm down, but she was gone.

Maru pinned his shoulder to the walkway.

"You're being tested," Maru whispered into his ear. "Do not give up. Do not falter. You're meant to be here."

Tears streamed down Jayce's face. He slapped Maru's hand away and rolled to his back. He crawled backward, his countenance dark with rage.

"She . . . she was right there!" he shouted.

"She was not." Maru shook his head. "You could not save her when she died, Jayce. You were a child. She died to save you, didn't she?"

Jayce stopped. He wiped his nose and spat over the side of the walkway.

"I could have done something," he said. "She didn't have to die."

"What?" Maru squatted down to look him straight in the eyes. "What could a child have done in a storm like that?"

"Anything!" Jayce beat a fist against the walkway. "Three days! Three days I clung to a piece of wood that kept me from drowning before I was rescued. You think I didn't—didn't . . ."

Maru extended a hand to him.

Jayce swiped at it. Maru took the hit and kept his hand in the same place. Jayce choked down his emotions and accepted it. Maru helped him up, then hugged him.

"You have no guilt to carry, Jayce. She died so you may live. There is no greater love."

"I became a river rat to save people." Jayce wiped another tear away. "So no one else would lose someone like I did."

"Then you are a good man and—" Maru raised his chin suddenly, then pushed Jayce back slightly. "Something's coming. We fight back-to-back."

Howls sounded in the darkness. Death cries from dozens of people. Jayce pressed his back against Maru's and the two readied their weapons.

"When I give you the signal, you run for the door. Do not stop for anything, you understand me?" Maru said.

"What about you?" Jayce asked.

"I don't matter now. Only you do. Claim a stone. Break your anchor and get back to the Sodality on Cadorra. The High Paragons will know what to do," Maru said. "Up high!"

Maru thrust his glaive straight up and speared an apparition through a gossamer burial shroud that flowed like it was underwater.

An alien skull with a thick jawbone and three eye sockets clattered over the side of the pathway. Bits of flesh still clung to its bones as it crawled toward Jayce. He cracked the skull with a downward swipe. The skeleton collapsed into individual bones and rolled around the pathway.

More apparitions swooped in and out of the darkness.

"Stay close, move with me." Maru swatted another ghostly attacker away. Jayce slid his feet back, bumping into Maru's back as the undead came for them. Howls swirled around them as gale-force wind whipped into a funnel around them. They stood in the eye of a storm as rotting visages cried out against them for living.

Jayce parried a stinger from a bleached white scorpion and twisted his sword around the length of small bones and severed the end with a flick of his wrist. He put a hand on the pommel and thrust the blade to his left blind, felt the tip crack bones, then readied the blade parallel to just below his chin and split a skull of some reptilian apparition between the eyes.

The laments of the dead grew louder. Above, hundreds more descended toward them, flowing down the whirlpool.

"Jayce!" Maru grabbed him by the shoulder and pushed him in front of him. "Run!"

"I'm not leaving you!" he yelled.

"I will be one step behind you. Run. Run!"

Jayce sprinted toward the bright light of the exit. He vaulted over an apparition that swung a bone scythe at his knees and pulled away from grasping hands that tugged at his arms and legs.

The pathway ended in the same polished stone as the plaza outside the pinnacle. Jayce slid to a stop and turned back. Maru was well behind him. The Paragon leapt and spun through the growing swarm of undead, his glaive tearing through them and keeping most at bay.

"Maru!" Jayce gripped the edge of the doorway and reached out to Maru.

The Wottan faltered as he stepped onto the polished stones and fell forward, out of Jayce's reach.

The dead piled onto Maru, tearing at his clothes and biting at his exposed flesh.

Jayce felt the ghost of his mother and their final moments together on the sinking ship so many years ago. He abandoned the doorway and swung his blade in a wide arc, dispelling the spirits into evanescent howls, and seized Maru by the collar. He hauled them both backward and fell through the doorway.

Chapter 26

✳

He remembered a face. One made of countless stars and nebula. He felt a warmth—caring from a complete stranger that would never harm him or put demands on a pure love he hadn't felt since his mother had cared for him after a nightmare.

The face faded into nothing, and cold came over Jayce. He gasped and kicked out. He lay on a smooth marble floor, a pulsing hum in his ears.

"Maru?" He coughed and felt something against his shoulder.

The Paragon lay on his side, deep purple blood dribbling from his mouth.

"Maru!" Jayce rolled him onto his back. Long gashes ran down one side of his face; a finger bone from a skeleton jutted out of his chest.

"Ah . . . I don't recommend that," Maru croaked. He looked down at the impalement, then at Jayce. "Pull it. Pull it so my other lungs . . . can . . ."

"OK." Jayce stood over Maru and pulled at the bone.

He lifted Maru a few inches off the ground and the alien groaned in pain. It was embedded too deep to come out easily.

"Hurr . . . eee." Maru's skin took on shades of alabaster.

"Forgive me." Jayce planted a boot on Maru's chest and pulled the bone out in wet spurts. It broke free and blood splattered against Jayce's face. He spat out something that tasted like oversalted spice broth.

"Better." Maru pressed a hand over the wound. "A little better."

"That was so gross." He blew a raspberry. "Are you . . . going to live? I don't know first aid for fish people." Jayce tossed the bone behind him. It skittered across the ground and bumped against the base of a pillar that twisted into a dark haze overhead. A glow shone through like a bright moon behind clouds.

"My kind is quite hardy"—Maru held a hand up to Jayce for help up—"but we are not invincible. My gills can take up the slack until that lung stops collapsing when I try to breathe."

"Drop your anchor, get back to the *Iron Soul* and—"

Maru looked past Jayce, his eyes full of wonder.

Behind Jayce, a dais rose atop layers of cylindrical steps. Two Veil stones circled each other at the summit, one obsidian black with thin lines of gold, the other ivory white cracked through with silver.

"Oh . . . they're beautiful," Maru said. "I never thought I'd see them with my own eyes. Master Zeist's hypothesis was correct. I need to tell him."

"This is the end? This is the Pinnacle?" Jayce asked.

"Indeed. Jayce . . . claim one. Hurry." Maru's knees

buckled for a moment and Jayce had to keep him on his feet.

"Which one?" Jayce asked.

"You . . . you know." Maru used his glaive as a staff to keep himself steady. "Go! Go before it's too late for any of us."

Jayce let him go and stepped onto the bottom step.

"Jayce?" a soft voice asked. It wasn't his mother this time, but he recognized it instantly.

"Leeta?" He looked to his right and the young woman stepped out from behind a pillar. She looked worn out, with dried cuts down one side of her jaw.

She laughed with relief and raised her arms to him.

"Maru! It's her!" Jayce stepped off and went toward her.

Maru's glaive struck the ground blade first between them. Jayce stopped, and Leeta flinched back. The Paragon wrenched the glaive out and leveled it at her.

"Stay away," Maru said. "This thing is not what you think it is."

"Jayce . . . Jayce, you said he'd help me," Leeta pleaded. "What are you do—?"

Maru shoved Jayce back.

"You can change your face, but I can smell the Tyrant's stench on your soul." Maru twisted his hands against the haft of his glaive. "This thing isn't what you think it is, Jayce."

"Please! I just need your help," Leeta sobbed. "Jayce promised me you'd—"

Light flashed from Maru's blade and Leeta raised her hands to shield her eyes. For the briefest of moments, her skin became the color of an approaching storm and fangs showed from her mouth.

The light died back, and Leeta's countenance changed from fear to disgust. Her hand slipped into her blouse and she flipped a dark metal hilt into her hands with a flourish. He'd seen the blade before, back on the docks where Kay had died.

"Leeta?" Jayce's jaw dropped.

"Thank you for bringing him over the threshold," she sneered at Maru as her skin darkened and her eyes filled with a red glow. "You proved most useful to Count Nabren ... and to me." Her arms and shoulders filled with muscle.

Maru thrust his glaive at her face. A segmented blade cast from her hilt and parried the blow high. She twisted her grip and the ridges crimped around the glaive. A forked tongue licked at the edge. Maru tugged at his weapon, but the hold from Leeta's weapon was absolute.

"Jayce, go! I'll hold her off," Maru said.

"Yes, go on." Leeta winked at Jayce. "I'll be right here waiting for you." She flung the glaive to one side and bent backward. Maru's quick swing sailed over her exposed midriff and she planted her hands on her sword against the ground and flipped back to her feet with an acrobat's grace.

Jayce hesitated at the stairs. Leeta and Maru traded blows, their blades sliding against each other with the sound of cracking glass. Maru deflected a strike meant to decapitate him over his head and slammed the end cap of his glaive haft against Leeta's foot. She snarled in pain and raked long nails down Maru's cheek. Jayce ached to help, but the two flowed around each other so fast he knew he'd only get in Maru's way.

Leeta shook her head quickly and her features transformed into a more masculine countenance. He finally realized who she was. Leeta was the Tyrant's enforcer who nearly captured him on the dock back on Hemenway. She was Lahash.

Jayce turned and ran up the stairs, taking two at a time. The pillar of light between the stones was blinding, and every step higher felt like he was moving through clay.

"I have to help him!" Jayce got to the top and the light from the pillar stung his eyes but didn't impart any heat. The ivory and obsidian stones swept past him, orbiting the pillar faster and faster as he hesitated.

"Jayce!" Maru cried out.

Jayce reached for the dark stone and missed. He moved his palm to intercept the white Veil stone and it smacked into his palm.

Power shot down his arm and every cell of his body felt like it was on fire. He held the stone with a death grip as color drained from his hand. He remembered the horror of the mystic who had died at the shrine but held on. A vibration began in his hilt and a warm sensation beat down his forearm with every beat of his heart.

Jayce wrenched the stone away and thrust it into the air. A ray of light struck down from the sky and hit the stone.

Light washed over him and the only sound he could hear was the clash of blades.

"Maru?" He shook his head to clear the disorientation and found the Paragon and Lahash still dueling. Maru was bleeding from deep cuts on his arms and legs, but the Wottan was still fighting. Lahash's body had morphed into

male proportions with wide shoulders and a thick neck
and an ugly, battered face.

Maru parried a high strike and used the long heft as a
fulcrum to parry his sword to one side. Lahash set a foot
against the base of a pillar and a look of actual concern
crossed his face.

The Paragon thrust his glaive at a downward angle at
her midsection. He jumped off the base of the pillar and
the thrust missed beneath him and glanced off it.

Lahash braced one foot against the pillar and used it
to propel himself forward. Maru was too slow with his
parry and his opponent's blade sank into his chest up to
the hilt.

Lahash twisted it hard, face-to-face with Maru. His lips
pulled back to flash bloodstained lips as Maru faltered.

"He lives," Lahash growled. "And I will tell him how
you died."

Maru spat blood into Lahash's face and spun his body
off the impaling blade. The motion ripped the weapon out
of his flank but he used the momentum to slice Lahash
across his sword arm and upper chest. The Tyrant's agent
screamed in pain. He struck out at Maru and the edge
caught Maru's anchor band. The device fell to the ground
as Maru fumbled for it, dropping his glaive in the process.
Lahash cracked the anchor with a flick of his sword and
retreated into the surrounding gloom, leaving a trail of
blood behind him.

Maru stared at the broken anchor and fell to one knee
as his life's essence poured from a deep cut in his flank.
He tried to rise, then collapsed to the floor.

Jayce bounded down the stairs, the stone in his hand

pulsing with power. He pressed down on Maru's wound to try and stem the bleeding, but his hand nearly slipped into the alien's chest.

"Maru? Maru, no!" Jayce put the Paragon's hand around his with the stone. "What can I do? Can this help you?"

"He's still close." Maru hacked up blood. "I-I'm sorry . . . Proud of you."

"I'll get you out." Jayce pulled off his own anchor. He wiped some blood off the talisman and stopped. There was a deep crack through it. It was either useless or would badly malfunction if used.

The wound in Maru's chest turned white and the fossilization spread slowly through his body as death overtook him.

"This is as far as I go. Farther than I ever thought possible. This is the Cycle. A life lost to save another is never wasted. This Sarai . . . she needs you. She's the other half, Jayce. You have to save her." Maru's eyes lost focus. "Go to the Sodality . . . they'll know what to do . . . with the stone. Tell Jessina I'm sorry. Sarai should . . . shh . . . it's cold, but least it doesn't hurt anymore."

The calcification spread up Maru's neck and his body went to an ashen gray. Maru slid off Jayce's knee. His shoulder struck the ground with a slight crunch; the stone broke into chalky clumps as it slowly degraded into dust.

Jayce stood, the stone in one hand and his lit blade in the other. Grief welled up inside him, but the threat of Lahash was still there. He heard something rustle behind him and spun around, guard high.

"No!"

Sarai stood in front of the glowing doorway, the shriek of banshees behind her and her jacket in tatters. She saw him standing over the dead Paragon, blade in hand.

"What have you done?" Sarai readied her weapon. The light pulsing off the blade bathed her face red.

"Sarai, wait!" Jayce kept his hilt at the ready while he backed toward a pillar to keep from being attacked from behind. Sarai advanced toward him, her anger rising. "There's someone else in here, she—he—works for the Tyrant and—"

"You expect me to believe anything you say? After you've killed him!" Sarai's gaze hung on Maru's crumbling body for a moment, then she turned and ran for the dais and ascended with determined speed. She didn't hesitate at the top and pried the obsidian stone out with a cry. The pillar of light jittered, the energy becoming more and more unstable.

Sarai pressed the stone to her chest and a column of dark light erupted from her mouth and eyes up and into the air. Her hand dropped and she stared at Jayce with pure hatred.

"You . . . you have taken everything from me!" she shouted. Her saber changed as dark motes ran from the hilt and formed a fresh edge.

"That's not what—Look out!"

Sarai raised her saber. She didn't see Lahash come up from behind her and jab a nail into the base of her neck. Sarai froze, then gagged like a fish with a hook down its throat as Lahash wrapped an arm around her waist to keep her from falling.

Jayce started up the stairs, but Lahash bared his fangs

and drew them across Sarai's neck, leaving two thin lines of blood. Jayce halted.

"I can only claim one of you." Lahash flicked the flower bracelet off his wrist, then plucked a talisman off the mesh of charms from the Docent divining rods. He flicked the case off an anchor and pressed it to Sarai's chest.

"She is far far more valuable than you. Thank you for leading me here. I'll tell my lord what a help you were." He snapped the anchor against Sarai and she vanished from the contact point out to the edges of her body, like she'd never even been there.

Lahash winked at Jayce, then cracked his own anchor with the same delicate gesture he used when they had first met.

The pillar of light grew wider and the dais cracked. The light expanded with each pulse, stinging his eyes and flashing heat across his skin. Jayce realized he had nowhere to run. He looked at the damaged anchor in his hand and ran a thumb over it.

"At least I have a chance." He broke the anchor and a pulse of cold passed through his body, and then everything was the same blinding light as the pillar.

Chapter 27

Ehran Tal huffed as he half jogged/half ran down a long passageway leading to docking bay 12. He'd been woken up in the middle of his well-known sleep hours. He was the Governance's senior-most bureaucrat for the fleet anchorage in Nashar's Star, and he expected a bit more deference and respect from the military—which he normally received!—but that damn Paragon had been most insistent on how *his* authority was different from Ehran's government rank.

Ehran wiped sweat from his pudgy forehead as a buzzer sounded down the empty passageway. This part of the station was closed off for maintenance but whatever emergency that Ehran simply had to handle insisted on docking someplace where the arrival could be obfuscated.

"It is entirely too early in the morning for this." He pressed his palm to a biometric reader and an access door slid open. The bay was empty, but the doors were already open to the void. An aquamarine ice giant turned in the distance; running lights on the orbital halos close to the visible pole blinked on and off as helium isotope harvesting continued.

Ehran put his hands on his hips and frowned. There was no one here. If this was all some sort of elaborate prank, the perpetrator would find themselves transferred to some crap world in the Deep and their finances audited after a series of phone calls. One did not poke a Governance civil servant of his stature without consequences.

The stars beyond the station wavered and a gunship de-cloaked as it slid through the force field. Heat-stained plasma cannons jutted out from beneath the prow of the ship; missile and torpedo ports closed as it sat down with barely a sound. A point-defense ventral turret slewed toward him and locked a pair of high-caliber coil guns on his august personage.

Ehran froze, unsure of what he'd done to bring such hostility into his life. One of his first official duties to the Governance was an incident and compensation report for a civilian ship that had "accidentally" been engaged by an Orbital Guard cutter's coil guns. Any attempt to avoid the gunship's fire would only expand the damage it would inflict on the station, and he wouldn't wish the excess paperwork on any civil servant.

He looked over the gunship's hull for any unit markings to complain to the commanding officer at least two levels above whoever was flying the ship. When he spotted none, his heart skipped a beat.

Things made much more sense now.

Ehran smoothed out his thinning hair over the top of his head and composed himself as best he could as a small ramp lowered from the gun ship. A pair of Marines in crimson Light Armor and coil carbines hopped off the ramp and swept the dock with their weapons. One had the common courtesy to *not* point his muzzle at Ehran.

A moment later and a man in the same armor, but different from the others' by a captain's rank pip, marched down the ramp and made directly for Ehran. He removed his helmet and the glower of a young man who'd seen far too much death and destruction for one life met Ehran's gaze.

"Well?" Captain Tarasin tucked his helmet under one arm.

"Yes? Yes! Sir, so sorry, I wasn't expecting an Umbral team here. At this hour. Or at all. I do have the requisite clearances and am aware that no records of your transit through this station are to be recorded or transmitted through any—"

"Was it you that sent the Code Nine Nine to my ship while she was underway?" Tarasin asked.

"Code Nine . . . Nine?" Ehran's mouth went dry and be began yammering. "Why would—No! It was absolutely not me. It was that Paragon! I didn't want him on this station to begin with and he's been nothing but a pest. To invoke that code is a massive—"

Tarasin put an armored hand on Ehran's shoulder. Gouges down the forearm plating spoke of a recent battle against something clawed and awful.

"I have an idea which Paragon summoned me," Tarasin said. "Take me to him. Now."

"But he's in the deep core with the way stone and— Right this way!" Ehran smiled.

∗ ∗ ∗

The way stone in the center of the space station had been recovered in the upper atmosphere of the nearby ice giant several thousand years ago. The alliance of space-faring races that preceded the Governance had gone to great lengths and risk to raise the stone from the clouds and then build a focusing chamber around the way stone, which was oval shaped and nearly three times the size of the humans and alien Paragons who recovered it.

The way stone hung in the crystalline focusing chamber, silver light glinting off its alabaster-colored surface, thin lines of gold creeping over the surface. Some claimed the future could be derived from the patterns and signs gleaned from the threads. Many had stared at the way stone until they'd gone insane in the process.

Captain Tarasin arrived through a short entrance. He wasn't sure if being required to crouch was done to force a sense of awe and respect for the way stone, or if the initial builders had just been rather diminutive compared to most species in the galaxy.

He straightened up and gazed upon the way stone. His jaw fell open as a wave of static washed through his nerves. The stone spun slowly, the gold lines skittering back and forth.

"It *would* be you, wouldn't it?" a voice asked above him.

Tarasin looked up, one hand going to an empty holster.

A Paragon in dimly glowing Light Armor floated several yards away from Tarasin. The alien sat in the lotus position. His skin was magenta colored, long dark hair bound into a ponytail to reveal sharp ears. A tail bent over the alien's left leg and wavered across his lap, at odds with his otherwise still poise. One leg was noticeably leaner than the other even in the armor.

"Kairos. I thought it might be you," Tarasin inched back toward the chamber walls. Squat pyramid-shaped panels stretched from the floor all the way through the domed enclosure; each panel had a veil stone tip that gleamed with different colored lights. "You care to explain why you sent my ship an emergency message while we were underway in FTL? My shipmaster cracked his stone rerouting us through a hazard-rated shunt to get here and she is *pissed* like I have never seen before in my—"

"You are disrespecting the sanctity of this chamber," Kairos said. "We rarely even allow your kind in here."

"My kind? You pompous—Why did you call me here, Kairos? We've made our hellos," Tarasin said.

"Does your shipmaster not feel it? She didn't warn you?" Kairos floated down. One leg unlimbered from the lotus position easily, the other moved slower and stiffer. The alien took a moment to steady himself, like a sailor coming onto dry land for the first time in months. He opened pale yellow eyes that glowed slightly.

"She was preoccupied with keeping the ship stone from shattering." Tarasin shook his head. "Out with it."

"There's an undercurrent beyond the Veil. I've never felt anything like that before. None of the other Paragons I've been able to contact through the way stones have either, but they do indeed feel it. How to explain it to someone without the sight . . . It's like that time we made planetary assault on Orgithan and the shuttle's engines failed. That moment between 'everything is fine' and 'something is wrong.' That feeling in your chest before the fear hits."

"You brought me here because of your *feelings*?" Tarasin crossed his arms over his chest.

"There's more than that." Kairos raised a hand and a faint aurora formed around his fingers. The golden lines shifted into space lanes through the sector. Motes pooled along the routes, the brightest one closed toward the Nashar system. "Fleets are moving, Tarasin. Fleets I can't identify or determine where they originated from."

"Mmm," Tarasin stroked his chin. He felt a slight stubble and chided himself for letting his discipline slip. "The Thirty-Seventh Fleet is anchored here. Did you think my Umbrals will turn the tide when there's a dozen battleship-class ships of the line along with—"

"Always the line between arrogance and reasonability with you." Kairos shook the aurora from his hand. "Do you know where Paragon Maru is?"

Tarasin's face hardened.

"No. Why?"

"Last word we had from him is that he's in this sector hunting down a gate world to escort everyone's favorite heir apparent to claim a stone. I've known him long enough that I can sense him beyond the Veil. I believe they entered through Besh VIII but I may be wrong." Kairos shook his head quickly. "I sensed him and then I was compelled to send a Code Nine Nine for assistance. Then you arrived and my faith is strengthened and my soul terrified by the implications."

"Wait. You were communing with the great... beyond"—Tarasin shrugged—"and you got some sort of magic tinglies to skip at least three links in the chain of command and Governance review to send a Code Nine Nine and you weren't sure *why?*"

"Yes. Precisely. Paragon Maru would understand. Any Attuned would understand, but your soul lacks the connection to—But *you* came. I sent the summons into the ether and it was your ship that answered and it is you that is here now. Not a coincidence."

"I have criticism that I will not say in this holy of holies of yours," Tarasin muttered. "So you're saying the Veil wiggled your nose and that's how I ended up here. That's the will of...whatever it is your types go on your Pilgrimages to see."

"You're accepting this better than I thought you would," Kairos said.

"I've served with enough Attuned to appreciate that strange things happen around you all. I'm here now. What do you need me to do?"

Kairos nodded. "I'm not entirely sure."

"What? What about that fleet on approach?"

"Not sure, but it would be prudent to have the Thirty-Seventh alerted. I just divined the threat a few moments before you arrived. Again, too fortuitous to be a coincidence. I've sent an alert to the shipmaster of the *Star Strider*, that's Admiral Julkatta's flagship."

"Do I...need to be in here?" Tarasin asked.

"Aboard the station? No...I'm rather surprised you came in here," Kairos said.

Tarasin flapped his arms against his sides in frustration.

"I'll contact the *Star Strider*...How's your leg?" Tarasin glanced at the Paragon's skinnier limb.

"Still artificial. Yes, I'm still angry with you." Kairos unhooked his hilt from his belt and tapped the end cap against metal within his pants leg.

"I saved the rest of you, didn't I?" Tarasin smiled.

Kairos did not smile back.

Chapter 28

※

Jayce felt a stiff breeze swirling around him. He opened his eyes and saw a perfectly normal blue sky and white clouds. He flipped over and saw the forest of Illara rushing at him.

He let out a series of panicky noises as his arms pinwheeled and the Veil stone in his hand flared with light. Dirt and broken branches exploded around him as he hit the ground.

He wiped soil off his face and looked around. He lay in a crater, a hiss of Veil energy surrounding him. The stone in his hand had dimmed, but its light was growing back. Something had lessened the impact of his fall, and he wasn't sure if the stone had done it or he'd willed that action into being through the terror of a sudden and fatal sudden stop against terra firma.

"Ow!" Jayce lifted his hilt to check that it was still there, then lay in the dirt for a moment. He rolled onto his back. The world felt correct, with the smell of rotting wood and mud all around him. The sky was blue and still, but for high wisps of clouds moving overhead. He'd escaped from the Veil, but he didn't feel like he'd accomplished anything.

Maru was dead. "Leeta" was really an agent for the Tyrant and he'd led the assassin straight into the Pinnacle. Sarai was this Lahash's prisoner. Jayce had no good idea of where he'd landed, other than somewhere on Illara after he'd broken his anchor. Where had Lahash taken Sarai with his own anchors? They could be close . . .

Jayce struggled to his feet. The stone had mitigated much of the impact but not all of it. He felt where bruises and sprains would begin to hurt once the adrenaline wore off.

At least nothing was broken.

"I need . . . Dastin. He'll know what to do. Everyone leaves at the same time when they break their anchors, right? So he's out here. If he's alive." Jayce climbed out of the crater and looked around. Insects buzzed in the swampy area, but there were no sounds of vehicles or other people. He had nothing but his weapon, the stone, and the clothes on his back. He fished out the water tube and took a sip, spat out muddy grit, then felt his back. The water blister had torn open at some point.

"I can't tell if things just got better or worse," Jayce said.

In the distance, a howl ululated through the forest.

"When am I going to learn not to say things like that?" Jayce tried to ignite his hilt, but he felt resistance from it. "What? I don't know how much of Sarai's dad is still in there, but I'm not going to abandon her. She's—she's probably on this planet. The Tyrant's soldiers followed us to this planet . . . she's still here."

The blade ignited. The edge was white hot and hurt to look at directly. The howling grew louder, and Jayce knew what was coming for him.

Jayce moved into a clearing. The Pinnacle stone was too large for the ring on his harness. He kept it in his hand and took a deep breath. He felt Reman bounding through the woods. The edge of his senses had an electrical static to them that he didn't understand.

Maru's warning about destroying himself with the power of his new stone was still with him. He wasn't sure which would be worse: the stone blowing up in his face or what Reman would do when he found him.

"I can't help anyone if I'm dead." Jayce beat the flat of his blade against his clenched fist around the stone. Plasma tendrils stretched from the weapon to his stone.

Reman burst out of the underbrush and landed on a fallen tree. His cybernetics had been replaced and a Veil stone glowed from his harness. The tips of his hackles pulsed with Veil energy.

"I still have your scent, meat!" The Draug's metal teeth glistened with spit. He flexed the cybernetic muscles of his right arm and Jayce noted how stiff the fresh implants were.

"Where's Sarai?" Jayce raised his sword. Light pulsed from between his fingers and Reman slunk back slightly. The alien wasn't as confident or aggressive as the last time they met.

"Duty demands I take that stone. I'll kill you for the fun of it!" Reman ignited long Veil-blade claws from his forearm rig and leapt at Jayce.

Jayce punched his stone-bearing fist at the Draug and

an energy shield cast from the stone and deflected the claws. He ducked under Reman and jabbed at him with his sword. The tip scraped against Reman's harness shield and the two swung back around to face each other for the next tilt.

Reman angled one leg behind him to hide whatever damage Jayce might have inflicted.

A buzz built in Jayce's ears and the stone in his grasp felt like it was about to burst into flames.

Reman rose to standing, head and shoulders over Jayce. He lunged forward and arced his claws downward at Jayce's face. Jayce sprang to one side and stabbed his blade into Reman's flesh-and-blood shoulder. Reman's harness shield flared again, and the alien snarled in pain. Jayce misjudged his next cut and it swept under Reman's arm. Claws raked at Jayce's face and the stone in his hand flared brightly.

He felt a sting across his forehead and blood seeped down his face, but he wasn't injured too badly.

The scent of blood triggered something inside Reman and he launched a flurry of attacks against Jayce.

Jayce intercepted the blows with his sword, slowing them just enough that his own shielding took the brunt of the force, but every hit still landed like a punch. Jayce thrust one leg back and stabbed weakly into Reman's stomach. The blade cut through the shield and cut a long gash down the Draug's abdomen.

Reman barked in pain.

Jayce hacked at Reman, beating him back. He jumped up and thrust his sword at his foe's throat.

Reman jammed his claws together, trapping Jayce's blade between them.

The two stared eye to eye for a split second. Something twitched behind Reman's real eye. A moment of fear and doubt. Jayce wasn't the easy prey he should've been.

"This is for Kay!" Jayce landed an uppercut against Reman's chest, and he felt ribs crack against the Veil-stone power in his fist. Reman's feet came off the ground and his claws deactivated. Jayce fell back to his prizefighting skills and beat Reman mercilessly with his one fist. He hooked a punch into the Draug's face and knocked metal teeth out of his mouth. He raised his hand up next to his ear and landed a downward-angled blow that sent Reman to his knees.

Jayce slashed his blade across Reman's throat, twisting around as blood sprayed into the air. He fell face-first into the bog and didn't get up.

Reman's limbs jerked and spasmed for a moment, then he went limp and sank into the mud.

"Ah!" Jayce's hand felt like it was on fire. He dropped his hilt and fell to his knees, then with his free hand gripped his wrist and fought to control the power coursing through him. The light was so strong that he could see his finger bones.

"No! I can't—can't . . ."

Through the pain, a melody chimed. Jayce sucked in a breath and began singing.

"Ahs sodame ko dahl . . . tad arima na egur methar . . ."
The power subsided with the pain and Jayce forced his hand open. He looked up, unsure who to thank for the inspiration to calm the stone. He picked up the muddy hilt and shook it clean.

Reman lay dead. Blood pooled around him in the bog.

"Which way?" Jayce looked around. "Which way did you come from? You must have gone in and out of the Veil through the same gate as Leeta—no, Lahash. There never was a Leeta."

A rumble of engines built in the distance. The skiff skirted over distant treetops, not on an intercept course for Jayce.

"Hey!" He waved his hilt overhead. "Little help!"

The skiff disappeared over the jungle.

"Ah . . . damn i—Oh, what is happening?"

Light broke over Jayce and a shunt portal formed over his head. It fell onto him and Jayce vanished from Illara.

Jayce fell onto the shunt platform aboard the *Iron Soul*. He coughed hard, then retched out what little water was still in his stomach.

"Jayce? Where are Maru and Sarai? Neither is at the gate." Uusanar leaned out of his command cradle. The alien's long neck swayed to and fro as he waited for an answer.

"Shunt Sarai up here." Jayce rolled off the platform, both arms clutching the tempest roiling through his stomach. "She's . . . she's got a stone like mine."

"I wasn't entirely sure you were you when I pulled you up," Uusanar said. "The Veil energy readings are enormous and—"

"Just do it!" Jayce's guts twisted like there was a knife in them.

"I cannot detect any other Veil emanations similar to yours." Uusanar blinked, and his eyes went milky white. "I do sense the same Tyrant battleship from Hemenway.

It is coming right for us and our escape window is closing."

"Dastin? Eabani?" Jayce set his face against the deck and appreciated how cool it felt.

"They've just boarded the skiff and will dock with us in the next two minutes," Uusanar said. "I'm violating a number of Pilgrim orbital regulations and I don't know what will be cheaper: a new black-market transponder or the fines. Where are Maru and Sarai? What happened in there?"

"Maru—Maru is dead. The Tyrant has Sarai." Jayce groaned in pain. "Why does this hurt so much?"

"Maru is gone? But I was just speaking to him before you all made planetfall. How can the Tyrant have Sarai? The Tyrant is dead by all accounts," Uusanar said. The deck canted from side to side, which only made Jayce's nausea worse.

"My shunt lock on you was imperfect as there was a high degree of interference from your new Veil stone. There should be no permanent damage," Uusanar said.

"I'm not cleaning this mess up." Jayce slunk to the deck. He gave Uusanar the high points of the journey through the Veil between coughing fits.

Dastin burst into the control chamber. He rolled Jayce over and grabbed him by the shirt and shook him hard.

"Where is she? Where is Sarai?"

"They took her," Jayce said. "I . . . I couldn't stop them. Maru's dead, Dastin."

Dastin froze in shock for a moment, then relaxed his hold on Jayce.

"As awful as current events have been"—Uusanar raised his four-fingered hands and tapped at holo globes spinning around him—"the Tyrant battleship is closing on us and if we do not engage FTL very soon our problems will compound. Who has command? As this ship is assigned to the Sodality, then Jayce has seniority."

"We have to—Mmrph!" Jayce struggled as Dastin slapped a hand over his mouth.

"No, he's not a Paragon yet," Dastin said. "Get us to Nashar's Star and then take the ley line straight to Cadorra. We have to tell the Sodality and Prefect Jessina what's happened."

"A most prudent course of action," Uusanar said. "Jumping to FTL in three . . . two . . . one."

Lahash removed his helmet as his skiff bounded over treetops. Sarai lay at his feet, her hands bound in thick metal covers, her wrists, knees, and ankles shackled together. A dark helmet covered her head and shoulders. Auto injectors hissed as they adjusted sedatives to keep her unconscious.

The dark stone pulsed from a box hanging from a chain around her neck. One of Lahash's soldiers had been disintegrated when he picked up the stone after Sarai came through the Aperture gate with Lahash, Reman, and the rest of her expedition. Lahash had used a small antigrav device to manipulate the stone into a containment vessel, then placed it around Sarai's neck.

"We've found him." The helmsman banked the skiff to port and stopped over the muddy clearing where Jayce had impacted.

"Too soon." Lahash jumped off the skiff and went to Reman's body. "You've crossed over too soon, old friend. The Tyrant needs his acolytes to be sharp and functional. You're better than a mindless beast."

He spread the coarse hair on the back of Reman's neck and watched as a dark gray metal pulsed through his spinal column.

Reman's arms jerked. One hand slapped the shallow puddle and flailed around. His cyborg shoulder twitched and spat out muddy water from the faux muscles. A moment later, Reman's head rose up.

His skin was loose; his flesh eye had sunk slightly in the socket.

"I'm alive." His voice rumbled in his chest.

"Your Grip has taken you closer to the Tyrant's dream." Lahash lifted his chin, examining the damage. "Your body is rotting away, old friend. We need to get you into containment before the degradation hurts you even more. Your form is too beautiful for the tanks."

"The whelp . . . he was stronger than I thought." Reman touched his chest and pressed broken ribs against.

"You went for him without my permission," Lahash said. "I tried to warn you."

"I felt him. If I hadn't hunted him, he would have slipped away for sure. The same ship must be in orbit. I will face him again and when I do—"

"Our mission was to capture the daughter and stop the traitors from seizing the Pinnacle stones." Lahash nudged Sarai with his foot. "We accomplished more than that. Now we return to the *Purgation* without delay."

"We can take them!" Reman brandished his claws in anger and one broken finger drooped toward the ground.

"No risks. Not now. Not when we're so close to final victory." Lahash shook his head. "The girl has a part to play in it."

Chapter 29

"Let me go back back!" Neff flapped his skin wings. Dastin, Eabani, and Jayce sat in the command chamber. Uusanar's attention was wholly on the holo globes. Jayce had a blanket over his shoulders and nursed a cup of steaming broth.

"How many times do I have to say this?" Dastin rubbed his temples. "We will get you back to your nest as soon as . . . feasible. Eventually."

"Tell us again what happened to Sarai," Eabani said.

"It's not going to be any different the third time," Jayce said. "It's my fault and I know it."

"You ever come across a shape-shifter like this Leeta before?" Dastin asked.

"Didn't even know they existed." Jayce sipped his broth. "She was so . . . I was just trying to help her."

"What do we do now?" Eabani asked. "We're supposed to keep her safe, Dastin."

"You think I don't know that?" Dastin shouted. "We couldn't get into the Pinnacle. That was for Maru and the rest of the shinies to handle."

"You're making excuses," the Lirsu said.

"Reasons, not excuses, but neither make any bit of difference. Maru is dead and the Tyrant has Sarai," Dastin said. "At least we have a kid with some kind of super stone, and he smells like fish."

"Why no no one worried about Neff?" The Docent touched his abdomen and the Veil flakes clinked in his stomach. "I have hatchlings to feed!"

"If I'd have left you behind, you would've been killed by other Pilgrims before you got back to the boomtown," Dastin said. "You're welcome. Stop complaining."

"Neff, what can you tell me about this?" Jayce opened his hand and light from the stone shone through the command chamber. Even Uusanar paused to wonder at it.

"Bad bad!" Neff tucked his head into his wings. "Docents never go to the Pinnacle. Never! Smells stronger than the way stones in nexus systems. Put away!"

Jayce closed his hand.

"Sorry, kid," Dastin said. "We've got to get you back to the experts."

The command center's light went amber.

"There is an issue," Uusanar said. "I am dangerously close to permanently damaging my stone to keep this FTL acceleration, but there's a problem at Nashar's Star."

A holo appeared. Red points pulsed over the fourth planet around a blue star.

"Shit!" Dastin touched the holo and more fields appeared. "Are you sure?" he asked Uusanar.

"My surety grows the closer we get," the shipmaster said.

"What do all the red dots mean?" Jayce asked.

"There's a star jammer in-system," Dastin said. "We can get in, but we can't get out."

"If I try to exit FTL now it will tear us apart," Uusanar said. "You wanted speed, you must accept everything that comes along with it. I have to use the way stone there to transition back to real space."

Dastin put his hands on his hips, then gave Jayce a dirty look.

"I'm starting to think you're bad luck," the Marine said.

"What's a star jammer?" Jayce sipped his broth, too tired to get worked up over the comment.

"Big ship that prevents ships from entering FTL," Eabani said. "They're rare and expensive. Most of the time they're used to keep a navy ships from escaping during an invasion."

"Nashar's Star is the Thirty-Seventh Fleet's anchorage," Dastin said. "Who's going to attack there? Some alien power we don't know?"

"As if things can't get any worse," Neff muttered.

"The distortion pattern is familiar," Uusanar said. "It's of Governance manufacture."

"Or Tyrant era," Dastin said. "He enjoyed using scramblers to lock down systems."

"It's worse," Neff whined.

"Our vector may be advantageous." Uusanar flicked a finger and a course appeared through the Nashar system. It passed close to the large pulsing dot of the scrambler ship. "Whoever is attacking did not anticipate reinforcements from the Deep."

"The *Iron Soul* have heavy weapons aboard that you've kept hidden from us?" Dastin asked.

"Not me—him." Uusanar pointed at Jayce.

"What?" Jayce glanced around.

"The reason scramblers are so expensive is the Veil-fleck resonance sheath," Uusanar said.

"You can get us that close?" Dastin asked.

"No, but the skiff can," Uusanar said. "Maru came to me because I could be quite sneaky when needed. It is time to utilize my entire repertoire."

"I am so lost," Jayce said.

"Is it ready?" Dastin asked Uusanar.

"Has been for days," the shipmaster said.

"Come with me." Dastin slapped Jayce on the shoulder.

Dastin opened the door to the ship's armory. Jayce followed behind him. He shivered in the cold room.

"You gonna be all right?" Dastin went to a computer panel and began typing.

"From the shunting or the disaster in the Veil?" Jayce shrugged. "I'm pretty miserable from both, tell you the truth."

"I'll get you some anti-inflammatory pills and water. Ancient Marine cure for everything," Dastin said. "Maru approved all the specifications before he sent it through the assemblers."

A panel on the bulkhead spun open and a Light Armor suit appeared. Its color was hues of gray, but Jayce felt a tinge of excitement when he realized it was for him.

"The mounting ring on the harness is too small." Jayce raised the fist gripping his stone.

"Easy fix." Dastin tapped on a screen and something buzzed and whirled inside the bulkhead.

"I don't . . . I don't know how to use it." Jayce touched the sleeve of the armor and ran his hand down the light weave beneath the forearm plate.

"Hey, some good news," Dastin muttered. "Maru always said the tech didn't require much thought. The stones are bonded to you shiny boys and it reads your thoughts and intentions."

Dastin tapped the metal plate next to his cybernetic eye.

"This just works." He clacked cybernetic fingertips together. "Same theory."

There was a *ding* and a small box popped out of the bulkhead.

"Get changed," Dastin said. "It'll fit over simple enviro layers so you can recycle your body's water. It's void-rated without needing to pull from your harness and it has integrated holsters for your hilt and sidearm. Mount points for carbines and battle rifles on the back."

Jayce tossed away the tattered jacket and trousers, then slipped into the Light Armor. He stretched his arms and legs.

"Pinches between the shoulders," Jayce said.

"It'll mold to fit you better with use. Hold still." Dastin unscrewed the too-small stone-mounting ring and replaced it with a new one from the box.

Jayce flexed one hand and looked at himself in a mirror.

"Hey now, you look like a hero." Dastin put his hand on the back of Jayce's neck and gave him a quick shake.

"I don't feel like one," Jayce said. "It's like . . . like the time I found some of my father's old clothes and put them on."

"Put the stone in," Dastin backed up.

"Worried?" Jayce smirked at him.

"No! No." Dastin took another step back.

Jayce turned the stone over in his hand, then brought it up to the ring. It hummed as it neared, then leapt on its own into the harness. The Light Armor tightened against Jayce's body, then the sensation faded away, like he was wearing simple clothes.

"The color permanent?" Jayce ignited his hilt and the light weave glowed along with the blade.

"Huh, you remind me of him," Dastin said. "Same weapon."

"This belonged to Sarai's father," Jayce said. "I'm not sure why it chose me."

"First time I saw that was when Taras cut through my cell door," Dastin said. "I'd been in and out of the Tyrant's arena on Pelen IX for days. The noble that ran the place loved watching the turn. Loved watching those of us who hated the Tyrant get turned to him. Taras got me and a few others out before we could amuse the nobles. My own fault for getting captured. Thing is, the Tyrant will have me in the end."

"What do you mean? The Tyrant's dead." Jayce snapped a punch out and smiled when there was a flash of power off the knuckles.

"Look." Dastin pushed the back of his high collar down and showed Jayce a spiderweb of flesh and metal fused to the back of his spine. "I have the Grip. Courtesy of my first hours in a Tyrant POW camp. There's no science or med tech that can pry it out. Not without killing me in the process."

"What . . . what'll happen?" Jayce asked.

"I'll die. Maybe today. Maybe tomorrow. But one day it'll happen. The newer it is, the longer it takes to fully compromise the nervous system. Soon as the Grip detects that my body can't keep my brain alive—" He snapped his fingers. "Part of me will still be alive, the part that keeps all my years of experience and some memories. But it will make me a slave to the Tyrant. That's not living, kid. I die, you finish me off good and proper. Decapitation. Wreck my brainpan. Whatever it takes. You promise?"

"That's a hard thing to do," Jayce said.

"The Grip takes me and the Dastin you know will be gone. Only an enemy will remain. Little miss and Maru are—were—willing to do it. Do you hate me?"

"What? No!"

"Then why would you let me spend the rest of who knows how long as a slave to Tyrant?"

"I wouldn't!"

"Then it's settled. Thank you." Dastin nodded.

"I—wait . . . wait." Jayce narrowed his eyes. "I may not have actually killed that Draug on Illara."

Dastin put a hand over his face.

"He was dead in the mud, but I didn't finish him off like you told me—"

Dastin slapped Jayce on the back of his head.

"Hey! Things were chaotic and sorry I didn't remember *everything* you told me. The Draug's going to come after me again, isn't he?" Jayce frowned.

"And he'll be a hell of a lot harder to kill . . . You know what? We're going to focus on the nearest lethal target before we come out of FTL." Dastin cocked his knife hand up, then forced it back down.

Jayce tapped the empty holster built into his thigh plate.

"When do I get a gun?" he asked.

"Did the Veil teach you how to properly use a firearm?" Dastin asked.

"No . . ."

"No gun."

"But Gunny! I'm wielding the power of the Veil with this super stone and I've got a Paragon hero's sword. You can definitely trust me with a gun." Jayce nodded quickly.

Dastin handed Jayce his coil pistol.

"Shoot out the light and I'll give you any weapon you want." Dastin pointed to the ceiling.

"Easy." Jayce accidentally pinched his finger between the trigger and the trigger guard. He pulled it out with a smile, then extended his arm up and pulled the trigger. There was a buzz and nothing else.

Jayce flipped the gun around and looked down the barrel.

"What's wrong with it?" he asked.

"It doesn't have a magazine loaded and the safety is still engaged!" Dastin slapped Jayce on the back of the head again and snatched the weapon away. He slid the chamber back and verified the weapon was empty, then re-holstered it.

"No gun for you! Not until you're trained. Now get your ass to the skiff before I kick it all the way there!"

"Yes, Gunny!" Jayce ran out of the armory.

Chapter 30

✳

Jayce stood on a small lift in the center of the upper chamber of the skiff. He was in full Light Armor with his helmet donned and sealed. He could feel the Veil slipping away as the *Iron Soul* transitioned out of FTL.

The crew had had a nervous energy to them that bordered on panic since Jayce had boarded the skiff. Petty officers had shorter tempers and the Marines aboard were oddly quiet.

"I'm picking up more ship-stone beacons," Uusanar said through a shipboard channel that came through Jayce's helmet. *"Sending you the best readings I have."*

A holo screen appeared on the inside of his helmet over one eye. A swell of red diamonds moved slowly to envelop a swath of blue squares near a star fortress in distant orbit around an ocean world. White dots dashed away from the battle.

A large yellow circle pulsed behind the red diamonds.

"Which ones are we?" Jayce asked.

"Red diamonds, enemy. Blue squares, friendly. White

dots, civilians," Eabani said from his turret. "You can't figure that out?"

"Yes," Jayce nodded quickly. "Just . . . making sure. The yellow's the FTL jammer?"

"This guy's the best thing we've got right now?" a crewman said over the skiff's channel. "He doesn't know his ass from a hole in the ground and *he's* our new hope to—what? Why are you tapping your helmet? Something wrong with your comms . . . No, I'm not on that chan— Wait. Ah, fu—"

"Jayce." Dastin's portrait appeared in Jayce's helmet. He was in the other dorsal turret, on the opposite side of the outer hull from Eabani. "You don't understand what you're seeing, do you? Do you know when the last time the galaxy saw a void battle this size?"

"No. Pretend I spent my whole life on a backwater fishing planet that didn't even get the good holo series."

"Not since the revolt. The Thirty-Seventh Fleet is fighting more enemy capital ships than other star nations even have," Dastin said. "I'll give you three guesses who's attacking the system."

"The Tyrant's loyalists? But Maru said they were weak. Only had a few systems under their control."

"It ain't just Maru that's often wrong. Seems our intelligence services are going to have some explaining to do," Dastin said. "What? Yeah, he's active in this sector. Seconded to the Thirty-Seventh last I heard . . . Then we better not screw this up. A mother can only take so much."

"*Prepare for FTL transition,*" Uusanar announced. "*I shall meet you all again on Cadorra, or the afterlife. I prefer the former.* Iron Soul, *out.*"

"This is already going great," Jayce muttered to himself. "I can tell."

The skiff lurched forward as the *Iron Soul* came out of FTL. The skiff spat out of the main landing bay.

Jayce felt like a weight came off his shoulders as the Veil's presence faded away. Something scratched at the edge of his consciousness, like a radio set between two channels or the screech of a rusty engine.

The holo changed to a map of the system. The skiff was a pulsing blue dot closing rapidly on the scrambler vessel.

"Stealth systems engaged," Dastin said. "Hold all fire. We're riding the scrambler's wake and that should mask us as we close on the target."

On the map, the *Iron Soul* banked hard and flew away from the conflict. Just another civilian vehicle that stumbled into a fight she wouldn't want any part of.

"Passive sensors active," Dastin said. "We're getting a look at . . . By the Veil!"

Transponders of dead and dying vessels appeared on the map. Jayce didn't recognize the names, but that the Governance had left a trail of destruction behind the main formation of the 37th Fleet.

"See those belfry carriers?" Dastin pinged the map for Jayce. "Same class the Tyrant built. Definitely a Tyrant fleet on the assault. They're not supposed to have this many ships."

"What does this mean?" Jayce asked. "Why now?"

"I'm not an officer, I don't worry about the 'why' so much as the 'have everyone do the right thing at the right time the right way so we accomplish the mission and maybe not die.' We get you to the scrambler ship, you disable it, then we get to the Governance fleet before it can FTL out and we're left smiling at the biggest Tyrant fleet I've ever seen. You get me?"

"I get you, Gunny," Jayce said.

"See? If I was an officer I'd still be blathering through the paragraphs of the operations order," Dastin said.

"You should put in a packet for officer candidate's school," Eabani said.

"No, I like working for a living," Dastin said. "We're inside their combat void patrol bubble. Eyes open for interceptors."

"What happens if they see us?" Jayce asked as the skiff closed on the scrambler ship. The holo in his helmet switched to a prow camera and he saw the aft of the interdiction ship. Three large engines burned deep blue, surrounded by smaller thrusters. He made out an elliptical shape to the aft against the light.

Ahead of the scrambler ship, fireballs and plasma bolts swept back and forth as the Tyrant's fleet kept up its pursuit of the Governance ships.

"It's all right," Jayce told himself. "I was on the hull during FTL. I can do this too."

"Hot mike," Dastin said.

"What? Does speaker have a safety switch like your gun?" Jayce asked.

"Where did we find this guy?" a crewman asked. "Oh right, a Deep fringe fish bucket. Good thing I've got the extra life insurance for the wife and kids."

"Break break break," Dastin said. "Keep chatter to a minimum. You're up, kid, make sure your maglocks are engaged or you're gonna have a real bad time out there."

Jayce pressed his heels down and his boots clamped against the lift plate he stood on.

"Set," Jayce said.

"Hydraulics engaged. We'll reduce relative velocity to the target soon as we clear the aft. We like you, kid, shame to see you smeared against the hulls," Dastin said.

The plate lifted up on guide rails and an iris opened overhead. The void above had a sheen of yellow particles from the scrambler ship's engines. Jayce ducked as the plate brought him out onto the upper hull just as the skiff passed under the much larger ship.

Dastin was in the turret next to him. He gave Jayce a thumbs-up through the ballistic glass, then pointed up.

The scrambler's hull had a lattice of Veil flecks and dust built into it. Larger stones formed bright nodes every few dozen yards. Jayce stood and raised his hilt up, but even without igniting the blade, he could tell he couldn't reach it.

"Closer!" Jayce yelled. "Get me closer!"

The skiff rose slowly and Jayce ignited his blade. He thrust it up and the tip scraped through the Veil lattice.

The skiff rolled sharply and Jayce's ankles nearly broke from the sudden strain. Neon-yellow plasma bolts snapped overhead and the port side of the skiff careened off the scrambler's hull. The skiff rolled the other way and a bay-winged fighter roared passed them.

"We're spotted!" Dastin called out. "Get level for another pass!"

Turrets on the skiff opened fire and a fireball erupted on the far edge of the scrambler's ventral hull.

"Why don't we just shoot the—Hey!" Jayce had to fall

to his knees as the skiff almost smashed him against the hull as it readjusted course.

"The whole lattice projects the scramble field. It's all or nothing!" Dastin swung his turret around and the double-barreled plasma guns almost clipped Jayce.

"Not the time for bright ideas." Jayce reached back and stabbed his Fulcrum into the hull. The Veil energy ran through the lattice, causing a chain reaction throughout the entire ship. A section of the enemy ship exploded behind them, and bits of debris and flame grasped at him. A burning, jagged line marked his passing along the hull.

Jayce's Light Armor glowed to life. He felt the pokes and jabs from razor-sharp hull fragments, but there wasn't any pain, no warnings that his suit had lost integrity.

He thought of Maru and the Pinnacle, and the power from the stone on his harness coursed through his arm and into his weapon.

The entire lattice around the scrambler ship overcharged and blew out in a shower of silver dust.

"Ah!" Jayce recoiled as he felt the Veil flutter behind his eyes. He crouched down, his senses spinning from the blowback.

"Hot damn, it worked!" Dastin called out. "Hang on, kid, I'll get you back inside in just a—Incoming!"

A neon bolt narrowly missed Jayce atop the hull. Another flurry of shots struck the starboard side and pierced through the upper cargo bay. The disc he was maglocked to came unmoored and Jayce floated off the skiff.

"Wait for me!" Jayce unlocked his boots and flipped over. His fingertips scraped against the skiff's hull as it accelerated away from him. Jayce stabbed his blade into the skiff and twisted it to anchor himself in place. The blade cut through the hull and stopped inches from Dastin's face in his turret.

Jayce swung his feet down and locked them against the hull as the skiff's engines flared with full power behind him. The portal he'd come out of was mangled metal.

"Dastin, how do I get back inside?" he asked.

"Ah . . . you don't. Not for a while," the Marine said.

"I'm just supposed to stay"—the skiff jerked from side to side as it dodged fire from fighters—"stay out here?"

"It's not much better inside!" Dastin let off a long burst from his turret and a pair of pursuers erupted into fireballs.

Jayce looked back at the scrambler ship. Its elliptical hull crackled with uncontrolled energy. He felt something there and the stone in his harness grew warmer against his chest. Jayce reached out through the Veil and grasped his hand toward the ship, then made a fist and tugged.

The scrambler ship imploded as the lattice contracted.

The battle around them faltered for several seconds as both fleets realized that the balance of power in the engagement had suddenly shifted.

"Flagship's still functional," Dastin said. "Get us aboard the *Star Strider* before they seal up the aft docking bay."

The skiff dove toward a Governance warship trailing the rest of the fleet. Her engines were dim, and smoke bled out from battle damage across the hull.

"You think she's gonna make it out of here?" the pilot asked.

"You think we can get to any other ship before they jump to FTL? More flying. Less talking!"

"Aye, Gunny!" The pilot pushed the skiff faster. "Squawking identify friend or foe, but we're not getting a ping back."

"Then get on standard channels and tell them we're coming. And tell them not to shoot us either!" Dastin shouted.

Jayce crouched low against the hull as a different make of fighter flew parallel to them. Jayce waved at the pilot, whose expression was unreadable behind his or her visor.

The *Nova's Glow*'s main launch bay ran the entire length of the ship, with hangars built into the ceiling and the side bays. Several ships were already parked on the runways, some of them burnt-out wrecks, others with the same dark metal coloring of the Tyrant's fighters.

"Got a blocked runway," the pilot said. "Coming in hot. Hold on!"

The skiff clipped the bottom of the launch bay and her prow dug into the flattop, sending out a shower of sparks. It veered toward a wrecked lander and Jayce released his maglocks. He went flying and a cocoon of Veil energy enveloped him. He skipped across the deck like a stone over a lake, then came to a spinning halt next to a makeshift barricade of ship tenders and cargo containers, manned by soldiers in dark void armor.

Jayce looked up at a pair of Tyrant soldiers who seemed more shocked to see him than he was to see them. He stabbed one through the chest with his Fulcrum, then snapped it across his body to cleave the leg off the other soldier.

More Tyrant soldiers stopped firing around the barricade and turned their attention to him. A jolt of aggression from the hilt spurred Jayce into the attack. What he lacked in grace and fluidity he made up for in brute strength. He shoulder-charged the nearest soldier and a blast of plasma off his Light Armor sent the boarder into a trio of his fellows.

Jayce cut down two more with a spinning attack and waded into a mass of black-armored warriors. He hacked and punched at them, feeling jolts of pain from coil gun hits that his Light Armor energy shielding mitigated to almost nothing.

A soldier grabbed him by the arm with his hilt and stopped a strike that would've killed another soldier with bright yellow stripes down his shoulder and arm. Jayce dropped the hilt and caught it with his other hand in a reverse grip and stabbed at what he guessed was an officer.

The blade slid off the officer's harness shield, leaving Jayce exposed. Another soldier tackled Jayce from behind and more and more of the boarders dog-piled on top of him.

The officer snapped a fist to one side and a punch dagger snapped from a forearm housing. He stabbed at Jayce's stone as the rest of his men held Jayce in place. The first blow was knocked back. The second scraped down the edge of his ribs. The officer stuck the tip over his stone and forced it through the shielding a fraction of an inch at a time.

Jayce struggled, but the Light Armor had lost too much strength in the fighting to augment the cybernetic muscles in his suit.

He made out dead eyes behind the officer's visor, his face swimming in some sort of a liquid within the helmet.

The officer snapped his head to one side as a red plasma bolt struck him between the eyes. Jayce fell to the deck as a storm of plasma bolts shredded the boarders, killing them all within seconds.

A bolt clipped Jayce's shin and he cried out in pain.

"Cease fire! Cease fire!"

Jayce deactivated his hilt and held up a hand. A Governance Marine stood over him, a rank starburst on his chest over a dead stone in his harness. His armor was pitted and warped from fire and plasma strikes.

Jayce stared down the barrel of the Marine's gun as both fought to catch their breath.

"Hi," Jayce said. "I'm on your side. See all this mess? Me. You mind not shooting me now?"

The Marine took his helmet off. His face was covered in sweat and a swath of nasty bruises marred his skin from the orbit of one eye to his ear. Jayce thought he looked like something off the old recruitment posters still hung around shanty floats back home. He holstered his coil carbine and shouted orders to other Marines as they swept through the bay.

"Where'd you get that?" the Marine demanded, pointing at Jayce's deactivated hilt.

"Maru said it chose me." Jayce waggled it. "Does everyone know it but me?" A pulse of thought and his helmet retracted from his face.

"Kid? Kid!" Dastin ran through the cordon of Marines, Eabani close behind him. "You hurt?"

Jayce looked down at the burnt cut across his shin.

"Any sailing you can walk away from . . ." He held a hand up to Dastin and the Marine hauled him up. Jayce thought he could put weight on the injured leg, but his knee buckled from the pain, and he stumbled into the Marine officer.

"Dastin?" The officer's face went pale. "What are you doing here?"

Dastin pointed at Jayce. He put Jayce's arm over his shoulder and kept him up.

"Captain Tarasin . . . what're the odds?" Dastin's face fell and his eyes filled with grief. "Sir, we need to get this one back to Cadorra ASAP. There's been some developments."

"You don't say." Tarasin's mouth twitched. "The sudden assault by a Tyrant fleet on a way-stone system was a change of pace this morning. And we're already in FTL." He tilted his head toward the forward bay doors as they closed. The swirl and streaks of the Veil boundary were broken up by the dark outlines of nearby ships.

The doors shut with a metal clang and cheers rose from the Marines.

"Where's Maru?" Tarasin asked.

Dastin shook his head.

Tarasin's face grew angrier.

"And where is my sister?" He grabbed Dastin by the collar and shook the Marine.

"Why does he think we know—" Jayce frowned and his eyes darted from side to side in through. "Who's his sister?" he asked Eabani.

Eabani raised a hand slowly, then clamped it over Jayce's mouth.

"They took her," Dastin said softly. "I wasn't there when it happened. I couldn't be there." He pushed a finger against his gunnery sergeant rank pin and it popped out. He offered it to Tarasin.

Tarasin slapped the hand away.

"*Who* took her?"

Jayce wrenched his face away from Eabani's scaly hand. "You mean Sarai? Is that the sister you're talking about, because she never mentioned you to me but—"

"Where did you find this idiot?" Tarasin asked Dastin.

"He washed up on a dock out in the Deep," the Marine mumbled. "Maru kept him because he's Attuned and things got even more complicated from there."

"Sarai," Tarasin said firmly. "My sister. Where is she?"

"One of the Tyrant's agents kidnapped her"—Jayce touched the soul stone he got from the Pinnacle—"after she claimed the other one of these. Maru says that these stones can bring about another Collapse like the one that destroyed the Ancients and—"

Tarasin balled his fists and looked like he was about to strike Jayce. There were muffled words from the captain's earpiece and his face softened slightly.

"Bastards are still in the lower decks." Tarasin put his helmet back on. "I'm going to kill them all, then you both will tell me every last thing that happened. Get him to sickbay."

The captain spun around and jogged off; his Marines followed him away.

"I've got a feeling he's still gonna kick my ass later," Jayce asked. "He strikes me as the overprotective brother type."

Jayce looked down at his hilt, which once belonged to

Tarasin and Sarai's father. He felt power returning to the Pinnacle stone every time he breathed.

"I'm a counterfeit of a much better man, aren't I?"

"You've done good, kid." Dastin slapped his shoulder. "We're alive. So's everyone else on the skiff, by some miracle. We're heading to friendly stars. Believe it or not, kid, this is winning. Now let's get you taken care of."

Chapter 31

Jayce scratched his heel against his shin. The new flesh on his wound didn't hurt, but the itching was starting to get to him. The shuttle rumbled as it flew through turbulence. High clouds around the shuttle were lit up from a sea of light beneath them.

The shuttle was small but comfortable, a departure from the military-grade utility Jayce had experienced aboard the *Iron Soul* and *Star Strider*.

Jayce wore his new Light Armor, now colored in shades of red and gold—the Sodality's colors. He wasn't entirely comfortable with the finished uniform. The Syndicate had strict and draconian measures against anyone who ever "repped the colors" without explicit permission and indoctrination. Dastin assured him that the Sodality wasn't run by thugs, and Jayce needed to present something to give those about to meet him a bump in confidence.

The gunnery sergeant sat next to him in the shuttle. He wore his dress Governance Marine Corps uniform and had a fruit salad of ribbons and medals. Captain Tarasin, despite being many years younger, was in the same uniform and sported several more rows of ribbons and a few more badges that Jayce didn't recognize.

Tarasin hadn't shown much interest in Jayce after the debriefing once he'd secured every inch of the *Star Strider*. He was a few years older than Jayce, but every time Jayce looked at the Marine officer an acute sense of inadequacy came over him. Tarasin always projected an air of calm and command around him. Jayce never heard a snide remark about the captain during the FTL passage.

He had his ankles crossed and his chin lowered to his chest. Jayce thought the man was asleep until he spoke.

"You ever been this far into the Core before?" Tarasin asked.

"Huh? No, sir, just my world and Illara," Jayce said.

"And the Veil. Not many get in there." Tarasin raised his chin, then tilted his head toward a porthole. "Take a gander. Governance won't allow landings in the Capital District during a state of emergency. Doubt you'll ever get another chance to see it like this again."

Jayce went to the porthole and his breath caught in his chest.

A city stretched beyond the horizon. Skyscrapers reached so high that lit beacons at the tops didn't shine from atmospheric distortion. Raised maglev highways spiderwebbed through multiple levels and into stacks of housing blocks and smoking industrial sectors. Running lights from police cruisers pulsed as they loitered over the never-ending city.

"How many people live here?" Jayce asked.

"Pointless to count," Tarasin said. "Soon as a census is

done, so many births and deaths have happened that that the number is useless, but most agree it's around ten-ish billion."

"Final approach to the Citadel approved," came over the speakers and the shuttle descended.

Jayce sat down next to Dastin, who had been unusually quiet.

"Gunny . . . what do I do when we land?" Jayce asked.

"Head down. Mouth shut until you're asked direct questions," Dastin said. "The High Chancellor isn't one to waste time. She'll know what to do."

"She's not always rational," Tarasin said. "Especially when she's right about something she warned others about. Prefect Jessina will probably be waiting for me—us—soon as we land."

The shuttle passed into a hangar and landed. Jayce heard the thump of blast doors closing. The craft powered down and a flight of stairs unfolded from a side hatch. Tarasin was the first out; Jayce followed.

The landing bay was sterile, with pristine lighting built into the walls and floor, but there were no other ships.

A tall woman with golden hair done up high, golden threading woven through the style to make it appear almost like a flower bouquet, was waiting for them. She wore a gown with small antigrav suspensors that kept the train and hem off the ground. A sash across her torso had a single large badge with the same seal as all the Governance flags Jayce had seen. Prefect Jessina, he assumed.

Marines in heavy armor were posted throughout the room. Two Sodality Paragons flanked the woman, each in

Light Armor that fit them far better than what Jayce wore. A Paragon with reddish skin and long black hair—and a tail—stood a few steps behind the reception.

Prefect Jessina opened her arms and hurried toward Tarasin.

"My boy." She hugged Tarasin and put a hand to the back of his neck. "When we heard of the assault on Nashar's Star I feared the worse."

"We expected reinforcements," Tarasin said. "That's why Admiral Julkatta tried to hold the system for so long."

"It wasn't just Nashar's Star the Tyrant attacked," said one of the Paragons, an elderly human man with a long white beard that hung to his sternum and was tied into a Veil-stone bead. "They struck three way-stone worlds at the same time. The decision was made to secure Khergova and Odush and prevent an attack here."

"Wise," Tarasin said. "Nashar's Star has fallen . . . Iridani as well, I assume."

"Perceptive as always," the Paragon said. He leaned to one side and stared at the stone in Jayce's harness. "By my ancestors . . . I didn't think a Breaking was this close. Who has the other stone, boy? Where is Maru?"

Jayce froze until Dastin nudged him.

"Sarai. She took it from the Pinnacle. Hers was darker, golden cracks in it," Jayce said. "Maru . . . died in the Veil. Killed by a shape-shifter serving the Tyrant. He also . . . took Sarai."

The prefect looked away.

"How bad is it?" she said after a moment. "Tell me, High Paragons, how long until the Tyrant can destroy everything?"

She stared into a face that was half skeletal, half rotten flesh and finally screamed.

* * *

The Shattered Star Legacy continues
in *The Light Asunder*,
coming soon!